The
CHARMER
in CHAPS

Center Point
Large Print

**This Large Print Book carries the
Seal of Approval of N.A.V.H.**

The
CHARMER
in CHAPS

JULIA LONDON

CENTER POINT LARGE PRINT
THORNDIKE, MAINE

This Center Point Large Print edition
is published in the year 2019 by arrangement with
Berkley, an imprint of Penguin Publishing Group,
a division of Penguin Random House LLC.

The text of this Large Print edition is unabridged.
In other aspects, this book may vary
from the original edition.
Printed in the United States of America
on permanent paper.
Set in 16-point Times New Roman type.

ISBN: 978-1-64358-247-4

Library of Congress Cataloging-in-Publication Data

Names: London, Julia, author.
Title: The charmer in chaps / Julia London.
Description: Large Print edition. | Thorndike, Maine :
  Center Point Large Print, 2019.
Identifiers: LCCN 2019016920 | ISBN 9781643582474 (hardcover :
  alk. paper)
Subjects: LCSH: Large type books. | GSAFD: Love stories.
Classification: LCC PS3562.O48745 C48 2019 | DDC 813/.54—dc23
LC record available at https://lccn.loc.gov/2019016920

Chapter One

WINTER

Everyone knows how intense a high school crush can be. When every waking moment is consumed with the awareness of the crush, when a smile, or a brush of the fingers from the crushee could carry the crusher for a day. Maybe even a week if you reexamined it ad nauseam with your best friend and roommate, Stacy, while your foster parents yelled at each other in the living room.

That's how Ella Kendall had felt about Luca Prince in high school. He'd transferred into Edna Colley High School in the middle of their junior year, coming from wherever insanely rich kids came from. He was tall and muscular, had dark hair streaked with gold, and had hazel eyes that changed from blue to green to brown. He was so handsome and so exotically perfect that Ella's hormones had stacked up like discarded tires and had burned for the next eighteen months. It was a fire that could not be doused.

Not that Luca Prince ever noticed.

Everyone in the town of Three Rivers knew about the Prince family and the famed Three Rivers Ranch for which the town was named. They'd filmed Hollywood movies there. They'd hosted a summit between the president of the United States and the president of Mexico about some trade thing. The ranch was massive in size and supposedly, if you wanted to see it all in one day, you needed a plane.

Ella and Stacy had never seen the ranch except in pictures, because they sure didn't run in the popular kids' circle. But they'd heard about the fabled fortress. It was tucked away behind a big fancy gate, nestled on the bank of the river at the foot of the hills. Mariah Frame, nee Baker, their only friend in high school, had seen the ranch, and she'd said it was a like a castle. A Spanish castle. "It's *so big,*" she'd said. "And it has *so many horses.*" Apparently it also had a pool, tennis courts, cars, and Ella could no longer remember what all. But she used to imagine that it was just like the castles in all the princess movies she'd watched as a kid.

Ella, Stacy, and Mariah had called him Prince Luca. He was so dreamy, with those mesmerizing eyes and wavy hair that brushed his shoulders. He and his twin sister, Princess Hallie, had ruled Colley High. They were the homecoming queen and king, a stratosphere of popularity so high above Ella that she must have looked like a speck to them.

Once, Luca had asked Ella for her notes from algebra, and Ella had gotten so tongue-tied that she'd just shoved them at him. And, of course, she'd completely lost her mind on the night of the senior dance when he'd grabbed her hand—without asking, now that she thought about it, but that was a minor detail—and pulled her onto the dance floor. And then, just like in the movies, after a bit of swaying around, he'd kissed her.

Out of the blue, with no warning, Prince Luca had *kissed* her, right in the middle of the dance floor, beneath the piñatas. Ella had been kissed many times since, but she remembered everything about that one. His hand had cupped her face; his other had rested on the small of her back. His lips had lingered on hers for what seemed like forever, soft and tender, like he'd landed there and liked it. He had *not* kissed her in the urgent, demanding way that Clint Adams had kissed her their sophomore year. Prince Luca's kiss was a proper knee-melting, heart-exploding kiss.

And then, just as suddenly, he'd lifted his head, touched her cheek, and walked off. He'd left her bobbing there like a tethered float in the Macy's Day Parade, unable to understand what had just happened. It wasn't until Frank Cash bumped into her that Ella had woken from that dream, still standing in the middle of the dance floor.

Naturally, she and Stacy had dissected every moment of that phenomenal event over the weekend that followed, and Ella was prepared for Monday. She knew what she would say. Stacy had coached her at flirting, because she and Mariah understood Ella was the *worst* when it came to flirting.

But Monday came and went, and there had been nothing from Luca.

He hadn't even looked her way. It was like he didn't even see her.

Then had come graduation, and they'd all gone their separate ways. Ella and Stacy had aged out of foster care, and she'd hied herself up to Dallas and college, later transferring to San Antonio on a scholarship to a small college. She'd worked a lot in the last twelve years, had struggled to finish her accounting degree, but she'd done it. She'd had a couple of serious boyfriends. There was Jake, who ended things with her when she wouldn't move in with him. Jake never did understand how she needed her own place after being moved from one foster home to the next since the time she was six.

The other was Mateo. About a year ago, Mateo told Ella that he felt like she was using him for sex and nothing more. "You don't really let me see you," he'd said.

Ella was a little stunned by that and swore it wasn't true. But later, she'd asked Stacy if it might be true.

"Oh yeah," Stacy had said. "You've got a wall up, El. I mean, everyone does, really, but yours is like, *super* high. Like border wall high."

"Okay, all right," Ella had said, not liking the idea of surrounding herself with a border wall.

Mateo was still her friend and, in fact, had gotten her the hostessing job at the Magnolia Bar and Grill when she'd moved out to the farm.

That had been it on the steady boyfriend front. She didn't have a lot of time for dating between her two jobs and trying to strike out on her own with a new bookkeeping and accounting business. And truthfully, no guy had ever made her heart flutter or her palms sweat quite like Prince Luca had. No guy had loomed as large in her thoughts—the legend of Prince Luca had lived on long after graduation, and he was still her ultimate fantasy. She hadn't seen him in twelve years, but she'd seen pictures of him online and had heard about him from time to time. Always with a beautiful woman, usually blond. Always at some swank location. Always gorgeous.

A prince.

So what were the odds that he would be standing before her now? How impossible was it that *he* would come riding to her rescue?

There was no mistake—Luca Prince was standing before her, here and now, and Ella felt like a ridiculous, dopey teenager all over again. A little thrilled, a little scared, a lot baffled. And totally afraid that if she opened her mouth, she might humiliate herself.

So she just stared at him, and he stared back at her. Which seemed like an odd thing for either of them to be doing on an old county road with nothing but buzzards around. Luca had come riding up on a horse across the open range wearing a white T-shirt, jeans so tight she wondered how he sat on that horse, and chaps. *Chaps.* He had a few days' worth of beard on his face, a hat stained with sweat around the crown. He looked like he'd come off a movie set. He'd ridden right up to her, did that acrobatic move off the horse, stuck his landing right in front of her, and said, "Well, *hello* there," like he'd been missing her all these years.

Here's the other thing about high school crushes. When you see your crush after twelve years, you're supposed to look amazing. He's supposed to realize he was an idiot back then. But Ella was dressed like a Dumpster diver. Not totally her fault, because she'd been caught up in a little problem prior to this meeting. Ella was a person who prided herself on having pulled herself up by the bootstraps and making her own way in this world. If she ran across a difficulty, she handled it, no complaints. She needed no one, expected nothing, and was, according to Stacy, self-sufficient to a fault.

Still, there were a few things Ella couldn't deal

with. Like snakes, thank you to Folsom Elementary and her second-grade field trip to the snake farm and the nightmares that had followed. Or liars. She definitely couldn't deal with liars. To paraphrase Mr. Darcy, once her good opinion was lost, it was lost forever. And she definitely couldn't deal with Mama Tia's taco stand on North Alamo Street in San Antonio. That place had almost killed her.

Last, but not least, she could not deal with cars. *Cars,* those stupid, lumbering, rusty, necessary beasts and their long slate of problems. She didn't care how vehicles worked. She didn't care how many horses they took the place of or how many miles she could get from a tank of gas. All she wanted was to get in her old SUV, stick a key in the ignition, crank it up, and go. Was that asking too much? Apparently so. The car gods were exacting their revenge on her for her less-than-stellar maintenance plan, because on top of the many, *many* home repairs she'd not counted on when she'd recently moved back to Three Rivers, she'd also had plenty of car trouble.

This morning, the faucet in the kitchen sink came off and sprayed water all over her. Ella had managed to turn the water off. She'd YouTube'd a video, "Repairing a Kitchen Faucet," and was on her way to the hardware store to get what she needed to fix that damn faucet when the check engine light came on and her car just stopped running. *While* it was running.

"Please don't do this to me," she'd begged, and had spread her arms across the hood and lay her cheek against the metal. "I am living on fumes right now."

When the car didn't answer, she'd kicked it. When the car still didn't answer, she'd shouted, *"Dammit!"* and gave the hood a whack with both fists. And then she'd looked around for her phone to call someone and discovered that of *course* she'd left it on the kitchen counter.

So her fists hurt and her car still didn't work, and she didn't have her phone. She'd climbed onto the hood and slumped against the windshield and pulled her hat over her face. "Okay, well, this is a good lesson on why you should always have a plan B," she'd said aloud. "You have to figure something out, because if you don't, you'll be late to work, and besides, there is a strong possibility you could be eaten by a coyote out here, because I know what I heard last night."

Ella had been talking to herself a lot since moving to the country, but sometimes, extreme situations warranted a full discussion.

Anyway, she'd sat up and stared down the road. It was what, a mile at most to the highway? She figured she could walk to Timmons Tire and Body Shop and get a tow. Or she could walk back to her house—a little more than a mile—and call someone to come get her. "But then your car is sitting here in the road," she'd pointed out to herself. "Okay,

Timmons it is." She'd slid off the hood, stomped around to the passenger side of her car; opened the door with a vengeful yank; grabbed her tote bag, which she slung violently over her shoulder; kicked the door shut; and stepped around to the road.

That's when she saw a horse and rider cantering across the field toward her. She'd been living out here only a couple of weeks, but she rarely saw anyone, and a slight panic suddenly surged in her—there was no one to hear her if she screamed.

"Don't be paranoid," she'd chastised herself. Just because a man was riding toward her didn't mean he intended to chop her into pieces and scatter the bits for the buzzards. A rider wasn't exactly uncommon around here either. Cows needed punching, and some places couldn't be reached by vehicle. She'd seen Three Rivers ranch hands on horses and all-terrain vehicles a couple of times out her back window.

As the person drew closer, she could see the cowboy hat, the white T-shirt, the chaps. She'd experienced a vague niggle in the back of her head that he looked strangely familiar. She'd lifted the brim of her sun hat to have a clearer look as the rider trotted right on up as if he knew her.

And then her belly did a somersault. The rider *did* know her, and she knew him. Holy hell, she hadn't seen him in a dozen years, but she'd known exactly who he was.

He lifted his hat off his head, dragged his fingers through his hair—still dark brown, still sun-streaked, still gorgeous—reseated the hat, then stuck his thumbs into the string that tied his chaps around his waist and flashed a dazzling smile, his teeth all snowy white against his tanned face. "Well *hello* there."

That was the moment the world stopped spinning and the sun shone brighter.

Ella wanted to speak up, but she was so stunned she couldn't stop gaping at Prince Luca. Her thoughts were doing a mad dash back to high school, slipping and colliding into each other as they went.

"Did I startle you?" he asked in a voice that was sexier and deeper than in high school.

Ella blinked. *Yes!* "No," she lied, in spite of all the obvious signs of being startled, such as eyes wide and staring and her heart fluttering so badly she could only sip in tiny gulps of air.

His gaze drifted down her body to the snow boots she was wearing. His smile deepened and his hazel eyes crinkled in the corners with amusement. "Expecting a norther?"

Ella glanced down. Oh no. *Oh God.* It was worse than she thought. Did she really have to rush out to the hardware store so quickly that she couldn't have at least put on a dry shirt or wiped mud off her thigh or dashed on a little mascara? And was it really easier to shove her feet into snow boots than to find some flip-flops? Because news flash, *it never snowed here.*

This, she decided, was the height of unfairness, for the universe to dump her out on this road like she'd been living in a cave just as her high school crush rolled up. "They were handy," she said vaguely. *Aaand,* here she was again, displaying her inability to be charming or erudite or even the slightest bit flirty.

Luca didn't seem to think that was a strange answer. He shrugged, and his gaze moved to her car. "Having trouble?"

"Umm . . . a little." God help her, but Luca the man was even sexier than the boy. He'd filled out in the last decade to the point that his T-shirt hardly fit across his chest and arms now. He was muscular, but not in a gym-rat kind of way. In a it's-natural-to-be-so-damn-strong kind of way.

"Do you need a ride?" he asked.

What she needed was a do-over. She would like for him to go back across the pasture, then come back when she was wearing the cute red dress she'd bought at the vintage shop in town and her hair was not a half-wet, half-frizzy hot mess and probably sporting a few cobwebs from her time under the sink.

"Hello?" he asked, dipping down for a moment so that they were eye level. "Are you okay?"

Ella snapped out of it. "What? Oh, yes. Fine. Um, thanks. No, ah . . . I'll just walk." She meant to point toward town but unthinkingly pointed toward her house.

He looked in the direction she pointed, understandably confused. "The old Kendall place?"

Well, of course the old Kendall place, seeing as how it was the only place out here, and she was a Kendall . . .

Wait just a dadgum minute. Oh God, no. *No!* She wanted to die. At least crawl under her car. Ella's heart slammed against her ribs, and she felt her face flood with the heat of embarrassment because *he didn't recognize her.* He had no idea who she was.

Okay, well, move over senior dance, because this moment was now the most humiliating thing that had ever happened to her.

And then she instantly chastised herself. *Jesus, Ella, why would he remember you?* He'd never noticed her, save that one night on the dark dance floor, and that kiss, while pretty darn memorable to her, what with all the fireworks and fizzy explosions inside her, had probably been one of dozens he'd bestowed on girls that week alone.

Ella thought she'd overcome all her high school insecurities, but they were suddenly roaring back to life and flaring into two spots of mortification in her cheeks.

"I can give you a ride if you need it," he said

16

again, and his gaze slid over her, taking in her floppy hat, her half-wet T-shirt cut off just above her belly button, her jeans similarly sheared off at the knees. And, of course, her snow boots.

Yeah, well, there was no way she was getting on that horse with all those muscles and abs as she recalled all the sparks he'd sent showering through her *twelve years ago* while he didn't remember her at all. "I'm good," she said with as much nonchalance as she could muster. She adjusted her tote bag on her shoulder. "I'm going to walk to town."

"You're at least a mile away," he pointed out. "That's a hike in snow boots."

Okay, buh-bye. She needed to get as far away from him as she could get before she started whimpering. "Nope. Not a hike. Okay! So, hi and all that, but I'm good. Have a good day," she said with moronic aplomb, and started walking.

"Hey, wait," he said, and the next thing she knew, he and his horse were walking along beside her. He was a mountain, a tall, fit, hot-as-hell mountain of a man, and her skin was tingling just being near him, just like it used to tingle when he sat next to her in algebra. She stole a look at his waist and had the insane urge to bury her face in his abs.

"I didn't realize anyone was living at the old Kendall place," he said. "I understood the owner had died."

"She did," Ella said.

"So, are you renting, or . . . ?"

Or what? Squatting? Did he think she was *squatting?* "Or," she said curtly.

"Okay." He bent his head in another attempt to make eye contact.

Ella looked down.

"You must think I'm pretty darn nosy," he said. "I don't blame you. I'm curious, that's all. My family owns the land around the Kendall place."

"I know," she said, and stole another look at him from beneath the brim of her sun hat. He was smiling, but his brows were dipped, as if he was unsure what he was smiling about. Even when he frowned he was good-looking. How did the Princes get so lucky? It wasn't fair.

She walked a little faster.

"That makes us neighbors," he said, easily keeping pace. "But I must be a pretty awful neighbor, because I've never seen someone so desperate to get away from me. If you weren't wearing those snow boots, you might have succeeded."

She laughed, the sound of it all *hahaha* like she was on stage. "I'm not trying to get away from you. I'm just in a rush," she said, and wished to God above he'd stop smiling like that. "*Super* busy," she added for emphasis.

"Are you sure that's all?" he asked with a lopsided smile. "Because I would hate to leave a pretty woman stuck on the road because she's upset with her neighbor."

Oh no. *No, no, no.* She would *not* fall for the random compliment tossed out to make her smile, to do the old, *"Who, me?"* Okay, so her heart had fluttered a little when he said she was pretty. But Ella wasn't crazy. She was a poster child for practical. And she was wise to the ways of the world. So she stopped midstride to face him. "Look, seriously, I'm not stuck. Thanks for stopping to check on me, but I'm good. And I need to run. I don't mean *run,* precisely," she said, bowing to his observation of her snow boots. "I mean hurry."

Luca Prince looked confused, as if he'd missed the stage instructions and didn't understand what was happening in his movie just now. "Well," he said, and swept his arm toward the road before her. "If you refuse the help of me and my trusty steed, then please, carry on," he said. "But do you mind if I ask a question before you go?"

His eyes were rimmed with dark lashes that made the hazel really stand out. Ella could remember staring at those lashes in science class. "Okay."

"When I was a kid, there was a natural spring behind the Kendall place. About the size of a small lake. Is it still there?"

"Ah . . . yes." She dropped her gaze to his feet.

19

In spite of how mortified she was, she was also suddenly and incomprehensibly horny.

"Mind if I come have a look at it sometime?"

Ella didn't understand him. Look at what? She glanced up. "Huh?"

His gaze fell to her mouth, and he said, "I'd like to have a look at your spring."

What did that mean? Was it a euphemism? Was she supposed to know what that meant like she was suddenly supposed to know what ghosting and submarining and breadcrumbing meant? "Umm . . . I guess?"

He smiled, and it was charmingly lopsided, a level of handsome that could not be fabricated or feigned, a smile that easily put him up against the featured actors and musicians on the pages of *Entertainment Weekly* she fantasized about while funneling corn chips into her mouth. "Thanks," he said.

"Okay, well . . ." She gave him a weird salute that she had never, ever done in her life, and started walking, this time with a determined stride.

"Will you at least tell me your name?" he called after her.

She paused. Her heart was racing again, and she imagined all the things he would say when he heard her name, how he would tumble over his own words trying to apologize. She glanced back. "Ella." *Ella Kendall. You kissed me at your senior dance, remember?*

But there was no flicker of recognition, no hand slapped to forehead with an *"Ah, of course!"* He just kept smiling sexily and said, "Nice meeting you, Ella."

He did not remember her. He had no clue who she was. He did not remember the notes, or algebra and science, or that kiss. Nothing. She was a big fat nothing in his memory.

Great.

Ella whipped around, determined to put as much distance between them as she could in the next five minutes so she could scream.

When she glanced back—because she couldn't help it, she had to have one last look at charming Luca Prince, had to know if he was watching her, had to know if this had really just happened or if she was suffering sunstroke—he was already on his horse, probably having somersaulted into the saddle, and was cantering across the pasture, disappearing into the winter grasses and oaks.

She wouldn't have been surprised to see the credits roll now to indicate the end of this little movie.

"Well, congratulations, Ella Kendall, once again, you've made a *smashing* impression," she muttered. She shifted her tote bag to the other shoulder and resumed her march toward town. She guessed a high school crush didn't go away over twelve years. It hibernated and came out hangry.

Chapter Two

When Luca was nine years old, he got in trouble at school. His mother, made hysterical by the words "inability to focus" and "may be held back," had accused Luca of a desire to destroy his future and, by extension, her happiness.

His father had taken a more practical, if somewhat unorthodox, approach. He'd asked Luca into his study, had poured himself three fingers of whiskey, and had offered Luca a sip, which he'd declined. His father had sat down in front of him, had templed his fingers, and said, "Son, very rich men with very good looks can get away with a lot."

Luca had thought maybe his father was confused about why they were having their chat.

But his father had leaned forward, and with a gleam in his eye, he'd reiterated, "A *lot*. You'll know better what I mean when you're a little older. But what I'm saying is, you need to find a girl and copy her homework. *Comprende*?"

Luca hadn't understood him at all, but he'd been afraid to admit it then and had nodded.

"Good, good," his father had said, and had leaned back in his leather armchair and picked up his whiskey. "Don't tell your brother what I said," he'd added before tossing the whiskey down his throat. "Nick's a fine-looking boy, don't get me wrong. But he doesn't have *your* looks, Luca. He's the smart one, so he'll be all right. You're the charmer, Luca. You'll go just as far."

Luca had considered his father's prediction without taking offense. He'd asked, "What about Hallie?" referring to his twin sister.

"Hallie!" His father had chuckled. "Hallie's a girl, son. That's a whole different ball game." His parental duty discharged, his father had patted Luca on the shoulder then said, "Go on, get out of here. But word to the wise, boy—I'd avoid your mother today if I were you."

Luca had left his father's study not under-standing what he was supposed to do. At nine years old, girls were still creatures that did not fit anywhere in his world view. But he was thirty now, and he got it.

He also got that he was lucky, first and foremost, blessed with both money and good looks. He could honestly say, and without much shame, that the last ten or so years of his life had been something akin to a perpetual airing of *The Bachelor*. He'd waded through so many pretty women with bikini bodies and Brazilian blowouts across Texas that they were all starting to look alike in his memory.

But it hadn't been all rose ceremonies either. Luca had made plenty of mistakes along the way, had probably been a dick more often than he realized. He wasn't proud of that and wished he could take back some of the things he'd said or done. *C'est la vie.*

He'd learned a few things, too.

One was to always listen when a woman spoke, which he was doing at this very moment, as Karen explained to him over the phone that she had better things to do than sit around and wait for him. He was due to be at her house in half an hour, but he hadn't even showered yet.

"I am a very busy woman, Luca Prince."

"I hear you," he said. If Luca was going to grade himself on listening—and he would, thank you, because he was not crazy enough to ask an ex—he would give himself a high score.

Except that he wasn't *actually* listening to Karen as she berated him, because he knew what she was going to say. She'd said it before. That was another thing he'd learned—women did not like to be stood up. Now, Luca had never actually stood a woman up, but on occasion, he had some time management issues that had kept one or two women . . . okay, a few . . . waiting past the point of forgiveness. He would have to grade himself as a "work in progress" on that.

This problem of his didn't just affect his personal relationships. He owned a car dealership

24

now—no thanks to Uncle Chet, who'd been trying to do him a favor, but had saddled him with a *car dealership*—and his inability to show up on time had caused some hurt feelings around the conference room. Honest to God, he wasn't doing it on purpose. It was like his internal clock was haywire, and when he thought he had plenty of time to get somewhere, he didn't.

Victor, his general manager, wore an expression of extreme crabbiness on those days Luca did show up to flip through catalogs and sign off on things. He said things like, "Should we schedule the meeting for Friday, or do you need more *time?*"

Yeah, he was not cut out to be a car salesman. Especially electric cars, even if they were better for the environment. He was all for the environment, but he'd rather have a tooth pulled than sell a car. And the Sombra electric car was still in its infancy. Designed and developed out of Mexico, it was supposed to be the car to rival Tesla. But it wasn't him.

Which logically led to the question, what *was* him?

Luca's internal jury was still out on that. All he knew was there was one thing he could be on time for, and that was the meetings that he and his lifelong best friend, Brandon Hurst, had been holding to explore the idea of how to rebuild the ecosystems on both of their family ranches.

Most people thought it was an odd thing for a couple of born and bred cowboys to be interested in, but they were two men who shared a love of the outdoors and a despair over the depletion of nature by the hands of humans.

"I'll be there in an hour," Luca promised Karen.

Karen sighed heavily. "If you're going to be even a minute longer than an hour, don't bother showing up."

"Thanks for understanding, Karen," he said, and hung up before she could object.

Some people thought Luca was irresponsible. His dad said he was a free spirit. The truth was that he was disorganized. He was late today, thanks to a date last night that had ended in his bed in his San Antonio loft. Three Rivers Ranch was the sort of mansion built to house generations of a family. He had plenty of space there, but like Nick, who lived in a smaller house on the opposite side of the ranch, Luca was too old to be living in the family compound. So he'd bought a loft in San Antonio. It came in quite handy for nights like last night.

He would make it up to Karen. A smile could go a long way toward easing a woman's ire, and so could cupcakes. Karen's sweet tooth was off the charts.

When Luca was showered and dressed, he passed through the kitchen, gave Frederica, the family cook, a big bear hug, and then went out to the multi-car garage that housed all their expensive vehicles. His mother's Mercedes. Hallie's Range Rover. His dad's King Ranch pickup, just like the one Nick drove.

Luca had a truck, too, which he much preferred. But as the owner of a Sombra dealership, he felt like he had to walk the talk.

He drove his Sombra into Three Rivers and parked across the street from Jo's Java. Jo Carol was behind the counter, a pencil stuck behind her ear and another pencil stabbed into the mess of platinum blond hair she wore on top of her head. On weekends, Jo Carol let that mane down, and she and her husband, Bill, did a little boot-scooting up at the Broken Wagon. "Good morning, handsome!" she said brightly. "The regular?"

"The regular," Luca confirmed, and eyed the cupcakes in the pastry case.

"Got your favorite," Jo Carol said as she filled a to-go cup with coffee. "Chocolate with crème filling."

"I might have to take about four of those with me," he said with a smile. "You know I can't walk away from your cupcakes, Jo Carol."

"You mean you can't walk away from a whole lot of woman," she said, gesturing to her ample figure. "I know your type, baby. If you want to play like it's the cupcakes you're after, I'll go along."

Luca laughed.

She fit the lid on the cup of coffee and reached for a sleeve. "Guess what? My daughter Hannah

27

is moving back to Three Rivers, all the way from Dallas."

"Is that right?" Luca asked. He quickly sorted through his ex file. Had he possibly dated Hannah from Dallas at some point?

"Yep." Jo Carol looked up and met his eyes as she handed him the coffee. She retrieved a box from the top of the pastry case. "You seeing anyone, Luca sweetie?"

Oh, so she wanted him to date Hannah, which meant he hadn't dated her. He smiled. "Now, Jo Carol. You know I'm never single."

She put the cupcakes in the box. "You're a dog, Luca Prince."

"Guilty," he agreed.

"But I've taught Hannah how to train dogs," she said with a wink. "I'll let you know when she gets in town. Put it on your tab?"

"Thanks," he said. He didn't really have a tab. Three Rivers Ranch had a running account with Jo's Java for meetings and charity functions. The ranch had accounts all over town. All over San Antonio. All over the state.

He turned away from the counter and was sipping his black coffee on his way out when he happened to spot Randy Frame sitting near the window. Randy was a big guy, hard to miss. He was married to Mariah Frame, who owned a little clothing boutique with an attached hair salon on the town square.

28

But what caught Luca's attention was who was sitting across from Randy.

It was *her* again. The woman he'd met with the broken-down car on the county road that cut through their land. He'd seen her since that afternoon. He'd seen her a lot and everywhere. It was like that phenomenon of seeing the same number everywhere you look, but in this case, he kept seeing the same woman. And every time he saw her, she either pretended she hadn't seen him at all or slipped away before he could speak. She was avoiding him.

Luca was starting to get a complex, and he did not get complexes.

He'd seen her at the corner gas station where everyone got their coffee in the morning. He'd pulled into the electric charge stations, and she'd been at a pump. He knew damn well she'd seen him, too, because their eyes locked. But before he could say a word, she had scrambled into that beat-up SUV (that by some miracle was even running) and had peeled out of there like he was carrying the plague.

Then he'd seen her coming out of the feed store as he and Nick were going in. She'd been struggling under the weight of a heavy bag of feed. "Hey," he'd said, but she'd ducked behind another man who was exiting at the same time and escaped.

Nick had looked at her sprinting across the

parking lot then at Luca. "Don't think I've ever seen a woman run from you, Luca. What'd you do?"

"Nothing," he said, truly baffled.

"You must be off your game, dude."

But he wasn't off his game. There were at least two women blowing up his phone right now, not to mention the wild sex he'd had last night. Luca didn't get it—why wasn't *this* woman behaving the way women generally behaved around him? He riffled through his mental catalog of women again—it was a big one and encompassed a huge geographical area—and he could honestly say he'd never known a woman to look at him in the way she looked at him.

It bugged him. It was like she found him . . . *revolting*.

Nah. What reason could she possibly have to be revolted by him? She didn't even know him.

As he was standing there staring at her, she happened to glance up, and then jerked her gaze back to Randy.

Okay, all right, that was just downright hurtful.

Luca decided to clear it up then and there, and started in the direction of their table. Little Miss Hates-Me sat up a little straighter. She looked pretty damn gorgeous today, definitely a step up from the Who from Whoville he'd met on the county road. His first impression of her that day was that she was cute. But this woman was *hot*.

Her coffee brown hair was in a sleek ponytail, and she was wearing a red dress that accentuated a very nice figure with curves in all the right places. He'd have to make a better impression, he supposed. What was her name? *What. Was. Her. Name?*

She was listening intently to Randy as Luca strolled up to their table. She did not look up, did not acknowledge him in any way. Her fingers curled tightly around her napkin.

Randy noticed him. "Luca!" He moved to stand up, but his bulk rattled the table, and the woman caught it.

"Don't get up," Luca said, and put his hand on Randy's shoulder. "I'm surprised to see you here. Didn't know you were a coffee man."

"I'm killing a little time," Randy said, and glanced at his watch. "Mariah and I have a meeting at the bank." He suddenly looked up, remembering he was not alone. "Oh, sorry—this is Mariah's friend—"

"We've met," the woman said cheerfully to Randy, still refusing to make eye contact with Luca.

Anna? Emma? Something like that.

"You have?" Randy asked.

"We sure have." She began to gather her things like a fire was spreading through the coffee shop.

"Where was that?" Randy asked.

"We met very briefly when I was riding the

west side acreage," Luca said. "She was broke down."

The woman smiled at Randy. "I think he means my car," she said, and picked up her purse.

Randy laughed. "Well, Luca, I hope you helped a lady out," he said. "Have a seat. We're just finishing up here."

"Have mine!" She stood, pushing her chair in Luca's direction. "I've got to run. Thanks again, Randy. I'll give you a call?"

"Sure," Randy said. "But hey, don't run off— Luca won't bite. Least not in public," he added, and chuckled hard enough to make his belly jiggle.

"Thanks, but I've really got to go," she said. "Super busy." She reached across the table to shake Randy's hand. She barely looked at Luca when she said, "Nice seeing you again," and started walking.

"Yeah, I . . ." Luca didn't finish his thought because she was already slaloming through the tables in her haste to get out of there, and he had hardly turned around.

What the *hell?*

Dumbfounded, he watched her walk out the door, and through the window he watched her jog across the street to her faded SUV.

"Close your mouth or you'll let the flies in," Randy advised.

Luca blinked. He gathered himself, hitched

up his cool guy pants, and sat down across from Randy. "How do you know her?" he asked.

"Mariah's friend," Randy said, referring to his wife. "She's looking for work."

"Oh yeah?" Luca asked. "What sort of work?"

"Accounting. Bookkeeping. She works part-time for some firm in San Antonio, part-time at Magnolia's Bar and Grill, but she's just moved out here and wants to hang out a shingle."

The sound of a motor that had seen better days roared to life. Her SUV began to coast down the street. As it passed Jo's Java, Luca could swear that Anna or Emma glowered at him through the driver's window.

"You offering me a cupcake?" Randy asked.

"Huh?" Luca turned his gaze from the window and glanced at the box. "Sorry, pal, those are for someone else."

"Oh yeah? Someone I know?" Randy asked, waggling his brows.

Luca smiled.

Randy laughed. "Going at it hard, huh?"

"Trying to," Luca said. "Speaking of which, I'm running late." He stood up. "Good seeing you, Randy," he said, and clapped Randy's thick shoulder before walking out with a wave at Jo Carol.

He drove to Karen's house by rote, because his mind was stuck on the fact that Anna or Emma didn't *like* him. He was mystified, could not

33

grasp why, could not fathom what would make a woman unable to bear even the *sight* of him.

Karen was standing behind her screen door when he pulled into the drive. She viewed the pink box he held in his hand with skepticism as he made his way to the door, one hand on her ample hip, one on the screen door handle, as if she were holding it closed. She stared hard at him. "Do you *honestly* think *cupcakes* are going to work with *me,* Mr. Prince?"

"I do not," he answered honestly. "But I'm optimistic and I've got nothing but hope going for me right now." He held up the box. "They're from Jo's Java House."

"I *know* where they're from," she said. "There's a big fat sticker right there," she said, pointing to the box.

"I'm sorry, Karen," he said. "I don't even have a good excuse for being so late. If you end this now, it's my own damn fault."

"Uh-huh," she said, and folded her arms across her chest.

Luca braced his arm high against the doorjamb and glanced self-consciously at his feet. Karen could read him like an open book. "I really am trying."

"Not hard enough," she said curtly. She shoved the screen door open hard enough to force him back. "Give me those cupcakes," she said as she grabbed the box from his hand, turned around, and marched off into the interior of her house.

"Does this mean I can come in?" Luca called after her.

"Just get in here!" she shouted from somewhere in the kitchen.

Once a teacher, always a teacher.

Luca stepped inside, put his hat on the little console next to the vase of paper flowers and beneath the hand-stitched sign that read, *Welcome to our happy, crazy, fun (loud) family home.* An array of framed family pictures cluttered the top of the table—pictures of Karen and her husband, Danny. Of her two grown kids, Dustin and Mandy, and their kids, a gaggle of babies and toddlers and boys in baseball uniforms and girls in dance costumes.

Sometimes, Luca fantasized about what it would be like to have lived in this little farmhouse as part of this family. He imagined home-cooked meals that were not a fancy chef's creation or pizza night when the strongest thing anyone drank was beer and there was no one to serve them. He imagined everyone sitting around the table doing homework or laughing at the day's events without fighting.

He followed Karen into her cheerful little kitchen with the strawberry print curtains, the tiled countertops, and the white GE appliances. As she fit the cupcakes onto a serving plate, Luca noticed the kitchen table had two pads of paper, one thick book, and a colorful chart next to a pitcher of lemonade.

"I've got to leave in forty-five minutes, so let's

make good use of our time." She set the plate down on the table and fit herself into her seat.

Luca took his place next to her. He reached for the chart, but Karen put a hand on his arm and pierced him with her brown-eyed gaze through her rectangular wire-rimmed glasses. "Now look here, mister. I've known you since you were in the sixth grade, and I know how you operate. I am not one of those silly girls who can be soothed with sweets and a handsome man's pouty lips."

"Pouty lips? I don't have—"

"You best be on time from here on out, or you're going to have to learn to read on your own."

He held up a hand, duly chastised and embarrassed for it. "Say no more," he said contritely.

She nodded to the chart. "Let's begin."

The chart was a rudimentary learning tool, one that connected sounds in common words to the actual letters. The sounds were illustrated on the chart with ducks and teddy bears, choo-choos and swings.

Unfortunately, Luca's lifelong battle with dyslexia had caught up with him as an adult. It was amazing to him that a man with all the advantages he'd had in his life could arrive at the age of thirty and not be able to read worth a damn. Oh, sure, he could make out a menu or a greeting card. But reading about adult topics with dense, tiny text was mind-boggling to him. The letters danced around on the page, shifting and moving so that he couldn't pin them down.

When he was diagnosed with dyslexia in the fifth grade, his mother was so relieved he wasn't a delinquent that she'd brushed off the learning disability. "You're just going to have to work extra hard," she'd said. "But you're a Prince, and that's what the Princes do—we work harder than anyone else."

"Leave him alone, Delia," his father had said, and had tousled Luca's hair. "He'll be fine. It wasn't like he was ever going to be book smart anyway, was it? Not my boy, Luca—he's destined for great things and won't have his nose in a book."

His father was right—Luca was never book smart, because he never really did conquer the dyslexia. He'd charmed his way through school, and when his charm didn't work, his parents' influence and a sizable donation had. He'd bounced from one school to the next, going wherever money could put him, until he'd run out of options and had to leave St. Mary's Hall in San Antonio and ended up at the public Edna Colley High School in Three Rivers. He'd graduated by the skin of his teeth.

His teachers, his parents, had all breathed a collective sigh of relief when he'd walked across that stage. All they'd wanted was for him to graduate—from their perspective, the hard part was over, the battle won. He didn't need to worry about his illiteracy anymore, because he was a Prince. His future had already been handed to him.

But it was at that point that he really started to bounce. From this so-called job to that woman. He never stayed in a job or with a woman long, because it was too shameful to admit he couldn't read. And Luca was self-aware enough to know that his family's wealth had made it possible for him to avoid settling on a life path. Otherwise, he'd probably be living on the streets of San Antonio about now.

Luca could point to the precise moment he knew he had to wake up and do something about his disability. It was when his uncle Chet, of Chet Applewhite Chevrolet fame, had saddled Luca with that Sombra dealership. Uncle Chet had meant well—it was a job that, in his eyes, married Luca's interests with an actual occupation. But sitting at a desk and selling cars was the last thing he wanted to do. He had realized that he'd be doing exactly that for the rest of his life if he didn't face his aimlessness, admit his true desires, and conquer his shameful little secret.

What he wanted was to be a naturalist. An environmentalist. A leader in ranchland con-servation. But he couldn't pursue that because he couldn't read. He might not be book smart, but he desperately wanted to put his nose in a book.

He would be eternally grateful to Karen, previously known to him as Mrs. Gieselman, his sixth-grade teacher. She'd taken a liking to him all those years ago and had finally agreed to tutor him as an adult after a fair amount of begging on his part.

"You've always skirted by," she'd said skeptically when he approached her about it the first time. "Why do you want to learn now?"

Because he'd grown up. Because there were things he wanted to accomplish, and he was being held back by his inability to read documents—his attempts resulted in a major headache and only a cursory understanding. Luca had ideas. He had dreams. He didn't know how he was going to do it all, but he wouldn't accomplish a damn thing if he couldn't even skim a contract for a new car. He needed to learn, to absorb.

So he picked up the color-coded chart and began to review the letters and sounds, stumbling more than once, feeling like an idiot when he did.

"Great job!" Karen said, grinning. "You're getting it. You ready to read?" She picked up the book he'd been struggling to comprehend. "Let's start where we left off last week," Karen said. "Do you remember what the chapter was about?"

Of course he did. "Conservation easements and Texas law." When Luca had borrowed the book from the Saddlebush Land and Cattle Company, the family business headquarters, his brother Nick said it was the most boring book in the history of books.

"Did you read it?" Luca had asked, surprised.

"Of course I did," Nick said impatiently, as if it was required reading for every man and Luca had missed the assignment again.

Luca was desperate to read it, to know what his brother knew. He wanted to know everything he could about land conservation and ecosystems and minerals and soil and grass and wildlife refuges. He wanted to do something meaningful with his life, and to him, that meaningful thing was taking care of what God had given them.

Karen helped herself to a cupcake, then held up the plate to him and said, "I still don't see why we can't accomplish your goals with a good romance novel or a mystery."

"Because I want to know this stuff," Luca reminded her. "I want to put these principles into practice."

She shook her head. "I always knew the Princes had more money than the US Treasury, but if you ask me, it's a waste of good land to let it sit and do nothing but grow weeds."

That's not what conservation was about, but Karen was not alone in her opinion. Everyone in Luca's family felt the same way—why conserve land when you could make money from it?

"All I know is, I am never going to get back the hours I've spent on this book with you." She winked at him. She was over her mad. "Turn to page sixty-three."

Luca forgave Karen her narrow view of the world. But he'd lived a good chunk of his life outdoors with Brandon. They'd camped out under the stars of Texas's big sky, searching for Indian hieroglyphics or arrowheads, inventing invading armies creeping toward them through the woods, imagining monsters clawing their way up from the spring. They would pull the stalks from the yucca plants and turn them into swords and guns. They rode horses down to the river and swam, hunted for rabbits and squirrels, and generally ran wild over tall grass prairies and wild-flowered hills.

He'd never tired of it. If anything, the land had only become more magical to him the older he got. But the land was changing. It was overused and depleted, beaten up by drought and erosion and rapid development. Wildlife didn't come around as it once had. Some birds and reptiles were in danger of extinction. Grasses didn't grow as tall. Trees were stunted and springs and lakes dried up.

He began to read, clumsily. Laboriously. "The Texas snow . . . bell, or *St-st wreck*—"

"Styrax," Karen said.

"*Styrax* is the . . . most . . . threet?"

Karen pointed to one of the sounds on the chart.

Luca stared at it. Then at the word. "Threat . . . threatened," he said, pleased with himself. "One of the most threatened na . . . tive . . . spee-sis."

"Species," she said, and pointed to the chart again.

It was so hard, like part of his brain was an unformed, unused blob. He thought of Hallie, who devoured novels, and wished reading came as easily to him.

He looked at the sentence he just read, his mind memorizing the letters. *The Texas snowbell is one of the most threatened native species.* He knew where a patch of it grew on the ranch. He knew where everything was on that ranch, all seventy-five thousand acres.

He had a painting that hung in his room at the ranch, rescued from a trash heap intended for burning when he was twelve. He'd shown it to his paternal grandmother, and she'd laughed. "This is the work of your great-great uncle, Leroy Prince. What a character he was! He used to take the farm girls down to the potting shed and diddle them there."

"Dolly!" his mother had yelled from her place behind the enormous, marble-topped kitchen island. "You do *not* have to voice every thought aloud to these kids."

"Oh, who cares," Grandma had said with a flick of her wrist. "Lucas will hear about it eventually."

"I don't know why he would, as you are the only person who keeps that sort of family lore alive, and for the thousandth time, his *name* is *Luca.*"

"It ought to be Lucas," his grandmother had said, and had winked at Luca as if they shared the same desire.

"For the love of God, you know I named him Luca because Charlie's cousin Lucy named *her* baby Lucas a month before I had mine. She did that on purpose," she'd added for Luca's benefit, pointing an accusing finger at him, as if he'd somehow brought this tragedy to her by entering this world a month too late.

"Good ol' Leroy," his grandmother had said, ignoring her daughter-in-law. "He wasn't what you'd call a good citizen, but he was a decent artist."

"I found it on the burn pile," Luca had reported.

"Right where I tossed it," his grandmother had said, and tapped her highball glass, indicating Luca's mother should pour a little more bourbon into it. "I figure we have enough landscapes hanging around this gaudy hacienda. This place used to look like a ranch house, you know. Now it looks like some antebellum mansion straight out of *Gone with the Wind*."

"Luca, honey?" his mother had said sweetly, as she'd swiped up her own highball of bourbon. "I'm going to walk down to the horse tank and hang myself. Tell your father," she'd said, as she sashayed from the room.

"You don't have to tell him," his grandmother had whispered conspiratorially. "She'll start to smell after a couple of days and he'll find her."

Luca hadn't paid either woman any attention. Their bickering was standard operating procedure around the house, and besides, he'd been too enthralled with his find. Even at his young age, he knew precisely the spot of Prince land his great-great uncle Leroy had captured. The painting depicted a natural spring, surrounded by natural grass, with bluebonnets and Indian blanket and Mexican hat and pink evening primrose wildflowers. A jackrabbit sat up on its hind legs and looked over a rusting plow at a pair of horses grazing in the distance. The sky was a splash of orange and yellow giving way to the pale pink and dusty gray-blue of dusk. In the distance were dark hills, dotted with cedar and oak, and on the top of one hill, so tiny that you had to squint to see it, a campfire.

He'd asked the family's majordomo, Martin, to hang it in his room, and there the painting had remained for nearly twenty years.

As the years passed, that painting had begun to represent an ideal to Luca, the way the land was supposed to look, the way God intended it to be. That was his goal—to convince his father to turn back some of the land the Princes had overused to its natural state. Not all of it—he liked money as much as the next guy—but enough that the wildlife would come back, and the wildflowers would grow, and the birds would nest. He could create a slice of heaven. He could do something meaningful, something he truly cared about.

But he had to learn it first.

No one but his twin knew about his reading lessons. Luca intended to surprise his family when he could finally read from this book. He intended to make a strong case for his vision, and he had just the place to do it. Brandon, who had become an environmental lawyer, had bought five hundred acres of parched ranchland out near China Grove. It was all used up, even sporting a couple of capped oil wells. It wasn't perfect for an ambitious environmental project—it was too small and really too far off the beaten path to get people out there to work. But it was all they had, and they were determined. They'd been talking about hosting a fund-raiser to ask for donations that would fund the equipment and manpower they needed to clear out invasive species and the cedars that suffocated everything green around them. To repopulate creeks and lakes, to clear out the silt and runoff that was choking the natural spring. To bring students and environmentalists in to study the effects of ranching and farming practices on the land.

It wasn't sexy, but it was the thing that made Luca want to get up in the morning. No matter how embarrassing it was to read like a first grader, he was going to conquer this hill.

Chapter Three

Ella pulled into the parking lot of Timmons Tire and Body Shop on the edge of Three Rivers and at the end of the unimproved county road that led to her house. She'd become quite friendly with her old classmate Lyle Timmons over the last few weeks, given the crap status of her stupid car.

As she climbed out of her car, the door between the garage and convenience store swung open and Lyle Timmons sauntered out, wiping his hands on a towel. No matter how hard Lyle wiped his hands with that towel, his fingers remained a peculiar shade of gray. He was wearing the greasy shop overalls he wore every day. He sported a ball cap on his head, the bill pointing backward, and a long ZZ Top–like beard cascaded down his front.

Funny how the people you least expected to change after high school did all the changing. Lyle had sat behind her in English class. He never uttered a word, had a military-cut hairstyle, and perfect penmanship. Now he looked like someone's fun uncle who carried Jolly Ranchers in one pocket, weed in the other, and played in a heavy metal band on the weekends.

"It's you again," he said. "If you don't cut this out, I'm going to have to start a customer rewards program."

Ella grinned. "It's so hard to stay away from all this rubber and chrome."

"Yeah, well, say the word, and I'll marry you and give you all the chrome and rubber you like."

"I wish!" she said brightly. "But my mom would have to live with us when she gets out of prison. Plus, I want at least six kids. Have I mentioned that?"

Lyle chuckled. "Well, I don't know if that shack out back would be big enough for your mom, but I'm willing to give it a shot if you are. And kids? Really, Ella? My sister has three, and they're a mess, into everything. I don't know why you don't settle for a pack of dogs. It'd be a damn sight easier. You can start with him." He pointed behind her.

Ella looked over her shoulder. The black-and-white dog that followed her everywhere was sitting patiently behind her on the asphalt, his big soulful eyes fixed on her, his tail swishing around enough to kick up dust. "Not again!" she groaned to the dog, and to Lyle, "He's not mine. He came with the house."

A couple of days after she'd moved in, she'd come home, gotten out of her car with her arms

47

full of groceries, and had been startled by a black-and-white dog loping toward her from the back of the house. She'd stilled. The dog stopped a few feet from her, tail high, alert, and Ella had prepared herself to be attacked. They'd stared at each other for a few moments until Ella said, "No one said anything about a dog."

The dog suddenly rushed forward, and Ella cried out, crashing back against her car but managing to hang on to her bags. The dog tossed himself onto his back, presenting his belly for a scratch.

"Oh. *Oh*," she'd said, her heart pounding. "It's like *that*." She'd obliged the dog. She'd put the bags on the hood and then knelt down to rub his belly. He had burrs in his fur and something that looked like grease streaked across his back.

Her belly rub must have been the best ever, because the dog never left after that. He'd joined the ranks of the abandoned pig that wandered around rooting for food, a cat that eventually sauntered out from under the barn as if he'd been there the whole time, then perched on the roof of her car to cast judgmental looks at the rest of them, and the three loose horses that appeared at the back fence in the mornings hoping for a handout. "Probably dumped there or left there by the last tenants," Lyle had opined once.

Paul Feingold was the attorney who had tracked Ella down to tell her about this house.

He'd shown up at the Magnolia where she worked part-time, handed her a manila envelope, and then asked for a menu. Inside the envelope was the news that she'd inherited the house from her grandmother, free and clear. Mr. Feingold explained that her grandmother's paltry estate had been rented out by a distant cousin to pay for her care in the Alzheimer's facility, and that the house and the patch of land it sat on was the only thing that remained after her death, and that her grandmother had left it to Ella. He'd explained everything in great detail—but he'd not mentioned a menagerie.

Ella frowned at the dog. His tail swished harder. "I have explained to him that he can't ride around with me, that I have to go to work. But he keeps getting in through the window and crawling in the back to sleep."

"Roll the window up if you don't want him in there," Lyle said, as if that very obvious solution had not occurred to her.

She gave him a look.

"Let me guess—broken?"

"Possibly. Probably. Definitely," she said.

Lyle squatted down and held out his hand to the dog. It obediently trotted forward with one ear cocked up, one down, and had a thorough sniff of his hand. "Have you named him yet?"

"No," Ella said, watching the dog wiggle around Lyle with undiluted pleasure once he'd passed the smell test. "He's probably passing through. Probably resting up before he moves on to find his master."

"That's one theory," Lyle said. "You feeding him?"

"Well, I don't want to be rude," Ella said.

Lyle gave her an accusatory glare. "Is he sleeping in your bed, Ella?"

She sighed heavily, as if he were trying her patience. "Maybe."

"Yeah, this canine ain't going nowhere. Give him a name. How about Rover?"

"How about fix my car?" Ella asked. "It's making that sound again."

Lyle clucked his tongue and stood up. "First your battery, then the transmission leak, and now the mysterious rattle. How much did you pay for the clunker again?"

"Twelve hundred cash," she said proudly. Proud of the cash part—it took a lot of will-power and missed opportunities at shoe sales to save that much cold, hard cash. She was not so proud of the car, however. It was a very old SUV and the beige paint was faded to an uglier beige. It served its purpose, but the back seat had a mysterious hole in the upholstery, the back passenger window wouldn't roll up, and she could not get rid of that mildew smell no matter how many Christmas trees she hung from the rearview.

"Twelve hundred for this death trap?" Lyle exclaimed. "If we did the math, you'd discover you're paying a whole lot more than twelve hundred," he said, and popped the hood of the car.

"Then let's not do the math," Ella suggested.

Lyle bent over the engine. "Here's your problem right here," he said, pointing at something. "Come over here. I'm going to show you how to stop that rattle when you hear it."

She followed Lyle, and the dog followed the scent of something around the corner of the convenience store. Five minutes later, Ella had learned how to tighten the clamp Lyle had put on a tube-looking thing. He tried to explain what the parts were for, but Ella waved him off. "No details, I beg of you. Just stop the rattle, please."

Lyle sighed and wiped his hands again. "You could stand to learn a thing or two about cars if you're going to drive this. I don't need you breaking down on the highway, because I don't run a search and rescue department here. You seriously need to think about getting something a little more reliable now that you're out in the country. It's not like you can call a cab, right? I can work a little magic on this piece of crap, but I'm not a full-fledged magician."

"What would you suggest I get?" she asked curiously.

"Well, now, the Princes have that fancy new Sombra dealership. I'm sure they could set you

51

up in a nice little electric car and you'd be the first in Cimarron County to own one."

She and Lyle simultaneously burst into laughter at the ridiculous impracticality of a car like that in the country.

"Let's take a look at your window," he said.

They walked around to the other side of the car to examine the problem. They had their heads stuck through the open window looking at the inside handle when someone behind them said, "Hey."

Lyle and Ella jerked up at the same moment, both of them cracking their head on the top of the window frame. They spotted Luca Prince at the same time, standing in front of a car that Ella assumed was a Sombra.

"Dude, you scared us," Lyle said, rubbing his head.

"Sorry," Luca said, and jerked his thumb over his shoulder. "Electric car."

"Try a horn tap, man," Lyle complained. "My heart's lodged near my eyeballs."

Ella hadn't eked out a word. His voice had startled her, and here he was again, all tall, delicious cowboy, wearing jeans, a Henley T-shirt beneath a denim jacket, and a knit hat that covered his dark hair. He'd tamed the start of a beard with a neat shave. She would seriously appreciate it if he would stop looking so damn sexy every time she saw him. Which was a *lot*.

She suddenly remembered her teenage self in English class, doodling his name entwined with hers. *Aaand* now her palms were slightly sweaty.

"How are you, Lyle?" Luca asked.

"Great," Lyle said.

Luca turned a smile to her, and Ella couldn't help it. She smiled back.

"Emma, right?" he said.

Emma! Her smile disappeared. She wished that she could waltz right past him, but she couldn't seem to move. She was mad at herself—she was a grown-ass woman and she shouldn't care if Luca Prince remembered her or not. So what if he'd kissed her once? She didn't remember every guy she'd ever kissed either.

Except that yes, she did. She remembered every single one.

Still, she was no longer a hormonal teenager, and there was no reason she should act like one every time she saw him. But come on, seriously? He couldn't remember her name even from a couple of weeks ago? Could he possibly make her feel any less significant?

Lyle took exception on her behalf. "It's *Ella,* man."

"Ella," Luca said with a wince. "Sorry."

"Ella Kendall!" Lyle said loudly, as if he were shouting at an elderly person. "You went to high school with her, dude."

Something flickered in Luca's lovely eyes—a

tiny pinprick of recognition. "Oh God," he said as that pinprick grew to full-fledged realization. He at least had the decency to look mortified. "Of course—*Ella,*" he said, and took a step forward, but the dog appeared from nowhere to sniff him and, thankfully, blocked Luca's path. Luca put his hand down and scratched the dog behind the ears without taking his eyes from Ella. "Ella, I am *so sorry*. I can't believe—I don't know what is the matter with me," he said as the dog trotted off to smell something else.

"Don't worry about it!" she said with false cheer. "It was a long time ago."

"It wasn't *that* long ago," Lyle said as the dog loped away. "I mean, she sat *right next* to you in algebra, remember?"

"I don't . . . I don't remember class so much," Luca said.

"Me either," Ella said with a flick of her wrist. In truth, the only classes she remembered clearly were the ones she'd had with Luca. God, she was pathetic.

She looked at her watch. "I've got to run. Don't want to be late." That's right, she didn't want to be late to the gallon of ice cream she was going to shove her totally forgettable head into. "Lyle, thanks loads for fixing that rattle," she said, and started to back away.

"But what about the window?" Lyle asked, gesturing to their joint project.

"Ooh, I'll have to come back for that one." She gave him a little wave of her fingers and avoided Luca's gaze altogether, even though he was staring at her with his hands on his hips now, which gave off the vibe that he was miffed she was leaving now that he'd finally, *finally* remembered her. Well, one thing *had* changed since high school—she wasn't willing to lick his boots and stick around. *No, sir. You had your chance, cowboy. You ridiculously handsome, insulting cowboy.*

"Come back any time, Ella," Lyle said. "Like I told you the other day, just say the word and I'll go down to Candy's Corner Café and fish the engagement ring out of the claw crane arcade box."

"You're such a charmer!" she called over her shoulder, hoping she sounded airy and carefree and *so unconcerned* about Luca Prince. She dove into her car, cranked it up, uttered a silent *thanks* to the universe that her engine didn't choose that moment to fall out, and got the hell out of there.

Emma!

She'd intended to go by the hardware store, but she didn't want to risk running into Luca again, so she took the long way around town.

That took all of five minutes.

Ella had forgotten how small Three Rivers was, even though she'd lived in this postage stamp of a town most of her life.

Just before she'd moved out to the farm, she'd been living in a bedroom community that had shot up on the outskirts of San Antonio, in a nondescript apartment with a guitar enthusiast overhead. She never saw anyone she knew in that subdivision, but in Three Rivers, as she'd gone around town trying to drum up a few clients for the accounting-slash-bookkeeping business she hoped to launch, she seemed constantly to bump into someone she'd once known. Even people who'd known her grandmother. And one person who, much to her horror, remembered her mother.

Three Rivers was so small that she had to wonder why Luca Prince was still here. She assumed people like him went on to bigger and better things. Shouldn't he be off skiing or doing whatever it was rich people did in the winter? She was pretty sure they didn't drive around little towns in electric cars.

Maybe they did if their family *was* the town. That was one thing that had changed since high school—the Prince family shadow had grown. The Saddlebush Land and Cattle Company, the mother ship of the Prince family business, had shiny, modern offices on the town square. Three Rivers Ranch Lumber was expanding. Prince Tool and Die cranked up every morning at seven o'clock sharp. She wouldn't be surprised if someone told her that the Magnolia Bar and Grill, which sat at the junction of River Road and the main highway, was owned by a Prince.

As she turned onto the county road that would take her home, she noticed the Sombra still sitting outside Timmons Tire and Body.

She could imagine Lyle filling Luca in right now. *Ella Kendall. Foster care. You remember, that green house on the edge of town with all those kids. The cops were there all the time, man!*

Was she going to have to see him every time she came to town? Maybe her friends had been right after all—maybe giving up her apartment and moving out here hadn't been such a great idea. Then again, she'd lucked into a house. How was she supposed to say no to that? Her friends said it sounded dodgy when she told them about her good fortune. *But it will be fun,* she'd said. *I'll always have a home,* she'd said.

Oh yeah, she thought, when the ramshackle old place came into view as she bounced down the pitted county road. *Just a barrel of laughs.*

When Ella learned she'd inherited the house, she remembered she'd last seen it when she was around six or seven. Since then, a life that was not in her control and painful memories had kept her from it. But her faded memory of her grandmother was warm, and she'd dragged her friends out at the first opportunity to have a look at the only real home she'd ever had.

Mateo, her ex, and Chrissy, a friend, had stared

at it in disbelief. "It's so far *out*," Chrissy said when Ella parked at the end of the drive to have a look. Chrissy was scanning the miles and miles of untouched land around them. "You're a city girl, Ella. You're not cut out for the country."

"What are you talking about?" Ella scoffed. "I was raised in Three Rivers. And it's so quiet and peaceful! Wait . . . do you hear that?"

Chrissy and Mateo each leaned forward, listening. Hearing nothing, they'd looked at her.

Ella grinned. "Exactly. No sirens, no one arguing outside my apartment. No planes or guitars overhead." They'd all looked skyward. Nothing there but some chemtrails.

"Yeah, but this house needs *so much* work," Mateo said. He'd been firmly against the move. Even though they'd broken up, he liked to look out for her. It was easier to do that when she lived in the same complex as him.

"I'm not afraid of a little work, you know," Ella said.

"Not until it comes to relationships," Mateo muttered.

"So what if it needs a few repairs?" she'd said with a shrug and a flip of her long brown hair over her shoulder. But privately, she acknowledged that the house was not the gingerbread house of her dreams. It was smaller and shabbier than what she remembered. In her memory, a huge porch wrapped around the entire house. The porch didn't wrap, and it wasn't very big. The paint was peeling, the roof was missing some shingles, and weeds had grown up where a yard had once been.

"Sorry, Ella, but this place is a dump," Chrissy had announced.

Ella couldn't disagree. But still, Ella had not been put off the idea of home ownership by the sight of the dilapidated farmhouse. "I'm going in," she'd said, and had gotten out of her car, marched up to the house, hopped over a broken porch step to the porch, and peered through a grimy window. She couldn't make out more than some dark shapes. She fit her key in the door. "Okay, this is it!" she'd said brightly to Chrissy and Mateo, who were standing off the porch, eyeing the house as if they expected the *Texas Chainsaw Massacre* guy to come bursting out the door.

Ella pushed the door open and was instantly overwhelmed with a smell so foul she'd taken an involuntary step backward. "What is that?" she cried out. "Is that *death?*"

"There's a *body?*" Chrissy had shrieked.

Turned out, there wasn't a body. It wasn't even death. It was a ham that had been left on a counter. The last renters had trashed her grandmother's house and had left Ella to clean it up.

That day, she'd searched the house for the

hooked rugs and worn furnishings she remembered, the two bedrooms with sheer drapes and chenille bedspreads. What she found was broken furniture. A heater than didn't work. A busted window.

As was often the case with Ella's life, what she envisioned and what was real were too vastly different things.

Nevertheless, this house, and the bit of land it sat on, was all hers. She had something that belonged to her, a home. A real home, and it was *hers*. But in her euphoria, several things had not occurred to her. Like the god-awful amount of work said house was going to need. Or that animals that had either been dumped out here or left behind would eat through her bank account at a nice little clip. Or how setting up a home office wasn't as easy as it sounded when you were so far out in the boonies that you could only get satellite internet that worked about every other Wednesday.

Or how about the icing on her little cake, that after all she'd been through in her life, after all she'd managed to accomplish in spite of it, and after all the crap and disappointment she'd put behind her, she could not shake a stupid, ridiculous, out-of-her-league high school crush.

That was quite possibly the most maddening thing of all.

Stacy. If anyone would appreciate her private little hell, it would be Stacy, who would *die* if she knew Prince Luca was wandering around Three Rivers. Ella needed to talk to her anyway. Her band, the Rodeo Rebels, was one of two accounting clients Ella had, and they needed to make a tax payment.

Her other client was the Little Creek Funeral Home.

Yep, she was living large out here. Between those two accounts, Ella made enough to splurge on a fancy bottle of wine. Which she'd done. And already drank.

As she gathered her things from the car, the pig came wandering out of the weirdly slanted garage Ella was afraid to use lest it fall over. The pig had claimed it for its hovel and shared it with the cat.

Ella walked up to the porch, hopping over the missing step. She pulled open the screen door and pushed the main door open when something large and out of place caught her eye. She slowly turned her head to see that her handiwork from this morning—a beautiful set of crystal wind chimes she'd hung *without instruction from YouTube*—had fallen. She couldn't actually see the wind chimes, because they were buried under the mound of rotted shiplap that had fallen from the porch roof along with them. "Are you freaking kidding me?" she said aloud.

She dropped her bag and picked her way over the debris to the end of the porch, where the

Esperanza grew so high that squirrels would swing from its limbs to the oak tree. She peered up. The whole roof looked rotted. "Is it *termites?*" she asked herself. "Please don't be termites."

She looked around, found one of the boards that wasn't too heavy, and with a grunt, hoisted it up. Balancing it precariously in her hands, she poked at the ceiling to explore the rot. There was a breeze, however, and her hair kept flying in her face, and she wouldn't know termites if she saw them anyway. "Maybe I should Google it," she suggested to herself, and dropped the board, which clattered loudly on the rest of the fallen soldiers, and fished her phone out of her pocket. She typed in *termites.*

"Hi."

Ella shrieked. She jerked around so quickly she stumbled over a piece of shiplap and landed on her elbow against the railing.

Luca Prince was standing next to his open car door. That fucking silent Sombra! He'd snuck up on her *again.*

"Jesus, I'm sorry—I thought you heard me."

It was a miracle there weren't reports of electric cars killing and maiming pedestrians across America, because who could hear the damn things? She pressed a hand over her heart, took a breath, then began to pick her way over the remains of her porch ceiling. "*What* are you doing here?"

He answered that by backing up and opening

the door behind him. Out hopped the dog. "You left your dog at Lyle's."

She glared at the dog as he trotted to an old tree stump in the front yard and lifted a leg. "First, he's not my dog. Second, I didn't *forget* him." She'd definitely forgotten about him, no thanks to Prince Luca. "We have an arrangement."

"Hmm," Luca said dubiously. "Lyle said he was your dog." He shut both car doors and sauntered after the dog as it sniffed its way to the porch. Luca stopped at the bottom of the porch steps, slipped his hands into his pockets, and stared up at Ella, as if he expected her to explain her poor dog management skills.

It was happening again, that tingly feeling she got when he was looking at her. "You really didn't have to bring him. He would have found his way back."

"Well, I'm a little particular about dogs."

The dog, all pleased with himself, trotted up the steps to the screen door, nosed that open, and carried on inside like he paid the bills around here.

"I think he thinks he's your dog," Luca opined, then looked at her porch. "You've got a mess there."

Captain Obvious to the rescue. "No kidding."

He stepped over the missing porch step, totally uninvited, and leaned forward to have a look. "You're gonna need to get that fixed."

Oh, dear God, did he think she didn't *know* that? "I kind of figured," she said. "So listen, thanks for bringing Dog, although—"

"Wait, back up—your dog's name is *Dog?*" he asked incredulously.

Ella hesitated. "For now. Thanks again, but I really need to clean this up before I go to work."

"Why doesn't he have a name?" Luca asked.

"Because he's not really my dog." She took a step backward, because the man was insanely magnetic. And she had an overwhelming urge to touch his plump lips with her finger.

"Then who does he belong to?"

"Good question."

He tilted his head to one side and considered her. Which actually meant his eyes took a little trip over her face, checking in at her forehead, her nose and lips, and even her ear. "So you're telling me that the dog that just went into your house is a dog you don't know?"

"Well," she said with a sheepish shrug. "I mean, I *know* him. Lyle said he was probably dumped out here. Maybe. Look, thanks again," she tried.

"I get it," he said, nodding. "You're *super* busy."

Ella blinked. "How did you know?"

"Seriously?" he asked with a chuckle. "Are you really surprised that I know you've been avoiding me? Look, Ella, we obviously got off on the wrong foot. But please don't hate me because

I didn't remember you from high school. To be honest, I don't remember much of high school."

"*What?* I don't hate you!" She laughed, too loud, too long.

He folded his arms, and all she could see were biceps bulging in his jacket. "Really? Because I think it's pretty obvious you're not a fan."

"That's ridiculous," she protested, although clearly, she'd been avoiding him like he was the Grim Reaper. "It's not that I'm not a *fan,*" she said. "It's because . . ." Whoa there, was she about to confess to being ashamed he didn't remember her?

"Because what?" he pressed her. "I haven't been friendly enough?" He moved up another step on the stairs so that he stood just below her, his eyes level with hers. He leaned forward and said, "Because if there is one thing I can say about myself, it's that I'm friendly." His gaze dipped to the hollow of her throat. "And I'm handy."

"How handy?" she asked.

"I could fix that mess," he said with a nod in the general direction of her porch.

"Well, so can I," she countered, puffing up a little. There was hardly anything she couldn't fix with YouTube and a hammer.

"It would go a lot faster with a friend."

"I have friends."

A slow, sexy smile appeared on his mouth. "So

what, you've bagged your friendship limit? Can't take any more without paying a hefty fine?"

"Why?" she blurted. "Why do you want to be my friend?"

"For starters, you're really pretty."

A slow heat began to build in her cheeks. She knew what he was doing, and she was *not* one of those girls who could be had with a compliment. She was *not*.

"Also, if someone doesn't want to be my friend, I want to show them they're wrong."

"It's nothing personal," she said.

"Oh, but it damn sure is personal, Ella," he said with a lopsided smile. "And finally, if I may be allowed to finish all the reasons why I want to be your friend, I think you're interesting. Plus, you have a dog."

The familiar grunt of her pig caused them both to turn. The pig had ventured out of his Leaning Tower of Barn and looked at her expectantly, expecting its snack.

"And a pig," Luca added. "Why do you have a . . ." He shook his head. "Never mind." He shifted his gaze to her again, his hazel eyes flecked with bits of gold and dark green. "So have I given you enough reasons that you'll consider giving me a chance?"

Teenage Ella was shrieking at her right now to accept his offer. Adult, distrusting, border-wall Ella was putting on her armor. Ella folded her arms.

"Here's the thing," she began, and wondered what the thing was. "I can't be played, Luca."

Luca blinked. He cast his arms wide. "Is *that* what you think?"

"You don't remember me, but I remember you. *Vividly.* And I can't be played."

"What you remember is a guy who was seventeen, eighteen years old with more hormones than brains. That was more than twelve years ago, Ella. And besides, I didn't even know you. Sitting next to you in class doesn't count. I had already checked out."

"Oh really?" she said. She had on her armor and she was working up a good head of steam. "You *kissed* me."

"What?" He laughed.

Oh yeah, she had him. *Player.* She nodded furiously. "Senior dance, right there on the dance floor, beneath the wild boar piñata that someone had hung upside down."

Luca stared at her. *Really* stared at her. She could almost hear the memory gears clicking in his brain. He slowly began to nod. "Yeah, okay." He smiled sexily. "No wonder you're so pissed at me."

Her skin was tingling. "You remember?"

His gaze slid to her lips and lingered there. *"Mmm-hmm."*

Holy smokes, her blood was suddenly boiling. In an insane split of feelings, she wanted to kiss him right now, to lay one on him he'd remember this time. And then she wanted to drop-kick him off the stairs and watch him go sailing over the trees.

"And it wasn't a piñata, it was a mirror ball. You were wearing a black dress," he said, and his gaze traveled down her body, as if he was remembering that black dress.

How had he remembered *that?*

"Tell you what," he said, slowly lifting a smoldering gaze to hers. "Let's start over. Let's be friends. I'll fix this porch for you."

Oh sure, Luca Prince was going to suddenly pop up in her life and fix her porch. "And in return?"

"Well now, Ella, real friends don't have to do the quid pro quo thing, right? But maybe in return you let me start over with a redo of that kiss."

"Are you kidding me right now?" she asked.

"You asked," he said cheerfully, and touched his fingers to her jaw. "I'd like to make amends, because let's be honest, that kiss was not my best. I've gotten much better at it. Now, if you don't want me to, I won't." He stepped up onto the porch. He was tall and fit, and her blood was suddenly rushing so hard she could hardly hear him. "But if you do," he said quietly, "I'll make sure it's a kiss neither of us will ever forget."

The blush in her cheeks turned to sunburn.

"You're *doing* it," she managed to whisper. "You're doing it right now. You're *playing* me."

"Nope. Just clarifying expectations for purposes of friendship."

"You're so good at playing people you don't even *know* you're doing it," she whispered.

He smiled lopsidedly again as if that amused him. "That's not what I'm good at, Ella," he said, and his eyes raked down her body, to the vee of her T-shirt just before he bent his head and touched his mouth to hers.

His kiss was so soft, so ethereal, that she had to grab his wrist to keep from toppling over. He teased her with his tongue, and she tipped right into some very serious sexual desire. Oh, but this kiss was *so much better* than the senior dance kiss. He kissed her so tenderly, and yet it was electrifying. It felt as if he was scarcely touching her, but he was touching her in all the right ways, and she was on fire, sizzling and breathless in her skin. He was luring her in, enticing her to some magical place that Ella very much wanted to go. *Right now. This instant.*

He moved her back, pushing her up against the screen door. He braced one hand against it and leaned into her as he slid his other hand down her arm, to her waist, and around to her hip. He was kissing her in the way she'd fantasized he would kiss her, with sex bombs detonating and rainbows and glitter falling on her.

The kiss rattled her to her core, threw her off her game, made her feel all fuzzy and giddy. When he lifted his head, he smiled seductively. He knew how good he was. "Now *that* was a kiss, Ella Kendall."

She was going to swoon all over the porch, right here, right now, and she didn't care if he saw it. She looked at his lips, remembering the feel of them on hers, and imagined being an impassioned kind of woman who took what she wanted, because she wanted him to kiss her again, and she was so close to reaching for him and going for it—but her phone rang and destroyed the moment. She turned her head, spotting her phone on the railing.

"What do you say, Ella?" Luca asked. "Can we start over and be friends?"

She hesitated. She glanced at him sidelong. "I'll think about it."

Luca suddenly smiled, and that single, lopsided, sexy smile was probably the nail in her armor's coffin. "I'll give you a call," he said.

"You don't have my number, player."

"Then I guess I'll have to show up when you're least expecting it, scaredy-cat."

He was playing her like a violin! She put out her hand. "Give me your phone."

He handed it to her, no questions asked. She tapped her number into his phone and gave it back to him.

He was still smiling, but his eyes had gone soft, and Ella was seriously on the verge of melting into an embarrassing puddle of delighted goo. "See you soon," he said, and twined his fingers very lightly with hers for the briefest of moments. It was a small touch, hardly a touch at all, and yet it set off a million little electric shocks through her.

The next thing she knew, he'd vaulted off the porch and was in his Sombra. It drove away without any sound but the crunch of tires as he turned the wheel.

Ella was still breathing hard. When she couldn't see his car anymore, she climbed over the shiplap, grabbed her phone, and saw she'd missed a call from Stacy. She punched the button to call her back.

Stacy was going to *die.*

Chapter Four

Ella Kendall.

The memory of the senior dance had come roaring back to him like some forgotten dream. Luca couldn't really recall her in any other setting, but the moment she'd mentioned that kiss, the pieces had all drifted into place, and he'd remembered. She was so pretty that night. Her dark hair was long and sleek, and she'd worn a simple black dress with a high neck. All the other girls had been dressed in sparkly, strapless pastels, their hair done up in elaborate coifs and held in place with more sparkle. Ella Kendall had stood out in her unembellished way.

Luca had taken Naomi Peterson to that dance, he remembered, a first and last date with the cheerleader. Naomi had flirted shamelessly with him in homeroom, and she had pretty brown eyes and platinum blonde hair, and—this was important to a seventeen-year-old male— big boobs. But Naomi had turned out to be a clingy, whiny girl who was darkly jealous of any attention he paid anyone else—even Hallie.

He remembered getting Brandon to dance with Naomi just so he could breathe, then escaping that pastel sea of girls, but stumbling over Ella on his way. Had she been standing in the corner? It seemed like it. He'd taken her by the hand— or had she taken his? Had either of them said anything? He didn't remember them talking. What he remembered was her slender hand in his, and stepping out on the dance floor for a slow dance.

He couldn't remember how or why he'd kissed her either. Probably just the constant revving of male hormones in him. He couldn't remember if he'd spoken to her before he kissed her, or if she'd just looked up at him with those pretty blue eyes . . . but he remembered that kiss. That surprising bit of heat beneath the mirror ball. Not a piñata, a mirror ball, because he could still see the little squares of light passing over her pretty face.

She was in one of his classes, wasn't she? Lyle said algebra. A class Luca practically slept through. And he remembered seeing her a Friday night or two on the main drag, come to think of it. With who? Mariah? Yes, Mariah. It was coming back to him—Ella was always in the back seat. She was a back seat kind of girl.

So that girl in the simple black gown with the oval face and pretty blue eyes was the same exotic creature he'd found on a county road wearing snow boots. She wasn't as thin as she had been in high school, but neither was he. Ella looked healthier now, all curves and glowing skin and shapely legs. And she was even prettier. Still in a simple, natural way. Nothing about her was made up. It was all right there. What you see is what you get, the perfect shape of a woman, and *damn,* he was attracted to her.

He was definitely looking forward to fixing that porch ceiling for her.

It was curious that she'd ended up in the middle of nowhere. Was she alone except for the dog and the pig? It was a pleasant little mystery he looked forward to solving. In the meantime, he would amuse himself with the image of her eyes and messy long brown hair, and the way those legs stretched a mile down the road.

He was still thinking about her when he arrived at the ranch. His sister, Hallie, was on her way out, dressed in a very short blue dress, her strawberry blond hair in a messy bun at her nape. "Where are you going?" he asked.

"Girls' night," she said. "What's up with you?"

"Not much." He looked curiously at his sister. "Hey . . . do you remember Ella Kendall from high school?"

"Ella Kendall?" She thought a moment, then nodded. "Yeah, I think so. She was pretty, right? But quiet. And very good at math."

"How do you remember that?" he asked, surprised.

"I don't know," she said with a shrug. "I just do. Why are you asking about her?"

"I ran into her," he said vaguely. He wasn't going to confess to Hallie the whole thing and how he hadn't remembered Ella at first. "I don't think she particularly likes me," he mused, more to himself than to his twin.

"What do you mean?"

"I mean, she doesn't *like* me," he said, and gestured to himself.

Hallie laughed. Actually, she howled.

"Okay, it's not that funny," Luca said, and when Hallie didn't stop laughing, he demanded, "What is the *matter* with you?"

"I'm just as astounded as you that there is a woman walking this earth who's not falling all over herself for your studly body, Luca! What is *happening* right now? What universe is this?"

"Okay," he said, nodding as his sister doubled over with laughter. "All right. Laugh all you want. But even you have to admit it doesn't happen often." He started to walk toward the house.

"Bye, Luca! Try not to cry yourself to sleep, because your eyes will be puffy in the morning!"

He rolled his eyes and walked on, muttering under his breath about the things he had to put up with around here.

The next morning, Luca called Brandon and arranged a happy hour meeting to talk more about the fund-raiser they were planning to get the ball rolling on Brandon's acreage near China Grove.

Three Rivers had only a few restaurants—most people wanting a night on the town splurged and went to San Antonio. There was a Mexican food diner on one end, Jo's Java in the middle, a couple of chain restaurants out on the highway. The closest they got to fine dining out here was the Magnolia Bar and Grill. It sat on the banks of the river, beneath the droopy branches of cypress trees and atop a gradual slope down to the river's edge. On summer nights, people would come out with their dogs and put blankets on the grass and listen to free music.

Luca was a little early and was texting Brandon as he walked into the restaurant to let him know he'd arrived. He hit the send button, then looked at the hostess. He was startled speechless for a split second, because Ella was standing behind the hostess stand. "Oh. Hi," he said.

She stared at him. Then she frowned playfully. "Seriously?"

"Seriously what?" he asked.

"You keep showing up where I am."

"Actually, you keep appearing wherever I am," he countered. "I didn't know you worked here."

She gave him a once-over. "Part-time," she said. "But I've never seen you in here before."

"I don't come around that often. But tonight, I'm meeting a friend." He smiled.

Ella looked around. "Do you see her?"

76

"Him," he said smugly. "And no, he's not here yet. I'm early."

"Okay," she said, and picked up menus. "Would you like to be seated?"

"I'd rather stand here and talk to you."

"Nope," she said without hesitation, and her eyes, he thought, looked like they were shining with a tiny bit of delight.

"It's early," he pointed out. "And you look like you're just standing around right now. Why not?"

"No," she said again.

He sighed. "Fine. I'll go to the bar. Come over and I'll buy you a prickly pear margarita."

"Very funny," she said, and pointed at the bar. There it was again, that dance of amusement in her eyes.

Sent off like a kid to time out, Luca went to the bar and took a seat. The bartender, a dark-haired, slender man with a full beard asked him what he wanted. "Do you have an IPA on tap?" he asked.

"Yep. Brewed in Austin."

Luca nodded. As the bartender poured the beer, Luca glanced over his shoulder at Ella. She was writing something on the seating chart.

"Don't waste your time," the bartender said.

"Huh?" Luca turned around as the bartender slid the beer across to him.

"She's hot, but she is a tough nut."

Luca glanced at Ella, then at the bartender. "What do you mean?"

"Foster care kid," he said with a shrug, and tapped his chest. "She holds it all close, and it's tough to get to know her." He grinned. "Trust me, I tried."

Foster care. That was a surprise and a new one for Luca—he couldn't recall ever knowing anyone from foster care.

"But she's definitely hot," the bartender said, and moved on.

"Luca!"

Luca swiveled around on his barstool with a grin for Brandon. They'd been best friends since almost before he could remember. The Hurst family ranch bordered the Prince land on the north side. Brandon was shorter than Luca and had a barrel chest that came from lifting a lot of weight. He had an infectious grin that Luca was sure helped him in court. Brandon came from a long line of ranchers and lawyers. His dad was a personal injury attorney—Thomas J. Hurst was one of the most successful personal injury attorneys in the state. There had been a lot of pressure for Brandon to follow his father into injury law, but Brandon had bucked his father and had gone into environmental law.

"Dude," Brandon said, and clasped Luca's hand, then chest-bumped him. To the bartender he said, "I'll have what he's having."

"How are you?" Luca asked.

"Great," Brandon said. As they waited for his beer, they caught up. When the bartender returned, Brandon tossed a twenty onto the bar. "Let's get a table."

Ella showed them to a table near the windows. She was handing them menus when they heard a loud, deep male voice.

Luca knew instantly who it was and suppressed a groan. Blake Hurst, Brandon's older brother, the sheriff of Cimarron County, was standing at the hostess stand in civilian clothing. Back in the day, Blake frequently tortured Brandon and Luca. He used to pinch them and twist their arms, all in the name of fun, but always to the point of pain. When they got a little older, Blake tortured them in other ways.

"What's he doing here?" Luca asked Brandon as Ella made her way back to the hostess stand.

"No clue," Brandon said. "I haven't talked to him in a while."

Luca had always suspected that Brandon disliked Blake as much as he did, but Brandon was a Texan, and blood ran pretty thick around here.

Blake spotted them. He waved lazily, then leaned against the hostess stand and spoke to Ella as his gaze unabashedly wandered her body.

Luca didn't appreciate the way Blake was leering at Ella. He waved Blake over just to force his lustful gaze away from her. Ella picked up a menu and led Blake to their table, and he sauntered along behind, openly ogling her ass. *Pig.*

"Hello, Blake," Luca said coolly when the sheriff reached the table.

"Fucking Luca Prince," Blake said, and clapped him hard on the shoulder, squeezing as hard as he could. "Buying my dinner tonight?"

"Wasn't planning on it," Luca said.

"Come on, you've got more money than a Russian oligarch. Help a public servant out."

"Knock it off, Blake," Brandon said, and cast an apologetic smile at Ella.

"Then maybe you will buy it, bro. You been avoiding me, or what?"

Ella smiled thinly and laid the menu down on the table.

"Ella, I should have introduced you," Luca said, standing up. "This is Brandon Hurst, and his brother Blake."

"That's Sheriff Hurst to you," Blake said, and slapped Luca on the back.

"Hi, Ella," Brandon said.

"Welcome to the Magnolia," she responded, and with a ghost of a smile, she walked away.

"How do you know her?" Brandon asked Luca as Blake put himself in a chair.

"Went to high school with her."

"Nice," Blake said. "Did you graduate?" He laughed.

"Don't be such a dick, Blake," Brandon said quietly.

"Oh, come on, I'm just teasing our old friend," Blake said, and once again, put his hand on Luca's shoulder and squeezed.

Luca shrugged him off and looked at the menu. "Are you going to join us, Blake?" he asked.

"I don't know," Blake said, and tossed his menu at Luca. "Read the specials to me."

Very few people in Luca's life knew that he couldn't read. Unfortunately, Blake Hurst was one of them.

"Read it yourself," Luca said, and shoved the menu back at him.

"Come on, Luca, read me the specials," Blake mocked him, and laughed as if they were all enjoying a hilarious joke. Brandon didn't laugh, and when Luca didn't pick up the menu, Blake retrieved it. "Just kidding around with you, Luca. You don't have to be so sensitive. But one of these days you're going to have to get that little problem fixed."

"Leave him alone, Blake," Brandon said.

Blake laughed. "No hard feelings, Luca. Look, don't sweat it. I'll read the specials to you."

"Fuck off," Brandon snapped.

"All right, all right," Blake said, and held up both hands in surrender. "Don't everybody get their panties in a wad." He grinned at the two of them and tossed aside the menu. "I'll let you two bricks have your dinner. I stopped in for a drink." He stood up and hitched up his pants, and with a survey of the dining room, he walked toward the bar. Fortunately, Ella was not at the hostess stand when he went by it.

Luca stared at the letters swimming around his menu. He felt like a child again, brought to the front of the class and humiliated by his inability to make sense of the letters he was supposed to put together into some sort of recognizable word. He was much better now, thanks to Karen, but at the moment, he couldn't make much out because he was seething. It had always been like this with Blake. Always needling them, always pushing them.

"Sorry about that," Brandon said sheepishly.

Luca smiled at his old friend. All their lives, Blake had made fun of Luca's inability to read and Brandon's weight. He was a bully. "Forget it," he said. He didn't want to think about it. "So get this—I've been in touch with the King Ranch Institute," he said, referring to a ranch management program. "They're interested in our plans for restoring pasture land and would participate in the fund-raiser."

"Fantastic," Brandon said.

Blake was forgotten as they ordered dinner and chatted about their project and fund-raising goals. They were looking at a late spring date for the fund-raiser. "Let's have it at Three Rivers," Luca suggested.

Brandon's brows lifted to his hairline. "Does Mama Prince know about this?"

"Not yet," Luca said with a grin.

When they'd paid their bill, Brandon and Luca strolled out of the dining room. At the hostess desk, Brandon stepped into the bar to say something to Blake. Ella glanced up at Luca as he waited.

"Got a hammer?" he asked.

"You don't need to hammer your way out of here. I'll open the door for you."

He smiled. "You're going to need one when we tackle that porch."

"Oh, right, the *porch*," she said, and leaned across her reservation book. "I thought that was all talk, cowboy."

"Nope. We're going to do it," Luca said. "I'll call you."

"Uh-huh," Ella said as a couple walked up to the hostess stand. "I'm not holding my breath." She turned away from him and said to the couple, "Welcome to the Magnolia."

Maybe the bartender was right—Ella was a tough nut. Fortunately for Luca, he appreciated that in a woman.

Luca and Brandon went on to San Antonio to meet up with some girls that Brandon knew. Luca always enjoyed a good flirt, but that evening, he kept seeing Ella Kendall's eyes sparkling at him, whether she meant them to or not. He spent the night at his loft, and the next morning, he went by his dealership and let Victor's resentment at his lack of managerial skills wash over him before heading back to the ranch. He had in mind to call Ella and arrange that porch date.

He drove down the tree-lined road to the compound, pulled around to the garages, and entered his personal garage. He was surprised to see Nick's pickup. Nick rarely came out to the house. He'd once confessed to Luca that after running the Prince family business all day— Dad considered himself "retired," which meant he meddled when he wanted to, disappeared when he didn't—the last thing Nick wanted to do was come out to the ranch and talk about it. He preferred his ranch house on the banks of the river on another section of Prince land.

Luca got out of his car and hooked it up to charge. When he stepped out onto the paved path to the house, he heard Nick call him. He turned around and saw Nick jogging his way up from the stables.

"Hey, bro," Luca said. "Just in time for happy hour. I've got some tequila that will put hair on your chest."

Nick didn't smile. He stared at Luca, his lips pressed together. He was stiff, like something hurt, and Luca's first thought was that maybe he'd put his back out. "What's the matter?" he asked.

"Luca . . ." Nick's voice trailed off, and he glanced away for a moment.

His demeanor was so unlike Nick that Luca instinctively knew—a shiver of dread ran down his spine. "Is it Grandma?" he asked. He didn't know why he said it, but something awful had happened, someone had died, and she was the logical one.

But Nick shook his head, and his clear blue eyes filled with tears. "It's Dad."

Chapter Five

Charlie Prince's last day on mortal earth was spent playing a high-stakes golf match with his best buddies. On the fourteenth hole, they said Charlie dropped an impossible eight-foot putt for five hundred dollars with skill he had never before possessed. And then *he* dropped, his brown eyes fixed on the sky above, the stogie still clamped between his teeth. It was quick, it was sudden, and it was devastating to everyone who knew him.

The memorial for Charlie went off without a hitch, in spite of the hundreds of mourners who'd tromped out to Three Rivers Ranch to ogle one of Texas's most revered families in their time of grief.

Cordelia, Charlie's wife—Charlie's *estranged* wife—knew the mourners were all waiting for something to happen, for some logjam of emotion to suddenly burst, for some catfight to break out. That was because where Charlie Prince was concerned, there was always something to see. He'd been larger than life, a rich Texas rancher with a penchant for pretty girls—the goddamn bastard—expensive whiskey, and big deals.

Naturally, their children, from oldest son Nick to the twins Luca and Hallie, took the news pretty hard. Charlie's mother, Dolly, took it quite hard, of course, but Dolly was old enough to have experienced wretched loss and knew how to numb herself with booze. Cordelia's children, not so much.

None of them took it as hard as Cordelia. She probably didn't show it—she could be an ice queen when she wanted to be—but she was nothing but ashes inside. It didn't matter that she and Charlie had been separated for the third time in their nearly forty-year marriage. Yes, of course she felt guilty that she hadn't been around to nag him to stop smoking those awful cigars and, for God's sake, to eat a vegetable now and again. But even though she and Charlie had certainly had their ups and downs, and he'd been a philandering ass, he'd also been the love of her life. She'd never stopped loving him, even when she'd wanted to kill him. And his death had absolutely flattened her.

Dolly had always said Cordelia was made of brass tacks, and she supposed she was. After her initial shock, she'd gotten hold of herself because she had to take care of things. She was the glue in this family, the hall monitor, the drill sergeant, the president. She gathered her children and her mother-in-law, and together they planned a good-bye that befitted the Texas titan that Charlie Prince had been. It was what people expected of the Prince family. It wasn't a memorial. It was an *event*.

So it was that on a beautifully mild winter afternoon, all those who mourned Charlie gathered at the famed Three Rivers Ranch compound. The ranch was set at the base of gentle hills and at the mouth of the river, amid ancient live oaks, acacia, and cedar, as well as the occasional patch of prickly pear. The old Spanish-style mansion had been the seat of the Prince family for more than one hundred years and was featured on postcards sold at Market Square in San Antonio. All twenty thousand square feet of the mansion looked like it belonged on the pages of *Architectural Digest*. Terra-cotta patios gave way to a modern, zero edge pool, and from every room, there were sweeping views of the more than seventy-five thousand acres of Prince land where cattle and thoroughbreds grazed.

Cordelia was dressed in a simple black shift that Zac Posen had made especially for her. She had her blond hair styled into a simple chignon and wore the diamond bracelet and teardrop earrings Charlie had given her after his last affair. She poured enough whiskey into her wineglass to float an armada. Cordelia wasn't a drunk—or rather, she hadn't been before Charlie died—but the days leading to the memorial had been a blur of pain and anger and numb acceptance, all made possible by the expensive Scotch whiskey Charlie was so fond of.

She walked out onto the balcony that over-looked the living room and stared down at the dozens milling about, drinks in hand. *Vultures.* They wanted to gawk? She'd give them something gawk at. This event was the send-off to top all send-offs. Not only had she cajoled her favorite chef to fly in from Los Angeles and cater the event, she'd hired waitstaff to walk around in formal attire with trays of canapés and French champagne. The plan was that after this so-called "celebration" of Charlie's life—that was what Hallie insisted they call it—the riffraff and gawkers would go home, and only the family would gather at the family cemetery to bury the urn that contained Charlie's ashes.

"Delia?"

Cordelia looked down to the left. Sarah Jenkins-Cash was waving at her, like they were at a charity function and Cordelia hadn't made her donation and was trying to slip out.

"How *are* you?" Sarah called up.

How the hell did she think she was? Cordelia put out her hand and gave her the universal so-so wave, then turned her back on Sarah. She hated people to see her pain. Charlie once told her she was too closed off. *"You don't give an inch, Delia. You're too damn hard."*

She wished she hadn't given him an inch. She wished she'd kept him home, with her. Kept him healthy. His veins free of plaque. She wished she'd been a better wife, a better lover, a better caretaker . . .

Wait. Why was she blaming herself? There was no one to blame but Charlie. She wished she could kick him just now.

Cordelia moved off the balcony and down the stairs, into the throng of mourners.

Charlie would have hated this. Every damn bit of it. It was as big a to-do as any of the charity balls Cordelia had ever hosted, and he'd always hated those, too, because Charlie was not that kind of man. He'd preferred to have a few friends over for barbecue and beer. She could picture him sitting by his grill, tossing a ball to one of the dogs while he entertained his friends with one of his ridiculously unbelievable tales. Even though Cordelia was an Applewhite by birth, she was the one who truly appreciated the Prince legacy. The family was big and influential, its roots sunk deep into every aspect of Texas history over several generations. People had come from all over the state of Texas to pay their last respects to Charlie—legislators, judges, lawyers, bankers . . .

And a few young women she didn't know and didn't care to know. Leeches.

More than two hundred people had been ferried

out to the ranch in tourist buses from town. Cordelia hated them all right now. Where had *they* been while Charlie's veins were clogging? Probably stuffing meat and cheese into him and watching him wash it all back with bourbon.

Fortunately, Cordelia had had enough to drink that she could smile at whoever stopped to tell her how *sorry* they were, and then turn away and mutter under her breath that they should go jump in a lake.

She watched the vultures circulate around the pool and pet the horses that meandered over to the fence looking for handouts. She watched them wander into her house, which *she* had completely redone when she married Charlie, because it had been one hot mess of vintage Texas and *Hee Haw*. She could see them googly-eyeing all the trappings of the Prince wealth, touching the marble and gold, the crystal, the silk. She could hear them talk about how great Charlie had been, and she hated them even more.

Charlie had not been *great*. He'd cheated on her, and he'd lied to her. But he'd given her three beautiful children and a life most could only dream of. He'd disappointed her, he'd surprised her, and he had always loved her, even when he couldn't love himself. She'd always loved him, too. Even at the end, when she'd hated him most, he could still bring her to her knees with a smile. *Stupid, stupid bastard.*

The afternoon continued to teeter along as Cordelia had planned. She imagined that everyone who was there would later say it was the loveliest good-bye they'd ever witnessed. She would be written about, sung about, and admired for her ability to honor Charlie even with the burden of her grief.

She would later wonder how she could pull off something so spectacular and still not understand it wasn't the mourners that would ruin it for her. No, they stood around, staring in awe at their surroundings. They'd come just to gawk. She would later realize things might not have gone haywire at all if she hadn't spent the day drowning the burn in her chest with whiskey. The *event* was just the icing on her little mourning cake. But the burial? That was the moment she'd been dreading, had been trying to numb herself to. That was when things went belly-up, when the light was fading from the day, and everyone had gone, and the family had trudged up the hill to bury Charlie's ashes next to generations of Princes.

Cordelia had a pretty firm opinion about how the burial ought to go and had envisioned it for days. The plan was that they'd each say a few words beneath the twisted boughs of the live oak trees while the family dogs lay obediently at their feet. She had imagined how, having spent untold thousands on her children's educations and elocution, they would each speak eloquently and say something profound. She had even planned that the last ray of sunlight would streak red and gold and orange across the sky when they released the Chinese lanterns, and somehow, Charlie would know how much she'd loved him.

But Cordelia hadn't counted on Margaret Sutton Rhodes and her son Tanner joining them like they were family. When she saw them walking up the path, her drunken fury had turned into a dangerous riptide. She'd swayed in their direction, determined to cut off trouble at the pass, but her brother Chet had stopped her.

Chet was a big man, taller than Charlie had been, broad across the chest. "He deserves to be here, Delia," he'd said. "I told him to come."

Cordelia thought her heart might explode out of her chest.

"Who deserves to be here?" Nick had asked.

Chet was referring to Tanner, Charlie's "other" son, and Cordelia glared at her brother—her kids didn't know that Tanner was their half brother. He was one of Charlie's dirty little secrets. Margaret, that bitch, had once been one of Cordelia's closest friends, up until the day she decided to sleep with Cordelia's husband. But Margaret's greatest mistake was walking into the family cemetery like a reigning beauty queen.

She should not have done that.

Cordelia was drunk, which, admittedly, was

93

not Margaret's fault, but Margaret should have suspected. Margaret had stolen Charlie from Cordelia not once, but *twice,* and she was not going to steal this final moment from her, too. Not to mention, Cordelia didn't think now was the best time to tell her kids they had a brother. So she did what any inebriated, grieving, angry woman of a certain age would do, and lunged for Margaret's throat.

She should not have done that.

Cordelia couldn't really say what happened next. She remembered Luca taking the first swing, because he was a loyal son, he loved his mother, and his mother was under attack. But Luca was more of a lover than a fighter, and honestly, Cordelia wasn't certain, but she might have been the one who was doing the swinging.

She knew that Tanner took the second swing and put Luca on his ass. To be fair, Tanner's mother was also involved in the brawl, and Tanner probably loved his mother, too, although it was hard to understand why, and he probably felt the same responsibility to defend as Luca had. Poor Hallie, who tended to act first and think second, didn't know who Tanner was, but no one was more important to her than her twin, not even her fiancé, Christopher, and Hallie had made a *towanda* sort of scream as she pushed Christopher over a chair in her haste to throw herself on Tanner's back and save her brother.

Chet pulled her off but clumsily tore her dress, which made Hallie shriek, which prompted one of the dogs to take a bite out of Chet's ankle.

Of course it was Nick, solid, dependable Nick, who grabbed his mother and held her back when George Lowe, the family attorney, appeared and threw up his arms and bellowed, *"Enough!"*

Everyone stilled. Cordelia looked around. Charlie's urn had fallen into its little coffin and had lodged crookedly, and Luca was trying to free it. The Chinese lanterns were crushed, the pastor had disappeared, and the dogs were so excited they kept jumping on Margaret.

George rounded them all up and pointed to the house. "Go," he'd commanded firmly. "We need to talk."

So the family had sheepishly stumbled down the hill to the house. Cordelia grudgingly agreed that Margaret and Tanner could come, too, when Nick told her in no uncertain terms that they were coming.

They gathered in the library. Things had calmed down considerably by then, as they were all too inebriated or too spent from the shock of losing Charlie and the grief, or just the general unfairness of life, to fight anymore.

Cordelia felt something odd and put her hand up. There was part of a Chinese lantern in her hair. Luca had a bag of ice cubes Frederica had probably given him—she'd always favored Luca—pressed to an eye that had swollen shut. Hallie's designer dress was slit up to her crotch. Tanner's lip was busted, Dolly was holding a broken framed picture of Charlie to her chest, and Nick had to stand between everyone and Margaret, lest anyone try and take her down again, because she kept saying, very loudly, that she *deserved* to be here.

Well, at least the worst was over, Cordelia figured. Her children now understood they had a half brother, and while she wished they had not found out like they had, she could at least mark that off her to-do list.

"I have news," George said, and his gaze flicked up to Cordelia, and he flashed a strange smile. A sad smile. Like he felt sorry for her. But not in a sympathetic way because she'd lost her husband—it was more piteous than that. "I don't know how to sugarcoat it, so I'll just say it. Charlie had a gambling problem."

Cordelia snorted. Was *that* all? She was well aware of Charlie's gambling, and his frequent trips to Vegas, his recklessness with betting. She glanced down at the dress Zac had made for her and noticed the seam had torn. She hoped he wouldn't ask for pictures.

"Now, don't misunderstand," George said. "It's not like you're poor."

Hello. That brought Cordelia's head up.

"But you're probably not as rich as you think,"

he said apologetically. "Well, frankly, I know you're not."

Cordelia's heart began to pound in time with her temples. "Wait just a minute, George," she said curtly, as if George was pranking them.

"You're going to have to start doing things differently," George said, pretending she hadn't spoken at all.

"Mom?" Hallie whimpered.

"How differently?" Nick asked.

"Don't spend as much," George said.

"What?" Hallie said, and looked wildly between George and her brothers. "I'm getting *married!*"

"George!" Cordelia shouted, alarmed. "You're scaring my children! You don't mean we can't *spend,*" she said with a bark of unbelievable laughter, and looked around the room for anyone to agree with her.

But everyone's stunned gaze was locked on George.

"Listen, all of you," George said. "Charlie was a good man at heart. But like anyone, he had his demons."

Cordelia snorted and looked at Margaret, who returned her glare.

"But he loved his family. Last time we updated his will, he made sure there was something in there for each of you." George looked at the paper before him and began to read. He didn't look up. He didn't make eye contact.

Cordelia knew her husband. And she knew before George ever uttered a word that the "something" Charlie had left for each of his family was not what they were expecting.

As if his death hadn't been hard enough, he would add this to it? She looked at the faces of her children, at the confusion and disappointment, and felt a new, fresh wave of grief. *Damn you, Charlie.*

She wanted to kill him all over again.

Chapter Six

It was Mariah's bright idea that Ella set up a booth at the Three Rivers Winter Carnival.

"You have to be kidding," Ella had scoffed one afternoon when she'd stopped by Mariah's beauty salon/boutique to beg her for work. "People aren't interested in accounting at winter carnivals."

Mariah had held up a black dress against Ella. It had big yellow daffodils printed on the full skirt, and Mariah had studied it with a critical eye.

"They are interested in games and beer and . . . winter," Ella had said as she glanced down.

"You'd be surprised," Mariah had said, and put the dress back on the rack. "Last year, Dr. Evans got two new patients. One of them didn't actually have many teeth, but still, he signed up for dental care at the carnival. That's how you reel them in." She'd picked up a light blue polka dot dress and held it up to Ella. "You would look *so cute* in this."

Ella had loved the adorable dress, but she'd pushed it aside. Unfortunately, the animals that congregated at her house were putting some serious hurt in her discretionary budget.

"That's not how you reel anyone in," she'd said. "Anyway, forget the carnival. Come on, Mariah. Are you going to give me your business?" She truly hadn't come to shop. If she didn't get her business off the ground, she'd be hostessing at the Magnolia and working part-time for strange Byron for the rest of her life.

Mariah had put the blue dress in front of her again. "Randy is skeptical."

"What? *Why?* I bought him a donut!" Ella had exclaimed, pushing the cute dress aside again. "Is it because I'm a girl? That's it, isn't it? That is so *sexist,* Mariah."

Mariah had returned the dress to the rack. "It's not because you're a *girl,* Ella. It's because you have no *clients.* You're untried. He says we don't know if you know what you're doing or not."

"I have a degree. I have experience. I am the accountant for the Rodeo Rebels," she'd pointed out.

Mariah had rolled her eyes at that. "Keeping track of nothing is a lot easier than actual money."

Mariah and Stacy had never been as close as Ella was to either one of them.

"Go to the winter carnival and drum up some business," Mariah had advised. "I'll even lend you a table."

So here Ella sat at the Three Rivers Winter Carnival, sandwiched between a brassy redheaded woman selling time-shares and homemade jam,

100

and a man with a faded plaid shirt and a cowboy hat that was as stained as her kitchen floor. He nodded in her direction, then looked away. He was too busy setting up a display of repurposed horseshoes. He'd painted a bunch of them orange and had soldered them together to make a pumpkin. He'd made some colorful horseshoe daisies, too, which he'd welded onto rebar poles. Ella assumed they were to put in a garden. He had wine racks, tables and chairs, crosses, toilet paper holders—whatever a person could possibly want, all of it made from horseshoes. And in the center of his table was what she thought was possibly his crowning achievement—a miniature horse made entirely of horseshoes. *Ironic.*

And Ella? Well, she had some brochures she'd made on her ancient laptop and had printed and folded at the local pharmacy and mailing depot for the outrageous fee of seventy-five dollars. And she had a bowl of Reese's peanut butter cups. Mariah had told her to do that.

Her table felt a little underdressed. Boring. Unnoticeable. So Ella walked around to the front of it to see if there was anything she could do to jazz it up.

The woman with the time-shares and jam stuck her hand out. "Barb MacKay," she said. "Recognize me?"

Ella was startled by the question. "Should I?"

"Sure! I'm a rural mail carrier and you're on

my route. At least I think you're the one holed up at the old Kendall place. Is that you?"

She wasn't holed up. "Oh," Ella said, and shook her hand. "Yes, that's me. I'm Ella Kendall."

"I know. I deliver your mail. Folks call me Big Barb on account of my personality," Big Barb said, and then laughed. "You'll see."

That would not have been Ella's first guess as to the reason for the nickname, as the woman was ample. "Nice to meet you."

"So how are you liking it out there?" Big Barb asked. "Pretty lonely living from where I'm sitting, sugar."

"Not at all. I have an entire animal kingdom to keep me company."

"Big Barb!"

Ella glanced over her shoulder—a woman with a flowery tunic top and two kids in tow was sailing directly for them.

"Marybeth Compton, how have you *been?*" Big Barb cried, and grabbed the woman in a bear hug.

"I'm good!" Marybeth said. "How are *you?*"

"Right as rain, I can't complain! I mean my fibromyalgia has been flaring up, but you just gotta work through it, you know? I'm not a complainer, mind you. I don't understand these kids today that gotta complain. You just do what you need to do, am I right?"

Marybeth was nodding along and asked Big

Barb if she'd been to see a doctor. The two women moved away from Ella's table to talk. The two kids remained behind and stared at Ella as if she were the creature from the Black Lagoon.

"Hi," she said.

The girl smiled shyly and lifted her hand.

Not much of a carnival for kids, Ella thought. One had to question why they called it a carnival at all. There was only one quasi-ride outside: four ponies walking around and around a maypole. Ella felt their pain.

Most of the carnival was taking place in a giant barn at the Expo Center. Outside, in addition to the ponies, there were fire pits, hot chocolate and hot dog stands, and animals to pet. Ella pondered whether or not she should have brought the pig to be petted. Maybe someone would have taken pity on her and taken that eating machine. Unfortunately, that pig was too big to fit into her SUV and probably would have eaten the upholstery on the way.

The barn itself was one of the giant halls where rodeo and cattle auctions took place. But this weekend, it had been cleared out, and someone had laid down a temporary dance floor. Across the barn from where the booths had been set up was a stage, and a local band was playing a two-step just now. Saturday night revelers were filling the place, and those who weren't stopping by to say hello to Big Barb were on the dance floor, moving counterclockwise in a giant circle of two-stepping. Temporary bars had been set up on either end of the floor, each of them hosting very long lines.

Lots of people wandered by Ella's sad little table, helping themselves to her peanut butter cups on their way to the repurposed horseshoes or the pottery down the line or the soaps or even Big Barb's jam. Only one elderly couple stopped by her table. He wore a Marine Corps hat, and her hair was snow white. They both had on wire-rimmed glasses and sensible shoes with Velcro straps.

"An *accountant,*" the woman cooed as she studied one of Ella's brochures.

"I am," Ella said. "Are you in the market for one?"

"Oh no," the woman said. "We use TurboTax. That's the easiest and the cheapest."

Well, yes, Ella was aware that her fees were a little higher than TurboTax. Unfortunately, not a whole lot higher.

The woman pocketed one of Ella's brochures all the same.

"You ought to get out from behind that table and dance," the old man said. "Pretty girl like you ought to dance."

"Leave her alone, Herb," the woman said. "Oh my, will you look at that? That pumpkin is made of horseshoes!" They moved away from Ella's table to ogle the horseshoe art.

After two hours of sitting there, Ella was thinking of packing up and heading home to send an appropriately worded text to Mariah when the music stopped and someone walked up on stage. He was wearing a western suit and bolo tie. Her first thought was that either a square dance or an auction was about to commence, and she was definitely getting out of here if that were the case.

"That's the mayor," Big Barb said, and came sliding over on her wheeled chair to be next to Ella. "Tom Franklin of Franklin Insurance. Know him?"

"I don't," Ella said.

"Well, if you ever need good insurance, he's your guy."

Mayor Franklin touched the microphone a few times to make sure it was working. "Hello! Hello, Three Rivers! Could I please have your attention?"

Everyone in the barn began to settle and turn toward the stage. Several people shushed others behind them and shifted closer to hear.

"I'd like to thank everyone for coming out to Three Rivers twelfth annual Winter Carnival! This is the biggest crowd we've had in our history."

This garnered a round of cheerful applause, because as all of them in attendance knew, small towns had to take the victories where they could get them.

The mayor had to use both hands to indicate everyone should quiet down again. "Now, normally, I wouldn't be up here to interrupt the fun, but down at city hall, we decided there wasn't a better place to do this."

As he spoke, a very fit woman in a sleek blue suit stepped onto the stage. She had gold-brown hair that was short and styled behind her ears. She was followed by a younger man who was tall and just as fit, with dark brown hair. An elderly woman was on his arm.

"I'm sure you've all heard that Charlie Prince passed away suddenly and unexpectedly about three weeks ago," the mayor said.

"Dropped dead on the golf course," Big Barb muttered.

Ella had heard about the death of Charlie Prince and had guessed—hoped?—that was the reason Luca had never called her. Of course he hadn't called her after his dad died . . . but she secretly hoped he'd meant to. The death of Charlie Prince was a big deal in Three Rivers. On the day of the funeral, Ella could hardly get through town because big buses were ferrying people from the civic center out to the ranch and back.

Behind the handsome man with the elderly woman came another middle-aged woman in a flowery dress, escorted by a handsome young man wearing a cowboy hat. And then, behind them, Hallie Prince. Ella hadn't seen Hallie in

106

twelve years, but she'd know her anywhere. She was still the prettiest one around. Behind her, hopping onto the stage as if he were running a little late came Luca.

Ella's breath hitched in her chest. He looked amazing, given what he and his family had gone through. He was wearing a dark blazer, a crisp white collared shirt, jeans, and boots. She wished she could speak to him, at least tell him she was sorry for his loss. She also wished she could think of something more comforting to say than that, but it hardly mattered. He was onstage and she was sitting in the back, in the shadows. He wouldn't even know she was here.

"Charlie Prince was descended from our town's founders," the mayor said. "He was a civic leader, a philanthropist, and an all-around stand-up guy."

"Well, well, that's Luca Prince, as I live and breathe," Big Barb muttered. "I haven't seen him in so long I thought he might have packed up one of those electric cars and moved out of state." She leaned closer to Ella and whispered, "Ever since Charlie died, I've been hearing things. People are worried about the Princes, you know?"

Ella blinked. She didn't know. She didn't even know what that meant.

"Quite a blow, losing Charlie like they did."

"Sure," Ella agreed.

"He was a gambler," Big Barb muttered, and looked around, as if to see if anyone could hear her. "Like a *big* gambler. I've heard there might be some trouble."

"As many of you know," the mayor continued, "it was Charlie's desire to see a new sports complex open up on the south side of town, and he donated the funds to make that happen."

A round of applause went up from the crowd. One of the men onstage put his arm around the woman in the blue suit.

"Now that's Nick Prince with Mrs. Prince," Big Barb said. "He's the oldest son. He's running the family company now, and Charlotte says he has been in a *mood* since his dad died," Big Barb said, waggling her brows at Ella.

"Charlotte?"

"You don't know Charlotte? I thought everyone knew her. She's the office manager at the Saddlebush Land and Cattle Company. It's been her and Nick these past few days."

"We had planned to unveil this plaque at the opening of the sports complex, but we thought we'd use this occasion to present the plaque to the family instead," the mayor said. "It commemorates the Princes' many contributions to our community over the last century," the mayor said.

As he spoke, two men rolled out a big lump of something covered with a sheet.

"Here to accept the plaque on behalf of the Prince family is Charlie's widow, Cordelia Prince."

The woman in blue stepped forward as everyone applauded.

"She's not handling it well," Big Barb said. "I heard she showed up to book club with a half-drunk bottle of wine and *store-bought cookies.* If you know anything about Cordelia Prince, you know she doesn't do store bought, no sir. She's always been proud that they have their own baker out there at the ranch, which, you know, always seemed a little over the top to me. Everyone around here would prefer one of Molly Maguire's cakes if I'm being honest."

Ella didn't know what Big Barb was prattling on about—she was fixated on what was happening on the stage. The men couldn't untie the rope around the covered object.

"Who's the guy in back?" Ella whispered.

"Oh, well, *that's* a story," Big Barb said with a gleam in her eyes. "Turns out Charlie had a kid he forgot to mention. That's Margaret Sutton Rhodes in the flowered dress, and the boy she had with Charlie. His name is Tanner Sutton."

The rope was undone, and someone pulled the cloth away from the thing underneath. It was a bucking bronco with a small plaque affixed to it.

Cordelia Prince leaned over and read aloud, "Dedicated to Charles Colby Prince, civic leader, benefactor, philanthropist, and friend to all."

Everyone applauded. Men whistled. Cordelia

Prince straightened and peered out stoically over the crowd.

"I heard they didn't even *know* about Tanner until he died. I bet that was some drama, I'll tell you what."

"Thank you, Mr. Mayor, and our friends," Mrs. Prince said. Her voice was smooth. She sounded practiced. "On behalf of my family, thank you for this dear commemoration. Charlie loved Three Rivers so much. Like his family before him, he never wanted to leave here." She paused to clear her throat and put her fist to her mouth a moment. "It's all still very new to us, but we wanted to be here to say thank you for remembering him in this way."

The crowd applauded again, and Cordelia Prince stepped back. But then the older woman darted past her to the microphone and tapped it. "I'm Dolly Prince," she said. "Charlie's mother. I just want you to know that my son would have wanted to be here tonight. He loved this carnival. He wanted to have it at the civic center, but oh no," she said with a shake of her finger. "The city council hates progress."

Luca and his brother Nick moved at the same moment, each of them grabbing an arm and pulling their grandmother away from the mic. Nick Prince said, "Thank you," and waved at the crowd before they escorted her to the back of the stage.

"That's Charlie's mother, all right. Little off her rocker," Big Barb offered.

"Oh," Ella said. "Dementia?"

"What? No!" Big Barb said. "She's just a crazy old woman, that's all. Nick, he's the only sane one of the group."

"Oh, I—"

"Cordelia is okay, but she's not the friendliest woman in town. Hallie, well, she's all about dresses and what not. Never had to work a day in her life. She's getting married soon and will end up on the high-society circuit in Houston."

How did Big Barb know all of this?

"And that Luca," she said with a snort. "He's easy on the eyes, but he's never gonna amount to much. Can't hold a job for more than five seconds, sleeps with all the girls in town but never for long."

Ella inwardly winced.

The mayor was speaking again, something about the parking lot. People were moving again, the band getting ready to play.

"Sure is sad what happened to old Charlie Prince," Big Barb said with a sigh.

"Big Barb, you still selling those time-shares at South Padre?" A man wearing suspenders had appeared at her table.

"You know I am, Ed. Are you finally gonna admit you want in?" she asked, and rolled back to her table.

Ella looked up to the stage. The family had gathered around the bronco to have a look. Luca stood behind them, his hands in his pockets. *Never going to amount to much.*

When you grew up in the Texas foster care system, you tended to take such proclamations with a grain of salt. Once, a police officer had come to talk to one of the boys in one of the places Ella had lived as a kid. The caseworker had met the cop, and they'd stood out on the front porch talking. Ella could remember their conversation like she'd heard it yesterday. The cop had told the caseworker that Bobby "was like the rest of them" and "was never going to amount to much."

"Hell," he'd said with a shrug, "the girls will end up pregnant, and the boys in jail. That's just the way it goes."

Which house was that? Number three? Number four? Ella couldn't remember anymore, but she could remember Bobby. He was painfully shy and couldn't look at anyone without the veil of his bangs over his eyes. He was a gifted artist. He drew scenes from the fantasy world that lived in his head. Dragons and warriors, damsels and castles. Two-headed beasts, forests glittering with fairies. They said Bobby was never going to amount to much, and maybe he hadn't. She didn't know what had happened to him, didn't know what had happened to anyone other than

Stacy. But she knew that, like all of them, Bobby was so much more than a foster kid. He was an artist. He could have amounted to a lot more than anyone knew.

She watched Luca leave the stage with his family. She didn't believe Big Barb. She thought Luca was already more than anyone knew.

She briefly toyed with the idea of walking across the dance floor and catching him to say hello. But he was with his family, and she didn't know what she'd say, exactly. So Ella instead gathered her brochures and her peanut butter cups.

"Wait! Where are you going?" Big Barb cried when she noticed that Ella was packing up.

"I'm calling it a day," Ella said. "No one wants an accountant."

"What you need is something to attract people." This came courtesy of the horseshoe guy.

Ella looked at him. "Like what?" she asked. "I don't have any cool horseshoe art. I have a head for numbers, that's all."

"Yeah, that's not very sexy," he said, and Ella wondered if she ought to be offended. "Anything would help," he added, and once again, she wondered if she ought to be even more offended. But that was her problem, in a nutshell. She didn't like attention.

"Here," he said, and reached down under his table then stood up, holding a small decorative bowl made of horseshoes. "Next time, put your brochures in that." He handed it to her.

"Oh! I couldn't," she said.

"Sure you can. I got plenty more where that came from. It's just a little something. If you don't use it for your brochures, put fruit or whatever in it, and next time, put it on your goshdern table."

"Thanks," Ella said. She took the bowl—it was heavy—and stuffed it into her bag. She smiled at him. "Appreciate it."

"Don't mention it," he said, and sat back down.

"Good-bye, Ella! See you on the route!" Big Barb said with a wave, and turned back to the couple who had come over to say hello.

With her new horseshoe bowl, and seventy-five dollars' worth of brochures in her bag, Ella headed out of the winter carnival. On her way to the parking lot, she decided she'd treat herself to hot chocolate and got in line. As she waited, she observed the kids going around on the ponies. She'd never been on a pony. She'd never been on a horse.

"Can I buy you a drink?"

Luca's voice startled her so badly that Ella whipped around and slammed him in the thigh with her heavy, horseshoe-laden tote bag.

Chapter Seven

"Ouch," Luca said, and rubbed the sting from his thigh. "What the hell do you have in that thing?"

"I'm so sorry! It's a horseshoe bowl."

Luca looked at the offending tote bag, not understanding. "A what?"

Ella pulled out the bowl made from welded horseshoes. A brochure fluttered to the ground, and he bent to pick it up, his gaze on the strange bowl. "That's . . . interesting."

"I'm sorry—you startled me."

"I gathered," he said. He'd already forgotten it, because Ella was cute. Pretty, cute, and sexy all tied up in one package. She wore her hair in two low pigtails, topped off with a newsboy hat. Her plaid skirt was ridiculously short, for which he was grateful, because her legs, for God's sake, were the best thing happening in all of Cimarron County.

He'd thought of her a few times in the last couple of weeks, of course he had, but was reminded now just how enticing she was. He hadn't called her like he'd promised. In his defense, he'd been seriously out of it. Drunk with grief.

It was unbelievable that he'd spotted her at all, really. As they'd been escorting his grandma from the premises before she made a scene about not being allowed to speak, he'd just happened to glimpse a woman with incredible legs walking out of the Expo, and there was something about her ankle boots that seemed sort of Ella-ish, and after they'd shoved his grandma into the limo, he'd gone after those legs, hoping it *was* Ella. He could use something else to think about instead of his dad.

"Hey," she said, as she slid the bowl into her bag, "I heard about your dad. I'm really sorry, Luca."

Every time someone said that, Luca inwardly flinched. It was like the news kept sucker-punching him over and over again. He hoped that wasn't obvious to her. He hoped he didn't look the mess he felt inside. "Thanks," he said, averting his gaze. "It was quite a shock." He glanced at the brochure he held and watched the letters dance around. He could have made it out, but it would have required concentration and a little time. "What's this?"

"Oh, ah . . . my accounting services," she said, and gingerly slid the brochure from his fingers and stuffed it back into her bag. "Mariah Frame convinced me I could drum up some business by having a booth here."

"And?"

"And no one wants to hire a bookkeeper or accountant at a winter carnival." She smiled.

"You're an accountant?"

"Yep, that's me," she said, and smiled tentatively, as if she wasn't sure what he would think of it. "What can I say? I love numbers."

Luca couldn't help a wry smile. "I didn't know anyone loved numbers."

"Oh yeah," she said, nodding. "Lots of people love numbers. They don't lie, you know. They are very definitely black on white paper. No gray areas to mess with your mind. You may not know where the road leads, but there is a sure path for getting wherever you need to go."

"You've thought a *lot* about numbers," he said. "Sometimes it's fun not to have a path."

"Hmm," she said, as if considering that. And then shook her head. "Nope. I definitely want a path."

He resisted the urge to touch her cheek. "Is it possible your path tonight leads to hot chocolate?"

"Oh. I, ah . . ." She squinted toward the parking lot.

"Let me guess," he said, and shoved his hands into his pockets so that he wouldn't touch her. "You're busy."

She gave him a sidelong look and smiled. "*Super* busy. There's a *Real Housewives of Atlanta* marathon happening tonight."

He had no idea what that was. "Then what are you even doing here?"

"Right? *Hashtag priorities* is all I'm saying."

His priority at that moment was prolonging this encounter. "Still . . . I'm surprised you don't want to buy me a winter carnival drink. I sort of thought you were falling for me."

"I *was,*" she said with feigned enthusiasm. "Totally! But then the housewives thing came up, and you know how it is. Plus, I have to feed a dog. And a pig. And some horses. And a cat. And some random chickens that are leaving eggs from time to time."

Luca glanced at his feet and tried to summon all his turbo sex appeal that Nick accused him of having. But he couldn't do it. He couldn't summon a playful retort or a line guaranteed to keep this going. He glanced up and said, "Look, Ella . . . I'm really sorry I didn't call."

"Don't be," she said instantly, her smile fading. "You obviously get a pass, Luca. Don't even mention it."

"Yeah, well, I appreciate that. But I really don't want to be that guy," he said with a slight wince.

"What guy?"

"You know, the guy who says he's going to call and never does."

"Oh, *that* guy. Well, never is a long time. I hadn't given up hope yet."

"But you weren't holding your breath."

"With all due respect, it was a good thing I wasn't," she said, and smiled softly.

He so badly wanted to touch her. Two fingers to her cheek, or her ear. "Did you get the porch fixed?"

"I did. Fortunately, there is nothing YouTube doesn't know how to do. Plus, I had a friend who owed me a favor."

"I feel bad about that. I practically made you go out and buy a hammer."

She shook her head. She glanced at the hot chocolate stand, then at him. Her expression was curious, and she shifted a little closer. But not too close, he noticed.

"How are you doing, really?"

"I'm okay," he said instantly, because that was what he'd trained himself to say these last few weeks, but he was looking at her eyes, and suddenly he had a strange compulsion to confess everything he was feeling to her, things he had yet to feel, past sins, future sins. There was something about her that made Luca believe that he could tell her anything.

God, he was a wreck.

He laughed self-consciously and ran a hand over his head. "The truth? Not great. A lot of stuff came up when my dad died, and I'm . . ." He paused. He was what? Barely making it through every day? Constantly standing in the middle of an argument between his mother and his grandmother, their grief so raw he could hardly cope with it? Letting Hallie cry on his shoulder while he wondered where the hell her fiancé was? Being the ear Nick needed to bend, because Nick was the one who had to pick up the burden of a family business he did not want?

Luca realized, standing there, that he didn't have a release from all of the grief and agony. He had nowhere to turn. Every which way he turned there was someone needing him to be strong.

The upshot was that Luca hadn't quite dealt with the loss. He wanted his dad back. Even a shadow of his dad would do at this point. He didn't want his dad to become just a memory. He didn't want to accept that his father was never coming back.

Never.

Never is a long time.

He felt something crack in him, the bitter acknowledgment that there were so many things he wished he'd said or done. He wished he'd been the good son. He wished he'd made his dad proud before he went to that big golf course in the sky. He could feel that crack widening, and it seemed to him as if all sorts of stuff was about to come flying out, like bats released from their cave.

"Are you okay?" Ella asked, and touched his arm.

Luca realized he was on the verge of losing it. He swallowed. He nodded. "Yeah, yeah," he said, and shook himself back to the present. "I've been thinking I need to take some time off and get out of town." The thought had just occurred to him, but it suddenly seemed imperative.

"That's a good idea," she said.

"Can we, ah . . . can we have a rain check on that call?" he asked.

"Sure," she said, and smiled sympathetically.

Luca's heart sank. He'd left her house feeling really good, and he wanted everything to go back to that afternoon. Before Nick met him on the drive.

"You know what? I think I should buy *you* a hot chocolate," she said.

"That would be really nice," he said, and to his horror, felt himself choking up.

"Stay right here," she said, and stepped up to the counter of a food trailer shaped to look like a giant coffee cup. "Two hot chocolates, please," she said, and began to dig in her tote bag for a wallet.

"Whipped cream?" the guy standing in the coffee cup asked her.

"Dude," Ella said with mock seriousness, "we're not Luddites. Of *course* whipped cream."

"So I guess that means you want the sprinkles, too," the guy said with a grin.

"Do you even have to ask?"

A few minutes later, Ella delivered Luca a paper cup of hot chocolate with a sturdy tower of whipped cream and rainbow sprinkles.

He tried to sip the chocolate. Ella laughed and, with the tip of her finger, wiped whipped cream from his cheek, then licked her finger. She took a bite of her whipped cream like it was an ice cream cone.

They began to meander along with their cups, headed in the general direction of the parking lot, their pace slow.

"May I ask what your dad was like?" Ella said.

"He was bigger than life," Luca said instantly. "I know that sounds trite, but he was." He didn't know how to explain that the force of one man's personality could have such an impact on those around him.

"A good dad?" Ella asked.

"The best," Luca agreed. "He wasn't a perfect man by any stretch." He gave a strangled little laugh at that overstatement. "He definitely had his issues. But yeah, he was a good dad, and I never doubted for a moment that he loved me in spite of . . ." He paused, once again uncertain what he was going to say.

"In spite of what?" Ella asked.

The fact that I can't read. That I'm not Nick. That I disappoint Mom all the time. He looked at Ella. "I meant no matter what."

She nodded and sipped her chocolate. "I'm sorry I never met him. He sounds like a great guy."

"He was," Luca agreed.

122

"I never knew my dad."

Luca looked up. "No?"

She shook her head. "Don't even know who he is." She smiled a little, as if she found that oddly amusing. "It must really suck to lose a dad, Luca. I can't even imagine it. But you're lucky—at least you have a ton of memories."

"True," he agreed. They had come to the split railing that separated the gravel parking lot from the Expo Center. He held up his cup and tapped it against hers. "Thanks for this."

"You're welcome."

Luca glanced at the cars, his thoughts spinning. Why did someone like Ella have to pop up on a country road at what would become the worst time of his life? "My timing sucks," he said.

He didn't have to explain—she understood. She nodded. "Life happens."

He looked at her again. *Really* looked at her. The dark lashes that framed her pretty eyes. The slight upturn of her nose. The dark plum of her lips. Yeah, his timing sucked, all right. He would have given anything to continue this thing they had growing between them, but it was impossible at present. He couldn't get out of his own head. "I guess I'll say good-bye." He didn't know what else to say. His game was so off it was in the locker room.

He couldn't exactly promise to call. He didn't know where he was going or which way was up right now. So he leaned in and softly kissed her cheek. Ella stilled. Her lashes fluttered, and then she closed her eyes. He lingered there, because she was soft, and her skin was warm, and he could detect a faint scent that reminded him of roses. She was a sweet summer dream, and for a moment, he was in that dream, flying back to the space he'd been in before his dad had dropped dead on the green.

Ella slowly leaned away and looked up at him.

Luca smiled. He tugged on the bill of her newsboy hat. "See you, Ella."

"See you, Luca," she said.

He stepped away, walking backward, not ready to relinquish the sight of her, then finally turned and began the walk back to the Expo Center where Nick and Hallie were presumably still waiting for him.

He thought he heard her say something, and he looked back. She was standing there, her arms crossed, the steam rising from her hot chocolate. But then she pivoted and disappeared between the cars.

And the warmth and kindness and understanding he'd felt in her presence disappeared with her.

Chapter Eight

SPRING

Due to a gig being canceled at the last minute, Stacy had a rare weekend to spend with Ella at her little house. They streamed movies and attempted to make pizza in Ella's ancient oven, but it wasn't heating right, and eventually, they gave up and ordered in.

The next day, they planned to go into town. The following morning, Dog's barking woke them. The horses had come up to the fence, annoying Dog. By the time Ella had pulled on some pants and run outside, the horses had moved away. So she sat perched on the fence, watching them from afar.

Stacy had followed her and was sitting on a tree stump painting her toenails, because nothing screamed spring quite like bright neon green toenails. Stacy had wanted to drag the picnic table out of the garage, but Ella had forbid it. "First, I think it's holding up a wall. Secondly, there might be snakes in there."

"Trust me," Stacy said, "if there were snakes, Big Bertha over there would have eaten them for a snack." She'd nodded in the direction of the pig, stretched out on its side, having a snooze just inside the garage.

Ella glanced at Stacy's toes, wincing a little at the color. "Remember the time you stole Pam's nail polish?" she asked idly, referring to the foster mother they had shared the last three years of high school. Before they were emancipated from the system and launched into the world to sink or swim. When the state's money stopped rolling in for their care, Pam stopped caring.

Pam and Gary had six foster children, the other four much younger than Ella and Stacy. It was always a little terrifying to Ella that people like Pam and Gary were allowed to take children in, given the amount of drinking and fighting they did. More than once, Gary had left Pam with a black eye. More than once, she'd threatened to stab him with a knife.

Stacy snorted. "Of course, I remember. It was one of the highlights of our time with Pam and Gary, trust me."

They were sixteen when Stacy swiped Pam's nail polish. But Stacy hadn't just painted her fingers and toes—she'd also painted some unkind things on the bathroom mirror. Ella loved Stacy like a sister, but one thing she'd never understood was why she liked to throw gasoline on established fires. What drove her? It was as if she was always looking for ways to make a bad decision, and if she made one, you could bet your last dollar she'd find a way to make it worse.

"Gary beat the crap out of me, remember that?" Stacy added as she squinted down at her left foot. She said it casually, as if she were asking if Ella remembered Gary ordering take-out that night.

"Oh, I remember," Ella said. She'd tried to intervene, and Gary had knocked her across the kitchen for it. "Sometimes I don't get you, Stacy. What did you think was going to happen when you painted those words on the bathroom mirror?"

Stacy shrugged. "You don't get me because you're the exact opposite of me. You'd rather stay in the background and hope no one notices you. I make sure everyone notices me. But that's okay—one of us needs to lay low."

Ella would rather lay low than intentionally make trouble. "You used to scare me to death, doing all the things that were so bad for you."

"Sweetie, I *still* do a lot of things that are bad for me," Stacy said. "But we're grown now, and you could stand to loosen your laces, you know? They're tied way too tight."

This was an ongoing debate between Ella and Stacy. Ella was the sober one, the responsible one, who made sure Stacy didn't spend all her money and paid her taxes. Stacy was the flighty, creative, not-so-responsible one who thought tips shouldn't count as income and liked to spend all her money on bling.

Secretly, Ella wished she could be more like Stacy. Secretly, Ella hoped to God she would never be like Stacy—her poor guarded heart couldn't take it. She did truly admire Stacy for her ambition and determination. But she did not care for the way Stacy skated on the edge of disaster all the time and seemed to get a thrill out of it.

"I wish the horses would come here," Stacy said, looking out past the fence. "I want to pet one. Can you pet a horse?"

"Why not?" Ella asked. She whistled to the horses, soft and low, because she'd never figured out how to do a shrill, look-over-here whistle. One of the horses lifted its head and looked at her, then went back to grazing. The other two didn't bother to look up.

The same three horses came around every day about this time. If Ella was inside, they would come to the fence and eat the feed she put out. If she was outside, they'd stay away and graze until she was gone, avoiding her like she was from the glue factory. The dog didn't like them. He barked every time they came around and raced out into the pasture. But the horses paid him no mind.

"They won't come anywhere near me," Ella complained to Stacy. "I'm starting to get a complex."

"They don't want to go back in a cage," Stacy opined.

"Do you mean a fenced pasture?" Ella asked dryly.

"Same thing. It's *confinement*. I hate confinement."

"Are we talking about you?"

"Shut up," Stacy said, and nudged Ella with her foot. She extended both legs and looked at her toes with a critical eye. "You didn't gush about my extensions." She pointed to the top of her head, where she had piled her glorious mane of blond hair she'd recently purchased. Stacy had called Ella at her accounting job the day she'd had them installed—in someone's garage in San Antonio's Southtown, by a woman without a license, but who "totally knows what she is doing" according to Stacy. "Tax deductible, right?"

"No," Ella had said.

"What?" Stacy said. "They are part of my stage costume and, therefore, tax deductible."

She'd badgered Ella until Ella had broken down and asked the advice of Byron, the CPA for whom she worked part-time. Byron was a one-man shop in a little two-person office on Broadway in San Antonio. He was always in his office, spilling over the arms of his chair, papers stacked around him from floor to ceiling. He had no social life that Ella could detect, and yet, he had a steady stream of clients, all of whom looked a little on the shady side.

When Ella had asked about the extensions, Byron looked at her with an expression that conveyed she'd failed him on every level, in every possible way. "I think you ought to reconsider your question," he'd said gravely.

Ella had reconsidered it and had slunk back to her desk.

"Don't tell me *Brian* is raining on my parade," Stacy complained when Ella reported back to her. "What does he know, anyway?"

"His name is Byron and he's a CPA," Ella had said firmly. "They look good," she admitted to Stacy now. "Very Carrie Underwood-ish. Where did you get them, again?"

Stacy sighed and stood up. "Never you mind, cupcake," she said, and then, "Are we going to Mariah's Easter sale or what?"

Ella cringed. That was not a good answer. Stacy was a law-abiding citizen for the most part, but from time to time, she had a slight problem with the *law* part of that. It had started in her teens with a little shoplifting. Ella remembered the first time she'd come home with some cheap earrings, slipped into her pocket at the dollar store. Ella had been shocked and alarmed. Stacy had thought it was funny. It happened several times, and she'd been caught more than once, had gotten into a lot of trouble that included a short stint in juvenile hall. Judges weren't very sympathetic when it came to stealing.

Twice, an unwitting Ella had been held with her. Guilty by association was a real thing. Both times, Ella had been let go because she wasn't a thief. Both times, she'd gotten a look from the officers that clearly relayed their skepticism about her innocence.

Talk about heart-pounding fear—Ella's worst nightmare was ending up in jail and sharing a cell with her mother. Everything she did was to avoid her mother's fate. But Stacy had seemed to think nothing of taking Ella down with her, or risking it all for so little.

That had been a long time ago, when they were juveniles. The stakes were higher now, and Ella worried that Stacy would push things so far she would get into serious trouble and disappear, just like Ella's mother had. She'd be devastated if that happened—Stacy was the closest thing to family she had. There were times she wished some Lilliputians would suddenly appear and lasso Stacy to the ground. Just keep her tied up so she couldn't shoplift hair extensions and earrings and whatever else she'd taken.

And yet, as much as Ella despised what Stacy did, she understood it in that strange, foster-kid way she had of seeing the world. People who grew up in foster care understood things that other people with happy childhoods couldn't possibly get. Being removed from a family and passed around screwed with a person's head. You learned not to trust anyone. You learned not to believe what adults told you. You learned how to cope without help from anyone.

Most kids figured out how to make it bearable. Shoplifting had been Stacy's way of making it bearable. Ella did not understand the psychology behind that, but Stacy's habit of stealing generally ramped up when she was under a lot of pressure. She was under pressure now—she and the Rodeo Rebels had no money but had a chance to sign with a record label if they could make it to Nashville. For all her faults, Stacy was an electric performer and an excellent singer, and she wanted that chance more than life.

"Stop it," Stacy said suddenly.

Ella looked at her.

"Stop *worrying* about me all the time."

Jesus, that was uncanny. Ella mentally instructed the Lilliputians to crawl back under their toadstools. "I'm not worrying. I'm imagining how wrong black-and-white stripes are with your coloring."

"I'm fine, Ella. Everything is *fine*."

So, in other words, everything was *not* fine.

"Are we going to Mariah's, or not?" Stacy asked impatiently.

"Yep," Ella said. "Let's go."

Chapter Nine

Just like Ella could not get over her high school crush twelve years beyond high school, Mariah could not get over being pissed at Stacy for stealing Cash Proctor from her. From Ella's vantage point, Stacy didn't really steal Cash Proctor, because Cash had never really seemed into Mariah at all and had in fact been stringing a number of girls along. And still, Mariah blamed Stacy.

Over the years, they'd been friendly. But not *friends*.

"Nice place you've got here," Stacy said, looking around. She'd never been in Mariah's shop and always had an excuse ready not to come.

"Thank you," Mariah said. "Nice hair extensions."

Stacy jerked her gaze to Mariah. "Thanks," she said uncertainly. "They're Russian."

Whatever *that* meant.

"So where's the sale I heard about?" Stacy asked, wandering between the racks.

"This rack is twenty-five percent off," Mariah

said, pointing. "That one is fifty, and the row of clothes at the back is all seventy-five percent off."

"I like seventy-five," Stacy said, and disappeared into the clothes.

Ella smiled at frowning Mariah. "So guess what? I might actually have a new client," she announced.

"Really?" Mariah asked, perking up. "Who?"

"Baptist Ladies Auxiliary. One of them was at the winter carnival." The elderly couple who didn't need Ella's services apparently were affiliated with a ladies group that did need her services. "The president is on a cruise or something right now, but when they start back up next month, I'm going to meet them. If I get the job, that will be *three* paying customers," she said brightly. "Tell Randy to put *that* in his no-clients pipe and smoke it."

Mariah laughed. "I'll tell him, I sure will. Who else have you got, again?"

"The funeral home," Ella said, holding up a finger. "The ladies group. And Rodeo Rebels."

Mariah glanced at Stacy, who was draping clothes over her arm, then leaned toward Ella and whispered, "Are they really making any money?"

"Yes, *Mariah,* we are making money!" Stacy called out in a singsong voice without turning from her perusal of a rack of clothes.

Mariah looked to Ella for confirmation. Ella shook her head. The Rodeo Rebels were not making real money.

Stacy sauntered to the front of the store, her arms laden with clothes. "Where can I try these on?"

Mariah pointed to a curtained cubby. "Let us see them on you," she suggested as Stacy sashayed by.

"Maybe," Stacy said as she disappeared into the changing room.

Mariah rolled her eyes when Stacy was out of sight. "Aren't you going to look at the sale? I've got some great pieces on the seventy-five-percent-off rack," she said to Ella.

"I'll look. But I'm broke," Ella warned her, and walked to the back of the store to browse.

She'd just found a purple dress with tiny gold puppies romping in sprouts of flowers when she heard the little bell on the shop's door jingle.

"Hallie Prince!" Mariah said, her voice full of delight.

Ella froze. *Hallie? The* Hallie Prince? Prince Luca's twin princess?

"Hello, Mariah. How are you?"

Ella quietly put the dress back on the rack and snuck around the end of it, trying to disappear.

"I'm really good!" Mariah said. "How are *you?* Oh, hey, I was so sorry to hear about your dad."

"Thank you," Hallie said.

"Hey, you remember Ella Kendall, don't you?" Mariah said.

Ella stifled a sigh and reluctantly stepped out from

135

behind the dress carousel. *Wow.* She'd seen Hallie up on the stage at the winter carnival, but up close, Hallie Prince was beautiful. She didn't look any older than she had in high school, but she looked more elegant. She was perfectly trim, dressed in a slim skirt and stiletto heels, a silk blouse. Her strawberry blond hair was cut in a perfect long lob. "Hi," Ella said.

Hallie slowly turned her hazel eyes—Luca's eyes—to Ella. "Ohmigod, *Ella?* Ella Kendall?"

"Um . . . yes," Ella said, and nervously pushed her hair from her eyes. For heaven's sake, why was she so nervous? She had to be the most socially awkward person ever.

"*Hi!*" Hallie said, as if they were long-lost friends and smiled. *Happily.*

"You . . . you remember me?" Ella asked stupidly.

"Of course I remember you!" Hallie said brightly, and shifted her Céline bag onto her shoulder as she came forward. "Why wouldn't I remember you?"

"Because your brother didn't remember her," Stacy's disembodied voice said, and Ella felt her stomach drop. Stacy and her big mouth.

"Who, Nick?" Hallie asked the voice.

"Luca!"

Hallie looked confused. "But he told me he ran into you."

"Hey, do you remember *me?*" The disembodied

136

voice of Stacy was dramatically revealed to be an actual person when Stacy threw back the curtain and stepped out in a slinky silver dress that was way too tight. But Ella could tell by the way Stacy posed that she loved it.

"Stacy Perry! How are you?" Hallie said.

"I'm great. And you're looking fine as usual, Hallie."

"Thank you," Hallie said.

"It's nice to see you, Hallie," Ella said quietly.

"You too, Ella," she said, and strangely, at least to Ella, she sounded as if she genuinely meant it. "I didn't know you were back in Three Rivers."

"She recently moved back from the city," Mariah said. "She has a place out in the country now. Actually, it's next to Three Rivers Ranch."

"It is?" Hallie frowned thoughtfully, then said, "Oh, of course! The old Kendall place!"

"That's the one," Ella said. "I inherited it from my grandmother."

"Oh." Hallie continued to look at her curiously, as if waiting for more information.

Ella tried to rattle a few coherent thoughts together by dragging her fingers through her hair. "She had Alzheimer's." She didn't know why she added that detail. It wasn't as if Hallie knew her grandmother. Ella had never been a chatty girl, because she had figured out at a very young age that the less she said, the fewer questions anyone asked of her. The only person for whom this rule

137

did not apply was Stacy, who knew pretty much everything there was to know about her.

"I'm so sorry," Hallie said. "That must have been hard."

This was exactly what happened when Ella opened her mouth. Now Hallie was looking at her with sympathy, and Mariah was looking at her like she was a dolt, and Stacy was looking at herself in the mirror. Ella didn't know how to explain that her grandmother's death wasn't hard, exactly, but more like a general disappointment that her life had ended like it had. General disappointment that Ella hadn't been a better granddaughter, or that there were such looming familial gaps in her life that she'd never be able to fill.

"We were really sorry to hear about your dad, Hallie," Stacy offered with a quick look at Ella. She always had Ella's back, always knew when the walls were closing in and stepped in to push them back.

"Yes," Ella said. "I am so sorry."

"Thank you," Hallie said. "He was here one minute and gone the next," She snapped her fingers. "It was lights out, just like that."

"That really sucks," Stacy said.

Ella ran her palm down the side of her skirt. She wanted to say something that conveyed that she felt bad for Hallie. She couldn't imagine what it was like to lose a beloved father like that. The closest she could come, besides her grandmother, was Mrs. Ellicott, her sixth-grade math teacher. And her tenth-grade math teacher. Ella had loved Mrs. Ellicott. She had skin as brown as the bronze statue of a mustang that stood outside the school entrance, and a wide, warm smile that she accentuated with bright red lipstick.

Somehow, Mrs. Ellicott had sensed that Ella was desperate for attention. Maybe she'd said something or done something, but in Ella's memory, her teacher was sitting beside her in class one day, telling her that she had a gift for numbers, that she was smart. That she could be anything she wanted to be. Mrs. Ellicott never failed to say hello to her each morning as she monitored the kids coming in for school. On those days Ella stayed after school to do her homework in peace, Mrs. Ellicott gave her hard candies and made her promise not to tell anyone because, she said, she couldn't give candy to all the kids.

Once, Ella had gotten in trouble for day-dreaming in art class. Or that's what her teacher had called it. The truth was that she'd been in a bad home placement, and she'd been exhausted and worried about what was going to happen to her there, and she couldn't care less how to make a pinwheel from construction paper. She'd been sent to the principal's office. Before the principal could do much other than admonish her, Mrs.

Ellicott had come riding in like a knight to convince the principal that she ought to "make" Ella help her sort through some lessons in her classroom.

So Ella had helped sort the lessons and put them in brightly colored boxes. Mrs. Ellicott sang while they worked and told stories about all the people in her life. It had sounded like a dream to Ella—a big, loving family, full of laughter and light.

That afternoon had been one of the best of her school days.

Mrs. Ellicott continued to check in on her as Ella moved through the years, and in tenth grade, when Ella was in her class again, she told Ella she was smart enough to go to college. "You're quick, and you're thorough, Ella. You could go into finance or accounting. Dream big, hon—there is nothing stopping you but your own doubts," she'd said, tapping Ella on the top of her head.

She'd continued to encourage Ella into her junior year. *Dream big, hon. Dream big.*

Then one day, Mrs. Ellicott wasn't at school. *Here one minute and gone the next. Lights out.*

Ella still thought of her. Still missed her smile.

"So what are you up to these days, Hallie?" Stacy asked with a quick look at Ella that told her to snap out of it.

"Well," Hallie said, a smile lighting her face.

"I'm getting married." She held out her hand to show them the ring. "With Dad gone we're sort of rethinking when and all, but hopefully this year."

She was sporting an *enormous* rock on her hand. "Wow, congratulations!" Ella said. "Who's the lucky guy?"

"Christopher Davenport. He's from Houston. He's a surgeon," she added proudly.

"Nice," Stacy said approvingly.

Hallie lowered her hand. "What about you guys?"

"I've got a band," Stacy said promptly and proudly. "The Rodeo Rebels. We have a show Saturday night and a rep from a Nashville recording agency is supposed to be there."

"How exciting!" Hallie said. "I always thought you were the best singer in high school."

"Thanks," Stacy said, her amber eyes lighting up. "I feel really good about it. I even got a new dress for the occasion."

New extensions, a new dress, and a dressing room full of clothes? Stacy was hardly making enough to cover her bills. Where was she getting the cash?

"What about you, Ella?" Hallie asked.

"I ah . . . well, I'm working at the Magnolia as a hostess a couple of nights a week," she began.

"She's an accountant!" Stacy said, and clucked her tongue at Ella.

"I'm trying to be," Ella corrected her. "I've been begging Mariah to take me on."

"What's Luca up to these days?" Stacy asked, clearly not wanting to allow Mariah into the conversation.

"Luca? Oh, he's, ah . . . well, he's been gone a lot," Hallie said. "He had to get away after dad died."

"Yeah, I heard," Stacy muttered.

"What?" Hallie asked.

"Is he seeing anyone?" Stacy asked.

Hallie blinked. Mariah looked like she might kill Stacy if she said another word, but she'd have to beat Ella to it. She mouthed the words, *shut up.* It was her own damn fault for opening her big mouth and gushing about Luca's visit. She wished she'd never told Stacy about running into him at the Magnolia and again at the winter carnival. She wished she'd never told Stacy anything, period.

Hallie laughed at her question. "Luca is *always* seeing someone. He hasn't changed at all."

"Really?" Stacy asked, and pulled her hair from its bun and shook it out. It hung almost to her waist. "I thought maybe he'd settled down by now. Frankly, I'm amazed he's still hanging around Three Rivers."

"Well, we're all trying to pitch in and help Mom, you know? Speaking of which, I need to get going. I just popped in to see if you carry

Spanx, Mariah. I've got to go to a charity thing in Houston this weekend and my dress is a little tight." She laughed self-consciously and rubbed her very flat abdomen.

"As tight as the dress Stacy has on?" Mariah asked with a mischievous smile. "Of course I do—it's my biggest selling brand."

"It was great to see you again, Ella, and you, too, Stacy," Hallie said as she moved to follow Mariah.

"Same," Stacy said. "Be sure and tell Luca that Ella and I said hello," she added, and winked at Ella before slipping into her dressing room.

Hallie had gone with a little wave by the time Stacy emerged from the dressing room wearing another dress. "Well *that* was interesting," Stacy said as she studied herself in the mirror.

"Why?" Mariah asked.

"Didn't Ella tell you? Luca Prince didn't remember who she was," Stacy said.

Jesus and Mary. "Stacy? Can you stop talking?" Ella asked, and looked at Mariah as her face heated. "He didn't remember me at first."

"I told you not to get too excited about him," Stacy opined.

"Ohmigod, seriously, stop talking," Ella said. "You never said that, and I was never *excited*. I was surprised."

"You were *so* excited—"

"I was intrigued!"

143

"Intrigued!" Stacy howled. "You practically had your wedding dress picked out after the senior dance!" She went back into the dressing room.

"What are y'all talking about?" Mariah demanded.

"Don't you remember, Mariah?" Stacy called through the curtain. "Luca Prince *kissed* Ella that night, and she's still swooning about it, even though he is clearly still a dog."

"Hey! Do not ruin my high school crush fantasy," Ella said, trying to make light of it. "I have very little to live for as it is."

Mariah waved it off with a flick of her wrist. "Who *didn't* have a crush on Prince Luca?"

"Me," Stacy said.

"Anyway, who cares," Mariah said. "High school crushes never turn out to be what you thought they were, right? It's like when someone dies young, and they could have grown up to be the biggest asshole, but people believe that only the good die young, and after time, that person becomes a saint."

"Huh?" Ella asked, confused.

"I'm just saying, people don't turn out to be who we thought they would be. Luca Prince was hot, but he barely passed his classes." She glanced up at them and said softly, "I've heard he can't even read."

"That's ridiculous!" Ella said with a snort. "That can't be true."

"But is it true?" Stacy asked as she emerged again with several pieces draped over her arm.

"That's what I've heard," Mariah said with a shrug, and took the clothes Stacy was holding to the counter. "Regardless, my point is, it's entirely possible he doesn't have a lot going on upstairs. You know, a beauty with no brains. He's no fairy tale, Ella."

Ella looked back and forth between Stacy and Mariah. "I don't believe in fairy tales. Of the three of us standing here, I am the *least* likely to believe in fairy tales." That was true—she really didn't believe in them. She'd always been the moon of a lesser planet, at the far end of the galaxy, and nothing had changed. She could go on with her life knowing that her high school crush had finally paid attention to her. They'd had a moment. But high school crushes weren't really *things*. They belonged in high school and not in real life.

No, Ella didn't believe in fairy tales. She wanted to. But she didn't.

"Okay, Ella, don't freak out, but I'm taking these two," Stacy said, pointing to two dresses on the counter.

"I'm not freaking out—"

"I can afford it!" Stacy said loudly. "And besides, I got a part-time job at the Cimarron County Sheriff's Office."

This was news, and Ella gaped at her. *"What?"*

Funny that Stacy hadn't mentioned it until this moment.

"How?" Mariah demanded.

Stacy laughed. "I am not without skills and/or charm, thank you. Ella said I needed a part-time job until the band takes off. So I got one." She shrugged.

"Congratulations!" Ella said, surprised that Stacy had listened to her. "Stacy, I'm so proud of you."

"Yeah, well, don't start turning cartwheels just yet. I start Monday." She pulled out her wallet.

They said good-bye to Mariah, and Ella drove a chatty Stacy back to her car. When she got out, she leaned into the window and lowered her sunglasses to look at Ella. "Had a great time," she said. "See you Saturday?" She had a gig at the Broken Wheel.

"Wouldn't miss it," Ella promised.

Stacy winked, and she moved as if she meant to go, but she suddenly dipped back into the car window. "You know what? If I were you, I'd forget about Prince Luca. Sounds like he's been up to his old tricks. You deserve better, Ella. You deserve . . . well, you just deserve the best."

Ella smiled. "Thanks. But I'm not thinking about him."

"Right," Stacy said, backing out of the window. "Just remember, it's easier to heal a skinned knee than a broken heart!" She wiggled her fingers at Ella. "Bye!"

"What?" Ella muttered as she waved at Stacy. "That makes no *sense.*"

Stacy truly didn't have to worry about her. Ella had made herself forget about Luca Prince the night of the winter carnival, when he told her his timing sucked, he was leaving, and he would take a rain chcck.

She knew all about rain checks. It never stopped raining.

Chapter Ten

It had been three months since Luca's father died. Three months of feeling numb, of waking up every morning and having to remember all over again that Dad was gone. Three months of having a new half brother Luca couldn't quite wrap his head around, and oh, right, three months of knowing his dad had also gambled away half the family's considerable fortune and owed a lot of money around the state.

It had been a lot to unpack.

Since the afternoon Nick had met Luca in the drive, it seemed as if Luca had been battling a dull headache. For a time, he thought maybe Tanner's punch had given him a concussion. But it probably had more to do with the drinking, which, of course, he'd done, in bars and honkytonks across Texas. Anything to get away. Anything to step out from under the collective misery that cloaked Three Rivers Ranch.

Or maybe his headache was due to the fact his usually robust libido was in the toilet and he wasn't getting enough recreation. He wasn't even getting it *up,* a disturbing and horrifying turn of events. Or maybe he was just losing his mind altogether—he'd been forgetting the dumbest things, like where he'd left his phone. Or where he'd parked his car. Or where, exactly, he was driving.

As the weeks passed, it had gotten a little easier, and the pain turned into a dull ache. Luca missed his father every day, but he was finally beginning to feel like himself again. He could keep up with his phone and his truck.

Last week, Luca had felt enough like himself to come home. He didn't know what changed, but one day, he woke up to a crisp, beautiful spring morning, looked out his window, and saw the blanket of bluebonnets that covered a dormant pasture, the Indian paintbrush and pink evening primrose filling in the holes. He'd looked at all the natural beauty and decided he was sick to death of grieving.

He wanted to be in the sun. He wanted to look forward, not backward. He wanted to know why his father had left him what he had. He wanted to get back to reading, to planning the fundraiser, to making phone calls and talking about sustainability. Was it ambition that drove him to snap out of it? That wasn't like him, but maybe.

The first thing he did when he finally came home was to call Karen.

"Come today," Karen had said. "Can't put off getting back in the saddle, you know that."

His mother had said the same thing about two months ago, one day before the winter carnival. He'd come in late after a night in the city, Brandon dragging him inside and depositing him in his bed. "*Get* up," his mother said, and punched his foot. "I don't pay Frederica to entertain Brandon over breakfast while he waits for you to get out of bed." She'd punched the button for the automatic shades to lift, and bright sunlight had spilled into his room and blinded him.

"Jesus," Luca had muttered, and had gone back to sleep.

When he did eventually get up, he'd found his mother sitting on the floor of the master bedroom with the wooden box Dad had left for her. Luca didn't know what was in that box, but whatever it was had upset his mother. Her face was puffy from crying, and she had a glass of Chardonnay in her hand even though it was only noon.

"Mom," he'd said, mildly alarmed. "Are you all right? It's noon and you're drinking wine."

"I'm fine. If I wasn't fine, this whole place would fall apart, wouldn't it? And it hasn't. Not yet, anyway. But you're *not* fine, Luca. You have a business that needs running." She'd said that in a shout that made her sound pretty tipsy. "Just leave me alone. I'll be all right." And she'd bent over the box.

Luca had left her alone that day. His mother was angry with his dad for dying. He understood that;

150

he understood her raging disappointment, because he felt it, too—disappointment that Dad had such a horrible gambling problem for which he'd not sought help. Wouldn't it have been better to get help than lose so much money?

Disappointment that he'd had a massive coronary event. He smoked cigars and ate like a trucker on the road. Would it have been so hard to hit the gym every now and again?

To Luca's way of thinking, Dad had checked out. He normally didn't go in for the hippy-dippy stuff, but he believed souls choose—they choose when to show up, they choose when to exit, and Dad's soul had chosen to exit.

The day Luca had woken up to the bluebonnets, his soul made a decision. He chose life.

He'd been home a week, and he felt good enough to ride out and look at the land his father had left him. Unfortunately, it began to rain, so Luca changed his mind. He decided to pay a visit to George Lowe, the family attorney. He needed to understand what his dad had left him and why.

He showed up at George's office with two cups of coffee from Jo's. George had made them all copies of the will, but Luca couldn't read it. He needed the CliffsNotes, to hear it straight from the horse's mouth, so to speak. So he told George it was too upsetting to read it and asked him to just go over it with him.

"It's pretty simple, son," George had said.

"Your father left you two thousand acres. You can do what you want on that land as long as you don't sell it and keep it in the family. And agree that no family money will go to whatever you do out there. You can use your trust if you like, but not the family money. Your old man wasn't crazy." He grinned. "But he was a softie."

"Why do you say that?" Luca asked. "Because he left land to me?"

"Well, now, he knew you weren't going to turn it into a cattle ranch or an oil field and make money off it, right?"

Luca and his dad had never had a conversation like that, but okay, fair enough. He wasn't a cattleman or an oilman.

"Now, there's a homestead out there, the Kendall place. It's about thirty acres right in the middle of the property. That's a bit the Princes never owned. But it's abandoned, so you should be able to pick that up for next to nothing if you want it."

"It's not abandoned," Luca said. He thought of Ella, with her dark hair and pale blue eyes. He'd thought of her many times, actually. Of her house, that needed so much work. Of her skepticism of him, which, of course, had proven to be a healthy skepticism. He'd wanted to reach out so many times, but every time he thought to do it, he imagined the phone call or the text, and he hadn't been able to face it. He couldn't follow through. And what was he going to say?

Hey, still floating out here in no man's land. Still raining.

"No, I'm pretty sure that old lady died," George said. "I'll have to do some digging."

"She died," Luca confirmed. "But now her granddaughter is living out there."

"Huh," George said. "Well, depending on what you're going to do with the land, maybe you can make her an offer she can't refuse. What *are* you going to do?"

Luca had some ideas. He smiled and said, "You'll see."

George looked at him for a long moment, then sighed. "You're not thinking of doing some environmental thing, are you? You know your mama isn't going to like it."

Luca wasn't surprised by this—George was practically part of the family. He shrugged. "My mama has never liked much of anything I do."

"Well, son, if you'd keep your pecker in your pants, that might help."

Luca was momentarily taken aback—he wasn't in the habit of discussing his pecker with anyone, especially George. Or his mother, for the love of God.

George colored and sat up a little straighter in his seat. "Sorry. I know Delia was fit to be tied about that party in Houston."

Luca had to think a moment about what he was talking about. Then he remembered—about a

153

year ago, he'd ended up in a River Oaks bedroom at a congressman's house with the congressman's daughter. The same daughter who was supposedly dating a general's son. Yeah, it had been a mess, Luca would be the first to admit. "I can't make any promises," he said with a lopsided smile. Give the audience what it wants, right? "I'll keep you posted on what I hope to accomplish with that land."

"If you need any help buying the old Kendall place, let me know," George said, and rose from his seat.

The thought hadn't even occurred to him. That was Ella's place, home to an assortment of abandoned animals.

Maybe it was time to see if he could regroup with her. The only problem was, he didn't know how to slide back into her life, not after an absence of several weeks. Ella had promised to show him that spring behind her house—maybe he could call her later and ask when he might come do that.

Luca got in his truck and turned onto the highway, mulling it over. But as he passed Timmons Tire and Body, he spotted her dog, trotting alongside the highway in the rain.

"What the hell?" he muttered, and pulled over ahead of the dog. He opened the passenger door and whistled. The dog trotted right up and jumped in, muddying his passenger seat, then shaking off his coat and spraying the rest of the interior and Luca. "What's with you?" Luca asked as he scratched the dog behind the ears. "Are you trying to get killed?"

He turned his truck around and headed for the county road that led down to the Kendall place.

The dog had just given him a reason to cash in a rain check—ironically, while it was raining.

Chapter Eleven

Once, when Chrissy had come out to see Ella, she'd said with a shiver, "I couldn't live out here by myself. I'd be a wreck."

"What is there to be afraid of?" Ella asked, sweeping her hand toward the dilapidated roof and sagging porch. "Other than the roof falling on your head."

She really did love the peace and quiet in the country. No planes overhead, no traffic from the nearby highway, no one arguing outside her apartment. So quiet that if there was the slightest breeze, the old windmill would creak and moan and wake her up.

All right, who was she kidding? *Everything* woke her up. Everything! That's why nights had taken some getting used to. Who would have thought there were so many things to be so loud at night? And coyotes! She could hear them calling to each other, and she imagined them advancing on her little house, closing in on the clueless pig, or worse, on her while she slept innocently and stupidly in her bed. She was startled awake by the strangest noises, and when she couldn't determine what a particular noise was, she was convinced robbers were in her house, and she pulled out her baseball bat—guns scared her—and tiptoed around her house while the dog trotted alongside her, hoping for some excitement.

She would find nothing amiss, and when the sun came up, she would remember that a robber would be pretty bad at his job if he went out of his way to rob *this* house, which clearly looked like it contained nothing of value. All her fears seemed ridiculous in sunlight.

But come the night, they loomed large again.

Fortunately, last night, steady rainfall had drowned out any other noises. She'd woken to the pitter-patter of rain against the window, and the steady *drip-drip-drip* of water into a pan in the living room where the roof had sprung a leak. But it was a pleasant drip, and she loved sleeping when it was raining, so she was very much annoyed when Dog began nudging her with his wet nose. It was hardly even dawn. Ella had stumbled sleepily to the door, had pushed him out, and had gone back to bed.

She didn't know what made her open her eyes again—a distant sound or maybe the windmill. But she slowly opened them, and through a tangle of hair she saw the big red number eleven glaring at her from the clock.

"Damn it!" She sat up, looking wildly about her. She *never* slept this late! But she'd been cajoled into going out with Chrissy and Mateo after work last night, and had come home in the wee hours to find Dog pacing the porch and eyeing her very judgmentally.

Thank goodness she had the day off.

Ella yawned and stretched her arms high overhead—and then froze. She heard something again. She leaned forward, straining to hear, and then realized it was the sound of a vehicle coming down the road to her house. Someone was coming *here? "No!"* She shrieked. She threw off the bedspread, vaulted out of bed, grabbed a pair of jeans from the floor, and pogo-sticked her way into them. She heard a vehicle door slam as she yanked off the T-shirt she'd slept in and pulled on a tank from the clean laundry she'd hauled inside last night.

Who was it? Was it *cops?* "Of course not!" she practically shouted at herself. She hadn't done anything wrong except grow up in places where police officers and social workers were the most common types of unexpected visitors.

She looked wildly about, grabbed the fake shotgun Mateo had given her when she'd first moved in, pushed the hair out of her eyes, and ran into the living room just as someone knocked. In her nervous haste, Ella nearly kicked the pan that was catching the water from the leak in the

158

ceiling, hurdling over it just in time and falling, shoulder first, into the door. "For God's sake," she muttered. She straightened up and yanked the door open, nearly taking it off its old, rusty hinges.

"Whoa!" A pair of hands shot up on the other side of the screen, and Dog, who was also there, went berserk, pawing at the screen door.

"Hey!" Ella shouted. "Hey, hey, hey, *stop!"* she cried. "It's okay, it's okay!" She managed to unlatch the screen door, and Dog took the opportunity to launch himself at her with his whole body, planting his muddy, wet paws on her shoulders. And his breath was atrocious to boot.

"Down!" a man commanded firmly.

Luca! He was here? *Now?*

Ella's heart was suddenly beating like a drum. She pushed the dog off her. Now that his enthusiastic greeting was done, he was happy to trot on to the kitchen to see if any morsels awaited him. She brushed at the muddy paw prints, only smearing them. *For Chrissakes, calm down.* She should be able to breathe. This was a surprise, okay, but she ought to be able to handle it. It was just that after the winter carnival, she really believed that little thing she'd had with Luca was done. She'd gotten her wish, and Luca had finally seen her, but then he said good-bye, and she had truly expected that rain check would never come. *Especially* on a rainy day. Was it even possible to collect a rain check on a rainy day?

159

Whatever he was doing here, she was blushing, and she probably looked a wreck because God knew she was not a pretty sleeper, and what was she supposed to say? She made herself look up into his hazel eyes as she tried frantically to catch her breath. "What—"

"Found your dog running down the highway in the rain," he said. "It's not safe."

Ella swallowed, willed her heart to stop beating so hard. "I had a talk with him about it. But he won't listen," she said. "He's pretty stubborn about his rights."

Luca ran a hand over his head in a manner that seemed a little anxious to Ella. "I had to bring him home. Because as I told you before, I'm pretty particular when it comes to dogs."

"Thanks," she said

He smiled lopsidedly, uncertainly, as if he didn't know what to say next, and it was so stupidly charming that Ella was certain he used that smile to great success all the time.

"You could have texted me before giving me a heart attack," she said sheepishly.

"Yeah," he said, nodding. "The thing is, I'm not a great texter. I do better in person." He smiled and shoved his hands into his jean pockets. Behind him, the rain suddenly began to come down in sheets. "For what it's worth, I come in peace, so maybe you could put your gun down."

Ella gasped. She had completely forgotten she had hiked it up under her arm. "Oh, sorry! It's not loaded."

"I would hope not. It's plastic."

She put her hand on the long barrel and dropped the butt to the ground. "You're not supposed to notice that. You're supposed to think it's real and be afraid."

The smile that lit Luca's face was slow and sultry. "Darlin', no one with half a brain would think that gun was real."

Darlin'. The word skied down her spine and landed on the flat of her groin with a *whoosh*. She tossed the stupid toy gun onto the floor next to some *People* magazines she had rescued from Byron's trashcan. Luca remained standing just outside the door, the screen door propped against his shoulder.

Ella pushed a hand through her hair and felt the tangles. Why oh why were the karma gods against her? Why was it that half the time she saw this man she looked as if she'd been tossed out the back of a moving truck?

She dropped her hand and looked him up and down. "I guess you're back," she said.

"I'm back," he agreed.

For good? Just passing through? And what in the hell was he doing *here* on this rainy morning?

"Umm . . . it's a little chilly out here," Luca said.

Ella's brows dipped. "Are you saying you want to come in?"

"I am. Unless you're saying you want to come out here so I can talk to you for a moment."

She looked past him to the rain and shook her head. She rubbed her hand on her bare arm and reluctantly stepped back. She wasn't thrilled about Prince Luca seeing her worn, threadbare house—it was inadequate for someone like him. It was decidedly unglamorous compared to Luca, who was virile and handsome and glamorous. But it was cold, and she was shivering, and she didn't know if he knew it or not, but the porch roof she and Mateo had repaired had sprung a leak very close to where he was standing. "Okay, come in," she said.

"Are you sure?" he asked uncertainly. "I don't want to bother you."

Ella didn't see how that was possible, since he was literally on her doorstep bothering her. "I'm sure. Come in—I could really use some coffee."

"Late night?" he asked, and smiled as if he expected her to say no.

"As a matter of fact," she said. *That's right, cowboy, you're not the only game in town. I haven't been wasting away out here, waiting for you to come back.* Except that her internal feminist declaration was not meshing well with all the butterflies in her stomach right now.

"*Well* then," he said, and his smile turned

curious as he slipped past her and into her house. His eyes flicked to her very thin tank top for a brief moment, and she felt her body perk up. She really wished she'd had time to put on a bra. "I'm not interrupting you, am I?" he asked.

"No. Be careful of the dip in the floor. The wood feels like it might give way there, and I have no clue what's beneath it." She darted past him and swiped up a hoodie from the couch and pulled that on over her tank.

Luca stepped over the dip in her floor to the middle of her living room. With his hands on his waist, he looked around at her sparse furnishings and the stack of work papers piled on one end of the couch she'd picked up at Goodwill. He looked at the novels on her Ikea bookshelf and then up at the leak in her ceiling. And then down to the pot on the floor, which had almost filled with rainwater. The dog paused to drink from it before disappearing into her bedroom.

"So, a good time was had by all last night, I take it?" Luca asked, and glanced over his shoulder at her.

What was *that* look on his face right now? He looked curious and interested and, if she wasn't entirely crazy, slightly annoyed. "Yep," she said, and rocked onto her toes and down again, and stopped short of hitching up her jeans.

"Huh," he said, and she could tell from his

blisteringly shiny hazel eyes he didn't like it. He seemed almost jealous. *Jealous? Oh please. Ella, get hold of yourself!* He was not *jealous.* What universe would that be? Would that be Opposite Day?

Ella pushed her hair from her face again. "Sorry about my house." She stepped around a box of books and some clothing she intended to take to Goodwill, or had picked up from Goodwill, she couldn't remember because she wasn't really thinking straight, and around a stack of mail she had not yet tackled, a yoga mat, and oh, look there, how convenient, a *bra.* "I've been really busy," she said. *In other words, I don't have maid service.*

"Another *Real Housewives* marathon?"

Ella shot a look over her shoulder. He smiled. So did she. A little, anyway. She hadn't quite decided what her demeanor was going to be just yet. She felt too topsy-turvy. So she padded into the kitchen, across the old linoleum floor, sidestepping a place where the linoleum had peeled back from the subflooring. She opened the back door in case it smelled as moldy in here as she feared. "When did you come back to Three Rivers?" she asked as she reached into a cabinet for her giant Costco-sized can of coffee and began to spoon it into the old coffee maker she'd picked up at the thrift store.

"About a week ago." He was watching her

like he'd never seen anyone make coffee before. Maybe he hadn't. Maybe he showed up in the dining room at Three Rivers ranch every morning and someone appeared with his coffee and eggs. That would be awesome, if all a person had to do was roll out of bed and someone had breakfast and coffee waiting for them.

"So how are you?" she asked as she put away the coffee and picked up a gallon of water to fill the coffee pot, because the kitchen faucet still wasn't working, and she hadn't had time to YouTube it.

"I don't know," he said. "I did a little traveling. This week, I've just been riding around on horseback like a fool."

"*That's* weird," Ella said. "Couldn't you just ride around like a cowboy?"

Luca chuckled. He leaned against the counter and folded his arms across his chest, relaxing a little. "I tried, believe me. It's funny, because when I was a kid, I rode every day. But it's been a while since I rode as much as I have this week, and I'm feeling a little cracked open."

"*Ouch,*" she said.

"Do you ride?" he asked curiously.

"Me?" She laughed. "No."

"You should try it," Luca said. "You can't have a ranch and not ride."

"A ranch? It's more like a waystation for misplaced animals."

"Maybe you could ride with me some day," he suggested. "I can teach you."

Was that an invitation? She looked at him from the corner of her eye to gauge just how serious he was, but he was looking up at her ceiling. She followed his gaze and winced. Water was bubbling in the corner.

"Maybe I will," she said. "I have horses, you know. I mean, I will if I can ever convince them to come back into the fenced pasture." She paused, thinking about that. "Actually, I'd have to give them away."

"What?"

"The horses," she said. "I can't keep them. I don't ride, and I definitely don't want to be cracked open." She laughed. And then instantly sobered, realizing how terribly sexual that sounded. She was *so bad* at small talk. She turned her back to him, pretending to do something with the coffee and closed her eyes.

"That won't happen to you," Luca said, letting the remark slide. "I had something to prove, so I rode a lot longer than I should have."

"Prove to whom?" she asked.

"To myself, I guess."

He was suddenly standing beside her, startling her. He leaned back against the counter and said, "I'll let you in on a little secret—I've lost my ranch muscle."

Ella didn't know what a ranch muscle was,

but he didn't look like he'd lost even a tiny bit of muscle. Anywhere. Not in his shoulders or his chest or his arms or his hips—Lord, his hips— or his legs. She swallowed and flipped on the coffeepot. "You don't look like you've lost anything," she said, and felt her cheeks flare with heat.

"Thanks," Luca said, and touched her hand. "But I can fcel it. I uscd to wail on thc punching bag at the ranch gym, then go out and work cattle or repair fences." He sighed and shook his head. "I'm determined to get it back, because I belong on that land. Not behind a desk."

This he announced as if he was talking to himself or making a case in front of a judge.

"I thought you had a Sombra dealership," she said.

He glanced at her curiously. "Did I tell you that?"

"Umm," she could feel herself color even more. "Lyle mentioned it. He's not a fan of electric cars."

Luca did not take offense—he laughed. "Lyle likes the smell of gas and a greasy motor. Not many people around here are fans of electric cars. It's really not my thing, either, but the dealership was a gift from my uncle Chet."

Ella was glad she was looking in a cabinet for sugar, because she was certain her mouth gaped open. She couldn't fathom getting a car dealership

167

as a *gift*. Who gave gifts like that? Only the Princes.

"I hate it," he said quietly.

The tone of his voice had changed slightly, as if he was ashamed to say so, and Ella had to look at him to make sure she'd heard him correctly. He was studying the back of his hand, and he glanced up, gave her a woeful smile. "I probably should not have said that out loud. I'm hoping it can stay between you and me."

Ella was dumbstruck. He hated being rich? Owning cars? And had he really just told her something he hadn't said to anyone else? "I don't know, Luca," she said. "I don't know if I can be trusted with the knowledge that you don't like electric cars. Maybe, and I'm just thinking out loud here, but maybe you and Lyle could form a support group for electric car haters."

Luca grinned.

"I won't tell your secret," she said. "If there is one thing I've learned in this life, it's how to keep secrets. And trust me, that is a secret I would have absolutely no one to tell."

He laughed. "Thanks. I feel like a total nerd now."

Oh, he was about as far from a nerd as a man could be.

A snort at the back door made Luca jump. Ella leaned around him to see the pig, just as she suspected, its snout pressed to the screen door. It was the same thing every morning—she opened the door, and the pig was there, ready for breakfast.

"Jesus," Luca said. "That thing startled me. Okay, Ella, I have to know—what's with the pig?"

"Same as the dog and the horses, I guess. Abandoned here. I'm not sure if the cat and chickens were left or if they wandered in to join the party." She poured him a cup of coffee and handed it to him.

"Thanks. Cats and chickens don't usually do so well together," he said.

"Right. But I don't think this cat is working with a full deck. Usually, he's lying in a mud puddle or on the hood of my car."

She held up the sugar container, but Luca shook his head no. She added plenty of sugar to hers and stirred, aware that Luca was watching her, aware that the butterflies were rioting in her belly. She was trying to pretend as if this were no big deal, as if it were perfectly normal for him to show up for coffee. She shouldn't have to pretend. It *shouldn't* be a big deal, because they were two adults now, not teenagers, and a man should be able to drop in on a woman to say hi, and she shouldn't get all weird about it.

But this was Luca Prince, and she'd been weird about it for a very long time. Some habits were very hard to break. She could feel herself getting wound up and tense because she didn't know what this was, and she was a black-and-white kind of girl. She needed to know. She suddenly blurted, "Okay, that's it." She put down her coffee cup and folded her arms across her body.

Luca tilted his head to one side. "You look kind of like you want to punch me."

"I kind of do. I don't know what you're doing here on a Thursday morning, without calling, instead of being wherever it is regular people go during the day. After . . . *weeks.*"

"Actually, it's midday Thursday for those of us who didn't have a late night."

Ella arched a brow.

"Okay," he said, and set his cup down. "Fair question, and one I don't have the answer to. It was a spur-of-the-moment decision on my part. I've been wanting to see you, Ella. And I saw your dog, and I . . . well, I acted impulsively. I have a habit of doing that."

He'd been wanting to see her? Really? For how long? When did it start? Was there a particular reason he wanted to see her, or was it the general, want to *see* her, see her? "You couldn't call first?"

"I'm sorry I didn't call first. But I've thought a lot about you in the last several weeks."

Could he see her heart pounding nearly out of her chest? Could he see how discombobulated she was? Better question, could she believe him? "Why?" she demanded.

He smiled with confused amusement. "*Why?* I don't know—why does any guy think about any girl? Is it so hard to believe I was thinking about you?"

"Yes! Yes, it is very hard to believe," she said adamantly.

Luca chuckled as if he thought she'd said it to be funny. But Ella hadn't meant it to be funny. She may be older and more mature, but part of her was still the same girl clutching a math book after homeroom hoping he would notice her.

He seemed to get it, because his smile faded and he looked at her intently. "Believe it. Believe it every time someone says it about you, Ella Kendall. You're smart. You're funny. You're so damn pretty. There are probably all kinds of guys thinking about you right now."

She rolled her eyes.

He leaned closer, his eyes locking on hers. "You interest the hell out of me."

The man was not playing around, and it was official, Ella was going to melt right here, onto this ugly linoleum. "Luca . . ." she said, her voice in a near whisper. "Are you doing it?"

"Playing you?" he whispered back.

She nodded.

He stepped forward, forcing her back a step, and she bumped up against the counter. He braced his hands on the counter at either side of her. "Look at me," he said, as if she could possibly tear her gaze away from him. "I am definitely *not* playing you." He didn't touch her, just stood so close that he could probably see every bit of her insecurity and fear swimming in her eyes. "I like you, Ella, and I want to know you. Things got a little derailed, but if it's okay with you, I would *definitely* like to get to know you. Is that okay?"

Her heart was galloping along, headed for the sunset, but a voice somewhere inside, buried under the debris of her life, kicked her. *Be careful!* "It's okay," she said. "But I should warn you, I'm not going to fall for you, Luca Prince, if that's what you think."

One brow rose slightly, and his gaze slipped to her mouth. "I don't think anything right now except that I want to get to know you better."

"I mean it," she said, her gaze on his mouth now. "You're so damn good-looking, and God, you're *hot*."

One corner of his mouth tipped up in an appreciative smile.

"But I'm not the sort who goes for that. I'm pretty careful."

"Are you always so certain about something before you even try it?"

"Yep," she said, and looked into his eyes again. "I know me."

He suddenly smiled and said, "Can't blame a guy for trying." But she could tell, by the way he was smiling at her, that he didn't believe her. He was smiling like he thought he had this in the bag.

Maybe he did. Ella wasn't sure she even believed herself. "I'm not flirting with you right now," she insisted.

"No kidding," he agreed cheerfully. "Okay, I heard you, Ella, loud and clear. You're absolutely not going to fall for a guy that, in your own words, is good-looking and hot, because you don't go for good-looking, hot guys."

"Right," she said with a nod for emphasis.

"Right," he murmured to her lips. "But we can still be friends, isn't that how it goes?"

She wondered absently if there were actual bluebirds chirping around her head or if that buzzy feeling was just the pheromones rolling off Hot Prince Luca. "Maybe. We'll see."

"Girl, you are *tough*," he said. "Well, you still owe me a look at that spring, remember?"

"What *is* it with that spring?"

Luca shifted closer. His head was next to hers, as if he intended to whisper in her ear, and if he turned even slightly, his lips would brush her temple. "When it stops raining, I'll show you."

She turned a fraction of an inch, so that there was nothing but a breath between her lips and his cheek. "I don't know if you noticed, but the rain is coming down pretty hard."

"There are plenty of ways to wait out a good rain," he suggested silkily.

"That's *exactly* what I'm talking about," she said, just as silkily. "I won't fall for a line like that." She wasn't about to let him into her bedroom, even if she did really like sex, because she wanted it too much, too hard. Wanting something too much was the kiss of death for Ella Kendall.

She could look back at her life, could see how the things she'd wanted the most had hurt her the most. Like the puppy her mother had given her. The same puppy Ella had watched a police officer put in the back of the animal control truck when her mother was arrested for possession and driving under the influence. Ella never saw the puppy again. Or how about Patience Montemayor, the young foster mother she'd had at house number three? Patience was beautiful and lively, and God, how Ella had loved her. She'd pretended Patience was her real mother, had told the kids at school Patience would adopt her.

And then Patience and David had split up, and the foster kids were shuttled off to new homes, and Ella had never seen her again either.

She had wanted those things too hard. It was her life—if she allowed herself to want something, to *really* want it, she was destined to lose it. And to want to be with Luca Prince as bad as she did felt awfully dangerous to the girl in the hallway still clutching her math book. She knew, even in this highly charged moment, that she ought to get out, but his breath was warm, and his lips brushed her skin, and a thousand little daggers of pleasure went skating across her cheek, and he asked, "Then what do you suggest we do while we wait?"

"I have an idea," she said.

Luca's smile was slow and sexy. "I'd love to hear it."

She dipped down and under his arm, and stepped away from the counter and him. She had an idea, all right. "Follow me," she said in the sexiest voice she could summon on short notice.

Chapter Twelve

She had him shoveling pig manure.

Sure, Luca had known the moment she'd opened the door and looked at him like he was a swamp creature that he wasn't going to get lucky, and really, that was not his intent or his modus operandi. He liked the connection to be mutual before he seduced a woman into bed.

But he damn sure didn't think she'd ask him to shovel manure out of a garage that looked like it would collapse at any moment.

He guessed he could be grateful she hadn't kicked him out.

The pig stood off to one side, short legs braced stoutly apart to hold up its girth, watching him. "What are you looking at?" Luca asked her.

The pig's snout worked, trying to smell him from a respectable distance.

"Would it be so hard to take your business outside like the rest of the animal kingdom?" he asked.

In response, the pig sat down in a pile of manure she'd left after eating the bucket of feed

Luca had given her. Luca was reminded of a brown Labrador retriever they'd once had on the ranch. Daisy had eaten and eaten until she could hardly walk. Luca and Nick had tried everything, but Daisy had a screw loose somewhere and couldn't stop, even when she was full and her belly as tight as a drum. She was fourteen years old when she'd wandered off the compound one day and never came back.

Amazingly, Luca's vision blurred thinking about Daisy. That was another of his little secrets—well, Nick and Hallie knew, because they were just as bad, but no one else—but Luca was ridiculously sentimental about his pets. Daisy had been gone twenty years, and he still teared up when he thought about her.

He pushed a pile of manure out of the garage and glanced up at the house. He could see Ella through the kitchen window. She'd showered and dressed, and her hair hung loose around her shoulders. This woman was undeniably beguiling. She wasn't the most beautiful woman he'd ever seen—he'd dated starlets and models, some of whom had altered their faces to the ideal. Ella didn't wear the spider lashes like so many women wore now, or a lot of makeup at all that he could detect. That was the thing— she was more alluring to him than any other woman because she looked fresh. *Truly* pretty. A completely unaffected, God-made pretty.

How the *hell* had he missed her in high school?

And why did he have to work so hard for her now?

Working hard for the affections of the opposite sex was not a landscape he'd explored before. Of course, there had been plenty of women along the way that hadn't been into him, but he hadn't been into them either, and therein lay the rub. With Ella, he felt like he was struggling to pass a test. To read the words right. To see what was right in front of him and failing miserably. But he wasn't running from the challenge anymore. Just like he was tackling the challenge of reading, he was going to tackle Ella. Unless she told him to take a hike, he was going to dig deeper into his bag of tricks.

A sudden shaft of sunlight skirted across the muddy yard. The rain was ending, and it looked like it would be a gorgeous spring day, hopefully with the sort of brilliance that brought artists to their canvases and cowboys to the outdoors.

The dealership flitted across his thoughts. He'd told Victor that he'd be in today. He hadn't been to the office in weeks. The people there could have robbed him blind by now, and he wouldn't know it. He knew he should go in, if not for all the obvious reasons, then at least for Uncle Chet, who really had tried to do Luca a solid with that business. But Luca stacked his hands on top of the shovel and through that grimy kitchen window,

178

he watched Ella doing whatever she was doing, and he was powerless. His desire to be here, with her, on this rundown little ranch, shoveling pig manure, was much more powerful than his desire to do the right thing and go to work.

He could work here, if she'd let him. Maybe not shoveling manure—he wasn't crazy—but he could patch her roof. He could fix her fence in the places the posts had fallen over. It looked to him like there was a very long list of things he could do here to be useful instead of trying to read things about electric cars.

The dog suddenly appeared from around the corner of the garage and trotted over to say hello. "Hey, buddy," Luca said absently.

The dog began to prance.

Luca looked at the wiggling ball of fur. "Are you a buddy?" he asked, and the dog's wiggling turned frantic. "Someone's called you that along the way, huh?" he asked, and went down on one knee to scratch the dog's ears. "Were you someone's buddy?" The dog rolled onto his back, presenting his belly. Luca laughed. "Let's make that your name, what do you say, Buddy?" he asked, and the dog leapt up into conniptions of joy. "We'll just tell the lady of the—"

He didn't finish his thought because he was bowled over by the pig, who also wanted love as long as he was handing it out. "You, too?" Luca asked, and scratched her rump before hopping to his feet and brushing off his knees. "Go on now, the both of you. I've got to get Ella to like me as much as you do."

He put the shovel away and walked out of the garage. The rain had turned to drizzle as the sun pushed through the clouds, and droplets of rain left clinging to the trees glistened like tiny crystals.

He walked up the back steps of the porch and sat down to remove his boots. He had one off when he heard the screen door open and close behind him. He removed his second boot, and in the next moment, Ella sat down next to him. She handed him a paper plate that held a ham sandwich on two thick slabs of bread, some chips, and a pickle.

"For me?"

"For you. I honestly didn't think you'd do it," she said with a smile. "You're easier than I thought."

He grinned at her. "Ye of little faith," he said, and picked up one half of the sandwich. "There's not much you can throw at me that I won't take on."

She smiled, her eyes crinkling in the corners. "Braggart."

"Honest," he said, through a mouthful of sandwich. And hopeful. He was very hopeful.

"Show-off," she said, still smiling.

"Gifted," he said with a wink.

Ella laughed.

Luca knew better than to read much into it, but when a woman made a man a sandwich and sat next to him teasing him while he ate it, some doors were cracking open. "Thanks," he said, holding up the sandwich.

"You're welcome," she said, and glanced away, as if she were afraid she might smile too much in his direction. *Smile at me at least a little.*

"The sun is out," he said. "Want to see the spring?"

"I've seen it, and besides, don't you have a job?"

"Yes. But I'm the boss, and you haven't seen the spring the way I see it. What about you, are you working today?"

She shook her head.

"Perfect. Then you have the time."

"Just because I'm not scheduled today doesn't mean I have the time," she said. "I've got errands to run, laundry to get to, a kitchen faucet that I need to YouTube—"

"Need to what?"

She waved her hand. "I have a lot to do. I don't have time for strolls through the park and picnics."

"I didn't say one word about a picnic," he said, nudging her with his shoulder. "Come on, Ella. Humor me."

She glanced at him from the corner of her eye.

He nudged her again. Ella sighed and shook her head. "I can't believe this. I can't believe Luca Prince is in my tiny little house, pretending he has nothing better to do than see a spring."

"Why can't you believe it?" Luca asked with all sincerity.

She rolled her lovely blue eyes at him. "You know why."

"No, I really don't," he insisted. "I think it's pretty obvious that I'm knocking on your door, girl."

She smiled prettily and studied him for a long moment. "Okay. If I go see the spring, will you quit asking about it?"

"Probably not," he said.

She laughed. "I like your honesty. I'll get my boots and we'll go see that damn spring."

"Thank you!" he said, and spread his arms wide. "I feel like I just won something here."

She smiled and stood up. "Don't get cocky." She disappeared into the house.

When she returned, she was wearing rubber farm boots and shorts, and a safari-type sun hat, and had draped a woven bag across her body, as if she was going to collect some herb specimens. He glanced at the bag, confused.

"Water," she said, and pulled out a bottle to show him. "And a phone, in case we get lost."

"We're not going to get lost," he assured her. "I know this land like the back of my hand."

"You can never be too safe."

"I think maybe you can," he said.

Ella picked up a thick walking stick that was leaning against the porch. When Luca looked at the stick, she said, "Coyotes."

He debated telling her that a coyote wasn't going to attack her unless it was rabid, and if it did, he was fairly certain she wouldn't be able to hold it off with a stick. He decided it was better not to chance spooking her—he was too happy she was going with him.

So they began the trek to the spring, walking along an old two-track road, each of them in their own track. The prairie grass between them had grown up so tall that it brushed against their thighs. The road was lined with wildflowers that seemed to have exploded overnight. Bluebonnets, Indian paintbrush, red poppies, and pink evening primrose. The pastures, long overgrazed and left fallow, were seas of yellow Blackfoot daisies and rain lilies. Luca thought there was nothing more beautiful than a Texas spring, even though the wildflowers were not as thick as they had been in years past due to long droughts. The land was too depleted and starved to produce a good crop.

The dog trotted ahead of them, nose to the ground, disappearing into the weeds and reappearing on the other side, then coming back again. "I think I have a name for your dog," Luca said.

"Oh yeah?" Ella asked, peeking up at him from beneath the brim of her hat. "What's that?"

"Buddy."

The dog stopped at once and whipped around, his tail wagging, looking eagerly at Luca.

"Buddy?" Ella said. The dog bounced back to her, tail wagging. Ella gasped. "How did you do that?"

"I didn't do anything," Luca said. "Someone must have called him Buddy enough times that now he's convinced it's his name."

"Hey, Buddy!" she said, and the dog began to wiggle around at her feet. Ella laughed with delight. She was stunningly beautiful when she laughed. Happiness shone in her eyes and glowed in her skin. Her happiness made *him* happy, made him feel soft. It also made him desperately want to make her laugh.

They walked on, reaching an old fork in the road. Luca pointed out that these old roads were originally the paths of Indians and Spaniards, and showed her the natural trail markers that would later guide people traveling west to distant forts with wagons full of supplies. He showed her switchgrass and Indiangrass, which could look alike to an untrained eye. Ella didn't seem bored by his talk—she asked questions and paused to examine everything he pointed out.

They reached a well-worn animal trail that cut

through the trees and went down a rocky incline. Luca started down that path.

"Are you sure?" Ella asked.

"I am."

She hesitated, then followed him into a thick underbrush. When the underbrush led into a copse of cedar, she paused again. "I don't know," she said. "This doesn't look right."

"I've been over every inch of this land," he said. "It's a shortcut to the spring." He offered his hand to her.

She didn't take it. "We can follow the road around, you know."

"If we go this way, you'll see the spring from a better vantage point. You can see just how big it is."

She glanced uncertainly at the path before them.

"Ella. Trust me," he said, and took her hand.

"That's asking a lot," she said, but gripped his hand as she picked her way down the path behind him.

They emerged, as he knew they would, onto a limestone shelf above the natural spring. To one side of the spring was a stand of pin oaks, the growth of new leaves a brilliant light green against the older, darker leaves. Below them, about a four-foot drop, was the water. The spring wasn't as large as it once had been, but at least the water was clear, a good sign that it hadn't been contaminated or clogged. He went down onto his haunches to look around. Ella sat down beside him and wrapped her arms around her knees.

"It looks healthy," he said. "No apparent contamination."

"Contamination!" Ella looked at him with surprise. "You sound less like a cowboy and more like a park ranger."

"I'm a little of both. Ecology and conserving the environment are my thing."

"Your *thing?*" She laughed. "Are you a student? An ecologist?"

"Not exactly." He knew how he sounded when he said things like that—God knew his family had accused him of being a bunny hugger more than once. "You see this spring? If it was properly cared for, it could revive an entire ecological system that has been lost because of poor range management and development."

Ella's eyes narrowed. "Who *are* you?" She shifted around so she could see him better. "I never expected to hear the phrase 'poor range management' come out of your mouth. So please, do go on," she said.

"What were you expecting?"

"I don't know, I thought maybe you wanted to swim. Or tell me something that happened here in high school."

"I don't remember much of high school. I'm

serious about this. The water that comes up here is fed from an underground lake. It's about sixty degrees year round. A little too cold for swimming today, but in August, you'll appreciate this spring."

She looked down at the water.

He was boring her. "I find it interesting, that's all. Don't feel like you have to listen to it. I am well aware of how boring it is to most."

"No, I *want* to hear about it," she said. "This is new and different. I may regret it, but right now, I want to hear it."

Luca was so used to people making jokes about his interest that he didn't quite know where to start. "Okay," he said. "But remember—you asked."

"I'm all ears," she agreed.

So Luca told her. About his love of the land. How his family had used it and abused it, and he'd gotten interested in the idea of conservation and rebuilding ecosystems after a particularly bad drought, when they'd had to ship their cattle north and wildlife had died and the land had not bounced back from that like it once had. He told her how hard it was to earn a living from cattle today, when the price per head was down but the cost of the land was up, along with property taxes and maintenance. How ranchers were diversifying, turning land into hunting and recreation leases, putting oil wells on the land

and selling mineral rights. How it wasn't what it used to be, and the Princes, like a lot of ranchers, had tried it all and had depleted the health of the land in some ways.

"We mined limestone until we used all that up. We drilled for oil until that was gone. We ran cattle until we'd overgrazed it. A lot of our land just sits now. Look at the wildflowers over there," he said, motioning to a field of bluebonnets. "See how they aren't quite as vibrant or as thick as you see in other places? The soil is depleted."

Ella looked at the field of bluebonnets. "I see," she said thoughtfully.

What Luca feared, he told her, was a move toward more development. What he loved about being the son of a rancher was the land. How he and his best friend, Brandon, who shared his love, had begun to look at ways to conserve something of what both their families had. He told her about the five hundred acres Brandon had bought for the sole purpose of seeing if they could revive it, but how they'd realized it was almost too small to really affect a change in an entire ecosystem. He told her how he'd been talking to Brandon about something a little different since his father had died.

"Different how?" she asked.

"My dad left me some land," Luca said. "Land that surrounds your house and includes this spring, to be precise. There is enough land here to test all the theories that Brandon and I have wanted to test. And my interest has only intensified."

"How much land did he leave you?" she asked curiously.

"Two thousand acres. Land south of the river, depleted of resources, too remote to be of use to anyone."

"But . . . why did he leave you depleted land?" she asked, her brow furrowing.

Luca told her about his dad's will, how he'd left something to all of his kids, but no one seemed to give much thought to the used-up, dried-up land he'd left for Luca. "No one in my family expects me to do anything they would find productive, like running cattle or selling the mineral rights or drilling for oil or gas, you know? To them, it's just barren land. But to me, it's a canvas."

He mentioned the painting in his bedroom at the ranch. He told her how he had longed for the land in that painting, to have what God had left here, appreciated first by the Indians, then the French and the Spaniards, then the Texans. He told her that when he'd learned his dad had left him *this* land, the worst they had, he'd felt despondent. "I didn't get it at first," he said. "I thought, *this* is what my dad put aside for me in case he died unexpectedly? *This* was his legacy to me? I get that he didn't have time to work out the finer details, but obviously he'd put *some* thought into it, and this is what he'd come up with? I thought maybe I'd offended him. Or disappointed him."

"That can't be true," Ella said.

Luca gave her a bitter laugh. "Oh, but it can." He realized he was saying things aloud to Ella that he'd never said to anyone else. Not even his twin. It felt good to get some of these feelings off his chest. "But then it hit me, Ella. One day I was staring at the painting. I've seen it a thousand times, but that morning, something suddenly clicked. I got it. Dad left me this land so I could try my hand at conservation like I'd been talking about since I knew what conservation was. He left me my shot."

Ella shook her head. "But the Prince ranch is so big. Couldn't you have conserved a piece of it before?"

Luca shook his head. It was difficult to explain how the Prince family thought, how it had been ingrained since they were children that the land was everything. It was their God, their savior, their only way. Every inch was supposed to make money. Not to mention, he wasn't able to follow through with any plans because he couldn't read.

"This has been my interest for a long time, but my brother Nick is the one who runs the ranch, not me. And every time I brought up the idea of conserving the land, at least some of it, the idea was too vague, and my parents—well, my mother—thought it was half-baked."

"Oh," she said, sounding surprised.

"I get it," he said with a shrug. "Ranching runs through our DNA. It's knitted into our membranes. I know how they think because I think that way, too. But I can see other possibilities. I remember a class I had in high school. It was for ranch kids, sort of like a 4-H class, but one particular lecture was about conservation. It was the first time I heard actual words put to the types of things I was feeling about our land. So I went home and told my folks that we should conserve." He laughed, remembering the skinny, freckle-faced kid. "I think I actually said, 'We should be good stewards to nature,' because I'd heard the teacher say it."

Ella laughed. "And what did they say?"

"Well, my grandmother said it was the dumbest thing she'd ever heard." Luca laughed, remembering his grandmother in her easy chair, her white Keds on the upraised footrest. "I asked, 'Why is it dumb, Grandma? Do you know how many cows we'd have to put on the whole ranch to make it economically viable?' or something like that, and she said, 'Well, it sure won't be economically viable with a bunch of tree-huggers dancing around the Maypole out there.'"

"Ah, okay." Ella nodded. "I see."

He smiled at her. "Right? But still, I kept at it for a couple of weeks. I tried to make the point that we could turn some of the land back

191

to its natural state, and lease it for hunting or, I don't know, let people just see and breathe and experience what God gave us before we ruined it. My mother wasn't having it. She said, 'It's *supposed* to look like a ranch. Maybe God gave it to us so we could turn it into the wealthiest ranch in Texas and not a fifth-grade science project.' "

Luca could still picture that evening, all of them sitting around the dinner table. His grandmother had snickered and said, *I didn't have a fifth grade. We all went to school in that little one-room schoolhouse out on Gonzalez Road until they found out the school superintendent was having an affair with the pastor's wife. Talk about an uproar.*

He could picture his mother, too, in her seat, holding her wineglass up, like she was contemplating hurling it against the wall. *Dolly? Could we please save the history of schoolhouse adultery for another time? I am trying to talk some sense into my son.*

Ella winced. "No one stood up for you?"

He shook his head. His dad had calmly carried on with his dinner without saying much, just sopping up the gravy on his plate with biscuits. "My dad told me that it cost too much money to conserve big chunks of land." He'd always believed his father had sided with his mother. Until his death. Until he realized his dad had left him this land to turn back to its natural state.

Ella laughed. "How can it cost money to conserve?"

"To do it right would require clearing out nonnative species. Planting native grasses and shrubs to take their place. Cleaning out the silt from waterways and building berms to stop erosion. For two thousand acres, that doesn't come cheap."

"So are you going to do it?" Ella askcd. "Are you going to . . . what's the word? Conserve it?"

"I want to. But what I want to do requires more than desire. It requires a lot of money and a lot of buy-in. Brandon and I were planning a fundraiser to do this on the acreage he bought. But this is a better place for it. We have the spring; we have the grassland and the hills here. We'll need even more money, but we're going to raise it."

"You're going to ask your friends to donate?" she asked, confused.

"Yes, but we're really targeting government agencies that are vested in the environment. And university types that study environmental change and ecological evolution. We're looking for grants and partnerships with university learning labs. Honestly, I'm not sure what all. I've still got some learning to do."

Ella looked out over the spring, to the land beyond.

"Imagine a flock of egrets and ducks over there," he said, motioning across the pond. "A healthy stand of cattails and water willows, ferns and water clover. Imagine a rabble of butterflies and wildflowers so thick that it feels like carpet under your feet."

She squinted.

"You probably think I'm crazy," Luca said. He didn't care, really—he was used to it.

"I don't think you're crazy. I think you're lucky."

"Right," he said with a snort. "Lucky Luca Prince with all that money to throw away—"

"That's not what I meant," Ella said. "You're lucky you have a dream. A lot of people don't. But you do, and it's a clear dream."

He glanced at her, surprised. Her praise swelled in his chest a little—he hadn't realized until now how much he'd wanted her to understand him. "Thanks," he said appreciatively. "But I've talked enough. What's your dream?"

"Mine?" She laughed. "It's different for me. My whole life has been about survival—Hey!" she said suddenly, and sat up. "There are my horses!"

Her survival? Luca wanted to know more about that but looked in the direction she was pointing. The horses, a little smaller and shaggier than those at the ranch, looked at them from across the spring before dipping their heads to drink. "Mustangs," he said. "They're feral."

Ella gasped. *"What?"*

He chuckled at her surprise. "Yep, those are wild horses."

"No way!" She clasped her hands together as if trying to contain her astonishment in a manner he found utterly charming. "No, Luca, they can't be. They come up to my fence every morning!"

"Sure they do. You're offering them a full buffet."

"Wait, wait," she said, and scrambled to her feet. When she did, the three horses turned skittish and galloped away. "But . . . how can you be sure?"

"Have you seen a brand on them?" he asked, coming to his feet, too.

She shook her head as the horses disappeared into the woods.

"I've seen them around. You can tell by looking at them. Their hooves are untrimmed, and they have thicker winter coats than horses who wear blankets or are stabled and brushed regularly."

"But wild horses? How is that even *possible* in this day and age?"

"Easy," he said. "Bad storms displace livestock. Three Rivers is thousands of acres. On a spread as big as ours, animals can get lost and stay lost, and then they breed and produce feral foals."

"I've been putting out oats for wild horses?"

"Looks like," he said, grinning. "I'll let my brother know. He'll send some ranch hands down to round them up."

"No!" she cried, looking alarmed. "What will he do with them?"

Luca laughed. "He's not going to send them to the glue factory, if that's what you're thinking. He'll break them."

Ella gasped.

"*Domesticate* them," he amended. "Better?"

"Hardly! They clearly like being free."

"Believe me—they would like to be fed on the regular, too. They'd like a farrier to trim their hooves. They would *love* a good brushing. It's a good thing." He held out his hand to her. "We should go back. But it's going to be tough to climb up that path in rubber boots."

She looked at the trail, then at his hand. She slipped her hand into his. "Just to get up the path," she said.

"Goes without saying. I wouldn't *think* of holding your hand a moment past the top. I'd rather chop off my own hand than hold yours a moment longer than necessary."

"Okay, then." She smiled.

But when they reached the top of the path, she did not pull her hand from his, and he did not let go of hers. They walked down the two tracks, this time on the same side of the grass and weeds, hand in hand. "I don't know about this hand-holding business," Ella said. "It feels dangerously close to teetering on a thing."

"God, you must be beside yourself," he agreed.

"What are you going to do about it?"

"I'm thinking about it." She glanced up at him, and her eyes were sparkling in the sun. "I could yank my hand free, but you'd probably get your feelings hurt."

"You could ease it out," he suggested. "Less room for interpretation."

"You could let go and save me the trouble," she suggested.

"Yeah, but that's the difference between you and me, Ella. I don't want to let go." He squeezed her hand.

And Ella squeezed back. And then she stopped walking, forcing him to stop, too. She turned toward him and glanced up, still holding his hand.

He eyed her warily. "Why do I feel something's about to happen that I'm not going to like?" he mused.

"Luca . . . I meant it. I'm not going to fall for you," she said.

"Okay, now you're just giving me a complex. I *know,* Ella, because you've already said it at least a dozen times."

"So whatever happens doesn't mean anything."

For Chrissakes, she made this hard. "It's just a *hand—*"

Ella caught him completely off guard. She suddenly threw her free arm around his neck, rose up on her toes, and kissed him. Or rather, she briefly pressed her lips to his, but rather earnestly, and then just as suddenly fell away from him and stared, wide-eyed. She had managed to surprise even herself.

But she'd only confused the hell out of him. "What the hell was *that?*" he demanded.

"That . . . that was impetuous," she said breathlessly.

He put his hands on his waist and stared down at her spring blue eyes. "So what . . . are you falling or not? Because a big bus of mixed signals just pulled up at my house, and I am more of the straightforward signals kind of guy."

"Not falling," she said, still breathless. "I just needed to get that off my chest."

For the first time since meeting her on that dusty county road, Luca had the clear sense that this woman could very well be the death of him. No woman had ever befuddled him quite like she was doing. He didn't know what to do with her. But he knew one thing—if he needed to kiss someone, it wouldn't have gone down like that. "Well, baby, the only thing I can say is, if you're going to get something off your chest, get it *off* your *chest,*" he said adamantly, and slipped his arm around her waist, yanked her into his body, knocked the sun hat off her head, and by God, he kissed her. None of this plant-one-and-get-out business. She was going to get a kiss that would hold her for the next twelve years if he had anything to do with it. He cupped her face, angled her head, and brushed his lips against hers. Just barely at first, just enough to let her know she had lit a fire.

Her lips parted. She grabbed his arm and dug her fingers into his flesh as if she thought he might let go of her and she would fall.

"You might want to close your eyes for this," he said, and brushed her lips with his again.

"I don't know if I can," she whispered to his mouth.

"Suit yourself," he said, and kissed her again, only this time, a little more urgently, his tongue slipping into her mouth. Her lips were velvety soft, and the touch of her tongue galvanized him and lit him up.

His fingers spread across her face and into her hair as the wave of lust and desire began to slink through him and curve around his heart, his lungs, his groin. It took a moment for Ella to see where he was going, but she caught on and began to respond, her tongue tangling with his, her free hand moving up his chest to his shoulder.

Luca's heart was thudding in his chest—her mouth sped him past all the usual vague thoughts about what's next. He was reacting from instinct, from a primitive place of desire. He pulled her into him, and she pressed against him, and his fingers tangled in her hair, and he could smell that faint scent of roses, and she felt so perfectly soft and ripe against him, and he was the one falling. He was falling over the edge, tumbling headlong into this want.

And then, with a sudden gasp as if she'd just broken the surface of the pool, Ella leaned back away from him and ended that kiss. It was agonizing—fire was burning through Luca's veins and pooling in his groin, and he wanted desperately to be in her, be *with* her. No one else, just her, out here on his land. He wanted her, and that wall Ella was so adept at putting up, that distance she would not let him cross, that mystery as to why, excited him to an unreasonable, indefensible degree.

"Did you fall?" he asked, hearing that he, too, was a little breathless.

"No," she said, her voice full of wonder. "But I almost did. I stopped just in the nick of time."

"Ella—"

She dipped down unsteadily to pick up her hat, which she stuffed onto her head. "Thanks for letting me get that off my chest," she said, and patted his chest. Her eyes were glittering at him, her smile luminescent.

Luca sighed.

Her smile deepened.

"Well, now you've gone and presented me with a problem. You're not going to fall, but I damn sure am."

Her smile was now beaming. *"Really?"*

He snorted. "Yes, Ella, really."

She laughed.

"Don't get cocky on me," he warned her.

"I wouldn't *dream* of it." She gave him a playful shove. "You have to go now."

"Let me guess—you're busy," he drawled.

"*So* busy," she said as they began to walk again. "I'm alphabetizing my salt and pepper today."

He grinned, and with a shake of his head he put his arm around her shoulders. "You're going to kill me, Ella Kendall."

She laughed, but he meant it. He could not recall a time he'd ever wanted a woman like he wanted Ella and didn't get his way.

Chapter Thirteen

Buddy was the one who took it the hardest when Luca left, chasing after his truck up the road for a time, then trotting dejectedly back to the house. Ella watched until they couldn't see the truck anymore. She wasn't even annoyed that he apparently had a nice big truck *and* a silent-but-deadly Sombra. Usually, she would have added that information to the con column, because no one that well-off should be hanging out with someone as poor as her.

She closed the door and looked around her cluttered little living room. Today had been such a nice surprise. It felt so good to be wanted, especially by someone who held a prime spot in her fantasy league of men.

She wondered if she ought to be concerned that he hadn't said when he'd see her again. She hadn't asked him. If she *had* asked, that would have made all the things she'd said today completely untrue. Like, how she wasn't going to fall. Asking would indicate falling.

"I'm *not,*" she informed Buddy. "I don't trust him. Not yet."

She still couldn't believe that this wasn't some weird little lark for him, a side note to an otherwise healthy love-'em-and-leave-'em lifestyle. She'd been around the block a few times. She knew how men could be.

And yet she drifted around the rest of the day, her head so far up in the clouds that it felt almost detached from her body, floating along while the rest of her tackled chores.

She wasn't any better the next day either, and she was working both jobs. First, she drove to her part-time accounting job, and Byron, from his throne in the smaller interior office, remarked that she seemed awfully chipper for an accountant in the middle of tax season. Ella had just laughed and asked if he wanted her to get some tacos for lunch. He did.

Later, when she showed up to work at the Magnolia, Mateo kept staring at her like he knew her from somewhere but couldn't quite place it. "What?" she asked laughingly. "Is there something on my shirt? Someone standing behind me? Wait! I know—I've won the *Reader's Digest* sweepstakes!"

"You look different," he said.

Ella glanced down at her black kilt skirt, the motorcycle boots she'd snagged off Craigslist, her flowered blouse, and the hair she had painstakingly braided into a fishtail to hang over her shoulder. "My hair is not in a knot for once," she said, and popped a maraschino cherry into her mouth.

"That's not it," he insisted, and gave her an appraising look. "You look like you're in a good mood."

She burst out laughing. "That's different?"

"Totally," he said. "You're usually worrying about something. Did you maybe pay off a bill?"

"You know I can't pay off my bills, Mateo." She smiled, swiped another cherry from the bar service, and went back to the hostess stand.

She smiled all night. She was happy to see everyone who walked through the door, even the Hanleys, who had a standing Friday night reservation so they could complain about everything. She complimented outfits, welcomed people back, welcomed new people.

Even Chrissy noticed her cheerfulness. "If you're on something, you better share."

Ella wasn't high on anything but life, and absurdly happy because of some kissing.

The next day, she still hadn't heard anything from Luca and still thought nothing of it. They weren't *dating*. They weren't anything other than friends.

She was humming when she went to pick Stacy up for lunch. She pulled into the parking lot of the new beige building that housed the Cimarron County Sheriff's Office. Stacy had been on the job a couple of weeks now, and Ella was eager to hear how she liked being gainfully employed. She probably didn't like it, knowing Stacy, but Ella had worked on the Rodeo Rebel books last night and, after their equipment rental costs, things were pretty dismal.

Stacy must have been watching for her out the window, because she hurried down the sidewalk in a cute yellow dress with white trim and wedge sandals. She wordlessly climbed into Ella's car, put her voluminous bag between her feet, and dug around in it for a minute, stuffing her ID inside it.

"What's up?" Ella asked.

"Why?" Stacy asked, glancing up.

"Because you didn't say hello and you look distracted."

"Oh," Stacy said, and shook her fingers through her long, platinum hair. "It's nothing, just this stupid job."

"You don't like it?"

"I *hate* it," Stacy said, and looked out the window. "The sheriff is an ass. Anyway, it's just a stupid job I have to do until we go to Nashville. Can we go?"

Ella put her car in drive. "What happened?"

"Nothing happened. But this job is not me, Ella."

Ella couldn't argue with that. "It's temporary, until you save the money to get to Nashville, right?"

Stacy suddenly gasped. "Guess who called me this morning? The record label guy. They want us this summer!"

"Wow," Ella said. "Fantastic!"

"We're going to cut a demo tape. We're doing 'Promise Me,' 'Kissing Kate,' and 'You Don't Make Me Feel.'" She began to hum "Promise Me." Stacy really did have a beautiful voice, and when she was onstage, she was amazing. Ella had always marveled at how she could get so lost in the music, how she could completely transform herself into such a mesmerizing performer. "You should totally come," Stacy said.

"What, to Nashville?"

"Move with us, Ella! You can be our manager," Stacy said brightly.

Ella wasn't moving to Nashville to be Stacy's manager. But she knew better than to say so at this point, and asked Stacy to tell her what the record guy had said.

They chatted about that until they reached the little café in a square blue-and-white building in Three Rivers. Jalisco's was authentic Tex-Mex cooking.

When Ella and Stacy walked in, several heads swiveled in their direction. Stacy was strikingly beautiful with her platinum blonde locks. And she liked to show off her great legs in skimpy hemlines. She was always fighting off admirers at her gigs.

Ella, on the other hand, was wearing cut-off shorts and a sleeveless embroidered Mexican peasant blouse that she'd picked up at the La Vallita Square one day. They'd been on an outdoor rack, going for five bucks each.

They ordered their food and chatted about life while they ate. When they were finished, Stacy touched up her lipstick, then folded her arms across the table and said, "So? What's going on with you?"

To Ella's dismay, she actually blushed. "Well, as it happens, I had a visitor."

"Your period?"

"Not that kind of visitor."

"The police?" Stacy asked matter-of-factly.

"No!"

"Social worker?"

"I'm almost thirty, Stacy. They social workers don't come around anymore."

Stacy shrugged. "Then who?"

Ella couldn't keep the silly little smile from her face. "Prince Luca."

Stacy gasped. "Get *out*," she said.

"I know, right?" Ella said, beaming like a seventeen-year-old.

"When?" Stacy demanded.

"He showed up one morning when it was raining. He found my dog on the road, and he brought him home. And then asked if he could come in."

"Okay," Stacy said, and gestured for her to speak, clearly wanting the good stuff.

Ella's smiled broadened. "He said he wanted to see me," she said.

"For what?" Stacy asked.

Ella gaped at her. "Seriously, Stacy? Because he *likes* me, that's why."

There was a long pause. A *long* pause.

"What's the matter, are you stunned into silence?" Ella asked. "So disbelieving that you're *speechless* for once?"

Stacy shrugged. "Maybe a little."

Now Ella was stunned into speechlessness. "*Wow,* Stacy."

"Don't get it twisted. Not because of *you,* Ella—any guy would be lucky to get you. You're gorgeous. But we're talking about Luca Prince. You know, the rich cowboy who, last we heard, was dating models in LA or socialites in New York? He's not the kind of guy to hang out with people like us, so I have to wonder why he is. Like, what's in it for him?"

"You are not making this better," Ella warned her.

Stacy took a breath. She pressed her palms to the table and said, "Ella. You're my best friend. You are the Gayle to my Oprah—"

"*I'm* Oprah," Ella insisted.

Stacy rolled her eyes. "I am *obviously* Oprah, but that's beside the point. The point is, you're like a sister to me. You are the most important person in my life, and I don't want you to get hurt."

"I didn't say we were dating!" Ella protested, and wished like hell she'd never brought it up. When would she learn to keep her mouth shut?

"You didn't say it, but your eyes are all twinkly, and I know how you feel about him—"

"Felt," Ella pointed out. "Like, twelve years ago. When I was a teenager. I'm a grown-ass woman now."

"Feel," Stacy countered. "Just look at you, all giggly and smiley. I mean, I get it," she said, pressing her hand to her décolletage. "He's super hot. He's a freaking charmer in chaps. But I don't want you to get your hopes up, because he's not going to stick around."

Ella's pulse was beginning to pound at her temples. She didn't know if she was thankful for Stacy's honesty or pissed that Stacy thought she was obviously not worthy of Luca's attention. "I didn't say I was expecting him to," she snapped. "And I'm not an idiot, Stacy. But you know what? Maybe he will. *Maybe* I'm not nearly the loser you think I am."

"El-*la!*" Stacy whined. "I knew you would take it the wrong way."

"How in God's name am I supposed to take it?" Ella insisted.

"You know what I'm saying. Okay, when is the

last time you saw a super rich, handsome guy fall in love with a very pretty, *wonderful,* but *poor* human being, who is essentially an orphan? Who is living practically in the middle of nowhere so she doesn't have to pay rent? Who doesn't even have running water?"

"I have running water!"

"Your sink is broken and your roof leaks."

Ella pressed her lips together.

"I'm just saying this sort of thing does not happen in our world. Everything that happens is because we had to claw and fight and scrape our way to it. You're not Cinderella, and this isn't a fucking fairy tale, trust me."

As furious as Ella was right now, she had to admit that Stacy had a point. She was dazzled by Luca, thrilled with his attention, but she didn't really know him. Still, Ella didn't like this lecture. She wasn't a fool, and she was generally a pretty good judge of character—the bad ones gave off a vibe. "If it's all the same to you, I'd like to swim around in my little fantasy while I can." She reached for the check. "I've got this."

"No! I called you. I'll get it—"

"No!" Ella said loudly. She paused, glanced around at the other diners to make sure no one had heard her outburst, then leaned across the table. "I balanced your books yesterday, and you don't have two nickels to rub together. Stop buying dresses," she said, gesturing at the one Stacy was wearing, "and hair extensions and whatever else, or you're not going to have enough for rent, much less enough to get to Nashville."

"All right, all right," Stacy said, raising both hands in surrender. "I'm supposed to get paid Friday. And we have a gig in Dallas this weekend that should be good money."

"Great!" Ella said, and stood up. Usually, when she and Stacy argued, she got over it pretty quickly. They had been thrown together at the age of fifteen, the two of them against the world, and they were in this life together. But today, Ella was so annoyed she could hardly look at Stacy. She knew deep down she wasn't right for Luca, but did Stacy have to be so damn eager to tell her so?

Stacy stood up, too, and hugged her. "I'm sorry, Ella," she said. "I just want you to know that I have your back."

Ella softened a little. "You have a funny way of showing it."

"Tact is not my strong suit," she said with a sheepish smile. "But I really believe you'll thank me for my honesty someday."

"Sure. And you'll thank me if you follow my advice and stop spending money you don't have."

"I'm *fine*," Stacy said.

At the moment, Ella didn't care if she was fine. Stacy had rained on her parade, and she was not going to let Stacy have her moment. The funny thing was, Stacy had been like that about Mateo, too, and Mateo was hardly better off than Ella. *He's not going to stick around,* she'd said to Ella one day. *Definitely a love-'em-and-leave-'em guy.* Ella remembered thinking that maybe he was, but she'd been enjoying it all the same. She was fond of Mateo, and they'd had fun. But it had never felt like the real deal.

It was too early to say what Luca felt like, other than a dream.

Chapter Fourteen

Cordelia Prince was sitting on top of Charlie's grave, her legs stretched before her, leaning back against the overly ornate headstone Dolly had insisted on ordering. *Son, husband, father, friend,* it said. Anyone seeing that would think Charlie had excelled at all of them. Well, he hadn't, and she'd come up here to remind him of the fact.

She hated the headstone. It was weirdly ostentatious for Dolly, given that she could never stop harping on Cordelia's designer handbags and shoes. But then again, Dolly had lost her son. She hadn't quite been the same since, dyeing her hair purple, signing up for tai chi at the senior center, and spending hours looking through Charlie's baby book. She was grieving as deeply as Cordelia.

Cordelia was quietly smug in the knowledge that she'd been the saner of the two in the months since Charlie died.

"You should see your mother," she said aloud to Charlie's grave. "She came home one day with purple tips in her gray hair like she'd gone all hippie. Let me tell you, it did not go unnoticed at church. It's your fault, you know. You sent your mother over the edge by dying." She paused, thinking about that. "Well, even more over the edge. You know what I mean."

She wished Charlie would answer. She wished she could hear him say, *I'm sorry I left you. I'm sorry I was such a rotten husband. I'm sorry you loved me so much when I didn't deserve it.* He didn't deserve it. But oh, she had loved him, and she missed him so.

"I don't know what to do about Nick," she said quietly, and opened her water bottle. "Yes, it's water," she added absently before drinking. Hallie had told her she was drinking too much, which of course Cordelia had not taken well, because what fresh hell had she entered where her own daughter felt the need to lecture her about drinking too much? But she thought Hallie might have had a point. She *had* been drinking a lot since Charlie died. She'd noticed her face was getting a little puffy. It had to be the wine, because Cordelia had quit crying all the time.

Anyway, Nick. "He's distant. He doesn't come around much, and when he does, he doesn't do much talking. He seems so angry, but you know what? I don't think he's angry with you. I think he's angry with *me*. I saw Charlotte last week, and she said he's been a royal pain in the ass, walking around the office with a huge chip on his shoulder. You know, the way you used to get when things weren't going your way." She gave a snort of indignation about that. "Yep, that boy is a chip off the old block, all right."

Maybe that was why she loved Nick so much. It was possible that Nick was her favorite. Not that she would *ever* really think that, but Luca and Hallie had each other, and Nick, well . . . she had Nick.

Cordelia loved all her children fiercely. But Nick was so much like Charlie that she'd always had a special fondness for him. Hallie was a dreamer, and it was easy to love her. Easy to worry about her, too.

An acorn dropped from the tree and pinged Cordelia in the head. "Dammit, I know that was you," she said, and flicked it off her lap where it had landed.

She drank more water, and then, from the corner of her eye, she saw Luca coming out of the ranch house. He was wearing chaps over his jeans and a T-shirt. He was carrying his hat, and his hair was brushed back. He needed a cut. Cordelia was proud of how handsome Luca was. She liked to think she'd played a significant role in turning out a child with movie-star good looks. Dolly said he looked just like Charlie's great-grandfather, and maybe he did, but Dolly would use any opportunity to take a dig at Cordelia. Still, there was no denying that Luca was *her* creation.

"I don't know what we're going to do with him," she said, pointing her bottle at Luca as he walked down to the stables. "Chet says he hasn't shown up at work in weeks. Where'd we go wrong with him, Charlie? You always said he was going to surprise us, but the boy is thirty years old, and he's spending his days riding around like he's twelve."

Another acorn fell, hitting her knee.

"You left me with so much *crap*," she said suddenly. "So many things to do and so many regrets, and I am still so *pissed*, Charlie! We never made up!" she cried skyward. "You died thinking I hated you, and I *did*, but I never got to tell you that I loved you so much more!"

Tears filled her eyes, and she swallowed them down. She was so sick of tears and regrets and trying to figure out how to carry on without him. And she was tired. So freaking tired.

She closed her eyes and leaned her head against the gravestone. Another acorn hit her in the chest. "I swear if you don't cut that out, I'm going to bust this tombstone into pieces," she muttered.

Chapter Fifteen

Buddy was not on the porch waiting when Ella returned from town one afternoon, but the pig came trotting as fast as she could. So did the three remaining chickens, running in crazy paths behind the pig. Ella didn't know what had happened to the other two. Lyle said probably coyotes.

"My God, you guys are transparent," Ella said as she lifted a box from the trunk. "Where's Buddy?"

No one answered, but the pig managed to get her snout all the way into the box before Ella realized what was happening.

She fed her herd, then finished unloading her car. She was walking up the steps of the porch when Buddy came loping toward her. He had nettles in his fur and was panting, as if he'd run home through the brush. She leaned down to extricate some of the nettles from his fur, but some of them would need to be cut out. "Where the hell have you been?" she asked the smiling, panting dog.

Almost as if in response to her, Buddy suddenly surged to his feet and barked. Ella looked up to see Luca on a chestnut horse, loping across the pasture toward her house.

Her smile was instantaneous. She hastily raked her fingers through her hair as she stepped off the porch to greet him.

Luca reined his horse to a halt. He dismounted and looped the reins around the railing on the steps. He was wearing a ball cap today, the bill facing backward, his hair gathered in a small ponytail beneath it. His dark gray T-shirt said *Renew Your World.*

"Hey," she said, hoping her grin wasn't too goofy. "I wasn't expecting you."

He held out his arms. "Surprise." Luca turned back to the horse and untied a satchel and a tool belt. He hoisted the tool belt over his shoulder and grabbed the satchel with his hand.

"What are you doing?"

"Forecast says rain this week. I brought what I need to patch your roof."

She gaped at him. "You're going to *patch* my *roof?*"

"Yep."

"Now?"

"If that's okay with you. Won't take long."

She didn't know what to say. She was immediately and deeply grateful—God knew YouTube wasn't going to patch her roof—and also con-

218

fused as to why this guy couldn't pick up a phone and tell her he was coming. "That's so *nice*," she said.

"You don't have to sound so shocked. I told you I'm a nice guy."

"Well, sure, everyone says they're nice. But you're, like, proving it. *Thank* you. I have to admit it's getting a little moldy inside."

"Don't mention it," hc said.

"I have to. It's *really* nice," she said, and when he arched his brow at her, she said, "Not that there is anything wrong with that. But dude, is your phone working? You keep catching me at my worst."

He smiled down at her with hazel eyes that were more green than brown or blue today, and said, "If this is your worst, I don't think I can handle your best. I told you I'm bad at texting."

"That's such a weird thing to be bad at," Ella said.

Luca's smile broadened, so warm, so brilliant, and she remembered the way he'd smiled at her in algebra just in passing, and she'd been beside herself with girlish glee. She was feeling that girlish glee all over again.

"Fortunately for you, I'm pretty good at things like patching a roof," he said, and dropped the satchel to remove his chaps. The denims he wore fit him so well that Ella couldn't help but look.

He glanced up at her and gave her a lopsided smile. "Look all you want."

219

Ella could feel her cheeks bloom. "You are so *conceited*," she teased him. "I was checking out your tool belt."

"Wow," he said with a shake of his head. "There are so many things I could say about my tool belt right now." His gaze skimmed over her, and he drew a deep breath. "Do you have a ladder?"

She wanted to hear about his tool belt. "Yes," she said. "It's wooden."

He looked skyward for a moment. "I guess we're going old school."

Ella couldn't help but laugh. "You have no idea how old school it is around here."

They fetched the ladder, and she sat on the tree stump and watched as Luca went up on the roof while Buddy snoozed on the ground beside her. He moved around, testing his weight in several places, then dragged the satchel across the roof to repair the hole.

It hardly took any time at all. When he came back down, she made lemonade. He took the glass she offered him and sat beside her on the top porch step.

"You ought to get some chairs for the porch," he suggested.

"I don't think the porch can hold the extra weight," she pointed out.

He nodded. "You might have a point."

Ella was acutely aware of every inch of him beside her. She tried not to ogle the beard shadowing his face. She tried not to think about how sexy he looked right now. She tried not to guess at all the things he could say about his tool belt.

"Okay, the roof. You want the good news or the bad news first?" he asked after he'd downed the lemonade.

"Always lead with the good," she said.

"Your roof shouldn't leak for a while."

"Great!" she said. "So what's the bad news?"

"You're in desperate need of a new roof."

Ella laughed. "Do they make used ones?"

"Ella," he said in all seriousness, "you have to replace that roof. I'm surprised you haven't lost half of it by now."

That roof could get in line behind the missing kitchen faucet, the sag in the corner of the front bedroom where the wall was separating from the floor, and pig feed. "Well, here's a surprise," she said. "I don't have the money to replace the roof."

He glanced over his shoulder at the house.

"I know," she said. "It's a wreck."

"It's not a wreck. It's just old," he said. "With a little help, you could make this a nice farmhouse again."

She didn't know if it had ever been a nice farmhouse. Her memories of it were very fond, but even so, she could remember wear and tear. Once, a floorboard had come up, and she had twisted her ankle in the gap. "Honestly, Luca, I can't thank you enough for patching that hole. You're a godsend."

"You're very welcome. But if you really want to thank me, you can meet me for dinner in town. I've worked up an appetite."

Ella's heart began to race. "Town. Three Rivers?"

"No, Dallas," he said, his eyes twinkling with amusement. "Yes, Three Rivers."

The nape of her neck began to turn warm. Dinner in town sounded so . . . real. "People will think we're dating," she said softly.

"My God, the horror," he said with mock concern. "How about we go to a taco stand? People wouldn't think we were dating at a taco stand. That's a meet and greet, not a date."

She smiled. "You're right. We couldn't *possibly* be on a date at a taco stand."

"Tell you what," he said. "I'll ride home, get cleaned up, and meet you there at seven. It's definitely not a date if I don't pick you up, right?"

"That puts it at chance encounter."

He slipped two fingers under her chin and turned her face toward him. "And I won't kiss you," he said as his gaze drifted to her mouth. "Because if I kiss you, we're probably almost certainly dating."

She felt flush. Slightly overheated and a little loopy. Her eyes fluttered shut as he leaned toward her and kissed her, his lips and the tip of his tongue as soft as marshmallows. All sorts of sparks flared through her.

Luca lifted his head and brushed her cheek with his thumb. "Deal?"

"Deal. We're not dating," she said dreamily, and ran her hand up his forearm, feeling the muscles beneath her fingers.

"We will *never* date," he agreed, and kissed her neck, sending more little shocks of sparks down her spine.

"We're just friends," she said with a sigh of pleasure.

"We're not even *friends,*" he said, and lightly bit the curve of her neck into her shoulder.

And then, quite abruptly, he stood up and jogged down the steps and picked up his chaps. "I'll meet you at the corner of Guadalupe and Blanco," he said as he put on the chaps, then unwrapped the reins of his horse from the railing. "Know where that is?"

"I think so," Ella said. She was still hovering somewhere between the clouds overhead and earth, because Three Rivers had like maybe twenty corners and she knew them all, but she could not think of them at this moment.

"Seven, okay?" he asked as he swung up on his horse. Buddy trotted down off the porch and stood ready to run alongside.

"Okay," she said, and leaned over the railing, trying quietly to catch her breath.

223

He smiled as if he knew he'd won this round, and then sent his horse trotting through the hole in the barbed wire fence that separated her house from the dormant pasture.

A moment later, Ella looked down to make sure she hadn't actually floated away.

Chapter Sixteen

Luca spotted Ella as soon as he got out of the Sombra. She was sitting at a picnic table, her hair down her back except for the bits she'd put up in two knots on the top of her head to keep it out of her face. Her posture was very prim, her knees visible through the rips in her jeans, her hands clasped in her lap. She looked wholesome, fresh, and pretty, like spring, when everything was so colorful and green and you could believe that a new start really was possible.

But at the same time, she was dead sexy. She was a siren behind a T-shirt and sweater and red Keds. He wasn't fooled.

He had to ask himself again how he'd missed her in high school. As a teenager, it seemed as if no girl—or rather, no parts of girls—went unnoticed by him, and yet he couldn't conjure up much more than a few fleeting memories of Ella Kendall in the background.

What a fool he'd been. Probably an ass, too, knowing himself as well as he did.

This was a perfect spring evening with a bit of

a chill in the air beneath the long, twisted limbs of the live oaks overhead. Clear globe lights were strung up in the branches to create a canopy of sparkly light. A smattering of potted flowers were scattered around to brighten things up.

Ella stood up as he walked across the lawn. She seemed slightly nervous, which was different from the slightly annoyed look he'd come to expect from her. *What's this, Ella Kendall? Did you decide it was a date after all?*

"You made it," he said.

"You shaved," she said.

"A beard can be a hazard when eating tacos. Speaking of which, what's your taco pleasure?"

She slipped her hands into the back pockets of her jeans and looked over her shoulder at the stand. "What have they got?"

"Miss Kendall, you are in for a treat. This is taco nirvana. These guys will put watermelon on your taco if you want it."

She laughed. "I definitely don't want a watermelon taco."

"Then let's check it out."

They walked up to the taco stand and perused the menu together, deciding, jointly, that the basic route—meat and cheese, lettuce and tomato—was the way to go. Luca ordered four, plus two beers, and when the man behind the stand turned to the cash register, he saw Ella slip her hand in her pocket. He caught her wrist. "I know you're not thinking of pulling money out of that pocket on the grounds that this is not a date."

"I am," she confessed.

"Yeah, well, I refuse to be insulted by a farm girl. I invited you to tacos, and I am springing for the twenty bucks this is going to set me back."

"Are you seriously going to make a big deal about twenty bucks?"

"Huge," he assured her.

She laughed. "Okay, cowboy, you win," she said, and pulled her hand from her pocket, holding up both palms so that he could see she had no money.

"That's more like it," he said, and gathered their food and beer.

They chose a picnic table right in the middle of the clearing. They sat on top of it, side by side, and watched some kids playing in a bocce ball pit. Ella took a bite of a taco and closed her eyes with a sigh of contentment. "Oh my God," she said.

"Didn't I tell you?" he asked.

"They're unbelievable," she said, and took another bite, filling both cheeks like a squirrel.

Luca laughed. He liked a woman who could eat, who wouldn't watch him buy a bunch of tacos and take only a few bites. It made him smile. He was always smiling around Ella, and he seriously tried to think of a time he had smiled quite so much in the presence of a woman.

He looked away to the bluebonnets in a grassy strip between the park and the parking lot. The bluebonnets brought to mind the spring behind the old Kendall place. A flurry of thoughts about what he could accomplish began to flit through his head. It felt strange to be turning all his attention back to the place he'd spent so much time as a boy, wandering around that spring, just a stone's throw from the old Kendall place. "How'd you end up at your farm, if you don't mind me asking?"

Ella delicately wiped a bit of sauce from the corner of her mouth. "Just did."

"Nope," he said, and put his hand on her wrist so that she couldn't keep eating her taco. She looked at him with surprise. "You're preventing me from devouring my taco."

"For the moment. Now listen, Ella, I've been doing my level best to scale the walls around you to know you. Are you going to tell me *anything* about you?"

She pulled her wrist from his grip and took another bite. "I've told you things about me. I told you I'm an accountant."

"You know what I mean," he said, and took her wrist once more, lifted her hand, and took a bite of her taco.

"Hey!" she protested.

"I'll eat the whole damn thing if you keep dodging me," he warned her.

"Fine," she said, and pulled her hand and taco

back. "But I should warn you, my life is not a happily-ever-after kind of story. Can you handle it?" She said it teasingly, but she glanced at him from the corner of her eye, as if she was worried he couldn't.

Luca snorted at that. If she only knew. "Trust me, I can handle it."

"Really?" she asked, and with the back of her hand, brushed a bit of hair from her cheek. "I'm not talking about being poor. You've had it easy, Luca. Easier than I have, is all I'm saying."

"Whoa, whoa, whoa," he said. "Who made you judge of easy? You don't know much about my life either," he said in all seriousness. "Okay, yes, my family has a lot of money and land."

"And businesses."

"And businesses," he conceded. "That's the easy part. But that doesn't mean my life has been charmed. And even if it had been all unicorns and ice cream, I can take whatever it is you want to tell me, Ella. I *want* to know. I'm dead serious—I want to know you. I want to understand you."

Her eyes moved contemplatively over his face. "Okay," she said, nodding. "Just remember, you asked."

"What, are you a cannibal or something? Hiding some bodies out there?"

"It's not *that* bad. But ending up at that run-down farmhouse is a full circle for me. I started there. It was my first home—I mean, at least to my knowledge. I don't really know, to be honest. I remember a time my mom and I lived with her parents, and my earliest and most enduring memories are of that house. But did I live there as an infant? I don't know."

How odd to think of her on that farm when he'd been running around on the fringes of it. "I was running around that house when I was a kid. How long were you there?"

She took a drink of her beer. "I was about six when child protective services removed me."

She said it so casually that Luca was momentarily startled. He knew she'd been in foster care, but he hadn't really thought about *how* she'd ended up there. Or when. Six years old? When he was six, he'd been wrestling Nick for control of the toy wooden rifle their grandfather had made them. "Why?" he asked.

"My mom got into trouble. She had a drug problem. And my grandpa was really sick, so my grandma couldn't take care of me and him. My grandma came to visit me at first, but I guess my grandpa needed all her attention. She stopped coming after a while, and then, the next I knew, she had Alzheimer's."

Luca stared at her. The emotion was gone from her voice. "You were in foster care all that time?"

"Until I was eighteen. A children's home at first, then different families. I never went home again." She shrugged. "And then one day, this

230

guy walked into the Magnolia with some papers."
She suddenly smiled. "Funny how something
happens, and you can finally believe in those
miracles everyone is always talking about."

"A miracle?"

"That's something a caseworker said to me
once."

"Okay, hold up," Luca said, and shifted so that
he was turned toward her. "You're going to have
to start over so I can keep up."

She looked at him with her spring blue eyes,
and he could almost see the internal debate about
how much to tell him. But then she said, "Once,
when I was maybe twelve, the state moved me to
another foster home. My third or fourth, I don't
remember that or why I had to move, but that's
just the way it was. Anyway, I had to leave my
blue bike and Tamir behind."

"And Tamir is . . . ?"

"Another foster kid in the same home I was in.
He was five. So *cute,*" she said, smiling. "I adored
him. He was my shadow." Her eyes shone with
delight. "I remember we were outside playing—I
was pulling him around in a wagon attached to
my bike. This woman pulls up, and she had a
puff of gray hair and so many bangle bracelets
that they sounded like wind chimes. She'd come
to get me, and I didn't even know I was going.
But sure enough, my bag was packed and ready
at the door." She glanced down. "It was horrible,

to be honest. Tamir didn't understand. *I* didn't understand." She shook her head and looked off to the bluebonnets for a moment.

Luca was appalled by the image her words had painted in his head. His heart ached for those two children.

"Anyway, this woman was trying her best to console me, and she said, 'Well, things happen for a reason, and although it seems terrible now, something good will come of it.' " Ella rolled her eyes. "She said, 'Sometimes, Ella, you just have to believe in miracles.' " She snorted. Then took another healthy bite of taco.

Luca tried to see the world through a lens he'd never tried on before. His family hadn't always been harmonious, but they were family, and he couldn't imagine not having them, couldn't imagine people showing up to take him away from them. "That seems a little too Pollyanna, given the circumstances," he muttered.

Ella laughed. *"Definitely.* And for the record, nothing good came out of that move or the one after that or the one after that. Nothing even remotely resembling a miracle came to me in all those years. Not until that day the lawyer walked into the Magnolia and handed me an envelope."

"Who was he?" Luca asked.

"Paul Feinstein, Esquire," she said with a flourish of her hand and a mock bow. "I had no idea who he was. He was wearing a tan suit and loafers with no socks, which is pretty racy for Three Rivers. He said, 'Are you Ella Louise Kendall?' "

"Let me guess—you refused to tell him," Luca said wryly.

She gave him a little shove with her shoulder. "As a matter of fact, I asked him *politely* who wanted to know. And he said, 'Cockrell, Hamblen, and Associates,' and asked me to call him after I'd had a chance to review the contents. And then he went into the bar."

"I would have thought I'd been served with a lawsuit."

"That's where we're different. I'm used to people I don't know showing up in my life. Until I was about twenty-five, there was always a social worker or a court appointee or prison advocate descending on me wherever I was."

"*Prison* advocate?" Luca said, and laughed.

Ella didn't laugh. She took a bite of her second taco. "I thought he was there to tell me my mom was up for parole again."

Luca had to rewind that statement. He looked for any sign she was joking. But then again, why else would she be in foster care? He didn't quite know what to say.

Ella said it for him. "It's okay," she said quietly as she studied her taco. "I'm far beyond being ashamed about it. It is what it is, you know?"

No, he didn't know; he had no clue. He was

as flabbergasted as he was fascinated. He ate his taco and tried to imagine his mother in prison.

Ella glanced at him from the corner of her eye. "Well?" she said lightly. "Don't you want to know?"

The impulse to pretend he didn't want to know sidled through his head—it seemed too personal. But she was being honest with him, and she deserved at least that much from him. "Yeah, I do."

"She'd been in and out of jail for most of my life for drugs, which is why she could never get her act together to come and get me. She'd get out of jail, and she'd say she was going to get a house for us and that things were going to be different. But she could never say no to using something, and she never could keep a job or keep up with her probation appointments or go to the parenting classes the state assigned her to. You know what I think? I think she just stopped trying after a while. But anyway, now she's in for aggravated assault with a deadly weapon."

He was stunned. It sounded like a *Dateline* episode. "Who?" he managed.

"Her husband. Apparently she caught him cheating and she was high, and she wanted to kill him. So she tried. She ran him over with a car. But she didn't kill him; she just maimed him pretty good from what I know."

"She ran over your dad with a car?" he repeated, aghast.

"Not my dad. I don't know who my dad is. I didn't know this man either. When it happened, it had been about three years since I'd even seen her."

Luca was losing his appetite and put his taco aside. She hadn't been kidding when she said her life had been hard. "Have you seen her since?"

"Once," she said with a shrug. "After she was sentenced she found Jesus, and she wanted to have a relationship with her daughter. The same daughter for whom she'd been unable to give up drugs, mind you, but I was seventeen, and I was curious. What I remembered about her was starting to fade. So I went to Gatesville to see her."

Luca knew enough to know Gatesville housed the state women's prison. "And?"

"And . . ." Ella looked him directly in the eye. "There was nothing there. It was like talking to a stranger, and a weird stranger at that. She was too eager, too religious." She shook her head and tossed the rest of her taco into the bag.

Luca did not know what to say.

"But *anyway,*" Ella said, making light of it, "fast forward ten years, and the man came to my bar with the envelope, and there it was, my miracle. It really was a miracle, Luca, because I was struggling to make ends meet. My hands got clammy, my belly did some loop-de-loops, and I,

235

Ella Louise Kendall, experienced my first bona fide miracle ever, because my grandmother had left me her house and her farm, which I didn't even know she still owned. Apparently, a cousin or someone kept it rented after Grandma went to the Alzheimer's home, and they used that money to pay for her care."

"That's . . . that's amazing," he said.

"I remember that house. I remember marking the walls in the front bedroom, and the marks are still there. I remember standing on the back porch and watching a breeze sweep across the prairie grass before I felt it in my hair and how Grandpa would push me in the old tire swing before he got too sick. Grandma would cook supper with food they grew right there, in the spot where the bushes have grown up now, and that house, believe it or not, always smelled like warm summer nights and hope and love." She smiled, the memories clearly still with her.

Luca knew that feeling, too, the feeling of summer. As corny as it sounded, it was a feeling he carried in his heart, and brought out and dusted off every year at the first breath of summer. What he remembered of summers was how their majordomo, Martin, would invite him and his siblings down to his house, and he would crank homemade ice cream on the back porch, and they would play games with Martin's kids. Other nights, his dad barbecued while they swam, and his mother would sit under the rose-covered trellis with a cocktail, laughing at his dad's jokes. And then later, they would lie on blankets and look at the blaze of stars overhead.

"So after all those years of moving around, I finally had a rundown place of my own." She laughed.

Luca picked up her hand and laced his fingers with hers. "You really have had a pretty rough life, haven't you?" he said.

Ella's smile faded. "Don't, Luca."

"What?"

She shifted around to face him. "Don't feel sorry for me. That is the *worst*. *I* don't feel sorry for me. I mean, yes, I've lost more Tamirs and grandmas in my life than I can possibly count, but I've managed. I have put one foot in front of the other, and I've wrapped up all my warm, fuzzy memories of my grandparents and taken them with me, and I've gone on. I've survived. I went to college; I got a degree; I'm working; I'm *fine*. But the one thing I can't abide, the one thing that I hate above all else is for someone to feel sorry for me. Because I made it, Luca. I made it in spite of everything."

"Okay," he said. He hated pity, too. He knew exactly what she meant, how it felt to be dealt a crappy hand and to make something out of it. "But I don't feel sorry for you," he said, squeezing her hand. "I admire you. I—"

237

"Luca!"

Both of them started at the masculine voice and turned toward it. Randy Frame was standing in front of them with a bag of tacos. "Hey, I guess you two know each other after all," he said, waggling his brows. "What's up?"

"Randy!"

Luca heard Ella sigh as Mariah appeared, holding two beers. She looked at Ella, then at Luca. Then at Ella. "Are you kidding me?" she said to Ella.

"Hello, Mariah," Ella said.

"Randy, sit," Mariah demanded, pointing to the table.

"Maybe we should ask if they mind if we join them," Randy said.

"We're sitting," Mariah said, and plunked herself down.

"Please, join us," Luca said, and mimed a look of fright at Ella before sliding off the table and sitting down across from Randy.

"What's going on here?" Mariah asked, giving Ella a grossly obvious wink.

What was going on here was that Luca was still falling, slipping farther and farther down the rabbit hole. "We're having some tacos, Mariah. Don't get any ideas."

"Too late!" she chirped, and beamed at him before turning that blazing smile to Ella.

Chapter Seventeen

This was exactly what Ella feared would happen if she came to town with Luca. Someone would see them, probably someone with a big mouth (Mariah), and knowing Mariah as well as she did, Ella was certain the whole town would have heard about their "date" by tomorrow afternoon.

And then, days or weeks from now, Luca would move on, and people would whisper, *Who does she think she is?*

That was really nothing she could control, and she understood that it shouldn't influence her feelings for Luca in the least, but Ella did *not* want to look like an idiot. She did *not* want to be the poor girl who thought she had a chance with one of the Princes. She knew better.

"So when did *this* start?" Mariah whispered excitedly as Luca and Randy talked.

"Nothing has *started*," Ella said. "He helped me with something at the house, and we had some tacos. That's it, the whole enchilada."

"The whole enchilada my ass," Mariah said. "How do you expect me to believe that?" she leaned across the table and whispered, *"Do you know how many times I had to listen to you pine for Prince Luca when we were in high school?"*

Ella stole a quick look at Luca to assure herself he hadn't heard Mariah. "Will you stop?" she whispered back. "That was a very long time ago."

Mariah leaned even closer and whispered, "So, what, you aren't into him anymore? What's the matter, did he get too good-looking for you? Because he's only gotten better looking—"

"Mariah, *stop,*" Ella said, laughing.

Mariah snorted. "I'm your friend. Why won't you tell me?"

"If I'm your friend, why won't you give me your business?" Ella countered.

"Not fair," Mariah said, and leaned back. She indicated Randy with her chin. "I have that one breathing down my neck." She grunted, took a swig of beer. "Okay, so don't tell me. But I thought we were friends. Speaking of *friends,*" she said, sounding a tiny bit surly, "remember the day you and Stacy came to my shop?"

That caught Randy's attention. He suddenly turned toward Ella and Mariah. "Yeah, Stacy," he said.

"Who is Stacy?" Luca asked.

"Oh, you remember, Luca," Mariah said with a flick of her wrist. "Stacy Perry. Blond hair. School choir."

"Oh, right," he said.

Well, great. Stacy, he remembered. "What about her?" Ella asked.

"Did you remember seeing a yellow dress with white trim?" Mariah asked.

Something tipped in Ella. She had a sudden vision of Stacy coming out of the sheriff's office in a cute yellow dress. Ella blinked. She lifted her bottle and drank.

Mariah's eyes narrowed. "Have you seen it, by any chance?"

Everyone was looking at Ella. She could feel the heat in her cheeks. Guilt by association all over again. "Umm . . . where was it?" Ella asked as she frantically tried to think of what to say.

"It was on the seventy-five-percent-off rack."

"I didn't go back to that rack, remember?"

"I know. But I'm asking, have you *seen* it?" Mariah asked pointedly.

Ella's stomach was suddenly churning. She wanted to throttle Stacy. She couldn't believe her! Shoplifting was horrible. But to steal from a *friend?* And when she was with Ella? Stacy clearly had no regard for Ella at all—it was like they were teens all over again. Stacy risking everything with no regard for how it would impact Ella if she was caught when Ella was with her. It had happened more than once, which meant Ella had also been taken into custody. *Guilt by association.* She'd been released when she had nothing stolen in her possession and Stacy had sworn it was just her, but it was harrowing all the same.

To know she'd done it again made Ella feel furiously helpless.

Her silence was enough of an answer. With a sigh, Mariah shook her head and looked away. "I knew it," she muttered.

"I didn't know, Mariah," Ella said. "I assumed she bought it in San Antonio."

The men had fallen silent, but not Mariah. "I know you had nothing to do with it, Ella, and I'm not mad at you. But I am *furious* with Stacy. When I think of all the times you two came over and my mom made supper for you. All the sleepovers we had so you two could get out of that house with all the fighting and drinking. We gave you and Stacy a normal life where we could, and this is the thanks I get?"

Ella wanted to crawl in a hole. She hated Mariah's review of her life. "I know, it's maddening," she said. "It's always been Stacy's way of coping—"

"Don't you dare defend her, Ella," Mariah said sharply. "Don't you *dare*."

"I'm not," Ella said evenly. "I would never." Her face was surely as red as a beet. She was so embarrassed that the person closest to her in this world was a common thief. What must Luca think of her now? "I know you're furious, Mariah, and

I am, too. I may understand why she does it, but I hate that she does it at all."

"Then *why* are you still hanging out with her?" Mariah asked plaintively. "You are so much better than that, Ella!"

"Come on, Mariah," Ella said softly. "You know why."

"Please don't give me that 'sisters' nonsense," Mariah said, making air quotes around the word *sisters*. "Because you're not."

"Okay," Luca said. "All right, Mariah."

Mariah glanced at Luca. She sighed, folded her arms over her body, and exchanged a look with Randy. A moment or two passed before Mariah sighed and looked at Ella again. "She put you in a terrible position, Ella."

"She did. She really did."

"I ought to turn her in. Which would be super ironic since she is working for the sheriff now," Mariah said with a snort. "But she is definitely not welcome in my store."

"No," Ella agreed. She was so livid she didn't trust herself to speak. There was no defense for Stacy.

"Okay," Randy said. "We've taken up enough of their time, Riah. Let's go." He stood up and picked up their bag of tacos.

Mariah got up, walked around the table, and bent down to hug Ella. "Don't take it personally," she said, and Ella wondered how she was not supposed to take it personally. She'd just dressed down Ella's choice of friends.

They said goodnight, and when the Frames had wandered off, Luca said, "Are you all right?"

No. "It's fine," Ella said, desperate to talk about anything but Stacy. "So it's getting late." She stood.

"It's not late; it's a little past eight."

She smiled. "I need to go."

Luca sighed. He stood up. "Thanks for coming out with me, Ella. I enjoyed it. Until the Frames showed up." He smiled.

She smiled, too. He put his hand on the small of her back as they began to walk toward the parking lot. "I'm glad you made me go," Ella said. "Thanks for the tacos."

"Thank you for sharing your story with me," he said as they reached the parking lot. "I know it wasn't easy for you to tell me. Or to take the flack about your friend."

She cringed inwardly. "Stacy has a bad habit. But she's really not a bad person."

"You'll have to tell me more about her sometime."

Ella smiled. "You'll have to tell me something about you sometime, too."

"That would imply you're up for a next time," he pointed out, and cupped her elbow.

"Sure," she said nonchalantly as he pulled her closer. "As friends." Luca looked so handsome in the sparkly light of the trees. So handsome that he made Ella feel achy and happy at the same time. Happy that she'd come with him after all. Achy that she longed for him so.

"Friends," he agreed, and he lowered his head, his mouth only a breath from hers, and lingered there.

Ella felt herself sinking into a little boat of pleasure. It wasn't fair, to be pushed from shore so easily. To like someone quite as much as this. She slowly lifted her chin, expecting, and wanting, to be kissed.

But he didn't kiss her.

She shifted slightly closer. *Kiss me already, cowboy.*

"I don't know," he murmured. "I'm not sure about this."

"Sure about what?" she whispered as he put a hand on her waist. *Come on already.* She was starting to feel a little on fire.

"I'm not sure if we're just friends."

It was her own damn fault for being so insecure that she'd started this friend business. She shifted again, so close that she was touching him. "Will you please stop talking and kiss me goodnight?"

He paused. He turned his head slightly so that his mouth was on her temple. "Okay, Ella," he said. "I will kiss you. But you enter this arrangement at your own peril." And then he took her head in his enormous hands and kissed her.

Ella didn't move. She opened her mouth to his as an image of him lying completely naked on her chenille bedspread flashed in her brain. His kiss was so tender and demanding all at the same time that she was on the verge of bursting into globs of gooey hearts. She put her arms around his waist and held on to keep that from happening.

He pressed the tips of his fingers to her cheek and lifted his head, his eyes searching her face. "You know we're kicking up some dust here, right?"

She was too impatient to analyze it. "It's just dust," she said, and nipped at his lips.

"Dust rises before a storm, you know."

She drew his bottom lip between her teeth and slid her hand down his rump. "So?"

He smiled, and then kissed her so steamily that she was a furnace of want, of hot, molten sexual desire. How could he make her feel so ravenous? How could he make her knees wobbly with a kiss? His kiss didn't feel just hungry and lustful. It was also reverent. He stroked her face. Her hair. His hand splayed across her face, not to move her head around to suit him, but to touch her.

And then, like a dream, he lifted his head, and it was over. He stepped to one side and opened the driver's side door of her vehicle.

Ella hadn't moved. She was staring at him, still deep in that heady space of desire.

Luca smiled, she thought, a little smugly. Like he knew the sort of knee-melting power he had over her.

Dammit. Damndamndamn. She'd shown her hand.

"Goodnight, Ella," he said as she forced herself to step around him and slip into the driver's seat.

"Goodnight, Luca," she said pertly, and cranked the engine. She gave him a cheery little wave out the window as she backed away, then roared out of the parking lot as she gasped for breath.

She drove home in something of a fog, uncertain about everything suddenly. She didn't know when she'd see him again. Or even if she should. She didn't know where this thing between them was going, exactly, or when it would end, but her fear of that had been dwarfed tonight by the desire to see him again, to feel his hands on her body, to see that shine in his eyes.

Imagining it made her shiver.

When she pulled up to her house, Buddy and the pig were stretched out on the porch waiting for her. She gave them both belly rubs, then walked into her rotting little house.

She shut the door and looked around at the furniture she'd salvaged from bulk trash by driving around the Terrell Hills neighborhood in San Antonio on pick-up day. The two blue-green totes stacked in the corner that carried her life's belongings. She'd learned at an early age to travel light, to keep possessions to a minimum.

She sank down on the couch and thought about the two La-Z-Boy armchairs that had stood side-by-side in this very spot when she was a child. The art had consisted of her grandmother's cross-stitched angels and snowy village scenes.

Ella was not as numb to her past or her memories as she'd claimed to be. She still felt her grandparents' loss. She felt the loss of her mother, and although it was a different loss, it ran just as deep. The truth, that Ella refused to let anyone see, was that searing losses burned in her gut and her head, and no matter how she tried to make it out as though her life had gone on and she was fine, those scars were with her every single moment. She once had loved her grandma, and her grandma had given in death the one thing she couldn't give Ella in life, the thing Ella had always craved—a real home. But she'd recently come to suspect that the only thing missing from this bona fide miracle was someone to share it with.

In all her wildest dreams, she wished it was Luca. In her wildest dreams, she knew that person was *not* Luca. Oh, she didn't doubt that he genuinely liked her and was attracted to her. But he was too rich, too important, from a family too powerful to ever be saddled with someone like her.

So what was she doing with him? Why was she

playing with a bonfire that would torch her in the end?

Her phone rang, causing Ella to jump. She smiled and dug in her pocket for it, expecting it to be Luca.

It was not Luca on her cell phone. It was Stacy.

Her warm mood quickly turned cool. Ella tossed the phone on the couch and stood up, walked into her bedroom, and ignored the insistent ringing.

Chapter Eighteen

Luca had just started up the Sombra when he got a text from his older brother. Where R U?

Town, Luca texted back.

Come out to the ranch?

Luca had planned to go to his loft, but he texted back a thumbs-up and headed out to the ranch.

He pulled into the garage and walked up to the house on a flagstone path that wended through palms and loquat trees, through azalea and bougainvillea, past shaped hedges, and through a stone archway into the pool area.

That's where he saw his sister languishing on a chaise longue near the pool. She was wearing a dress, and she had a stiletto heel on one foot; the other foot was suspiciously bare. Her hat, like something he'd seen women wear to a garden party, was pulled down over her face so that all he could see was the ends of her strawberry blond hair.

Luca headed over to the chair. When Hallie did

not look up, he nudged her. "I thought you were in Houston."

"I was. Go away," she said, without removing the hat from her face. "I'm having a pity party, table for one."

"Is everything okay?" Luca asked.

With a sigh, Hallie removed the hat and looked up at him. "I don't know. I'm just thinking, Luca. Or maybe I'm not thinking at all. Actually, what I'm doing is feeling sorry for myself and I'd like to do it in peace, so if you don't mind, go away."

Luca knew his twin pretty well. He pushed her legs to one side and sat next to her on the chaise. "What happened to your other shoe?"

Hallie's gaze shifted to the pool. Luca followed her gaze, leaned over her legs, and spotted a shoe at the bottom of the pool, its red sole clearly visible.

"Don't ask," Hallie said.

He was not about to ask—if there was one thing he'd learned through the years, it was that when a woman said don't ask, either do as she asked or get ready for a tongue-lashing. Whatever was behind this shoe business, it seemed like a job for Hallie's fiancé. Speaking of which, he asked, "Where's Chris?"

"In Houston." She covered her face with the hat again.

"How did you get here?"

251

"Nick flew in to get me."

Luca thought he'd smelled jet fuel. They had a small airstrip nearby and a hangar on the other side of the stables for the two Prince planes. He was about to ask Hallie what had happened in Houston, but she suddenly removed her hat and peered closely at him. "Where have *you* been?"

"In town."

"Three Rivers? Who were you with?"

"Why are you so nosy?"

Hallie's gaze narrowed accusingly. "Who was she?"

"Who said it was a she?"

"You look cute, Luca. And you're in a fairly good mood, which is kind of noticeable around here these days."

Hallie knew him too well. "Ella Kendall."

Hallie gasped with surprise, and her eyes lit up like it was Christmas morning. She pushed herself up in the chaise and tossed her hat to another chair. *"Ella Kendall,"* she said gleefully. "I thought she didn't like you."

"I've been working on that."

She gasped. "Are you *dating?*"

"No," he said, and pointed at her. "Don't, Hallie. I helped her out around the house, and then we had tacos. End of story." Jesus, he sounded like Ella.

"But why were you helping her at her house?" she asked, waggling her brows at him.

"Because I wanted to see the spring."

Hallie's smile faded, and she sank back against the chaise. "When are you going to tell Mom what's going on with you and that land?"

"When the time is right," he said. Hallie was the only person Luca had told about his and Brandon's plans. He hadn't intended to tell her at all until everything was ready to go. But she was at home the day he'd looked at the painting in his room and had understood what his dad had done. He'd pulled Hallie into his room to take a look with him and tell him he wasn't crazy.

"So?" he'd asked her after she'd stared at it for a good long minute. "Am I crazy?"

"You're not crazy," she'd confirmed.

That epiphany had opened up his grief, had found a fissure and cracked it open to let some sun in. In hindsight, it was so simple. When they'd first heard about the will, Luca had understood immediately why his dad had left Nick the running of the family business—he was the oldest, the heir apparent. Nick had been looking to get out of the ranching business before his dad died. He wanted to fly. Literally fly, as in big planes, private jets, anything. But for now, Nick was stuck, at least until he could convince their mom to hire a manager.

And then there was Hallie of the one shoe. She'd been moping around since she'd learned she wasn't going to get her Big Society Wedding that was supposed to have been featured in *Bridal Guide* magazine. Not only had Dad's gambling pulled that rug out from under her, he'd also left her the headache of a few empty warehouses near San Antonio. *Warehouses.* For a woman whose life goal had been to be a ballerina, leaving her empty warehouses didn't make a whole lot of sense to Luca. Or anyone else, for that matter.

Dad had also left Tanner Sutton some land that he owned free and clear of their mom—Luca wasn't sure how that had come about—but it was land along the highway, and his mom and grandma were certain "that upstart" was going to build apartment buildings and "ruin our lives" with it.

Last, but not least, he'd left the two thousand acres of crap land to Luca.

"I like her," Hallie said thoughtfully.

"Ella? Did you know her in school?"

"Not really," she said. "But I always kind of liked her. She was one of those people who always struck me as a little mysterious, you know? Like there was a lot more going on with her than anyone could guess."

His sister was perceptive.

"You have officially ruined the end of my pity party, you know. Nick is waiting. He wants to have a family meeting."

"Great," Luca muttered. He looked at the house. Lights were blazing in the more than a dozen windows that faced the pool area. "So, tell

me the truth. Does Mom suspect anything about what I'm doing?"

"Oh, George may have mentioned your visit with him. And, of course, she sees Mrs. Hurst all the time, so I am sure she's heard about the land Brandon bought and what he meant to do with it. But she doesn't know what you're up to, Luca." She pinned him with a look. "You better tell her," she warned. "Because she will really come unglued if she thinks you've been doing this behind her back."

"I *have* been doing it behind her back."

"So you better tell her if you don't want to spend the rest of your life listening to her complain about the time you planned a fund-raiser without telling her. Help me up," she said, pushing him off her chaise. She slipped off her shoe and dangled it from one finger as they walked to the house.

They made their way inside, walking down a long hallway on hickory floors, past paintings bought at art auctions in New York, beneath a pair of crystal chandeliers that had been shipped from the Island of Murano in Italy. The hickory gave way to marble in the foyer, which paved the path to the spacious, sunken family room with commanding views of the ranch. Here, the floor was thick planks of hand-scraped oak. The ceiling soared overhead, a boxed beam construct. The furnishings were fine leather and the rugs hand-knotted wool and silk.

If there was one thing their mother did well, it was display the Prince wealth.

Luca's mother was seated in one of two overstuffed leather chairs near the windows. His grandmother sat in the other one, her feet on the ottoman, the bottoms of her shoes facing them all. Nick was behind the small bar their father had installed one particularly wet winter. He lifted his chin in greeting when Luca and Hallie walked in.

Hallie headed for the couch, plopping down on her back, stretching her legs out, and taking up most of the space.

"What have you been up to?" Nick asked Luca when he stepped behind the bar.

"Not much. I'll take a whiskey, barkeep. Something tells me I'm going to need it."

"You might need two," Nick said drily.

"You're going to ruin that pretty dress," his mom said to Hallie. "That's no way for a lady to sit."

That was his mother's job in this family as Luca saw it—to make sure everyone knew what they were doing wrong.

"Perfect. I don't feel much like a lady today," Hallie shot back.

His mom turned her gaze to the window, surprisingly unwilling to argue.

"I don't like wearing dresses, myself," his grandma said. "Never did. Too much fuss. Give me a pair of Levi 501s, a nice linen shirt, and I'm fine."

"I like 501s," Hallie said absently.

"They don't make 'em like they used to, you know," his grandma said.

His mother sighed wearily, then stood up from her chair and wandered over to the window.

"They used to be made so well that if someone tried to get in your pants, it wasn't going to happen. Not like today with all that Lycra."

"Dolly, please?" his mom asked wearily.

"Now I'll tell you what I don't like," his grandma continued, ignoring her daughter-in-law. "Those cut-off shorts all the young girls are wearing now. They're *too short*. You can see all of China and all of France."

"Maybe we could save the discussion about denim for another time," his mom suggested.

"Anytime you like," his grandma said. "Make me a martini, Delia, please."

Luca noticed his mother's shoulders seemed to sag a bit, but she dutifully walked over to the bar. Her gaze flicked over him as she picked up the shaker. "You look nice."

"Thanks. So what's this party about?" Luca asked.

"Money," Nick said. "What else?" He came out from behind the bar with Luca's whiskey. Nick was an inch taller than Luca. And a little broader, although that didn't stop him from helping

257

himself to Luca's shirts when he was at the ranch.

"Do we have to talk about money again?" Hallie complained. "It seems like every time I am here, we are talking about money."

"Oh, we have to talk about it," Nick said. "You, especially, Hallie."

"Me!"

"You shop too much. How many handbags does one person need?"

"Hey!" Hallie snapped, and sat up. "Who gave you the right to look at my receipts?"

"Dad did when he died, that's who," Nick said calmly. "I keep an eye on the Prince books now, and your money, like all our money, comes from the Prince Family coffers. You've got the trust Grandpa left you if you want to own that many handbags."

"But that's for my future," Hallie said.

"Yeah, well, the family account is for all of our futures," Nick said. He paused, took a sip of his whiskey. "I've been working with our CPA to get a handle on our cash. Our property tax has gone up quite a lot. Not to mention the estate tax. The upshot is, we're all going to have to tighten our belts."

Nick actually looked worried. Luca couldn't recall ever seeing him so concerned. "What's going on?" he asked.

Nick sighed and ran his fingers through his sandy brown hair. "We're pretty low on cash. We—"

He was interrupted by Mom's suddenly loud and vigorous shaking of their grandma's martini. She looked as if she'd heard it all before.

When she finished, Nick said, "We have a lot less than I thought."

Less money was not something that was ever discussed at Three Rivers Ranch.

"But we're rich," Hallie said unnecessarily. "I thought we were the one percent of the one percents."

"I don't know where we fall in the rankings," Nick said with a look for Hallie. "And I'm not saying we're destitute. We're rich in assets, but not so rich in cash. Dad . . ." Nick paused. He glanced down, his jaw working a moment, as if he were having to swallow something bitter. "Dad had a lot of debt," he said. "He took a big chunk of our cash reserves to pay off some of his debt, but he had even more debt because of gambling losses and bad investments."

"Well now, that's your opinion, Nick," their grandma said a bit defensively. "They were good investments when he made them. He couldn't help it that other people are sorry crooks."

"I don't like it either, Grandma, but they were bad deals."

His mom handed his grandma the martini she'd requested. "You know how impulsive Charlie could be, Dolly."

Hallie had come up on her knees on the couch. "Okay, so what does this mean, Nick? How are we supposed to tighten our belts?" she demanded, as if Nick's suggestion that they live like most people was impossible.

"I mean don't spend so much. Don't run up your credit card and expect that it's going to be paid, no questions asked. Don't fly off to New York or LA on a whim."

"Those trips were *not* whims," she said defiantly, then sank back. "This *sucks*. First Dad dies, and now we have to tighten our belts?"

"It's not like I'm asking you to shop at a thrift store, for Pete's sake," Nick said.

Hallie gasped softly but wisely said nothing.

"And you, Luca. Stop staying at the most expensive hotels and having them cater your parties."

Luca felt slightly warm under the collar. It was true that he'd gone on something of a bender after his dad's funeral. He hadn't known how else to grieve. *None* of them had. Nick walked around pissed all the time. Mom drank. Hallie shopped. Grandma was turning her hair purple and pink and blue.

Their answer to all their problems had always been money. They didn't know how to not have it. "It couldn't have been that much," he scoffed. At least he hoped not, but honestly, he was uncertain. He never looked at the bills. Just

260

signed them and went on to the next diversion.

"Would you like me to announce how much?" Nick drawled.

Luca gave him a withering look. "I get it, Nick. I understand."

"If you understand, Luca, how about you stop chasing this ridiculous dream of creating some sort of new ecosystem?" his mother asked, and turned from the window. "We don't have the money for that. Or this . . . *party* you want to have."

"What party?" Nick asked, looking between Luca and Mom.

"Can't we sell some stock or something?" Hallie interjected.

"Then we'd have to pay more taxes. What party?" Nick asked again.

"Ask your brother," Luca's mother said, and sat heavily in the chair next to Grandma.

Nick looked at Luca.

This was not the way Luca had wanted to have this conversation. "Brandon and I are planning a fundraising event here at Three Rivers—"

"Here?" his mother exclaimed sharply.

"Here," Luca said evenly. "We're bringing together researchers, environmentalists, and academicians to pitch turning some land into a conservation ranch."

"What land?" Nick asked.

"The land Dad left me."

261

Nick stared at him, as if trying to process this news.

"If we need money, we damn sure don't want to spend it on some fancy party. We need to sell that land," his mom said flatly. "Tell him, Nick."

"You do *not* sell land," his grandma said in a moment of fierce clarity. "And besides, Charlie already gave enough land away to that bastard kid of his."

"His name is Tanner, Grandma," Hallie said. "Tanner Sutton. And he's a nice guy."

Everyone paused to look at Hallie.

"What?" she asked. She stood up and walked to the bar. "I ran into him at Jo's Java and said hello, and he asked me how I was, and we sort of talked about losing Dad." She dipped down, then stood up again with a bottle of wine.

"I'm going to nip this in the bud right here, Hallie Jane Prince," his mom said. "We are *not* inviting that man into our lives."

Hallie rolled her eyes. "I didn't invite him to dinner, Mother. I just said hello." She poured wine to the rim of her glass.

"Can we please stay on track here?" Nick asked.

"Yes. The track is that I say we need to sell the land your father left to Luca," his mother said. "That's useless acreage to us."

"It's not useless," Luca said quietly. "And I'm not selling. I just told you, I'm hosting a big fund-raiser here hoping for general buy-in from environmentalist investors. Brandon's working on the paperwork to establish a foundation to support the transformation and maintenance of the land."

"How are you going to pay for that?" Nick asked.

"The trust Grandpa left me. My income from the dealership. But mostly with the money we raise."

"Your *trust?* The money my father worked hard all his life for?" his mother exclaimed.

"Leave him alone, Delia," Grandma said.

"This is not your business, Dolly," his mother snapped, and turned her glare to Luca. "I want to know how much, Luca. I think we *all* want to know how much money you are going to waste on land that could produce income for us. This is a serious family issue."

Luca tossed the whiskey down his throat. "You just said the land was useless, Mom. But here's the thing—that land is mine, and I'm sure George told you that I can do what I like with it. I can build a space ship and launch it from there if I want."

"That sounds like fun," his grandma said in all seriousness.

"Dad's will stipulated that I can't use family money for anything I do there, so you don't have to worry about it," Luca added.

"I can't believe you're going to waste your trust fund that *my father* left for you on this stupid idea of creating some wondrous natural oasis. Well, guess what, Luca—we live in South Texas. The land is never going to be pretty to look at."

"That depends on your perspective," Luca said tightly.

"*My* perspective is what is right for this family. What is *right* for this family is that we sell that land because it *is* worthless. That's why your father left it to *you*."

Something hard and cold stirred in Luca. He glanced at Nick, who looked as stunned as he felt, then looked at his mother again. "What do you mean by that?"

"Did you think your father would leave you valuable property?" she asked. "Of course not, because you never stick to anything."

"*Mom,* stop," Hallie said irritably. "We all know you're furious with Dad, but you don't need to take it out on Luca."

"Actually, Mom," Luca said, surprised by how deadly cool his voice was, "this is an idea I've stuck with since I was a kid. It is the one thing I've been consistent about. The one thing I've wanted to do."

His mother suddenly sighed, and her shoulders drooped as if he'd just informed her one of the horses had died. "Oh, Luca," she said sadly. "I know you want to save the world."

"Nope. Not the world. Just our ranch."

"But don't you see that what you want is impractical?"

"That's not true," he said, and for a moment, a slender moment, he thought he might get through to her, might convince her to look at it another way. "I've been studying up, and I think—"

"Studying up? My God, Luca, you can't even *read.*"

Her remark was met with stunned silence. Luca could hear his heart pounding, could hear Nick's breath coming hard and short, like he was about to blow.

"I shouldn't have said that," his mother tried, realizing, too late, her mistake. She opened her mouth again, but Luca put his hand up, stopping her from botching any attempt at an apology. She'd done enough damage. "No need to explain, Mom. It's never been a secret what you think of me."

"What?" She looked around the room for support and found none. "Don't be like that, honey. I love you. I have always only wanted the best for you—"

"Sorry," Luca said, cutting her off. "It's too late for that." If he stood here another second, he feared he would detonate. He put the whiskey glass on the bar, with a finger of whiskey still in it. "We can wrap this up right now. That's *my* land. Not yours. Not Prince family land. And I'm not selling it. Now, whether you or anyone else believes it is a good idea or not, I don't give a good goddamn. It's none of your business. Brandon and I would like to host the fundraiser here in early June, just so you know. I'll work the dates and details out with Martin."

"Luca, I'm sorry," his mother said again, pleading now. "I shouldn't have said that. I'm just concerned! You're going to need money to do anything with that land. You can't use up your trust like that, and Chet says you never show up for work as it is."

"Good *Lord,* Delia, if I were you, I'd shut up about now," his grandma said.

Luca looked at Nick. His brother's eyes were locked on their mother, and his expression was dark. "Anything else, Nick? If not, I'm going to get out of here."

Nick turned his gaze to his brother and shook his head. "Nope. Just let us know the date, so we can plan to attend."

"Great. Well, thanks, all, for another delightful evening," Luca said, and turned around and strode out of the family room.

"Luca, wait!" Hallie called after him.

He ignored her and kept walking, across the marble foyer, down the hickory planks of the long hall, through the sunroom, past the pool, and along the flagstone path to the garage.

He was driving before he realized it, his elbow out the open window of his truck, the sunroof retracted so he could breathe in the cool night air and calm himself down. He wasn't angry. He was disappointed. Definitely numb. But mostly, he was so damned determined to prove his mother wrong that he suddenly crashed one fist down onto the steering wheel.

At the end of the drive, as he waited for the gate to roll back, images from his life kept racing through his head. Of all the disparaging things his mother had ever said to him. Of all the times she'd claimed to be looking out for him.

When the gate opened, he drove through, his intention to head to his loft. But when he reached Three Rivers, he looked at the clock. It was half past nine.

He was about to pass Timmons Tire and Body when he abruptly pulled into the lot and parked.

He wasn't thinking straight, but he suddenly had a deep yearning to be with someone whose last name wasn't Prince.

He picked up his phone and studied the screen a long moment, debating. He clicked the text icon and typed, U up? His thumb hovered over the send button for what seemed like several minutes before he finally sent it.

A moment passed. And another. Three dots popped up on his screen. Who's this?

Luca groaned and dropped his head to the headrest, his eyes closed. But then his phone pinged again and he glanced down.

Jk. ☺. Maybe I'm up. Why?

Luca knew what the text said, but he sounded out the letters in his head to make doubly sure there was no mistake, and then slowly smiled. He searched through the emojis until he found one that looked slightly thoughtful, sent it, then turned his truck and crossed the road, heading down the old county road to Ella's house.

Chapter Nineteen

What was that? Ella wondered. A confused face emoji? A thinking face emoji?

What was she supposed to make of that?

She was *so* bad at this. Flirting was beyond her. When it came to men, she was the type of woman who needed to know exactly what was happening. She liked black and white, no gray, everything by the numbers, just like her accounting. She needed a text like this one spelled out. *Which of these best describes the purpose of your text: This is/is not a booty call. Circle the one that applies.*

Was it a booty call? Because honestly, in spite of what she had thought about Luca being a player all these years, she was beginning to believe that maybe he wasn't that kind of guy after all. And then again, maybe she was kidding herself. Maybe she was just full of green hope.

But she'd had such a great time tonight, a casual evening with a handsome, considerate man who had not seemed the least bit appalled by her past. She'd told him things she'd not said out loud in a very long time, things she liked to keep buried and forgotten. The amazing thing was that it had been surprisingly easy to tell him. She didn't sense any judgment from him, got not one whiff of superiority that his life had been "normal."

She wouldn't have faulted him if he had. She got it—people with more traditional lives couldn't fathom what it was like for kids like her, who'd grown up in the foster care system because her mother was in prison. People who did all the things they were supposed to and went to church and raised their kids right and maybe had too much to drink on occasion but were generally responsible, were sometimes quick to make judgments about people like the Kendalls.

Her family had been easy to judge, her mother especially. But Ella had come to terms with it along the way. Her upbringing had been very unconventional, but that didn't make her a bad person. Her mom's mistakes were not hers. If other people couldn't see that, it was their problem. Not Ella's.

And yet, it hadn't been easy, and Stacy was right, Ella had built some pretty high walls around herself as a result. Still, she'd managed, and she was both grateful to Luca and relieved that he hadn't looked away, hadn't stopped touching her when she'd told him about her life. She appreciated that he'd let her talk, because once that floodgate had opened, she'd wanted it all out there in the open.

She'd liked being with him so much that she'd come home feeling slightly bereft. To be honest, she hadn't been ready for the night to end, and if she were a go-getter, a girl from a country western song, she'd have made her own booty call.

So if his text was the call she was too chicken to make herself, she was open to it, and she wouldn't hold it against him, because she was *really* into this man.

Ella went into the bathroom to check herself out and make sure she didn't have taco on her face or something just as embarrassing. She brushed her hair while the practical voice in her head warned her that she shouldn't go in so deep, shouldn't let her heart fill up, because eventually, their worlds would collide, and her heart would burst when it was time to acknowledge there was no future with Luca Prince for a woman like her.

"For the love of God, shut up," she said to her practical voice, and glanced down at Buddy, who was all ears. "Could I possibly, just once, loosen up and go with the flow?"

Buddy cocked his head to one side, as if considering her question.

"Could I, for once, be the one to win the prize?"

Buddy kept listening.

"I *know* I have issues," she said to the dog. "It's

not rocket science, right? I have serious trust issues and always fear the consequences, because my rug has been yanked out from under me time and time again, am I right?"

Buddy gave her several resounding and affirmative thumps of his tail against the floor.

"Maybe," she said, squatting down to scratch his ears, "this time, I could not worry so much about what is going to happen tomorrow and just enjoy the ride?"

Buddy scrambled up to lick her face. *You like him, Ella,* she thought to herself. *You really like him. You like him in a jittery, please-don't-ever-end way, and not in the usual yeah, maybe, we'll-see-what-happens way. You, my friend, are standing on the edge of a diving board ready to take a headlong plunge into the deep. In the dark. And there are rocks at the bottom. But go ahead, knock yourself out.*

It was too late to back out even if she'd wanted to—she heard the truck before she saw the lights on the road. Buddy heard it, too; his ears pricked up, and he launched himself at the door.

"Oh, so it's like that, huh?" Ella said, and stepped over his wiggling body to open the door. Buddy burst through the screen door and bounded down the steps, scrambling to the driver's side of Luca's truck and planting his paws on the door before Luca could put the thing in park.

Luca got out and gave Buddy the intense

272

attention he was looking for, rolling him onto his back and scratching his belly with both hands. He stood up and smiled at Ella on the top step of the porch, then sauntered sheepishly forward. "Hey," he said.

Ella nervously slipped her hands into her jean pockets. "You keep showing up at my house," she said.

Luca shrugged and smiled. "What can I say? That's where you are."

Okay, all right, that sort of talk made her feel all woozy and soft inside. She wished she could think of something funny to say, something completely charming, right out of a romantic comedy movie script. But she couldn't think of a single thing so she just grinned back at him like an idiot.

"How is it you look even better now than you did earlier?" he asked as his gaze moved over her. He put a sneakered foot on the bottom porch step, and she wondered how many times in his life he'd charmed the pants off a girl. She decided she shouldn't let it be so damn easy. "Hey, how many girlfriends have you had?"

Luca paused and gave her a funny look. "Is that a trick question?"

"Just curious."

"Okay," he said warily. "In my lifetime?"

She had to think about that. She'd had a boy-friend in the first grade—at least Angel Martinez had pronounced her as such. "Starting with your sophomore year in high school. I don't need to know about the earlier crushes."

He arched a brow. "Got it," he said, and settled back against the porch railing. "So do you want to know how many crushes or girlfriends I've had?"

"Good point of clarification, thank you," she said, bowing her head in acknowledgment. "Both."

"Softball question. I've had a *lot* of girlfriends. But to my recollection, I've only had one true crush." He smiled slowly, his eyes dancing with challenge. "Does that answer your question?"

Ooh, but that was a funny little slide of heat through her. She nodded dumbly. "Yep."

"Your turn. How many have *you* had?" he asked.

She was feeling a little loose in the knees and wrapped her arm around the porch railing post. "Four real boyfriends, not counting Angel Martinez. We were only seven."

"Crushes?" he asked.

She pushed her hair back and took him in. "Only one. One big, fat crush."

"Isn't that interesting," he drawled. And then he laughed.

"What?"

"You're blushing."

"I'm not blushing—"

"You're as red as a tomato."

"That's just the porch light," she said, and rubbed her fingers on her cheeks, as if she could somehow rub the blush out of them.

"I'm starting to figure you out, Ella Kendall, you know that?" he asked.

"Please," she said. "There is nothing to figure out. I come home and feed animals. That's about it." *That, and I am wild about you.*

"You know, when I was a kid, Hallie and I had this picture book. The first page was a drawing of a framed picture with nothing in the picture but a red door. Turn the page, and the picture was the red door and a window. Turn another page, it was the red door, a window, a rug. Every page added something until the picture was a room with furniture, a cat, a teakettle and muffins, some books on a shelf, and a little old lady sitting in a rocking chair, knitting socks."

What was he talking about? "Is that supposed to make sense?"

"You are a lot like that book, Ella. Every time I see you, something else gets added to the picture."

"Wow," she said, and felt the smile curving on her lips. "I didn't know I had so many layers. I haven't figured out anything about you," she said. "Other than you're ridiculously handsome."

He grinned. "As delighted as I am to hear that, I hope you've seen more than that."

"Yeah," she said thoughtfully. "I have. You're persistent. And surprisingly consistent."

"Those sound like excellent traits for a tax lawyer. Anything else?"

She smiled a little lopsidedly. "Well . . . you're not a douche," she offered.

He laughed with surprise. "I didn't know that was on the list of possibilities."

"Dude," Ella said, and smiled sheepishly. "That is *always* on the list of possibilities." She wanted to touch the dark tress of hair that had fallen over his brow. "But you've been a perfect gentleman. You're even a gentleman when you make, umm, you know," she said, whirling her hand, "an evening call."

"A what?"

"Otherwise known as a booty call?" She imagined herself leaping onto his body—swiftly followed by a fleeting image of them tumbling down the steps and each breaking a leg.

But Luca didn't smile like she thought he would. He frowned. "What?"

Had she been too blunt? She seriously needed flirting lessons.

"You think this is a *booty* call?"

"Wait, what?" she echoed, confused by his confusion. "Isn't it? You texted me."

"Yeah, I texted you, but I didn't mean *that,*" he said, looking slightly offended.

Oh, good *Lord,* had she really misunderstood

him? "But you texted 'you up,' " she reminded him. "Who texts that in the middle of the night if it's not a booty call?"

"Ella, it's nine thirty. I meant are you up, am I bothering you," he said, and took her hand in his. "And as much as I would love it, I didn't come here to get you into bed."

Well, *that* was disappointing news on the surface and all subterranean levels. She had imagined him taking her in his arms. *She* was supposed to protest, not him.

"I have too much respect for you to try something as crass as that," he added.

Ella wanted to crawl in a hole. She glanced around for one.

"I wanted to see you," he said earnestly. "I texted you because . . ." He paused. He pushed a hand through his hair, and he looked, she thought, almost distressed.

"Because?" she prodded him.

"Because things have been pretty intense at the ranch lately, and I was on my way to my place in San Antonio, and I thought, maybe . . . I don't know . . ." He shrugged.

She was so confused as to what was happening. "Thought what?"

"That we could talk? Just talk, Ella—that's all I intended."

Talk. Huh. She believed him. She was a little disappointed, but she believed him. "Maybe next

277

time be a little more explicit in your text, so a girl doesn't get the wrong idea," she muttered.

"Yeah, about that," he said, and squeezed her hand. "Can we take a walk? I want to tell you something."

"Sounds ominous," she said as he tugged her down the steps. "Are *you* a cannibal?" she asked, teasing him about what he'd said to her earlier in the evening.

"Not yet," he said with an enigmatic smile.

"Are you sick? On the lam? Oh, I know! You're poor."

"No, no, and no," he said, and put his arm around her waist as they walked along the moonlit path they'd taken to the spring.

"You're moving," she said. "You're going to raise goats in the Andes Mountains."

"If I was that into goats, I'm not sure why I'd go all the way to the Andes Mountain Range to raise them when I could do that right here. But that's not it either."

"Then what is it?"

He sighed. He stopped walking and turned her to face him. "I don't text very often. Only in emergencies."

Ella almost laughed. "*That's* what you want to talk about? That you prefer calling to texting?"

He said nothing.

She couldn't suppress her laugh. "Whew!" she said, and pressed her hand to her heart. "I thought you were going to tell me something huge. Okay, you're a caller, not a texter. Message received. But not by text." She giggled at her joke.

Luca didn't smile. "The reason I don't text is because I'm, ah, dyslexic," he said, and pushed his fingers through his hair again, a habit she had come to recognize as a telltale sign of his discomfort.

"Okay." She didn't understand why that was a big thing either. Lots of people were dyslexic.

He drew what sounded like a tortured breath. "The truth is that I can't actually . . . read," he said softly.

"You can't read?" she repeated. Luca didn't smile, and Ella's heart fluttered. "You mean you're a slow reader," she said, attempting to explain it for him.

"I mean I can't read," he said flatly. "If you ask me to look at a menu, I can make it out. But a book? A message scrawling along the bottom of the TV screen?" He shook his head.

"Oh," she said, and meant to offer her empathy, but he was already nodding.

"I know," he said instantly. "It's unbelievable. But it's true, Ella, and you should know that about me. I'm functionally illiterate, and I can't text very well, and honestly? I'd rather tell you I'm a cannibal than I'm illiterate."

Ella's chest filled with disbelief and compassion. She couldn't imagine not being able to read. She couldn't imagine how hard it would be to admit it. How was it possible that a man from the Prince family couldn't *read?* "But . . ." She paused, uncertain if she should ask how he'd graduated without the ability to read.

"I skated by in school," he said, anticipating her question. "I picked up a lot by listening. Every time it looked like I wouldn't pass, my parents sent me to another school. No one was going to hold a Prince kid back, not even for a legitimate reason," he said, and sounded a bit resentful. "When I got older, I faked my way through."

Ella remembered all too clearly the charming way he'd hung around with girls who were known to be smart.

"But as an adult, I'm determined to change it." His tone was earnest, as if he thought she might doubt his determination. "I've hired my sixth-grade teacher to teach me, and I'm learning."

"Really?" Ella was surprised.

"Look, I know no one wants to be with an illiterate man—"

"I didn't say that," she protested.

"You don't have to. I get it. In the world we live in, in a country like America? Illiteracy is inexcusable."

"I wasn't thinking that at all, Luca," she said, and took his hand in both of hers. "I was thinking what a terrible burden this must have been for you as a kid. How hard it must have been to try and make your way through school and . . . and *hide* it, right? How hard it must have been for you to tell me."

He curled his fingers around hers. "You have no idea," he muttered. "When I was in middle school, a teacher, a counselor—someone—thought I ought to be in special education. My parents lost their minds. My mother hired a tutor, but that guy was a joke. She hired another one, a college student, but the drive from San Antonio got to her and she quit after a few weeks. My mother was so frantic that no one from Three Rivers find out about her illiterate son that she didn't get anyone else. I think she mostly hoped I'd grow out of it. When I had problems at school, Dad made donations."

"What sort of donations?" Ella asked.

Luca put his arm around her and nudged her to walk with him. "Remember the new football stadium they finished our senior year?"

Ella remembered it, all right—football was sacrosanct in Texas, but for the size of Edna Colley High, it was a monstrous stadium, big and flashy. Regional play-off games from much larger schools were played there. She remembered a plaque on the outside stadium wall commemorating the Prince family and their contributions to the school district. Someone had tagged it with graffiti. "Your father built a football stadium just so no one would know you couldn't read?" she asked incredulously.

"Let's just say that my father's contribution got the school district over the hump and made sure they had enough money to finish the stadium. And then I was passed to our senior year."

Ella couldn't fathom it. Had she suffered from a learning disability, no one would have cared. The goal of every foster parent she had was to get her to her eighteenth birthday and out the door, no matter if she had a diploma or a baby or a job or a criminal record.

"It's a little sickening," he said.

"Sickening? No," Ella said. Luca didn't know how fortunate he was that he had parents who actually cared so much. "I'm sure they thought it was the right thing to do for you," she said. "I'm sure they cared if people knew, because people can be so cruel. Whether or not they did the right thing, I don't know, but it's in your hands now, and you're learning. What are you reading?"

He laughed. "Conservation law. Best land management practices."

"Oh my *God*," she said, and laughed up at the sky. "I'm *so* glad I'm not your tutor. What does your mom think of what you're doing?"

"She doesn't know," he said. "I haven't told anyone but Hallie."

"Are you going to tell her?" she asked.

"Not right now," he said. "I wasn't kidding when I said life has been pretty intense out at the ranch lately. My father's death left us with some unresolved issues, and feelings are all tangled up in them. It's like walking through barbed wire at home right now."

"So when will you tell her?"

"At the fund-raiser Brandon and I are planning," he said, and for the first time since he started this conversation, he smiled. "My plan is to read from some notes. She'll hear it along with everyone else."

"Well, that ought to bring down the house," Ella said.

He grinned. "Dramatic, huh? We're firming up a date in early June. Maybe you could come?"

The thought of going to Three Rivers Ranch was a little scary to her. "You know what, Luca? I'm, like, totally proud of you," she said. "I know it's not my place to be proud of you, but I am, because it's really incredible that you're taking this on without a lot of support."

He gave her a thin smile. "I should have done it a long time ago."

"*Aah,*" she said with a shrug. "You're doing it now. So hats off to you, cowboy."

His smile deepened. "I have an extra incentive now—I want to get my texts right so there is no misunderstanding between us."

"Very important," she said. "You can't rely

283

on eggplant emojis alone. Too much room for interpretation."

He laughed and laced his fingers with hers. "There is one small thing I'd like to ask you."

"Okay," she said. "But I've told you everything. You know about my past. You know my best friend is a bit of a klepto. Admittedly, I didn't mention the leak under the bathroom sink, but you would probably find out on your own if you need to use it."

He tucked her hair behind her ear. "This is a very important question."

"Great," she said, sobering. "What is it?"

"You said you thought I was making a booty call."

"Who wouldn't?"

"As I said, it was most definitely not a booty call. Nevertheless, you seemed on board for it." His eyes moved to her mouth. "Were you?"

A smile slowly curved on her lips. "Busted."

His eyes moved down her chest.

"Unfortunately, you didn't come for that," she reminded him.

He lifted his gaze, cupped her chin, and stroked her cheek. "Good news—I'm pretty flexible. I can change my plans when necessary."

Ooh, her belly was doing cartwheels. She settled her hands on his waist. "Are you changing them now?"

"Well, that depends on you. Now, we could

take this real slow. Maybe wait until some of those walls come down a little," he said, tapping her chest.

"We could." Her heart was beginning to pick up speed, *thump-thump-thumping* along.

"Or . . ." He paused to kiss the corner of her mouth. "I could help you kick down one or two of those walls tonight." He kissed her again, and an eddy of tingling flared across her skin. He smelled like cardamom and horse and a little bit of Buddy. He smelled like a man and Ella was certain she must smell like raw desire. She closed her eyes when he kissed her neck. "Did you bring your tool belt?" she murmured. "Some of the walls might require extra effort."

He chuckled against her neck. "Baby, I brought the biggest tool belt I could find." He slid his arm down to her hand and laced his fingers with hers. "Back to the house?"

She opened her eyes. Her breath was already short, her body already desperate for his touch. It was alarming how much she wanted him. "Are we doing this? Are we taking the next step?"

"I'm in, Ella," he said. "I'm all the way in."

She slowly released her breath. "I'm in, too."

He grinned. "Then saddle up, girl."

Chapter Twenty

Luca didn't know exactly how they'd made it to her bedroom, how exactly they'd managed to walk as they'd kissed and their hands had explored. But here they were, standing in the dark of her bedroom, lit only by moonlight.

The room was small, but he liked it. Ella had left the windows open, and a breeze lifted the sheer drapes, making them look like ghostly dancers that brushed against them from time to time. There had been no words since they'd come in and kicked Buddy out. They didn't need to speak—the energy flowing between them said everything there was to say. This felt right to Luca. This felt new and exciting and meaningful.

Ella looked up at him with eyes turned gray in the moonlight. Her breath was shallow as she reached for his shirt and began to unbutton it. How odd that a strangely vulnerable feeling swept through him. For the first time that he could recall, he was concerned that a woman might not find him attractive. It had never been so much as a thought before—previously his focus had always been on the act of sex itself, on enjoying the ride to the top. Not whether a woman liked the way he looked. But with Ella, it mattered, and Luca was at a loss in that moment to understand why, really, other than he truly, genuinely cared about Ella. A lot. He had feelings about her and for her that made his head spin, but above all, he wanted this moment to mean something.

Shut up, he told his head. *Shut up, shut up. Just go with it.*

"Are you okay?" she asked as she slid her hands up his bare chest.

He was better than okay. His heart was pumping, his body ready to explore. "Yep," he said, and shrugged out of his shirt, letting it fall to the floor. He ran his hands down her arms. "Are you?"

She stepped back from him to her bedside table and opened a drawer. When she turned around, she held up a condom.

Luca drew her forward until her body was touching his bare chest, took the condom from her hand, and kissed her. His natural instincts took hold, pushing his overactive brain out of the way. He slid his hand down her back, to her waist, and moved his hand into her jeans, squeezing the warm, supple flesh of her hip. Ella unfastened her jeans and stood still as Luca pushed them down, so she could step out of them. He wanted to bite the red bikini panties from her, but instead reached for the hem of her shirt, and she lifted her arms overhead so that he could pull it off, and then she removed her bra.

Luca paused a moment to take her in, admiring the swell of her breasts, the soft roundness of her belly, the flare of her hip into a trim waist. He loved women of all shapes and sizes, but there was something about this particular woman that appealed to him beyond the visual. His reaction was visceral, hitting him square in the gut. The sight of her went to the heart of him, a place so primal and apparently, so needy, that it took his breath away. She was so natural in everything she did, in every way she looked. Her body was not perfect, but it was beautiful, as God had intended—the only form that would slake a man's internal thirst.

With a sigh of longing, he drew her to him. He could feel the beat of her heart melting into his. He swept his tongue into her mouth, nibbled at her lip, filled his hand with the heavy weight of her breast, kneading it. Her smooth skin aroused him to hardness, attraction buzzing like a beehive as it spread through his limbs. His pulse was beginning to thrum in his temples and his groin, and he unfastened his jeans, then let her go a moment to remove his shoes, hopping around like a loon in his eagerness to get them off before falling backward onto her bed.

Ella fell beside him, laughing. No matter how

this had happened, no matter what he remembered of her or what she remembered of him, this moment was all that mattered. It felt as if she was the one he'd been waiting for. She was the girl he had always hoped would show up at a party, at a bar, in the showroom of the Sombra dealership. She was the girl he had always imagined would come and claim him.

He kicked his jeans away and rolled on top of her, holding himself above her so that he could look at her. Her hair spilled around her, her eyes glistened with delight and desire. He sensed that she wanted him with the same intensity he wanted her, and moved his palm up her body and over her breast. He kissed the hollow of her throat before moving his hand down again, between her legs.

Ella seemed to undulate against him as her mouth moved over his skin, to his neck. His chest. He languidly caressed her, trying to keep a lid on his desire, struggling not to rush, to push—but the need was building. Their caresses became more urgent, their kisses deeper. "This is crazy, Ella," he said between gulps of breath.

"It's insane," she agreed, and raked her fingers up his back and gripped his arms, pulling him to her, pressing against his erection. Luca's imagination was racing ahead of his body; he could see himself sliding into her, his cock as hard as marble, his hips clenched as he tried to restrain himself from driving into her. But then she took him into her hand, and he lost all rational thought, drifting into the ether of their lovemaking, completely submerged in the sights and sounds and scents of it.

He crumbled on the inside and slipped away from his invisible harness. He took her breast into his mouth and moved between her legs and, with his knee, pushed them apart. Ella hooked one leg around him and pressed against him. The desire for her burned through him—this woman was driving him to madness. He was afraid of his own strength, of wanting her so desperately and overpowering her.

He stilled himself to take a breath, to get a grip. He looked into her eyes—which shone back at him with the same hunger he felt inside himself. She seemed to understand his hesitance, seemed to feel his restraint. She put her hand on his hip, gripping it, and pulled him toward her.

Luca closed his eyes and guided himself into her. The sensation of her body around his stole his breath. He'd hardly moved, and he was already flying. A demanding rhythm began to beat in his veins, and as Ella pressed against him, he began to move, pushing them both toward the peak, stroking her with his hand and his body at the same time.

It was quick and furious. Ella arched her back, her hands seeking his flesh, her heels digging into his back. Her body was damp, her breath warm on his cheek, and there was nothing more erotic, nothing more arousing than this. His blood flooded through his veins, his heart boiled just beneath the surface of his skin. He groaned as she caressed his body and her mouth moved along his jaw. As his body slid in and out of hers, he could feel the massive release building in him, the increasing pressure in his body, and when Ella suddenly gasped and shuddered around him, Luca's body and heart felt as if they exploded away from his thoughts, releasing into the air, soaring away from him like a rogue balloon.

Several moments passed as they both struggled to catch their breath. Her body was limp, one arm slung overhead. Luca rolled onto his side with her, wrapped his arms around her, and closed his eyes. "Unbelievable," he said.

"I have no words," she said into his chest. "No words."

They lay there, not speaking, until their breathing had returned to normal. Ella reached for his hand and squeezed it. "Should we have a snack and then try again?" she asked.

He grinned up at the water-stained ceiling. *A woman after my heart.* "I *definitely* think we should have a snack and then try again." He hugged her closer to him. "So, are you falling for me yet?"

"Absolutely not," she said, and kissed his chest.

"Just checking," he said, and sighed with a

contentment that had settled into his marrow.

Ella extracted herself from his embrace, picked up his shirt from the floor, and shrugged into it as she disappeared into the other room. "No, Buddy," he heard her say when she opened the door, then he was rudely startled by the snout of that dog on his bare skin. When Ella returned, she was carrying a bottle of water and a bag of potato chips. She kicked Buddy out of her room, closed the door, then leapt onto the bed, stepping over him before collapsing, cross-legged, onto her bottom beside him.

It was the best after-sex glow he'd ever experienced. They ate potato chips and laughed about high school, the people they'd known, the things they'd done. And when they made love again, the bag of potato chips sliding off onto the floor, it was slow and easy. They took their time, taking care with each other.

When they at last slept, she was wrapped in his arms.

Luca was awakened the next morning by a phone ringing somewhere. Ella sat up, her hair tangled around her. "Who *calls* this early?" she demanded, and climbed out of bed. She was still wearing his shirt. She opened the door, stumbled into the other room. Luca heard her mutter under her breath, and then the ringing stopped. Ella returned to the bedroom and jumped on the bed, straddling him, bouncing up and down. "Time to get up, cowboy. I have to go to work." She jumped off and, whistling as if she'd just slayed a dragon or two, waltzed out of the bedroom.

Luca slowly pushed himself up on his elbows. He was still thinking about last night, a delicious swirl of memories and sensations in this bed. He thought of the way she'd taken him into her mouth, her lips and tongue swirling around the tip of his cock until he couldn't stand it another moment and had dragged her on top of him to ride. *Saddle up,* she'd said with a laugh.

He remembered the way her hair fell wild around her shoulders, teasing her nipples. He remembered how she'd tossed her head back the moment she came, and how he'd had to hold her hips to keep her from falling off when she did.

Ella Kendall was a sorceress—she had cast some sort of magical spell on him, had turned him around and upside down, and had crumbled up all his rusty, dusty emotions and rearranged them so that they all felt fresh and new. He felt like a teenager who was just discovering how exciting and consuming adoration could be.

He sat up, ran his fingers through his hair, then sleepily looked around him, seeing the small room for the first time. Their clothes and shoes were scattered about the floor. There was a basket of folded laundry near the closet. Novels and jars of creams covered the small bureau. On the wall, a pair of paintings, one the Riverwalk in downtown San Antonio, a very colorful, tropical place with palms and a rainbow of umbrellas. The other was of a windmill. He recognized it as the broken windmill behind this house.

This room was Ella's world. This was what she saw when she woke each morning. God knew it wasn't as luxurious as the surroundings he awoke to each morning, but her essence was here, painted into every corner, woven into the fabric. He didn't want to leave it. He wanted to stay in this bed for as long as he could.

Unfortunately, he had things to do.

Luca got up, found his clothes. "Would you mind if I used your shower?" he called out.

"Help yourself!" she called back. He heard the screen door slam, and glanced out the back window. Ella was walking barefoot down to the chaise, a cup of coffee in her hand.

He showered quickly—and examined the slow leak under the sink—then dressed. Then he went in search of her and his shirt. As he grabbed a cup of coffee in the kitchen, he heard Ella shouting. "Buddy, no!"

He found Ella standing at the fence, waving at Buddy. But Buddy was running with the wild horses, barking.

"Bad dog!" Ella shouted.

Luca slipped his arms around her waist.

"Buddy is scaring the horses away!" she complained.

"Nope. He's playing. Watch," Luca said.

Two of the horses had moved down into a gulley, but one of them was loping around the field beyond the fence in big circles. Buddy wasn't chasing the horse—he was running alongside, barking gleefully, his tail high. The horse changed direction. So did Buddy. The horse suddenly went another direction, and Buddy wasn't as quick to change. He raced around, catching the horse near the gulley, then running alongside him again. They did this two more times, and then the horse disappeared over a hill. Buddy sat down, watching his playmate go.

"Oh my God," Ella said, her voice full of amazement. "You mean all this time Buddy was calling *for* the horses? I thought he was trying to scare them off."

"Buddy likes horses," Luca said, and kissed her nape. "You've seen him with my horse. He likes to run beside him."

"Oh my God," she said again, her voice full of wonder. "How did I not see that?"

Luca slid his hand beneath his shirt, to her bare belly. "As much as I hate to do it, I'm going to need that shirt."

"Oh yeah?" She turned around, looped her arms around his neck.

"Yes. I have a reading lesson at eleven," he said. "What are you doing today?"

"Work," she said with a sigh. "My part-time

accounting job, then hostessing at the Magnolia."

Back to reality, he supposed. The night had definitely turned to day.

They walked back to the house, and Ella changed clothes, returning his shirt to him reluctantly. She followed him onto the porch.

Luca went down the steps and turned around. Dressed in cut-offs and a cropped T-shirt, Ella stood watching him. Buddy was lying beside her, panting, his tongue long and pink. The pig had come around, too, and was nosing around Ella's pockets. "I'll call you later?" he asked.

"Text me," she said with a wink.

Luca groaned. "You might not understand it."

Ella grinned. "I'll figure it out."

Luca shook his head. He still didn't move. He kept looking at her, almost fearful that he would forget a freckle or the tiny scar on her collarbone. "You're something else, Ella Kendall."

"Around here, we call it poor," she said, and laughed. Her phone began to ring. She sighed, pushed her hair from her face, and said, "Bye, Luca Prince." She stepped inside.

Luca headed to his truck. He got in and cranked the ignition and looked at that ramshackle little house before putting the truck in gear. He was falling for this woman. He was falling hard.

He just hoped that after last night, Ella was starting to fall a little, too.

Chapter Twenty-one

The next three weeks were a gauzy dreamscape for Ella. She and Luca were together as much as they could be between her work schedule and his efforts to pull together a viable fund-raiser. They weren't dating, exactly, but getting to know each other. Hanging out. She didn't want to define it or put expectations on it.

Luca showed up almost every day, generally bringing something she desperately needed. Like feed. And a kitchen faucet, which he easily installed. Ella was especially grateful for that—she had not realized what a huge difference running water made in her life. He repaired other things around her house, too, like the bathroom sink. They would laugh at how the moment one thing was fixed, something else would break or malfunction.

They took long walks around her property, and Luca pointed out native plants or showed her landmarks that had guided travelers for centuries. His knowledge of the evolution of this land was fascinating and impressive. He showed her where vaqueros held their version of a rodeo, the *charreada*, for bragging rights. He understood ecology, why some plants flourished and some didn't. He knew the wildlife, down to the beetles scurrying between prickly pear cactus. He cut the fruit from one very large complex of cactus and peeled it for her. "Eat it," he said.

Ella ate it. It was delicious.

She realized during one of those walks that he had shown her ancient Texas and what this land had looked like to the Native Americans and Spaniard and French explorers. Then to the hardscrabble people who had come west and eventually settled this land. When she saw it through his eyes, it was amazing, so much more than trees and cactus and grass and a natural spring. It was a living, breathing thing.

Luca also talked about his lessons, and the things he was learning from the books he was reading on conservation. He talked about the work he and Brandon wanted to do, and how much effort and money it would take to see it come to fruition. He told her again how costly it could be. "Reclaiming the land from an invasive species that has choked it is not easy," he'd said. "And it's not cheap to remove old oil wells or seed entire pastures. Or construct natural barriers to prevent soil erosion and protect watersheds. There's a lot that needs to be done."

He talked about where they hoped the money would come from to realize their vision.

Environmental groups. Universities. Philan-thropic organizations. "But not," he'd said with a laugh, "the Prince family foundation."

"Why not?" Ella had asked.

Luca had sighed. "It costs a lot of money. The board—mostly family—prefer to see our money go to things that might shine with the Prince name. Like hospital wings or women's shelters. Ecology and conservation is a little out there for them."

Ella didn't know squat about family philan-thropic organizations, but that sounded terribly unsupportive to her. "So if you manage to do all that you want with the land, then what happens to it?" she asked.

"Hopefully, it will attract scientists to study the ecology and renewal of the land. And hunters and recreationists, too. What I want is for everyone to be able to see what the land is in its most natural state. What it should look like."

Everything hinged on the fund-raiser. He said if they could get the buy-in from universities, environmentalists, and government, they had a chance at some real funding through grants and charitable donations without depleting their bank accounts.

Luca Prince was nothing like what Ella had assumed when he'd come riding out of the landscape to help her that day on the road. He'd talked about her layers, but *he* was the one who was the evolving picture book. She'd always thought him a jock, and while he was very athletic, he was so much more than that.

It was also astounding to her that for a man who couldn't read, Luca knew so much. He had failed to learn in the traditional way, but he had forged a path around it, had learned in spite of his glaring disability. She'd thought that, with all of his family's money and influence, Luca was the sort of man who could move through life doing what he pleased, with any woman he wanted. His privilege far exceeded that of those around him. She never would have guessed he had viewpoints that were at odds with his entire family.

And neither was he a player as she had always assumed. He was respectful, and he cared in a way she couldn't really fathom.

They rarely ventured away from her little house. They ate tacos from the taco stand and barbecued once until they discovered the pig was not deterred by fire. Ella wasn't much of a cook, but she made a batch of enchiladas two nights ago—thank you YouTube—which Luca very gallantly proclaimed the best of his life.

"You are such a liar," she'd said, and Luca had pulled her onto his lap.

"What, me lie? I freaking loved those rock-hard enchiladas," he swore, and kissed her. Before long, they were on the couch like a couple of teenagers in a desperate hurry before curfew.

Surprisingly, Luca had a trick or two up his kitchen sleeve. "Frederica taught me," he said, and told her about the cook who had been with them longer than he'd been alive.

He talked some about his family, mostly Hallie and his brother Nick. He didn't say much about his mother. His grandmother, he said, was two-thirds crazy.

Ella told him a story or two from her time in foster care, too, but mostly, the time they had together was spent in the moment, enjoying each other, making love, laughing at silly shows on Netflix at night when the satellite passed over.

Neither of them mentioned the future. Neither of them asked what their relationship meant or where it was going. And for that, Ella was particularly grateful. She didn't want to think about those questions just yet, because she feared the answer. She just wanted to live this dream for as long as she could.

As she dressed for work one morning, she happened to look at Buddy lazing in front of the screen door. That was his preferred spot in the house now. He was the first to know if Luca was coming, either by horse or by Sombra or by truck.

As she walked out of the bathroom, the dog lifted his head and gave her the once-over.

"What are you looking at?" she asked.

Buddy thumped his tail.

"Well, take a good long look, pal," she said, throwing her arms wide and twirling around. "This is me in an extremely good mood. I know, unbelievable," she said, and laughed as she went down on her knees to vigorously rub Buddy's ears. Then she popped up, dusted off her knees, and grabbed her bag. "Don't wait up." She waggled her brows as she opened the screen door to shoo him out, then locked the door behind them.

"Good-bye, Priscilla!" she shouted as the pig came running forward with the evergreen hope of more food. They had named the pig after Luca declared it was either name her or eat her. "That's the rule for farm animals," he'd said.

"That is a *horrible* rule," Ella had exclaimed.

"So name her," he'd said with a shrug. "I like Priscilla, because she's a little prissy when she's had enough to eat." As if to prove his point, that afternoon Priscilla had been doing some hopping and rolling around in the dirt.

Ella grinned as she recalled that conversation and climbed in her vehicle. "Yeah, you're high on life all right," she said to herself. "If I didn't know me better, I'd think I'd never had great sex."

Well, she certainly hadn't had sex as great as what she'd been having the last three weeks—that was for damn sure. Luca was the best lover she'd ever had, which, granted, was not a large pool. But he knew his way around a woman's body, knew how to make it hum. Every time he touched her, she felt like she might disintegrate. Every caress of his hand, every brush of his lips against every body part sent white-hot charges running through her. He had explored every crevice, every crease, over and over and over again.

It was hard to not want him all the damn time.

Ella started up her car and listened for any rattles. She heard none today. They seemed to come and go. Maybe, things were finally turning around for her. Because she'd never felt quite as sunny and pretty and invincible as she had these last few weeks, and she *liked* it.

The only cloud that seemed to occasionally drift over her sun was Stacy. She hadn't seen Stacy since Mariah told her Stacy had stolen the dress. She'd let Stacy's calls roll to voice mail. She'd exchanged a text with her here and there, usually citing how busy she was. Ella generally liked to deal with issues head on, but she was so furious with Stacy that she wasn't ready to speak to her yet.

She couldn't avoid her forever. But she hadn't wanted the shadow of Stacy to rain on her Luca parade.

Ella drove into town whistling "La Bamba," the earworm stuck in her head since it had played at the Magnolia a few nights ago, and some of the bar patrons had broken into mangled Spanish, trying to sing along. She would be grateful for the day she had a working car radio.

She pulled into Lyle's for gas. She got out and stuck her card in the reader. Lyle walked out of the shop, rubbing his gray hands on a rag that he returned to his back pocket. He reached for the pump.

"You don't have to do that," she said as she punched in the obligatory information.

"I know. But I'd hate to see you spill gas on that dress."

Ella glanced down at her vintage store special, red and blue stripes with a cinched waist. She smoothed the lap of it as Lyle filled her tank, then looked up and noticed Lyle eyeing her suspiciously. "What?"

"I don't know," he said. "Something's a little off about you lately."

"Off!" Ella laughed. "You are mistaken, sir. It's a beautiful spring morning—what could possibly put me off?"

"Are you stoned?" he asked.

"Yes. High on life," she said, laughing. "Of course I'm not stoned."

"Well, something's made you awfully perky lately. I'd finally gotten used to Miss Grump pulling in here every other morning."

Ella laughed brightly at that absurd depiction of her morning somberness. "How many times must

I explain that I am *not* grumpy in the mornings? I just need coffee before I can function."

"Oh, you're grumpy," he said. "A month ago you threatened to punch me in the mouth when I offered you a donut."

"Okay," Ella said, lifting a finger, "to be fair, you suggested I take a few donuts to keep me warm at night, because obviously something needed to."

Lyle suddenly grinned. "Well, chica, it appears I wasn't wrong," he said, and winked at her.

Ella flushed and averted her gaze. She hadn't told anyone about Luca, but Lyle was very good at reading people. Plus, he probably saw Luca's various vehicles turning down her road on a regular basis. "Shut up, Lyle," she said playfully.

"I don't know what you've got going on exactly, but it's put a spring in your step. I just want you to know if it doesn't work out, my offer still stands. Think about it—unlimited access to Funyuns."

Ella laughed. She had a huge soft spot for this gray-handed man. "As enticing as that sounds, I'm going to keep to myself and my house for now."

"I'll get through to you one of these days," Lyle said, and slipped the nozzle back into the pump.

Lyle was right, there was a spring in her step. More like a Tigger bounce.

Ella said good-bye, then got in her car and drove to the Baptist Church. She was finally meeting with her potential new client—the

Baptist Ladies Auxiliary club. Then she was scheduled at Byron's office, followed by the Magnolia.

Luca was not a frequent visitor to the Magnolia, but last night, as he was leaving her house, he'd complained about her busy day, then asked if she would mind if he showed up at the Magnolia tonight. Ella had felt an instant twinge of reluctance. It had taken her a moment to understand why—but then she'd realized she didn't want the real world to intrude on them. "And do what?" she'd asked, pretending to be distracted.

Luca shrugged. "Look at you."

"That would be kind of weird and stalkery."

"I'll bring Hallie," he suggested, and had kissed the hollow of her throat.

"How will that make it less stalkery?" she'd murmured dreamily.

"Because I won't look like a stalker. I'll look like a good brother. Let me come, Ella," he'd said quietly, and damn it, he'd kissed her softly on the mouth.

"Okay," Ella had said at last. "But don't be weird."

"Not to worry, darlin'. I won't be any of those things, because we are not dating."

"Never," she said, and taking him by the hand, had escorted him to the door and waved good-bye to him.

Ella's initial meeting with the president of the Ladies Auxiliary went well, and the president promised her she would invite her to meet the whole group. Ella drove into San Antonio, said hello to Byron, watered his droopy plants, then sat down to work. Her phone pinged, and she glanced at the ID. It was Stacy. She texted At work. Can't talk.

Stacy did not text back, and Ella forgot about it.

She left Byron's office late in the afternoon with a cheery wave and a "see you Friday." Byron just looked at her, then picked up a cupcake that had seemingly appeared out of thin air.

When she arrived for work at the Magnolia, Mateo was already behind the bar. He gave her a look when she came in. "You look cute," he said.

"Thank you." She curtsied.

"Hey, Ella!" Chrissy appeared from the wait station carrying a tray. "You look so pretty today! I love that dress."

"Vintage," Ella said, and gave the hem of it a swing.

Chrissy nodded approvingly. "Looks like country living agrees with you after all."

"You know what? I think it does, too," Ella said, and then, before she could catch herself, she laughed.

Chapter Twenty-two

When Luca pulled up to the gate at Three Rivers Ranch and waited for it to open, he noticed a Jeep barreling down the road toward the gate in the opposite direction. As the gate opened, the Jeep pulled alongside him. The magnetic sign, RURAL MAIL CARRIER, was attached crookedly to the Jeep's door. The window on the driver's side came down, and a brassy red head popped out of the window. "Luca Prince, how the heck are you?" Big Barb shouted at him. She plunked her arm down on the open car frame and leaned out.

"Hello, Big Barb," he said. "How are you?"

"I'm great! Been out of town?" she asked, squinting at him.

"Excuse me?"

"I only ask because I haven't seen your truck the last few mornings when I've brought the mail. But I've seen that Sombra!" she announced. "Guess you've got the only plug in Cimarron County." She laughed loudly.

Luca had to suppress the urge to roll his eyes.

"I thought maybe you were staying up at your place in San Antone," she said.

Good Lord, Big Barb was the most meddlesome meddler south of the Red River. "Nope," he said.

"Oh, I figured out you hadn't been, cuz I'd seen your truck at the Gieselman place. Every Tuesday and Thursday, about the time I deliver the mail." She cocked her head to one side.

Luca said nothing, refusing to give her anything she might repeat around town, and waited for her to make her point.

But Big Barb was a pro at the gossip game and changed course. "Your poor mamma seems to be doing better. She didn't yell at me today."

"Then I guess things are looking up," he said.

"I gotta say, I've been worried about her. I heard that Sarah Jenkins-Cash heard from someone in her bridge group that Margaret Sutton is going round saying your dad ran through all his money and left y'all with nothing."

Luca's grip tightened on the wheel. "You probably shouldn't believe everything you hear."

"Oh, well, I *don't,*" she said cheerfully. "I don't believe anything *anyone* tells me. You have a great day, Luca!" she sang out, and pulled her Bozo head back into the Jeep and drove off.

Luca was used to talk about his family, but he was so annoyed with Big Barb that he gassed the truck and peeled away from the gate, rocketing down the drive to the house.

After he'd parked, he wandered around inside looking for a sign of anyone before he found Hallie in the kitchen making scrambled eggs.

"Hey, I'll have some of those," Luca said. "Where's Frederica?"

"Mom reduced her schedule. She's here three days a week now."

"Wow," Luca said, and looked at his sister. "After all these years? Is that really necessary?"

"There's no talking to Mom about it," Hallie said with a sigh. "So where were you last night? I could have used some company."

"I was out," he said, and went to the fridge to pour himself some milk.

"With Ella?"

"Maybe."

"You two are a thing?" she asked.

"Hallie—"

"I'm just curious, Luca. I like her. I'm sort of surprised, that's all."

"Why?" he asked, a little more sharply than he intended.

"I don't know," she said. "Because she's not like the other women you've gone after. You know, tall, blonde, and leggy."

"Ella is very attractive," Luca said.

"I know that," Hallie said. "I'm just surprised *you* see it."

He cast a withering look at his sister, although

he supposed she had a point. He had always drifted toward the model types. Or the types that showed up to the parties he tended to frequent. "I like her, okay?" he said, and tugged on an end of Hallie's hair.

"You what?" She looked up at him, her eyes searching his. "Luca . . . that is *great,*" she said quietly.

"Don't get excited," he said, then instinctively looked over his shoulder. He preferred to keep his life private. In other words, his love life was not up for discussion with his grandma or his mother. "Don't say anything," he muttered.

"Why not?"

"You know why," Luca said. "Have you met our mother? Where is she, anyway?"

"In her room," Hallie said, and shoveled eggs onto a plate. She took the carton from the fridge, pulled two more eggs from it, and dumped them into the hot pan.

"Hey, I've got good news for you," Luca said as he took a seat at the bar. "I'm going to take you out to dinner tonight."

"What? No," she said with a shake of her head. "I have plans."

"I thought Chris was in Houston."

"For your information, I happen to be in the middle of bingeing all four hundred seasons of the *Bachelor*. It's taking a lot of time that I don't have." She sniffed.

"Come on. This will be more fun than that. I'm going to call Brandon and have him meet us. We'll talk about the fund-raiser. It's coming up, you know."

"That's right, and you're going to be very happy you agreed to let my wedding planner manage this event," she said, and turned off the flame and dumped the second batch of eggs onto another plate. "She has the best ideas."

Hallie had told him about the planner after the family meeting, and he'd said okay, but he was afraid to think of how much this was going to cost him. "Are you coming or not, Hallie? I haven't seen you do much of anything lately but open bottles of wine."

"Hey!" she said, and jabbed a finger in the air in his direction. "Do *not* judge my coping mechanisms!"

Luca ate his eggs and did not judge her coping mechanisms.

"Where are you going, anyway?" she asked as he stood up to bring his plate around to the sink.

He grinned and turned around. "I knew I could talk you into it."

"I haven't said I would come."

"You're the best, Hallie," he said, and caught her with one arm around the belly and kissed the top of her head. "The Magnolia."

She slapped his arm away with one hand while the other held a fork full of eggs.

"Get away from me, charmer."

"I'll pick you up at seven," he said, and sauntered out of the kitchen.

On his way to his room and a shower, he passed the master bedroom and paused to peek inside. Seeing no one, he took a few steps down the hall before he heard his mother call him back.

Luca backed up and went into her room. She was sitting in the bay window, her legs stretched in front of her. On her lap was the mysterious wooden box his dad had left her. "What are you doing, Mom?" he asked.

She looked out the window, to the vast expanse of Prince land. "Thinking."

Luca shoved his hands into his pockets. "About . . . ?"

"Life. Death. You know, all the important things." She sighed and shifted her gaze to Luca. "How soon is too soon to start drinking?" she asked idly.

"Mom," Luca said.

"I'm kidding," she said. "Sort of." She stood up and put the box aside. She walked over to Luca and put her arms around him. He couldn't remember any longer at what point he'd grown so much taller than her, but she seemed so small to him now.

"I owe you an apology," she said.

"For . . . ?"

"The things I said to you that night."

Christ, not this again. Luca had no desire to talk about it. "You already apologized," he said.

"I did, but your grandmother said my apology was like the apology of a guilty person on *Dateline* and that no one believes courtroom apologies."

Luca smiled. His grandmother was right about that.

His mother dropped her arms and walked across the thick carpet to the long bench at the foot of her bed. "I know I've always been hard on you, Luca, but it's because I love you so much. I want you to succeed."

"I know, Mom."

"Chet says you're not going in to work," she said, and glanced up at him.

Luca shrugged. "Victor has it handled. He doesn't need me to interfere."

"That doesn't matter. You're the boss, and that's your business."

"Actually, it's really Uncle Chet's business. He's still involved." He sighed and ran the palm of his hand over his crown. "You know as well as I that he never trusted me to actually run that business. He and Victor don't need me, and honestly? I'm in the way. I don't want a Sombra dealership."

His mother sighed wearily and looked down at her feet. "You could learn it. You have to have

314

a purpose in life, Luca. People who don't have purpose end up drunk and old."

"I *have* purpose," he said stiffly.

"I wish my father had never set up those trusts for you kids. It makes it too easy not to pursue—"

"Mother," he said quietly.

The tone of his voice prompted her to stop speaking and look at him.

"We're not going to do this again," he said firmly. "I don't want to hear it anymore. I know who I am, and if you don't like it, that's your problem. Not mine."

"That is *obviously* not what this is about."

"That's what it's always about," he said. "The fund-raiser is happening. The conservation is happening. You may as well accept it." He didn't wait for her to argue—he turned and walked out of her room.

She did not call him back.

Luca went to his room at the end of the long hall. What she thought of him shouldn't matter to him at this point—he was a grown man, long past the point of needing his mother's approval. And yet, like the little boy who used to sing silly songs to make her laugh, he still craved that approval.

He understood that his mother would never be proud of him. But he had resigned himself to the fact that he would never stop wanting her to be proud of him.

· · ·

The Magnolia Bar and Grill seemed awfully crowded at six on a Tuesday. Ella was at the hostess stand when Luca and Hallie met up with Brandon. She was always beautiful when she smiled, but tonight, she was glowing as she chatted with Hallie. Luca had not seen the dress she was wearing before, and he had a hard time looking away from it. It fit her so well that he idly began to think of her body and the way they fit together when they made love.

"I've got a corner booth if you'd like," Ella said when another couple entered the restaurant. With her head, she indicated they should follow, and led them across the room to the booth. She introduced them to Chrissy, the server, and with a quick little smile for Luca, she returned to work.

Brandon watched Ella walk through the throng of tables.

"Eyes front," Hallie said. "She's spoken for. Luca saw her first."

"I'm starting to figure that out," Brandon said, and turned his gaze to Luca. "You're dating her?"

Funny that he and Ella hadn't exactly defined what they were doing. It was a running joke between them, but frankly, Luca hadn't felt the need to define it. Brandon's question made him wonder. "We're hanging out," he said with a shrug.

"You?" Brandon said again.

"Would you please not say *you* like you

316

discovered I'm the one that pissed in your cereal? Is it so hard to believe?"

"Well, yeah, a little," Brandon said. "You generally don't 'hang out,'" he said, putting air quotes around the word.

Did *everyone* think he was a player? "Well, I am now. I like her," Luca said, and his gaze fell on Ella again and the swing of her hair around the middle of her back.

"She's pretty," Brandon said.

They ordered dinner and drinks, and talked about life since Luca and Hallie's father had passed away. When Brandon asked Hallie about Chris, Luca was surprised to hear her hesitate—she was always so effusive in her praise of him. "He's good," she said with a shrug, and looked away.

It was half past nine when Luca waved Ella over and convinced her to slide into the booth with them next to Hallie, where she could keep one eye on the door. The establishment closed at ten, and Three Rivers typically rolled up the streets by eight. The place was beginning to empty out.

Brandon leaned across the table and fixed his gaze on Ella. Luca feared he'd had enough wine to wander past charming and into the territory of annoying. "Ella, right?" he asked.

"Yep. Ella Kendall."

"She's living out at the old Kendall place," Hallie said.

Brandon suddenly sat up. "What, you live

there? We used to run wild around that place," he said.

"Has Luca told you what they are planning for the land around your house?" Hallie asked.

"He has," Ella said.

"Great! So you'll be at the fund-raiser, right?" Brandon asked.

"Well, I, ah—"

"You have to come," Brandon said. "You've seen Three Rivers Ranch, haven't you?"

"No," Ella said, and seemed to shrink a little in her seat.

"What? Luca, what's the matter with you? Take her to Three Rivers," Brandon said to Luca, clapping him on the shoulder and squeezing hard. To Ella, he said, "You won't believe the views. It's one of the biggest ranches in Texas. You have to see it to appreciate it."

"So I've heard," Ella said.

Funny, they'd never talked much about the ranch. Luca didn't know what she knew about it.

"That's why we're having the fund-raiser there," Brandon said. "Potential investors will come, and they'll see that view and hear what we have to say, and voilà. If anyone can charm them into opening their wallets, it's Luca Prince," he said with a wink for Luca.

"Yeah," Ella said. She tucked a bit of hair behind her ear. "It sounds . . . fancy."

"Oh, absolutely!" Hallie said. "Black tie,

cocktails, fancy food. Mom taught me that a long time ago—when people get all dressed up, they think that what they are doing is really important. And honestly, we need a good excuse for a party at home, don't we, Luca? It's been a mausoleum out there."

"Ella, you need to come," Brandon said earnestly.

"You do," Hallie agreed.

Ella looked startled. "I've never been to a fund-raiser."

"This should be your first," Luca said. "We nailed down the date this morning—June tenth. I would love for you to come, Ella, and meet the family."

Ella's eyes widened.

"That's perfect!" Hallie said. She looked at Luca and Brandon. "Remember that summer we were all in Cabo? That's when I introduced Chris to the family, remember?"

"I remember. His boat was a lot bigger than yours," Brandon said.

Hallie clucked her tongue. "His family sold it. They're getting a yacht."

"So back to the fund-raiser," Luca said, uninterested in Chris's boats. "I heard back from the US Department of Agriculture, did I tell you? Their conservation arm is studying soil erosion and the protection of water reserves. They are very interested in attending."

Brandon wasn't listening. "How big is the yacht?" he asked Hallie.

"I don't know, seventy-five feet?"

"Nice," Brandon said, nodding approvingly. "We should all get together and fly out and have a look."

"Hey!" Hallie said brightly. "Let's do it! You, too, Ella. You'd love our villa in Cabo. It's not huge, but it's right on the beach."

Ella looked like she wanted to sink below the table. Luca loved his sister, but sometimes, she could be a little insensitive. Did she or Brandon really think that Ella could just call into work, then fly out to Cabo the next day? To see a *yacht?*

"Actually, I should get back to work," Ella said.

"Stick around," Luca said, and had to resist the urge to lunge for her, to keep her there. "We're through talking about yachts."

"We're starting to close down, and I need to help." She stood up. "It was nice seeing you all tonight."

"You too, Ella," Hallie said cheerfully. "Hope to see you at the ranch!"

The three of them watched Ella return to the hostess stand, then Hallie turned to Luca. "What just happened? Was it the yacht?"

"Maybe," Luca said.

"Maybe it was mentioning your family," Brandon responded. "That would scare anyone away."

Luca and Hallie laughed.

But Luca considered that maybe Brandon was right. Maybe it was too soon to have suggested meeting his family, and Luca shouldn't have so casually tossed it out there. He was rusty on the rules of relationships. He didn't do relationships. He never thought about bringing a woman to Three Rivers, because he never went out with a woman past two or three dates. That was the point at which it became impossible to hide his affliction.

Ella was at the hostess stand when they left, and as they walked out the door, Luca lingered. "See you tomorrow?"

"Maybe," she said, smiling.

"Just a maybe?" he asked, and touched his fingers to her hand.

"I'm meeting the Ladies Auxiliary in the morning, and I have some errands I need to take care of." She gave him a half-hearted shrug.

"Luca!" Hallie shouted at him from somewhere outside.

"Text me," she said.

He wanted to say something. His chest felt funny, but he couldn't quite determine what it was. So he kissed her cheek and backed away from her, unwilling to lose sight of her just yet. Ella laughed at him. "You're going to trip."

"I don't care."

"You promised you wouldn't do anything weird."

"Remind me not to make any more breezy promises," he said.

She waved at him, and he turned around and walked out to the parking lot, trying hard not to appear as besotted as he felt.

That's when he realized what the sensation in his chest was. It felt like the bulb of a plant, like all the thoughts and emotions that formed the idea of settling down with one person, of committing to one, were beginning to knit together into a bulb and take root.

That realization was a little stunning.

He was going to need another drink to absorb such significant changes in his cell structure.

Chapter Twenty-three

Ella locked the door of the bar and turned, almost colliding with Mateo. "Jesus, you scared me. You shouldn't sneak up on people."

"I didn't sneak up on you, I walked to the door. Maybe you were distracted." He'd donned his dark leather jacket and ball cap, and he was looking past her, out the door. "So that's the new guy, huh?"

Ella looked over her shoulder, but of course, everyone had gone. "No," she said, and inwardly winced at her lie. "I mean, sort of. It's new. Actually, it's not really defined, it's just . . ." For heaven's sake, she sounded like a babbling idiot. Why was she so hesitant? Why couldn't she just own it? She wasn't worried about hurting Mateo's feelings—they had definitely moved on from each other. No, this was something else entirely. Part of her thought Mateo wouldn't believe her. Part of her didn't believe it herself. Damn it, but she still felt unworthy of someone like Luca Prince. *Still.*

"You know the guy he's with, right?" Mateo asked.

"Brandon? Do you know him?"

"I don't know *him,* but his dad is that guy in the TV commercials. 'If you've been hit by a truck, call four-four-four,'" he said with a roll of his eyes. "I heard the old man commutes from the Dominion to his downtown office every day in a helicopter. Can you imagine the scratch you'd have to have for a daily helicopter?" Mateo stepped around her to the door. "So who's the guy?" he asked.

"His name is Luca. Luca Prince."

Mateo stilled a moment. *"Whoa,"* he said. "Figures—the two families with all the money in Texas. Well, lucky you, Ella."

"Money doesn't have anything to do with it," she said, exasperated by the insinuation.

Mateo gave a dark laugh. "Are you serious? Money is the way of the world, or haven't you been paying attention? Those that have lots of it get to do what they want. And then there are the rest of us. We're just mortals," he said, and winked at her before he pushed the door open. "Good luck running with that crowd," he said, and walked out the door.

She locked the door behind him.

Good luck running with that crowd.

The words rattled around in her head, refusing to settle. It was the same thing she'd thought privately, especially when they'd started talking about Cabo. *Hey, let's jet down to Cabo this weekend and see some guy's yacht. You, too, Ella!* Then again, why *not* run with that crowd? She wasn't a peasant. But she couldn't jet off to Cabo, and she would never have the kind of money the Princes had. Still, she was proud of what she'd accomplished. She was proud of finishing college while working two jobs. She was proud that she had a degree in spite of her shaky beginnings.

Meet his family? She was not ready for that. In spite of Ella's confidence, there was something about the perfectly put together Princes that made her feel less than adequate. She didn't want to meet his family. She didn't want to step off her little farm and be reminded of who she was not.

She glanced heavenward, looking for help she was not going to get. She was so stupid, living for the moment, pretending the outside world didn't exist. She still hadn't gotten used to the idea that she and Luca were kind of, sort of, seeing each other, or know what it really all meant past their little bubble.

But what really annoyed her was that she was thinking that way at all. She had believed she was well past the point of caring what others thought of her. She was supposed to be a self-assured woman, and mostly, she had been. She had been right up to the moment she was faced with the prospect of actually going to the famed Three Rivers Ranch, and had promptly tumbled into a pit of insecurity that felt as big and deep as it had when she was in high school.

"Damn, I annoy me." With a shake of her head, she went to the back to help Chrissy close out.

Later that night, with Buddy stretched out beside her and snoring loudly as if he'd worked cattle all day instead of lazing around on the porch, Ella cranked up her laptop and Googled Brandon Hurst to see if what Mateo said was true.

She discovered that Brandon had not followed his father into the apparently very lucrative practice of injury law, which had sprouted offices in San Antonio, Austin, and Houston. There were several articles about his father's high-profile injury cases and multimillion dollar settlements, as well as his family's high profile charity events. Thomas Hurst had two sons. The oldest, she knew, was the Cimarron County sheriff, who had an entirely different set of articles, mostly to do with drug busts, traffic accidents, and burn bans.

There were a few articles about Brandon, too, and his efforts in environmental law. He was not as visible as his father or brother, but he had been involved in the successful litigation on behalf of some rice farmers who'd sued an oil company that had failed to adequately clean up a spill.

Next, she Googled Luca. Stacy said one should never date a man without at least a cursory Google check, but Ella had never really checked

326

on Luca past scrolling through some social media and Google references. But she hadn't clicked on the articles that popped up. For one thing, it felt invasive. And she was busy. And her internet connection was so primitive as to be considered third world. And she was afraid of what she might find, other than him with a bevy of beauties.

She held her breath and hit the return key. Oh, but the beauties popped up, all right, going back ten years. The things written about Luca were very different from the news on Brandon. There were no accolades for his performance in a courtroom, no distinguished honors at a school or in a profession. There were, however, quite a few mentions of him in conjunction with his family's philanthropic foundation, and many, *many* pictures of him at high-society parties. There was Luca in a tuxedo, a little glassy-eyed, holding a highball glass on a rooftop in New York. There he was again, his arms around two men on either side of him, on a Caribbean beach. There he was with a beautiful blonde at what looked like a debutante ball. Another woman at an opera in Paris. At a boat show. At an art gallery opening in Los Angeles.

Good luck running with that crowd.

Ella's head was beginning to hurt. She closed her laptop and went through the motions of getting ready for bed while Mateo's words played on repeat in her mind. She tried to read to quiet her thoughts, but it was a long time before she fell asleep.

The next morning she woke up groggy and out of sorts. She dressed and made her way to the Baptist Church to meet with the Ladies Auxiliary.

"As long as no one objects, you have the job," Mrs. Wilson, the president of the group had said when Ella spoke with her earlier in the week.

The board met in what turned out to be a rather dusty, stuffy basement room of the church. Someone had set up metal folding chairs in a circle. On a table against the wall was a cornucopia of carbohydrates—cookies and sheet cakes—baby carrots and broccoli that no one touched, and—there seemed to be a bit of a row about this—sugary punch instead of tea. From what Ella could gather, Mrs. Rosenholz had defied the wishes of the food committee and brought the sugar punch instead of tea.

But the ladies gamely carried on without tea, filling their plates with cookies and cake, and settling in. Ella took a seat in the designated guest spot and was pulling out her notes when she heard a familiar name: Cordelia Prince.

"I'm telling you, he sees Cordelia Prince up there sitting on his grave in the early evenings. I mean on *top* of the grave. Like she's made herself a bed there."

"Oh, how she must miss him," said one of the

ladies. "I still miss John, and he's been gone thirty-two years now."

"Well, I wouldn't piss on Charlie Prince's grave if he were *my* husband," said another.

"A man like Charlie Prince would never have been your husband, Willa."

"Betty!" Mrs. Rosenholz said. "That's not nice."

Willa didn't seem terribly offended. She said, "He ran around on Ms. Prince all their lives! He had that kid with *Margaret Sutton* of all people, and let me tell you, that woman has said some things that would curl your hair."

"Did you know that Margaret and Ms. Prince were best friends once?" Mrs. Rosenholz asked slyly.

"That Charlie," said another of the ladies with a tower of cookies that looked precariously close to toppling over. "He was good for nothing. Nearly ran the Prince name into the ground."

"Ladies," said Mrs. Wilson primly, "this is a house of worship, not a coffee klatch, and we have a lot of business to get to. And besides, it's all just gossip. None of us knows the truth of what happened between them. Now, I found Charlie Prince to be a good Christian man. We wouldn't have that cross out front if it weren't for him!"

The cross she was referring to, Ella gathered, was the one that was almost as tall as the church.

"That's true enough," said Betty. "He was a sinner, but he was a good man, too. His kids are another story," she added with a snort.

Everyone giggled.

Ella could feel heat creeping into her cheeks.

"I like Nick," said Willa. "He seems responsible. Not very friendly, but responsible, and someone has to be with that kind of money floating around. I tell you what, the way Hallie shops is something else. Big Barb says she gets boxes and boxes from New York and Paris all the time."

"It's their money to do with as they please," said Mrs. Wilson, and sat in her chair. "Can we please call to order? I am sure Miss Kendall has better things to do than listen to gossip about the Prince family."

Actually, she did not.

But the group settled into their seats and began to review the books and what Ella could do for them.

The books, she discovered, were a hodgepodge of handwritten notes, receipts, and a meeting agenda from two years ago. It was a nightmare for Mrs. Wilson, and even Ella would be challenged to make sense of it. But she liked a challenge, and promised to clean up their accounting and present them with a new spreadsheet that showed exactly how much available funding they had at the next monthly meeting.

"Well, then I guess you're hired, hon," said Mrs. Wilson, then looked around the room. "Any objection?"

The other ladies shook their heads.

They moved on to the next item, and Ella walked out to her car, still digesting all the talk about the Princes. It was stunning to hear them so openly discussed. In her car, she checked her list of things she had to do today and saw she had a missed call from Luca, followed by a text that said, Cal me?

She smiled. He was getting better about texting, although his spelling needed work. She decided she'd call him when she got home. She put her phone on the hands-free device and backed out of her parking spot. It rang as she was backing out, and she hit the button to answer, assuming it was Luca. "Hey there," she said.

"Oh my God, *finally*," Stacy's voice shouted into the space of her car.

Ella suppressed a groan. "Hey, Stace. What's up?"

"What's *up?* Are you kidding me? You've been avoiding me, that's what is *up,* Ella!"

"Are you going to start this conversation by yelling at me?"

"I'm not *yelling* at you. I'm pissed! Why haven't you taken my calls?"

Ella slammed her car into drive, her errands forgotten. "Because I'm pissed at you, Stacy!"

"What?" Stacy asked, sounding perplexed. "What'd I do?"

"Are you kidding me right now? You stole a dress from Mariah!"

That was met with a slender moment of silence, and then a dismissive, "Oh, *that.*"

Ella's fury soared to new heights. "Yes, *that,*" she snapped. "I'm done, Stacy. I'm really, seriously done this time! I've never been able to stand your stealing, but now, I refuse to put up with it. If you're going to shoplift from our *friend,* then you are on your own."

"I'm sorry!" Stacy wailed. "I swear I won't do it again. And besides, it was just a stupid sale dress. Seventy-five percent off."

Ella banged the steering wheel with the palm of her hand several times. "Do you *hear* yourself? It doesn't matter that it was on sale! You stole from Mariah! Your good friend *Mariah.* Don't you have any remorse?"

"Of course I have remorse," Stacy said, her voice quieter. "Actually, I feel really bad about it. But you know I can't help it sometimes."

Ella rolled her eyes. That was always Stacy's excuse. She couldn't help it. "Yeah, well, *I* can help it, and I'm not your mother, and I don't want to be around you at all if you're going to steal."

"O-*kay,*" she said. "Look, I'm sorry. I'm not perfect, okay? I know you're pissed, but I—"

"Uh-uh," Ella said. "Nope. Not listening. And I won't until you apologize."

"I just did! I'm sorry. I'm sorry!"

"Not to *me,* Stacy, to Mariah. You have to apologize, and pay for the dress. You have to make this right!"

"Okay," Stacy said. "I will, I swear I will, but Ella, will you please listen to me?"

Ella sighed. She knew how this would go. Stacy would apologize. She might even apologize to Mariah and make good on the dress. She'd swear she'd never do it again, but something would happen, and instead of facing her demons, she would shoplift again and say she couldn't help it.

"Are you there?" Stacy asked plaintively.

"Yes. Fine, whatever. What do you have to tell me?"

"You know the sheriff?"

"No. I mean I've seen him, that's all."

"Sheriff Hurst is his name."

"Right," Ella said.

"He's the one who hired me, which, you were right, I really needed the job, because it looks like me and the guys are going to Nashville in a couple of weeks. Anyway, I need my paycheck to help move us, but the sheriff has been harassing me."

Ella pulled up to a stoplight. "What do you mean?"

"You know what I mean," Stacy said

impatiently. "He's handsy. He remembers me from something that happened a long time ago, and he's using it against me."

"What happened?" Ella asked, confused.

Stacy sighed. "It's a long story. I took something. Can't I tell you over drinks?"

Ella didn't want to have drinks with Stacy. She didn't want to hear about another theft.

"Ella, please. I need you."

She hated when Stacy appealed to her sense of loyalty. "Why am I still your friend?" she groaned.

"I don't deserve you. I really don't. And I wouldn't ask you, but honestly? I'm a little scared. This guy won't leave me alone, and I really don't like where it's going."

"Okay," Ella said, giving in. "Okay, Stacy."

"*Thank* you!" Stacy said in relief.

"You promise you'll apologize to Mariah?" Ella demanded.

"Yes, I will! Tonight? I mean, can I meet you tonight?"

"Not tonight. Friday. Come by the Magnolia at five. That's an hour before my shift starts."

"Okay. Thank you, Ella!"

"Call Mariah!"

It was too late—Stacy had already hung up.

Ella muttered a few things under her breath about Stacy, then drove home, her errands forgotten, her mind a million miles away, back in that foster house where Pam and Gary fought like cats while Stacy and Ella hid under a cover with a flashlight, trying with everything they had to pretend all was normal. When Ella graduated from college, Stacy was there, cheering loudly. When Stacy played her first big gig, Ella was there. She loved Stacy; she really did. But why did Stacy have to steal?

Ella was mulling it over as she turned onto the county road that led to her house, wondering if it was even possible that Stacy could change without a major intervention, like therapy. Or worse—jail.

She didn't see Luca's horse when she pulled up under the oak tree. She didn't see him until she was walking up to the house and saw him on her porch steps. He was wearing a dirty white T-shirt, jeans and chaps, and a cowboy hat. And he was clutching a bouquet of wildflowers.

Ella's heart began to skip through its own field of sunflowers. She smiled at him sitting like a poster child for sexy, romantic cowboys.

She forgot about Stacy.

She forgot what Mateo had said.

No matter what she thought of her and Luca's situation, or whatever it was they were doing with each other, she was still mentally pinching herself with happiness every time he came around, and she didn't want to stop until she was black and blue.

Chapter Twenty-four

Luca stood up as Ella walked up to the porch. She shielded her eyes from the sun with one hand and looked at the bouquet, tied with a string. "Are those for me?"

"For you," he said. "But you may have to fight Priscilla for them. She thinks they're her afternoon snack."

Ella gazed up at him as she took the flowers from his hand. Her blue eyes were shining with pleasure, and Luca thought he could spend the rest of his life doing nothing but putting that smile on her face.

"I'm going to put them in some water. Come in," she said. She was still smiling as she went up the steps and around him, her arm brushing against his before she unlocked her door and walked inside.

Luca followed her. He would follow this woman anywhere.

She went to the sink and filled a Mason jar with water. As she began to stuff the flowers into the jar, Luca walked up behind her and put his arms around her waist and kissed her nape. "I probably smell like a barnyard," he muttered.

"You smell like sun and air," she said.

He moved his mouth to her ear, and she bent her head to give him room. "I've missed you, Ella."

She laughed softly. "You saw me just last night."

"Yeah, but there were other people around us. It's not the same."

"No," she agreed. She finished arranging the flowers in the jar.

"So," he said, wondering how best to speak of things that rattled around in him. "I had a good time last night."

"Yeah, it seemed so," she said.

Her response, on a scale of one to ten, ten being a trip to the moon and one being a funeral, was about a three.

She stepped away from him with her jar of flowers to set them on the scarred bistro table she'd dug out of some trash heap.

Luca studied her, trying to gauge her mood. "We talked a lot about the ranch," he said.

"Yes," she said.

"We sprung the fund-raiser on you, too. I know I mentioned it before, but now we have a date. I would really love for you to come, Ella."

"Oh, you don't need me there," she said, and gave a bit of a laugh.

Something uncomfortable fluttered in Luca's heart. As if his heart had detected the unspoken subtext he feared. "I don't *need* you there. I want you there."

She winced. *Winced.* "I've never been to a fund-raiser or a fancy party—"

"It's just a party," he said quickly. "No big deal."

She looked at him as if he had lost his mind. "You mean it's no big deal for you."

Luca didn't understand what was happening right now. Was the idea of a party at his family's ranch that upsetting to her? Or was it something else? She had never once given him any reason to suspect she was intimidated by his name or his wealth. That's what he appreciated about her— she knew who he was and cut him no slack for it. And she'd seemed so interested in what he was trying to accomplish. At least he thought she had.

"Is it my family?" he asked, landing on that idea. "I know I haven't said a lot about them, but they are good people—"

"Luca," she said quietly, cutting him off. "It's not your family. It's that I don't belong at your house. I don't want to go and meet a bunch of people I will never see again. I don't have the fancy manners for an affair like that. I'm liable to do something I won't even know is wrong. Use the wrong fork or something."

"What are you talking about?"

"We're so different," she said. "We come from

very different backgrounds and life experiences and world views. And that . . . that world is nothing to do with me."

It was his privilege, then. This was his fault—he'd been so caught up in her, and in the little fantasy he'd been living in here at the old Kendall place, that he hadn't really looked at it from her perspective. He couldn't begin to guess what she'd heard about Three Rivers Ranch and the Prince family. He glanced at his watch. "Do you have someplace to be in the morning?"

"Not until tomorrow afternoon. Why?"

"I would like to take you to dinner. I'm going to ride home and get cleaned up. Then I'm going to pick you up. Wear a dress."

"Wait, what? I've got some things I have to do—"

He shook his head. "This is my fault, Ella. I haven't taken you on a proper date. I haven't shown you my world. I have loved every minute being here, with you, away from all that," he said, gesturing vaguely in the direction of Three Rivers Ranch. "I didn't think about what you might need from me. I'm going to change that. Tonight. We can stay at my place in town."

"Tonight?" She looked around her little kitchen. "What about the animals?"

He laughed. "They survived until you showed up to save them, didn't they?"

"But I have to work."

339

"When is the last time you took a day or two off from your work?"

She paused as if trying to remember her last vacation. "Give me a minute."

"That's what I thought." He drew her into his arms. "Come on, baby—put on a pretty dress. Let me take you out and try to impress you."

A very tentative smile began to curve her lips. "I'm pretty jaded, you know. I'd hate to see you get all dressed up and then I'm not impressed."

"I love a challenge," he said, and kissed her before she could refuse him. Luca was fundamentally an optimist. He believed that if he just hung in there, Ella would eventually see that what they had together was pretty damn great, and his wealth, and her lack of it, had no bearing on that. None. So he kissed her slowly and thoroughly, hoping he chased every doubt from her head. When he finally pulled away, he said, "I'll be back in a couple of hours. Does that give you enough time?"

"I didn't say I was going," she said.

Luca groaned playfully. "At the risk of seeming too aggressive in this day and age, what if I say I'm not going anywhere until you say yes?"

Ella's eyes sparkled with amusement. "A good feminist would advise you to rethink that. Lucky for you, I'm a mediocre feminist—so mediocre that I will ask you what sort of dress should I wear?"

Luca smiled with relief. "I am also only a mediocre feminist. Wear any dress you like— you look fantastic in everything, including snow boots."

"Now you're trying to butter me up," she said with a broad smile. "You have to give me *some* clue. Are you picking me up in your truck or your Sombra?"

"Sombra," he said without hesitation.

"Ooh, so it's a *Sombra* kind of evening. That's a different kind of dress altogether."

"Does this mean you are officially agreeing to go out with me?" he asked.

"I'm going to let you try to impress me," she said. "But it's not a date."

He snorted. "I wouldn't even *think* of dating you." He kissed her forehead. "I'll be back."

"You said that like a thousand times already," she teased him.

"Repetition is my only hope of getting through to you."

She followed him to the door and leaned up against the post on the porch railing at the top of the stairs, watching him jog down to his horse and swing up on its back. He pulled the reins into his hand and turned his mount around. "See you soon," he said.

"For heaven's sake, go *on* already," she said, laughing, and wiggled her fingers at him in a playful wave good-bye.

Luca rode full bore back to the ranch, even opting to cross the river at a low point rather than ride around to the old trestle bridge.

It was a running gag, this business of not dating, but he was beginning to feel a little anxious. He had the unsettling feeling that she would bolt on him if he wasn't careful, and run off like a skittish fox. Maybe he was imagining things, but something was telling him that he and Ella were not quite on the same page.

The idea that she might not be feeling all the things he was feeling alarmed him. Which is why he intended to pull out all the stops tonight.

If she was going to bolt, at least he'd make sure she knew what she was bolting from.

Chapter Twenty-five

Ella had once read in a magazine that all a woman needed in her wardrobe was a good pair of jeans and a little black dress. She'd taken the advice to heart. She had lots of jeans, and after searching sale racks and thrift stores, she'd finally found a lovely black dress in a resale shop. It was sleeveless, made of silk and chiffon. It skimmed her legs just above her knees and had a V-neck so deep that she had to wear a special bra.

She put her hair up in a messy chignon just like she'd seen Stacy do with her hair extensions, and clipped on some fake pearl drop earrings that had not lost their luster. She added a delicate gold chain and heart necklace, the one Stacy had given to her when she'd graduated from college. *I am so proud of you, Ella,* she'd said. And then had promptly produced the receipt, in case there was any question about where she'd gotten the jewelry.

Ella slipped her feet into a pair of black stilettos and winced. She rarely wore heels this high and hoped she didn't have to walk too far, because there was a strong possibility she'd hobble herself if she did. In her bedroom, she squinted at her reflection in the tarnished mirror, turning one way, then the other. "Okay," she said to Buddy. "I think I'm ready. What do you think?"

His tail bumped hard against the wood floor.

"You probably say that to all the girls," she said.

She gave the dog a biscuit, then made sure Priscilla had plenty of water on the back porch. Then she went outside and sat carefully on the steps of the porch to wait for Luca, because God knew he'd sneak up on her in that Sombra and probably find her hiking up her Spanx. She decided Luca was right—this sagging porch would be a lot more comfortable with a couple of chairs.

Her instincts were spot on, because she saw the Sombra before she heard its faint hum. And then Luca stepped out of the car.

She was not expecting *this*. She was not expecting her heart to leap right to her throat or her stomach to flutter quite so much. The man was truly stunning, and she felt seventeen all over again, all fluttery inside. Normally, she thought there was nothing quite as sexy as a cowboy in a faded T-shirt and dirty jeans, the sign of a man who worked for a living. But *this* guy, this handsome, debonair man walking toward her now blew the cowboy out of the water.

Luca was dressed like a man of the world, in

slim black pants that fit him like a second skin, a dark blue checked jacket, and a dark blue collared shirt. He had brushed his hair back behind his ears and had shaved, and he smiled at her, all snowy white teeth and shining hazel eyes. He was breathtakingly beautiful. He looked like a real, honest-to-God prince. All he needed was a sash across his chest and a sword on his hip.

Ella slowly stood up, holding on to the railing to keep the fluttering from carrying her away.

"Wow," Luca said. He walked up the steps and took her hands in his, spreading her arms wide and smiling as he ran his gaze over her. When he lifted his eyes to hers again, he gave her a sheepish smile. "Ella . . . do you have *any* idea how beautiful you are? Bella Ella."

Bella Ella. "Thank you," she said shyly. "And *you* have outdone yourself, sir. Very dashing."

"Thank you," he said with an incline of his head. "You have no idea how badly I want to zip that dress off you right now."

"No way," she warned him, and pressed a hand to her abdomen. "I put on *Spanx* for this, and I worked up quite an appetite squeezing into this dress. You have to feed me, as promised."

He grinned. "Anything you want, Ella. Anything at all."

The fluttering in her belly morphed into what felt like a vortex of geese. No one had ever said that to her before, and she didn't know if he

345

meant it or if it was just talk, the sort of thing men said on a fancy date, but he had a way of looking at her and speaking to her that made her feel as if she mattered. As if she truly meant something to him.

And she had never meant anything to anyone.

Luca tucked her hand into the crook of his elbow and escorted her to the infamous Sombra.

On the way into the city, she examined the car and its various features. She was amazed by the technology alone. "My car is so old. I didn't know they make them like this," she said as she leaned forward to check out all the features on the dashboard.

"Your car is so old, I'm surprised you don't have to hand crank it every morning," he said, and folded her hand into his, resting it on the console, and continued to hold it for the thirty-minute drive into San Antonio.

At the Riverwalk, he pulled up to a valet stand outside a French restaurant. He tossed the key fob to the kid who jogged around to the driver's side while another attendant helped Ella from the car. "The usual place, sir?" the young man asked.

"The usual place," Luca said, and winked at Ella. With his hand on the small of her back, he escorted her inside. She breathed in the rarified air of a restaurant with tuxedoed waitstaff and tables covered in crisp white linens. It was the most upscale restaurant she'd ever been in.

"Good evening, Mr. Prince," the maître d' said. "We have your usual table ready, if you would care to follow me." He began to walk, and Luca took Ella's hand as they followed him.

"You have a usual *table?*" she whispered.

"I do," he whispered back.

The table was set before a curved booth covered in red velvet. The view was of the Riverwalk, and the doors were open to the evening air. Two young men appeared and, in a flurry, put napkins in their laps and arranged china and silver and a variety of wine glasses. The last glass of wine Ella had drunk was out of a red Solo cup.

Another man appeared before them and bowed. "I will be your wine steward this evening, Mr. Prince." He presented a menu to Ella that looked two feet long, with a double column of wines.

When the steward stepped away from the table, she looked at Luca in a slight panic. "I have no idea," she said.

"Let me show you a couple of tricks an illiterate cowboy has learned along the way," he said, and took the menu from her hand. When the steward returned to the table, Luca handed it to the steward. "Bring us your best French champagne," he said.

"Very good, Mr. Prince," the steward said.

Ella giggled as the steward stepped away. "Is *that* what you do?"

"I have for a very long time, yes, and I can say

I've had some interesting wines along the way," he said. "But I'm reading menus now," he added with a wink. He stretched his arm across the back of the booth.

Ella looked at the suave man beside her. She couldn't help but imagine how difficult it must have been for him, how many situations he'd had to learn to handle, and she felt a surge of sympathy for him.

The champagne was quickly served, and Luca touched his glass to hers. "To you," he said.

Ella smiled. "To *you*," she responded. *To us,* she wanted to say, but there was still the tiniest shadow of doubt in the back of her head, still a fear that this would all come crashing down.

The waiter appeared with the menus, but Luca waved them away. "Tell us what you recommend."

Ella almost laughed—he certainly had this down. When the waiter had gone through the options, and they'd ordered and sent him off, she said, "I'm impressed, Luca."

"Don't be," he said, grinning.

"I can't imagine how hard it must have been for you all these years."

"I've had a good life. I can't complain."

"But still," she said.

He considered her a moment. "Do you want me to say it's shameful? That I have died a thousand deaths? That every time a teacher called on me to read something or write something, I almost pissed my pants?"

"Is that true?" she asked.

He lifted his champagne and touched his flute to hers. "To a certain extent. It's kept me from relationships. From pursuing things I would have liked. Every time I got close to someone, it wasn't long before the truth reared its head, and my response was to walk away rather than let anyone know that I was afflicted with something as embarrassing as an inability to read."

"But you told me," she pointed out.

"I told you because there is something different about you, Ella. You never seemed judgmental, even when you didn't like me. You're compassionate."

Ella had never realized what a compliment it was to be called compassionate. She lifted her flute. "That might be the nicest thing anyone has ever said to me."

Over dinner—after he showed her how to use a fish fork and knife—he talked about growing up a Prince. Trips to Europe in the summers. Pursuing any hobby that struck their fancy. Nick pursued flying. Hallie pursued dancing. He pursued rodeo.

"Rodeo!" She laughed. "You never mentioned rodeo."

"I didn't? I'll have to dig out my lariat and show you a few tricks," he said with a wink.

The talk turned to her life, too. Luca wanted to know more about the various homes she'd lived in, how the stigma of not living with her parents affected her in school. He was surprised to learn the state had paid for her college tuition as it did for all foster children who wanted to go, but that she almost hadn't gone because she hadn't known what to do. There had been no one to guide her. The only guidance she'd had at all was Mrs. Ellicott, who had urged her to study accounting or finance.

Their conversation was, as always, easy and interesting. Ella loved listening to Luca talk about the land where he'd grown up. He glowed with excitement when he talked about the fundraiser and how many positive responses he'd received. "It's going to be a bigger event than Brandon and I ever anticipated," he said. "Who knew that there were environmentalists starved for a project like this?"

"That's great, Luca."

"I'm going to give a speech," he said, and smiled self-consciously. "You won't want to miss that, me and my note cards."

No, she did not want to miss that, his crowning achievement.

When Luca asked about her new client, the Ladies Auxiliary, Ella's tongue had been considerably loosened with champagne, and she blurted the talk she'd heard about his family. "I don't know why I'm telling you," she admitted. "But I don't want to have that sort of thing in my head without you knowing."

He tucked a bit of hair behind her ear that had come loose from her chignon. "Don't worry about that. Someone is always talking about the Princes. There is something online or in a paper all the time."

"Doesn't it bother you?"

"A little, maybe, but all of that gossip is just that—gossip. Most of it isn't true. People assume a lot. So I ignore it. Besides, it doesn't do me any good to let it bother me."

After dinner, when he handed off a card to the waiter without looking at the bill, Ella had to fight the urge to call the bill back so she could go over it to make sure they hadn't charged them for two bottles of champagne instead of one. Luca suggested a walk, and with his arm around her waist, they went out the river side of the restaurant and took a languid stroll along the Riverwalk. It was a gorgeous evening. Ella had been on the river many times, but it had never seemed quite as glittery or colorful as it did tonight. Strains of music drifted out at them from various music venues, punctuated by the clinks and din of people dining alfresco.

They strolled along, pausing to look at a display of piñatas, and then some pottery. But when they reached a red brick building that looked as if it had been turned from industrial to chic, Luca took her by the hand and walked into the lobby.

"Hello, Mr. Prince!" said a cheery, heavyset woman behind the reception desk.

"Hello, Jan. How's your mom?"

Jan?

"Oh, thanks for asking. She's much better. The girls were in today, so your place should be sparkling," she said, and got up, walked to the elevator banks, and punched a button.

"Thank you," he said, and tugged on Ella's hand so that she would move.

When the elevator doors closed, she said, "Where *are* we? Who is Jan?"

He smiled enigmatically, punched a code into the keypad, and continued to smile until the doors opened onto a loft.

Ella's mouth gaped. She'd seen lofts like this in movies—floor to ceiling windows, hardwood floors, and thick iron posts holding up the tall ceiling. In the center of the room was a grouping of overstuffed leather furniture on a thick shag rug. A kitchen to the left was gleaming with stainless appliances, marble counter tops, and sleek gray cabinets. And while Ella was no connoisseur, the modern art on the walls looked to be originals.

"Is this *your* place?" she asked in absolute awe.

Luca shrugged out of his jacket and unbuttoned the top of his shirt. "Yep."

She turned in a full circle to take it all in. It was

so modern, so cool. If this was his place in the city, what must Three Rivers Ranch look like? She was dumbstruck by the opulence and moved to the middle of the loft, studying the industrial ceiling with the exposed ducts, the thick windows, the hand-scraped floors. It was grander than any house she'd ever been in. She was almost afraid to touch anything. "It's amazing," she said, and turned around to face him. "It's incredible, Luca."

He seemed almost embarrassed by her awe. He went into the kitchen, opened a cabinet—when he did, the shelf automatically slid out—removed two glasses, and closed it again. "Want a nightcap?"

"Sure." She walked to the windows and leaned forward as he prepared the drinks. She could see people moving around below them on the Riverwalk like little armies of ants. She heard the clink of ice into the glasses. She heard the click of his shoes on the floor as he moved across the room. He set the glasses down, and a moment later, he was behind her, his arms around her waist.

Ella closed her eyes and leaned back against him, trying to envision nights like this. A *life* like this.

"What are you thinking?" he asked.

"That this has been a fairy-tale evening. What are you thinking?"

"How beautiful you are," he muttered, and kissed the nape of her neck before pulling free the barrette she'd used to hold her hair in place. Her hair tumbled down around her shoulders.

He moved one hand up her abdomen, to her breast. Ella opened her eyes and looked out at the night sky, the stars twinkling above all the glittering lights below. It was as if Luca's house was in the clouds, shimmering along with the rest of the world.

He slipped his hand into the vee of her dress, his skin warm. She was beginning to stir, the movement before the boil. She felt above the clouds, too, as if she were floating along in all those lights on a raft of sensation and want.

Luca slid his hand down her side and around, sliding in between her legs. "Let's go to bed," he said low.

"No," she said. "Let's stay right here."

She felt him pause, felt him lift his head from her neck and look out the window. He reached for the hem of her dress.

Ella would never know why that moment, of all the moments in Luca's company, would possess her so completely as it did, but she felt as if she was in a waking dream, drifting through snatches of imagery. A strand of lights here, a heavy cloud there. As his hands stroked her body, she felt herself flying higher and higher above the city.

Luca kept his grip on her waist, as if he feared

she would leap from the window and fly. The pleasure in his caress tormented her. She was moved by the evening, moved by his regard for her. She could feel her border wall cracking, could feel the warmth of the sun as it shone through the cracks. Something was happening to her, something that felt profound and life altering.

Her dress slipped off, and Luca tossed it onto a chair. He was not intimidated by her undergarments, sliding his hands into them and pulling them off. She was naked above the city, her hands pressed against the cool glass, her gaze on the dazzling lights below.

Luca seemed as lost in the moment as she was. His clothes had come off, too, because she could feel the heat of his skin at her back, the hardness of him against her hips. His fingers tangled in her hair, then scraped down her body, between her legs.

When he lifted her leg and slid into her from behind, Ella's heart began to race. She pressed against the glass, gasping for air, her heart feeling as if it might burst and rain down on the people below. "My God," he breathed. He pressed a hand against hers, gripping her fingers against the glass as he moved inside her.

Ella closed her eyes and dropped her head back, giving in to the night, to her soaring desire, to her affection for him, feeling it all spill through the cracks in her wall and shimmer in her blood, in her groin, in the air around them.

Luca suddenly pulled out of her and turned her around, putting her back against the window. He framed her face with his hand as he entered her again. Ella wrapped her legs around his waist, pressed herself against him, and kissed him with the heat of her desire. Their lovemaking turned ferocious, both of them striving, moving hard against each other, battering down all the barriers that remained between them. It was urgent, and when they reached the end of that ride, she burst into the rich light of a sun-filled Texas day.

They collapsed against each other, emptied of their physical desire for the moment. Luca swept her up and carried her to the couch, and the two of them fell on it, breathless and perspiring. Her arm lay limply across his chest, his foot draped hers.

She was speechless. The light was still glistening in her, and she believed in that tender moment that she really could have this life with him. That she really could run with his crowd.

He caressed her face and her hair. "This has been the best date of my life," he murmured.

"It's been the best date of my life, too."

"Did you say date?" He slowly lifted his head to look at her, and a slow, sultry smile lit his face. "Ella Kendall, are you finally *falling* for me?"

"Maybe a little," she said, and giggled.

He laughed. "Then I guess I need to get to work and push you over the edge," he said, and kissed her into oblivion.

The next morning, Ella woke up to the sound of water running and realized that Luca was in the shower. She groggily sat up and looked around her. In the daylight, she could see just how richly appointed this loft was. Everything in here was beyond what even HGTV had taught her to imagine. Last night was beyond her imagination, too—she never would have dreamed that a girl like her could end up with a man like Luca Prince, in a place like this.

They grabbed a couple of breakfast tacos on their way out of town. Ella had to work later, and Luca had a meeting with Brandon. At her house, he got out and opened the car door for her, but he didn't move toward the house. It looked so tiny and ramshackle compared to where they'd just been.

"I'm sorry, but I have to run," he said, and lifted her hand to kiss it.

"Me, too." She rose up on her toes and put her arms around his neck. "Thank you so much for last night. I had the best time."

"Thank *you*, Ella. Does this mean you'll come to the fund-raiser?"

"Luca, I don't know. I have nothing to wear to an event like that," she pointed out.

"Are you kidding? Wear what you've got on. You look like a million bucks."

Ella looked down. She loved this dress, but a fancy black tie event?

"Please say you'll come," he said. "I need you there. I need to know you're in my corner."

She *was* in his corner. "Okay," she said.

He paused. "You'll come?" he asked skeptically.

"I will."

Luca sighed. He gathered her in his arms and kissed her, hard. "Thank you. I'll call you later," he said. "I've got to run—I'm already late."

She watched him get in the Sombra and drive away, then turned toward her house, smiling to herself. She felt on top of the world. This had happened to her, and it was glorious.

Ella floated to the door and fit her key into the lock. She realized, as she pushed the door open, that the happy she was feeling was not normal for her. But oh, how she wanted it to be normal, because it felt so damn good.

She walked into her house, shut the door, turned around—and screamed.

"Don't be mad," Stacy said. She was sitting balled up on the couch, Buddy beside her. She looked gaunt. Her hair extensions were gone. Her face was red and puffy and streaked with tears.

"What the hell?" Ella demanded, her heart still

pounding from her scare. "Could you not have texted me? How did you get in?"

"I threw my phone away," she said tearfully. "And I got in through an open window in the kitchen. I really need to talk to you, Ella."

She reached down to her purse on the floor and picked it up, then tearfully, carefully, removed a revolver.

Ella cried out with alarm and fell back against the door. "What are you doing, Stacy? What have you done? Put that thing away, please! I don't want a gun in my house."

"I don't want it here either, but I need to do something with it. You have to help me, Ella. Something's happened and I'm in horrible trouble."

Ella's heart plummeted. So many familiar emotions began to bubble in her. Fear. Loathing. Compassion. *Loss.* She'd just lost the happiness, the dream, she'd walked in the door with, and she knew it.

Her little fairy tale had come to an end, and she was right back in foster care number two, the children's home. The children's home where a boy would come in several nights a week and do something to the girl in bed next to her. Ella had been seven years old and hadn't known what to do. And the girl—Ella couldn't even remember her name now—hadn't known what to do either. Her eyes had looked so dull, as if the light had gone out of them. Snuffed out by a boy in the dark. *It wasn't right. It wasn't right.*

Stacy's eyes looked just like that girl, and Ella had to figure out what to do.

Why an image of Luca should loom over her, she didn't really know, other than that vague feeling of knowing all along that whatever they had could not last.

Chapter Twenty-six

Luca met Brandon and Dr. Greg Castillo at the Hurst family ranch on the other side of Three Rivers. The Hurst ranch was old, too, like Three Rivers. The heir, Thomas Hurst, had built a bigger, grander home north of San Antonio, in the very upscale Dominion. Now, the only person who lived here full-time was Brandon's grandmother and a couple of ranch hands.

The Hurst ranch had been famed in the mid-century, but it showed signs of aging. Mrs. Hurst apparently liked the rustic charm. "It's like she's living at the Ponderosa," Brandon had once groused.

Dr. Castillo was a young environmental scientist from Trinity University in San Antonio. He was enthusiastic about what Luca and Brandon wanted to attempt with Luca's land. "This is fantastic," he said. "There are certainly opportunities for grants and outside funding. I can tell you that the university has been searching for an outdoor environmental laboratory for our students for some time."

"That's exactly the sort of thing we're hoping for," Luca said. "Conservation and the study of the environment and ecology."

"When can I take a look at your land?" Dr. Castillo asked.

They agreed on a time that they might ride out and have a look. As they were wrapping up, Blake Hurst sauntered in wearing full sheriff gear and a smug look. How he'd managed to get himself elected sheriff of Cimarron County was a mystery to Luca. He'd always been a bully. And his ridicule of Luca had been a life-long endeavor. Once, when Blake was a teen and was driving Luca and Brandon somewhere, he'd pulled up to an intersection in Three Rivers and said, "Well, look here, boys, we're lost. Luca, I'm gonna need you to read that sign over there."

Luca could remember shooting a panicked look at Brandon. Brandon had turned red and sullen, and had slid down in his seat, afraid to confront his older brother.

"What's the matter, boy? Can't you read? Cuz we're going to sit right here until you read me that sign."

Luca couldn't recall any longer how that particular day had ended, but he remembered clearly the humiliation he'd felt. Blake was still that bully, but he'd gotten good at putting on a public face and playing the role of public servant, here to protect us all. Brandon, on the other hand, was not like Blake or his father. He didn't have the physical stature or the killer instinct those two shared. When they were kids, Brandon opted to stay home with his mom when Mr. Hurst and Blake went hunting. He read books while his brother shot deer.

"What's going on here?" Blake asked congenially.

Brandon introduced him to Dr. Castillo and told him a little about what they were discussing. Blake laughed. "Still determined to find some land for tree huggers and liberal flower children, huh?"

"You like to hunt, Blake," Brandon pointed out.

"Yeah, we'll see if there's anything out there to hunt other than bunnies," he said, and chuckled as he settled himself into a seat and picked up a magazine.

"I should go," Dr. Castillo said, looking at his watch.

Brandon showed the professor out, leaving Luca alone with Blake.

Blake never looked up from his magazine.

When Brandon returned, he was holding a couple of beers. "That went well, don't you think?" he asked Luca.

"I do," Luca agreed. He didn't say more—he didn't want to talk about their plans and listen to Blake's negative opinions.

"This fund-raiser is going to be fantastic," Brandon said, and tapped his beer to Luca's. "Is Ella coming?"

"I think she will."

"Who's Ella?" Blake asked, looking up from his magazine.

"You met her at the Magnolia," Brandon reminded him. "She moved out to the old Kendall place."

Blake seemed surprised and then thoughtful. "The Kendall place," he repeated. "I thought it was abandoned. Ella Kendall?"

"Right," Luca said, feeling strangely uncomfortable. "Do you know her?"

"Nah," Blake said, and looked at his magazine. "But I know someone who talks about her a lot."

"Who's that?" Brandon asked curiously.

"Doesn't matter," Blake said.

Brandon rolled his eyes. "So, Luca, I've got some time tomorrow if you want to go through the presentation. Are you free?"

"Sure," Luca said, and stood up. He didn't like being around Blake and his strangely aggressive energy. "I'll call you," he said to Brandon.

"You didn't finish your beer," Brandon complained.

"Sorry, man. I didn't see the time." He left as Blake pretended to casually peruse his magazine.

On the drive home, Luca phoned Ella, but the call rolled to voice mail. He didn't leave a message—she would see he called, and he would try again in a couple of hours.

He called Hallie next, who was meeting with her wedding planner about the finishing touches for the fund-raiser. "Luca!" she said excitedly. "This fund-raiser is going to be *dope!*"

Luca held his phone away from his ear and looked at it. *"Dope?"* he said, and put the phone to his ear again. "I've never heard you use that word."

"You don't understand, Luca. There will be trees and lights and *two* bars, and the food will be to die for!"

"Wait," Luca said, feeling a small tic of alarm. His sister could spend money like it was her job. "How much is this going to cost?"

"Don't worry about it. We'll make it back in spades with all the money that's going to roll in."

"We are not *making* money, Hallie. We are asking for grants for specific purposes." But Hallie was still talking, oblivious to the fact that Luca wasn't on board with everything she had planned. When Hallie took on a project, she took it *on.*

She was *still* talking when he pulled up to the house at Three Rivers. "Hallie. *Hallie,*" he said, a little louder.

"What?"

"I've gotta get off the phone. My ear is burning."

"Fine, go. I've got this, Luca!"

That's what he was most afraid of.

His intent was to make a quick change of clothes and then go to Ella's. But as he walked through the garden, he came upon his mother and grandmother. His grandma was sitting at a table under an umbrella, sipping lemonade and reading *People* magazine. Her hair was pink now, he noticed, and she had taken to wearing shiny gold Nikes.

But it was his mother who really caught his attention. She was down on her knees, planting something in a freshly emptied bed. He had never seen her garden before. Ever. They had staff for that sort of thing. Or, at least, they had before his father had died. "What are you doing?"

"Planting the roses I wanted here and your father didn't, that's what," she said pertly.

"He didn't want them there because they won't get enough sun, Delia," his grandma said without looking up from her magazine.

"Says you," his mom responded.

"Says me and the landscaper Martin hired to create this garden."

"They'll grow," his mother said stubbornly. "Just you hide and watch."

"Frankly, I'd rather watch dust collect in my navel," Grandma said, and put down her magazine. She propped one gold foot on the table. "Lucas, did I ever tell you about Maria Ford? She lived down Parker Lane."

Luca and his mother looked at each other. "There's nothing down Parker Lane, Grandma. It's just a pass-through," Luca said.

"Exactly," she said, with a nod. "That's how spooky she was. She lived down there somewhere, no one knew where, and she grew these giant roses the size of salad plates. Everyone said it was impossible to grow them that big, but here she'd come to Saturday market with 'em."

"And your point?" his mom asked as she dug another hole.

"Just that there is nothing but sun down there. She grew those roses in sun. You know what else she grew down there, don't you? Wacky weed." She laughed. "I swear on the grave of my husband you could smell it all the way over here."

Luca's mother used the back of her hand to wipe perspiration from her brow. "That's at least five miles from here," she said. "You couldn't smell it."

"Damn sure could. Had to send my kids to bed early so they wouldn't notice it. They say that weed is a gateway drug, you know."

"Well, Luca, it looks like your grandmother is now an expert in gateway drugs," his mother said.

"Now, truth be told, Grandpa and I didn't mind a little bit of the wacky weed now and again."

She waggled her brows at Luca. "That was the sixties for you."

"And that's your grandson you're bragging to," his mother said.

"Well, I know, Delia. I can see him plain as day. Anyway, Lucas, roses need sun, that's all I'm saying."

"Okay, Grandma," Luca said with a grin.

His mother looked at him, eyeing him curiously. "What are you doing?"

"I'm going to change clothes, then head out. I've got some things I need to do."

"Hallie says you're seeing someone," his mother said bluntly.

Great. He would thank Hallie for this later. "Mom? I'm thirty. I see lots of people."

"What, I can't want my son to have a love life? When do I get to meet her?"

"Maybe when you stop taking naps on Dad's grave and planting rosebushes where they don't get any sun," he suggested.

His mother blinked. She turned her attention back to the flower bed, and she looked a little stung. Luca instantly regretted his tone. "I'm bringing her to the fund-raiser," he said.

"Oh, goody," his grandmother said. "I can't wait. I like to cut a rug."

"It's not that kind of party, Grandma."

"Who says we can't make it one?" she asked cheerfully.

"I do," Luca said sternly. "No shenanigans from you, Grandma. This is a big deal for me."

"I guess it is for me, too, if you're bringing your girlfriend," his mother said, and began to dig with a vengeance. "You never bring anyone around. I wish I'd known it was because of my flower beds, because I would have put them on hold."

Luca sighed. "I'm sorry, Mom. I shouldn't have snapped. I better go. I'm running late," he said, and walked on to the house.

"Chicken!" his mother shouted after him, and his grandmother laughed.

After he changed, Luca tried Ella again and still got no answer. He decided she must be working. He'd try her again after he ran by the Saddlebush offices. He'd made an appointment with Charlotte, the office manager, to go over some of his finances.

In the foyer of the Saddlebush offices—made to look like a rustic barn at a cost Luca could not possibly fathom—Charlotte met him with a smile. "Hey, Luca, it's so good to see you," she said. "It's like old home week—your uncle is here, too."

"Chet?" That would save Luca a trip—Uncle Chet was his second errand of the day.

"Yep. He's in with Nick."

Luca walked back to his dad's old office. The door was open, and he could see Nick in the chair his father had once occupied, one boot up on the desk, his cowboy hat tossed onto the desk. Luca had never really noticed how much Nick looked like their father.

Uncle Chet was sitting across from Nick in one of the leather seats. "Hey!" he said when Luca entered. "Look what the wind blew in, will you?"

"Hey, kid," Nick said.

Luca sat down and asked how they were. The three men chatted about the family business— Nick's angst had been quietly ratcheting up, and he was in the midst of asking Uncle Chet for advice to improve their cash flow.

Uncle Chet ran through various options, then said, "It all comes down to diversification, Nick. Just like our boy, Luca, here," he said with a grin.

"Yeah, about that," Luca said, and dug into his pocket for a key. "I was coming to see you today, Uncle Chet. I've got something for you."

"What's that?"

Luca handed him the key to the dealership. He didn't know if it was a symbolic key or real— he'd never been in the office before or after hours—but it was the one Chet had given him when he'd gifted him the Sombra dealership.

"Is that what I think it is?" Uncle Chet asked.

"Yep."

Uncle Chet sat up. "Why are you giving it to me?"

"As much as I appreciate what you did for me,

I have to give it back to you, Uncle Chet. I'm not running it. You and Victor are running it. And Victor is great at his job. He should be the general manager. Not me."

"Luca," he said, already sounding disappointed. "You'd be great at it, too, if you'd show up—"

Luca shook his head. "It's not for me."

Uncle Chet frowned. "Luca . . . you need *something*. What's better than the electric car that's going to rival Tesla? It can be lucrative, and it conserves energy like you like—"

"But I've already got something," Luca calmly reminded his uncle.

"Is it the reading thing? Because if it is, Victor can brief you."

Luca glanced at Nick, whose expression suggested that he, too, wanted to know if it was the reading thing. Luca swiped up a paper from the desk and read, haltingly—but *read,* "Hey . . . Nick ran into . . . Thompson last week," he read. *Was that how you spelled Thompson? What was the H for?* "He said you've got a deal on some . . . pal . . . pal-o-minos."

His reading was met with silence for a moment. Then Nick lowered his foot, planted his arms on the desk, and said, "Knock me over with a feather. Are you kidding me, Luca? Did you just read that?"

Luca tossed the paper down and looked at his uncle. "It's not because I can't read. It's because

371

I hate it. I'm not a car guy, Uncle Chet. I'm not a salesman."

Chet's mouth gaped.

"That doesn't mean that I don't appreciate all you've done for me," he hastened to assure his uncle. "In fact, I can't ever thank you enough for it. But it's not my thing."

"What is your thing, Luca?" Uncle Chet asked. "Letting two thousand acres go wild? I get it, son, but you can't make a living that way. You'll go broke before you've turned it around."

"I may already be broke after letting Hallie plan the fund-raiser," Luca said with a wry laugh. "But I don't think I will. I can make money with hunting and recreational leases."

"Those won't pay enough," Uncle Chet said with a flick of his hand.

"I agree, they won't pay the kind of money the Princes are used to. But I ought to make enough to get by. And if I lose it? Well, I will have lost it on something that means a lot to me. It's mine to lose."

"Luca," Uncle Chet said, and rubbed his face with his hands in a manner that suggested he was trying to keep his cool. "For heaven's sake, I wish Charlie was here to talk some sense into you. Listen, kid, all your life you've been flitting from one thing to the next. This is the craziest yet. Tell him, Nick."

Luca braced himself to hear Nick's opinion.

But Nick looked at him and shrugged. "I think if Dad were here, he'd say do whatever makes you happy, Luca. A lot of us don't get the chance to do what we love." He gestured to himself in that chair. "You've figured out how to have your chance, and I say, go for it."

Uncle Chet glared at Nick. "Are you yanking my chain?"

"Nope," Nick said. "I'm disagreeing with you."

Luca gave his brother a smile of gratitude. "Thanks, Nick. See you at the fund-raiser?"

"I wouldn't miss it," Nick said.

Luca stood up and hugged his uncle to take some of the sting out of his disbelief. He left the two men to meet with Charlotte. Two hours later, he walked outside and called Ella. No answer.

She didn't answer that night either. Or the next day. Luca tried not to read too much into it. It had only been a couple of days. They'd gone that long without speaking before. But the difference was they'd gone that long without speaking before the night in San Antonio.

It seemed off.

He began to imagine all kinds of things, like she'd gotten hurt out there by herself, or her car had broken down somewhere and she was stranded. So the following day, he rode out to Ella's house, traveling through cedars and the marshy part of the river. He was wet to the knees and sweating when he finally rode across the dead pasture to the Kendall house.

Buddy saw him first and came bounding off the porch, eager to see his old pal, Ranger, the horse. Buddy loved horses. He probably thought he was one.

A moment later, Ella walked out onto the porch barefoot, in a summer dress, and with her hair piled on top of her head. His heart skipped around, relieved that she was all right. He was eager to touch her.

She smiled as he swung off his horse and looped the reins over the fence.

"You're okay," he said. "I thought something might have happened. You haven't returned my calls."

"What?" She laughed. But it was a laugh Luca had never heard from her before. "I'm fine!"

"Then maybe you've been avoiding me," he said, and smiled.

She laughed again in that strange way, too loud, too much. It was odd. "Not at all. I've been busy."

That phrase sent a paroxysm of dread straight through him. He walked up to the porch steps, his smile gone. "Super busy?"

"You would not believe," she said with a shake of her head. "I had to watch some paint dry yesterday. Took all day." She smiled thinly and looked down. To avoid his gaze?

374

"You must be exhausted," he said, and rubbed his hand on his nape. "Any reason why you couldn't pick up a phone while you were watching it dry?"

"Oh." She plucked at the seam of a pocket on the front of her dress. "It was dead. I didn't know it was dead."

He didn't believe her. But he also couldn't believe she would lie to him about something so benign. A thousand thoughts riffled through his head, and he rubbed his nape again, trying to work it out. She wasn't talking, just watching him, fiddling with the seam of that pocket. "Mind if I have some of your good well water? It's getting hot."

"Oh." She glanced over her shoulder at the house. "Sure. Come in."

She acted as if she was hiding something. It was bizarre—what could she possibly have to hide? Luca followed her inside and looked around. Everything looked the same. The door to her bedroom was closed, maybe to keep Buddy out of there. There was a purse on the kitchen table and one in a chair, which seemed like one too many purses to him, but who knew with women and their purses? Hallie had dozens.

He followed Ella into the kitchen. She turned on the faucet, and he put his arms around her middle and kissed her cheek. "I've missed you," he murmured.

"I've missed you, too," she whispered.

He kissed her neck. "Why are you whispering? Is it a secret?"

She just laughed and turned around, handing him the glass of water. But Luca put it aside and kissed her. She felt the same, tasted the same, responded the same by curving into him and sighing into his mouth. What was happening? What was so different about her? Luca lifted his head and took her by the hand. "Come on," he said, and tugged her away from the counter, intending to take her to bed.

"No," she said quickly, and pulled him back. "I, ah . . . I've got a bad headache," she said, and winced.

Luca stared at her, stunned. "Did you seriously just use the I've-got-a-headache excuse?"

"It happens to be true," she said, and winced again. Not as if she were in pain. As if she felt sorry for him.

Something inside Luca detached and fell, some piece of him knocking against his organs and sending a shock up his spine. This was so wrong, so off, and he didn't get it, and he knew instinctively that she was not going to tell him. He felt like an idiot. So he said, "Okay," and leaned in and kissed her.

Ella lingered, folding into him, as if she wanted him to kiss her, as if she wanted him to make love to her, and Luca was so flummoxed that he stepped back, downed the water, and without a word, walked out of her house.

She followed him, and on the porch, she slipped her fingers into his. He clutched her hand as they walked down the steps to his horse, where Buddy was stretched out in the shade the horse provided. Luca racked his brain—had he said anything? Done something to offend her? But finding nothing, he took the head-on approach. "Is there anything you want to tell me, Ella?"

Her lashes fluttered, and she averted her gaze, looking at the ground. "No, nothing. I'm sorry," she said, and lifted her gaze to him. "I'm just having an off day."

"Is it your period?" he asked, hoping that he wasn't out of bounds.

She shook her head and looked at the ground again. "A headache."

"Ella," he said, and dipped down so that he was eye level, forcing her to see him. "You can't even *look* at me."

"Yes, I can," she said, but she was looking away. "My head is killing me, Luca. I'm so sorry, but I don't feel good."

He did not believe her. Not for a moment. But he swung up on his horse and leaned down one last time to kiss her. "Call me when you feel better, okay?"

"I will," she said, and she looked as if she wanted to cry.

Luca reined away from her and spurred his horse to a canter.

He already knew she wouldn't call. He had rarely been on the receiving end of a breakup, so he was no expert, but this had all the signs of it, and he felt like he would be sick.

For the first time ever, he wasn't ready for a relationship to end. And he didn't have a clue how to stop it.

Chapter Twenty-seven

Ella stood in the very spot Luca had kissed her before he mounted his horse. She watched him ride across the field, wanting to shout at him to come back. Wanting to drop to her knees and confess everything.

But she didn't.

She wrapped her arms around her and went back inside. When she shut the door, Stacy came out of the bedroom. "Was *that* a booty call?"

"No."

"No!" Stacy laughed with disbelief. "What else do you call it? He rode over here in the middle of the day like the Marlboro man because he wanted to fuck you."

Ella winced at her choice of words. "Please don't say that," she said. "It's not like that."

Stacy stared at her. "Oh my God, Ella . . . you're not really falling for his bullshit, are you?"

"It's not bullshit—"

"Sure, you tell yourself it's not," Stacy said. "But we both know it is."

This was so typically Stacy—every man was

a dick. "Why are you doing this?" she suddenly exploded. "Could you for once let me have something without ruining it? Just once, Stacy!"

Stacy gasped. *"Wow,"* she said. "So I ruin everything, is that it?"

Ella groaned. She didn't want to fight. "I'm sorry—"

"No, don't be sorry," Stacy said with a dismissive flick of her wrist. "The truth comes out when we're pissed. And honestly, I'd rather know the truth from you than have you be another liar in a long line of them," she said, and marched into the kitchen.

Ella marched after her. "You want the truth? Okay, here it is—I'm pissed that you have to run it down because I really like Luca, Stacy." She more than liked him. She thought she might actually love him.

"I'm not running it down, Ella. I'm giving you a freaking reality check, okay? Because I don't want you to get hurt! I know you better than anyone else, and I know you keep your heart so guarded because it breaks so easily, and trust me, *that* guy," she said, jabbing her finger in the direction of the door, "is going to break your heart." She reached into the fridge for a soda.

"No, he's not," Ella scoffed.

"Okay," Stacy said. "So where is it going with you two? Do you think he'll actually marry you?"

"I don't know!" Ella said angrily. She had not

allowed herself to think that far ahead. "You don't even *know* him."

"I've known a dozen Prince Lucas. The music industry is crawling with them. They wine you and dine you, but they only want one thing, and when they get tired of it, they get tired of you. The moment you tell them you don't know who your parents are, they get tired of you. The moment you tell them about the time your foster dad touched you, or admit that no, you weren't a cheerleader because you were in juvenile detention, they are through with you."

"That's you, Stacy," Ella said. "Not me."

"Oh, really?" Stacy asked with a withering look. "So have you told him about your mother?" she asked, and brushed past Ella on her way to the living room. She plopped down on the couch. "You'd be doing yourself a huge favor if you forget this high school fantasy and come to Nashville with us."

"Are you crazy?" Ella cried. "How do you know you won't be in jail?" This had been an ongoing theme since Ella had found Stacy in her living room, hiding from the sheriff of Cimarron County. Stacy tried to paint it as the two of them united against the world. Ella kept reminding her that she was the one who had fought the sheriff, taken his gun, and threatened him with it.

It didn't matter that the sheriff had tried to rape her. It was Stacy's word against his.

"I believe in karma," Stacy said. "You can be our accountant slash manager. Managers make good money."

"I don't know anything about managing a band," Ella impatiently reminded her. Stacy seemed to think all she had to do was say she was a manager, and voilà, Ella suddenly possessed knowledge and skills.

"We don't know anything about the recording industry either. We're all learning as we go. Come on, El, what are you going to *do* here? Live in a house that's falling down around your ears and pick up more church-lady clients?"

How was it that every time Stacy talked about Ella's life, she made it sound so sad? "Stop," Ella said sharply. "At least I don't have a sheriff looking for me right now. Maybe don't worry about me and worry about what you're going to do with yourself."

Stacy's face suddenly fell. "I know," she said morosely. "You're right. I've been thinking about what happened, and what to do. But the thing is, no one will believe me. You know they won't."

Ella didn't want to say it, but she was right— no one would believe Stacy Perry.

Stacy had told her everything, beginning with how the sheriff's sexual harassment had escalated. All those weeks Stacy was trying to talk to Ella, and Ella had been avoiding her, Stacy had been fending off his advances. The night Ella had been living a dream in Luca's loft, Stacy had worked late, trying to make some extra money. The sheriff had stayed after everyone had gone, and when Stacy refused his blatant advances, he'd gotten angry and tried to rape her. But Stacy was a street fighter, and she'd fought back. Somehow, in the struggle, she'd grabbed his gun. And then she'd pointed it at him and threatened to shoot him.

The sheriff was furious and swore he would lock her up for good. He told her he could easily trump up some theft charges, because everyone around town knew she was stealing.

"Mariah must have told him," Stacy had said tearfully. "I can't believe she ratted me out!"

The sheriff had mentioned some other things—a bracelet, a pair of shoes, someone's phone—that Stacy swore on her life to Ella she'd not taken as she'd dabbed at her tears. "I swear it!" she'd said when Ella appeared dubious. "But it doesn't matter! He'll make sure there is evidence to support whatever he arrests me for."

"Is there anything else?" Ella asked. She'd been trying to assess the damage, to understand how much trouble Stacy really was in—and by extension, herself.

"No," Stacy had said, and had buried her face in a pillow and sobbed.

Over the next two days, as they'd debated what to do, Ella had determined that the biggest problem was the gun. She tried to convince Stacy

383

to turn it in anonymously. "Leave it on the office doorstep," she said.

"I think I should dump it in that lake behind your house," Stacy argued.

Ella instantly thought of Luca and how he'd talked about the delicate ecosystem in that spring. "Great, and when you're gone and they find it, they charge me?"

"You'll be long gone," Stacy had said.

"No, Stacy, I won't!" Ella had shouted at her. "This is *my house*. I'm not leaving it."

"Why are you so married to this house?" Stacy demanded. "Because it's not much of one, Ella. It's like you're clinging to an empty box, some place to hide yourself from the world. It's basically just another wall, don't you get it? Come with me to Nashville. Start fresh."

"I am clinging to it because it is mine, Stacy. No one can move me to another foster home. I belong to this house, and it belongs to me."

Their arguing had bled into today, and it had only gotten worse. Stacy had begged Ella to pick up a prepaid cell phone for her. Ella had finally given in. Stacy had called Wells, the guitar player in her band. Wells reported that a sheriff's deputy had pounded on his door this morning asking if he knew where she was. "He said they've got an arrest warrant," Wells said.

"No, they don't," Stacy had scoffed, but had pulled a face of sheer panic to Ella.

She ended the call, tossed the phone into her purse, and said, "I have to get out of here. I'm going nuts."

"Could you get a lawyer?" Ella asked. "Tell him or her what happened?"

"I hardly have enough money to *move*, Ella. How am I going to pay for a lawyer? Anyway, I'm not missing my chance to go to Nashville."

It was as if she thought if she made it in Nashville, all would be forgotten. "You can't run from this, Stacy."

"Like hell I can't," Stacy had muttered. "I didn't do anything wrong. I was defending my—" She suddenly paused and slapped a hand to the window, peering out. "Oh my God," she said. *"Oh my God!"*

"What?" Ella ran to the window to look out and saw what had Stacy hyperventilating next to her. A sheriff's patrol car was coming down the road to her house. She and Stacy turned stunned gazes to each other. Then Stacy ran into the bedroom and shut the door.

Ella tried to calm her heart. She walked in a tight circle, shaking her hands, taking deep breaths. *Pretend it's drama class.* The shut of the patrol car door made her jump.

"You're in a play. You're acting. Act!" It was a trick she'd taught her teenage self—never let them know how you really feel.

She heard the footfall on the steps, the creak of the porch under a man's weight. And then the inevitable knock on the door. Ella's heart was beating so hard that she was certain he would be able to see it leaping out of her chest. She took several deep breaths, then went to the door and opened it. She said nothing but stared at the sheriff through her screen door.

"Hello," he said, and cupped his hand around his eyes, leaned forward, and peered in. "Ella Kendall, right?"

"Yes. Why?"

"You have a couple of minutes, Miss Kendall?" he asked congenially.

"I really don't," she said, and looked at her watch. "I have to get to work."

"Do you? Because I swung by the Magnolia and they said you weren't on the schedule."

She wanted to kick herself. "I'm also an accountant."

The sheriff gave her an oily little smile, yanked her screen door open, and stepped inside, almost knocking her over as he pushed past her. "By all means, come in," she said wryly.

"I'm looking for a friend of yours," he said, as he looked around her cluttered living room.

Ella saw Stacy's purse on the chair. Her purse was on the kitchen table. Her palms turned damp. "Who?"

"Stacy Perry," he said, watching her closely.

Ella furrowed her brow. She shook her head. "I haven't seen her in weeks."

"Have you talked to her?"

"Nope." Ella slipped her hands into the pocket of her dress and hoped he couldn't see her shaking. She felt like a quivering mass of gelatin.

"You sure about that?" He hooked his thumbs into his gun belt and glanced around the room, his eyes lingering here and there.

"Yes."

"Not even a phone call? A text? I thought you two were friends." He looked at her again.

Ella's heart was racing ahead of her thoughts. "She's been calling, but I haven't picked up."

"Why not?"

Ella could feel the panic growing in her, slowly clawing its way up her throat. Any moment now, she would be choking with it. "I'm pretty mad at her right now, to be honest. I don't want to talk to her. Why are you looking for her?"

"Why are you mad at her?" he countered.

Ella sized him up. "She doesn't like my boyfriend."

He gave her that snakish smile again. "Who, Luca Prince?"

How did he know that? Ella did not move. She refused to give him any more than he already knew.

"I'd really like to talk to her. I don't like people stealing in Cimarron County, Ms. Kendall."

"Stealing!"

"You heard me." The sheriff moved closer to where she was standing. He was a big man and a rapist, and he was looming over her. "You know what I hate worse?"

Ella shook her head.

"Someone who helps a person like that."

How she managed to keep her composure, Ella couldn't say. But she responded, "You and me both, sir," as if they'd both appeared at her house riding the same high horse.

The sheriff's eyes took on a sheen she didn't like, and his gaze drifted slowly down her body. "You like Luca?"

That caught her off guard, and her mask slipped. "What?"

The sheriff smirked. "I'd be careful if I were you. I wouldn't want him to hear anything bad about you. Anything that might cause him to push you off the gravy train."

The swell of indignation in her was so swift she had to quickly swallow it down to keep from punching him in the mouth. "And what would that be?" she asked as casually as she could.

"Like . . . you're harboring a fugitive from the law."

"Except that I'm not harboring a fugitive."

"Well, if that's true, you won't mind if I have a look around, will you?" he said.

"I mind your being in my house at all, sir.

I've done nothing wrong and I don't like the insinuations. Don't you need a warrant or something to come in here?"

"Don't get uppity, Ella," he said smoothly. "I've been looking at some records, and you and Miss Stacy have been in trouble more than once."

She stilled. "I haven't been in any trouble."

"Not you? Then why is your name on the incident report at the Dollar Store?"

This was exactly what Ella had tried to make Stacy understand. She had not been arrested, only because they found no merchandise on her. But she was guilty by association. She narrowed her gaze and said, "Are you talking about something that happened thirteen years ago? I'm sorry, sheriff, but unless you have a warrant or whatever, I need you to go. I have to go to work."

He chuckled as if she amused him. "Okay, Ella. I'll come back when I have that warrant. In the meantime, I'll be watching every little thing you do. I'll see you at the Magnolia Bar and Grill." He smiled and looked around her living room again, his gaze lingering on the closed bedroom door, and then sauntered out.

Ella was shaking so badly that she could hardly lock the door behind him. She grabbed the windowsill to keep from collapsing and watched him drive away. When she was certain he wasn't going to turn around, she shouted, "Okay!"

Stacy quietly opened the bedroom door. "We have to get out of here," she said.

"No, *you* have to get out of here," Ella countered. She picked up Stacy's purse from the floor and pushed it against her. "I'm not going to jail for you, Stacy. Get someone to come pick you up."

"Who? And how?"

"He knows you're here!" Ella exploded, her arms flailing as she pointed at the door.

"No he doesn't—he's too stupid."

Ella gaped at her. Stacy lived every day as if she were a fugitive. She didn't take life seriously; she just flitted about, expecting that everything would work out like she wanted. She was always criticizing Ella, telling her that she had this giant wall around her, and maybe she did, but at least Ella took her life seriously.

It had been only a couple of days ago she'd had that magical, beautiful evening with Luca. She had never felt that alive in her life. Like she *mattered* to someone. Like she could be normal for once in her life. And here was Stacy, ready to bring it all crashing down around her. "I don't know how you do it, Stacy, but I want you out."

Stacy's bottom lip quivered. "Are you kidding me?"

Ella shook her head.

Clutching her purse, Stacy twirled around and marched into Ella's bedroom and slammed the door. "That's my bedroom," Ella said after her, but fell on the couch, knowing Stacy wouldn't come out until she was ready.

The thing that sucked the most about this was not the fear of what could happen. Fear was something Ella had lived with all her life. What sucked the most was Luca. She had begun to believe that she could really have something with him, but Stacy was right—she couldn't escape her past or who she was. Neither could he. It was better to end it now, before she was in too deep. Before this thing between them seared her and left a lasting scar. And it was better that she not see him abandon her, because that would be the death of her. She couldn't bear that much hurt. Better to get ahead of it.

He would hate her, but he'd get over her.

Ella wasn't sure she could say the same for herself.

Chapter Twenty-eight

She could have predicted Stacy wouldn't leave that night. She did her fair share of stomping around to make sure Ella knew she was mad that Ella wasn't being as understanding as Stacy thought she ought to be. Ella didn't have time to care about Stacy—she was living on a razor's edge, waiting for the sound of sirens and then patrol cars to roar up to her house and surround them.

She was due to go to work the next day but called in sick.

"You're just raising suspicion," Stacy said. "You have to act normal or everyone will think you're hiding something."

"Okay, hold that thought," Ella said. "I just need to take some notes here about how to act when I'm literally hiding something."

Stacy glared at her.

"I can't think," Ella said. "It's bad enough that I'm trying to do some bookkeeping while you're here. I've probably made all kinds of mistakes."

"Well, pardon me for breathing!" Stacy snapped.

When they weren't arguing, Stacy was practicing her singing, as if *she* had nothing to fear. Only Ella.

But the sheriff didn't come.

The next day, Ella made herself go to work. Byron looked at her strangely, as if he couldn't quite make her out, then shrugged and handed her some files. She worked at her desk, but every car that pulled into the parking lot was a cop. Every person who walked past the door was Sheriff Hurst.

She drove home in a mood, her thoughts full of doubts and questions about how in the hell she was going to get rid of Stacy and that damn gun. So much so that she didn't notice Luca's truck parked under the oak tree until she was right up on it. She panicked. If he'd seen Stacy, it was the beginning of the end. He was sitting on the porch, his elbows on his knees.

Ella cautiously stepped out of her car and looked around, not entirely certain that Luca hadn't brought Sheriff Hurst here with him. "Hey," she said.

"Hey." He wasn't smiling. He looked dark as he stood up from the porch. "You could really use some porch chairs."

He didn't sound angry. Maybe disillusioned? "Have you been waiting long?" she asked.

He shook his head.

Ella made herself walk around the front of her

car. She hated being caught off guard—her tongue felt thick in her mouth. Luca had been a constant thought the last few days, swimming around the edges of her consciousness. She'd been so stressed about being caught hiding Stacy that she hadn't been able to think past missing him.

"I thought I might have heard from you by now," he said. "And when I didn't, I came to see if everything is okay. That must be some headache."

"What?"

He lifted his chin slightly. "You said you had a bad headache."

"Oh." She unthinkingly pressed two fingers to her forehead. She'd forgotten what she'd said; her mind had been a jumble. "I'm sorry—I've had a lot on my mind."

His hard expression softened. "Is there anything I can do?"

Oh, how she wished he could help. But she wouldn't dare tell him. She wouldn't risk him going to his friend, the sheriff. She wouldn't dare risk making him a party to this awful, horrible mess she was in. She shook her head and tried to smile. "It's nothing."

Luca stepped down from the porch. "Well, it's not nothing, Ella. What's going on? We had a great date. We've had a great *month*. And then suddenly, you disappear on me. You practically ghosted me."

"I know," she said, nodding, and pushed her hand through her hair trying to think of how to say it. "I guess I've been trying to avoid this. Luca . . . I can't go to your fund-raiser." Her voice sounded pathetically small and weak. "I can't . . . do this."

Luca's face paled. She had stunned him. "Why not?"

"I just can't," she said. "It's not me. I don't belong there, I—"

"Will you stop with that horseshit?" he said sharply. "You belong there. You belong anywhere you want to be. I won't accept that as a reason, Ella. So, is it me? Have I offended you?"

"No!" she insisted. "Luca, you've been amazing." He'd been so amazing that he was wrapped around her heart, which made this all the more painful. "But I warned you, Luca. I told you I wouldn't fall."

He looked sick, as if she'd kicked him in the groin. "So the takeaway is that the last few weeks with us have meant nothing to you, huh? It's all been fun and games?"

"I didn't say that—"

"Yeah, well, you don't have to, Ella," he said coolly. "It's obvious I don't mean to you what you mean to me."

"We had a great time—"

He threw up a hand between them to silence her. He swallowed. Twice. "I laid everything on the line with you. I have told you everything about me. *Everything.* I've done everything I know to show you that I care about you. I thought we had something special. If you don't want it, then for fuck's sake, say so. But you've been sending so many mixed signals I don't know which way is up."

She felt the first tear slide down her face. She'd read a long time ago that in order to understand true love, you had to once be broken by it and had to once do the breaking. She was doing the breaking, but she felt broken. "I'm just not good at being part of a *we*."

His expression shuttered. He glowered at her, unsatisfied with her response, as well he should be. He stepped around her and walked to his truck.

"Luca?"

When he reached the driver's door, he turned around and pointed at her. "I love you, Ella Kendall. Is that what you needed to hear? I *love* you."

Well, there it was, the cleaving of her heart in two.

"I don't know why I do, particularly given the way you've treated me the last few days. I don't know what the fuck I will do now, but you need to know that I have fallen in love with you. Personally, I think you are so afraid of letting anyone get close to you that you can't see over all the damn obstacles you keep putting in the way."

"That's not true," she insisted.

"Deny it, then. Tell me that you're not fearful that if you love me, too, I will walk away. Tell me the reason you refuse to fall is because you're afraid you will end up in pieces."

How was he so perceptive? She put her hands behind her head and tried to think.

"*Everyone* fears that. But it doesn't stop most people from going for it because the alternative is so good. I'm telling you—I've *been* telling you—that I'm not walking away from you. If you fall, I am here to catch you. I will catch you, and I will hold you close."

"Luca, I—"

But he wasn't finished. He took a step toward her. "You know who the player is here, Ella? It's *you*. You play with people's feelings. You say you're not into me, and you kiss me, and you make love to me, and then you push me away without any reason." He laughed bitterly. "And I'm the stupid fool who keeps taking it. I keep wearing my heart on my sleeve. And by the way? Your timing is the worst. In two days, I am going to get up on a stage in the biggest classroom I've ever been in, and I'm going to read. I really hoped you'd be there so that you could see all that I have worked to achieve, but more than that, because I need you. I want someone who believes in me to be there, rooting for me, because I promise you, everyone else in that crowd will be waiting for me to falter. But standing here, right now, I'm glad you won't make it. You don't deserve to see me."

He was right. He was *so right.* "That's what I've been trying to tell you, Luca. I don't deserve it."

He made a sound of disgust. "Have fun feeling sorry for yourself," he said, and got in his truck.

She watched him drive away, the dust billowing up in a great white cloud so that she couldn't see the vehicle. She finally waved the dust away and turned around.

The front door opened, and Stacy stepped halfway out of it. "Are you okay?" she called to Ella.

The last person Ella wanted to talk to at that moment was Stacy. She ignored her and walked to the back of her house and down to the fence where the horses would come in the afternoon. They weren't around, naturally. Neither was Buddy. Only Priscilla wandered over, pausing to sniff at the chickens.

The horses. Ella was just like them. Wild and feral, skittish and distrustful. They'd been left to fend for themselves, and so had she most of her life. And it had cost her a love.

She had no one to blame but herself. Stacy may have been the catalyst, but Ella had been convinced from the moment she'd laid eyes on Luca that she wasn't worthy, and she'd willed their relationship to end this way. She was incapable of tearing down the walls around her heart.

The sobs began to rumble from somewhere deep in her body, erupting from her mouth and pushing her to her knees. She hated herself right now, but she didn't know how to stop being who she was. She didn't know how to tear down her walls.

Chapter Twenty-nine

On the afternoon of the fund-raiser, there were so many people at Three Rivers Ranch running around and setting up tents and bars that Cordelia went to Charlie's grave. This was not her event— Hallie had made that very clear, taking over in a way that reminded Cordelia of herself many years ago, and annoying her as she had surely annoyed Dolly. Actually, what Hallie said was, "Thanks, Mom, for your suggestions. But I think you would be more helpful in your room right now."

Cordelia knew when she wasn't wanted, so she'd walked up the hill.

She had installed a folding lawn chair that she'd picked up at Walmart last week. Cordelia had never been in a Walmart before then and, frankly, was amazed at all Walmart had to sell. Everything a person could want was there, brightly crammed into what seemed like five hundred separate aisles. She'd walked up and down those aisles like a wanderer, picking up things, examining them, putting them down.

When she left, she had a lawn chair, a bird feeder, and a cooler that also acted as an end table.

Cordelia was seated in her lawn chair with a drink in hand. A screwdriver, if anyone was interested. So shoot her, already—it had been a stressful week and a stressful day, and she was allowed to self-medicate in the middle of the day if she wanted to. "Who's going to stop me?" she asked Charlie.

Predictably, Charlie didn't answer.

She watched men moving around their expansive lawn, setting up what looked like circus tents. Fitting. Tonight was going to be quite the event, apparently—Hallie said they were expecting three hundred people.

"You know what? I'm proud of Luca," Cordelia said, and sipped her drink. "Yes, I know, I've been hard on him, I don't need you to tell me that. But you and I both know Luca always needed a push."

She could almost hear Charlie telling her to go easy on him. *He's a free spirit, Delia. He has a big heart.*

"He's worked hard for this," she said. "Hallie told me he's going to make a speech from prepared remarks." She got a little misty-eyed. Her son had suffered ridicule all his life, and she had to admit, it was a ballsy thing to do to stand up there and attempt to read his notes. She sipped more of her drink and waited for Charlie to say, "I told you so."

"Delia?"

Cordelia was so startled she spilled her drink on her leg and the grass as she jerked around. She put her hand over her heart and closed her eyes. "You almost killed me, George," she said.

"Sorry." George Lowe had been the family's personal attorney since the day she married Charlie. He wasn't much older than her. He looked it, though, huffing his way to the top of the hill.

"I don't have an extra seat," she pointed out.

"That's okay," George said, and braced his arm against the tree and breathed heavily for a moment.

"You should go to the gym," Cordelia observed.

"Yeah, I probably should," he agreed.

"So what's up?" she asked.

He shrugged. "Just thought I'd check on you. Ms. Dolly said you were spending an awful lot of time up here."

"Yep," she said. "All I need is a fridge and I'm all set." She lifted her glass in a mock toast. She was not going to entertain any discussion about it. She didn't need anyone to tell her that it was weird that she came up here and talked to her dead husband. Her dead *estranged* husband. But there were so many things that she never got to say.

402

"Hallie asked me to tell you that it's time for you to get ready," George said.

"When did she become the boss of me?" she asked curiously. "Was there a ceremony that I wasn't invited to? Someone obviously passed her the torch because she has been free with her advice lately." She eyed him suspiciously. "Was it you, George?"

"You know I wouldn't do that, Delia. I think maybe she cares," he said kindly.

"Mmm-hmm." Cordelia stood up and took the arm that George offered her, looping her hand into the crook of his elbow.

As they started down the path, George said, "I want you to know that I'm going to make a pledge to Luca's foundation tonight."

Cordelia looked at him. "You *are?*"

George smiled. "I believe in that kid."

"He's not a kid," Cordelia said. That was her issue with Luca—he wasn't a kid anymore, he was a man, and he ought to have a man's job.

"No, I guess not," George agreed. "But he knows what he wants and he's going for it. He's been studying."

Cordelia was reminded of what she'd said to Luca that night in the family room, and she felt a sharp pain in her side. Oh, but she could be awful sometimes. Years ago, Margaret Sutton had told her she could slice right through a person without even knowing she'd done it. Well, she regretted what she'd said to her son. More than regretted—she hated herself for it. "You think this could actually work?" she asked curiously. "That he won't throw all his money down a black sinkhole?"

George sighed. He put his hand on hers and patted it. "Every rancher in this state is trying to make something work, Delia. Ranching isn't what it used to be. Who knows if it will work? But he's got a great head on his shoulders, a good family to back him up, and most importantly, he has the desire. And let's be honest—he never was going to be a nine-to-five kind of guy."

George was right about that. Since he was a boy, Luca had always had big dreams and a vivid imagination.

Maybe she was the one who lacked imagination. She was the one who had pigeonholed him. Charlie used to tell her to let Luca have his head, that he'd run to something. She should have listened to Charlie.

Chapter Thirty

Karen made Luca stand in the front window of her living room and go over his note cards, as if he were addressing a crowd. "I feel ridiculous," Luca complained.

"Do you want to go out and give your speech without rehearsing?" Karen asked.

He did not want to do that.

"Let's do this," she said, and propped her feet on an ottoman. "I don't have a lot of time. I have a hair appointment so I'll look good tonight." She beamed at him.

Luca took a breath. He began to recite his speech. He had note cards that he read from to remind him of the points he wanted to make. It was a short speech, thankfully, and Karen kept barking at him to stop moving around, to make eye contact. After they'd gone through it three times and he'd nailed the last one, she stood up and applauded.

Luca bowed grandly. "Thank you."

"I am busting my buttons I'm so proud of you. I wish your dad was here to see you."

"Me, too," Luca said.

"Well, you go home and do whatever it is people do at enormous ranches to prepare for big events. But I want you to take a moment today to think about what you've accomplished, Luca. It was no small feat to pull off this fund-raiser and learn to read all at the same time. Most people would have crumbled."

He didn't know about that, but Luca promised her he would reflect on it. He *was* proud of himself. Only a few months ago he would never have believed this day would come. What he and Brandon had worked so hard to build might actually come to fruition. And he, hopefully, would put to bed the rumors that he couldn't read.

He'd worked hard for this moment, and yet, it was tarnished because Ella had given him the boot. He never knew it could hurt so bad. He wondered if *he'd* ever hurt someone as deeply as this.

He hadn't slept worth a damn since he drove away from her house. He'd paced his loft, thinking back on every word. Should he have seen it coming? Did he push her? Did he do something to turn her off? Was it possible that he misread things so completely? Because it had seemed to him they were on the verge of something pretty amazing that night in his loft. They'd had great conversations, and their bedroom was on fire.

Maybe it was her. Maybe she was just too damn stubborn, too fearful.

He was driving himself crazy trying to figure it out.

He drove to the ranch, went to his room, and sat on the end of his bed, his note cards clutched in his hand. He should review them again, but he couldn't get his mind off Ella. He was crushed by her, but he was also furious with her. She'd let him go down a path, knowing he was blinded by his feelings for her. And then, when he wasn't looking, she'd pushed him off a cliff.

He jumped a little at a knock on his door. Before he could answer, Hallie pushed the door open and stuck her head in. When she saw him sitting there, she bounced in, her smile beaming. "This is going to be *amazing*," she said. "Did you see the magnolia trees we brought in?"

"Yep."

"It looks like we're going to have three hundred people, Luca! Are you ready?" she asked, and hopped onto the bed beside him.

"As ready as I can be," he said.

Hallie's smile faded. She peered closely at him. "What's wrong?"

"Nothing."

"Bullshit, Luca. Don't lie to me."

There was no hiding anything from his twin. "I'm a little bummed because Ella isn't coming."

Hallie stared at him, her brows slowly sliding into a vee. "Ex-*cuse* me?"

He shrugged. "She broke up with me."

Hallie's eyes widened. "She *broke up* with you just before your big event?"

"Don't make a big deal of it, Hallie," he said wearily.

"Make a big deal of what?"

Nick appeared in the doorway of his room. He had a garment bag slung over one shoulder.

"Ella *broke up* with him," Hallie said with incredulity. "Just before his big event!"

Nick looked from one to the other. "Who's Ella?"

"Nick, seriously?" Hallie complained. "Are you really so out of touch? His girlfriend!"

"I've had a lot going on, Hallie," Nick said defensively, and to Luca, "You have a girlfriend?"

He was silenced with a glare from Hallie.

"Man, that sucks," he said.

"Well, I'm not having it," Hallie said, and stood up.

"Hallie. Leave it alone," Luca warned her. "Go arrange your magnolia trees."

"Nope," Hallie said, and marched to the door, pushing Nick out of the way. "This isn't going to work for me," she said, and flounced out of the room.

Nick watched her go, then turned back to Luca and winced. "I am sorry, bro," he said. "Maybe when this is behind you, you can fill me in."

Luca forced a smile. "Plenty of other fish in the sea."

"Well . . . hang in there," Nick said awkwardly, and walked on.

Luca got up and quietly closed the door. He turned his back to it, folded his arms across his chest, and sighed. Then doubled over. He felt empty. Nothing felt as if it mattered. This fundraiser didn't matter. It was grief all over again, pushing him down, making him want to sleep and drink and forget about the rest of life. But his grief was different than he'd experienced with the loss of his father. This felt like the kind of grief that he couldn't get over.

Chapter Thirty-one

Stacy had packed up her few things, but she couldn't get her band mates to respond to a call or a text. She paced around the house, in and out of the bedrooms, in and out of the kitchen, that throwaway cell phone to her ear.

"What are you going to do with the gun?" Ella asked for the hundredth time when Stacy threw her phone at her purse with a grunt of frustration.

"I'll cross that bridge when I get to it. Where *are* they? Why aren't they answering?"

The sound of tires on the drive brought Buddy out of a dead sleep, and he leapt up and raced for the door. He missed Luca more than Ella did.

Stacy ran to the window and looked out. "Oh my God," she said. She suddenly lunged for her bag and pulled out the gun.

"Put that away!" Ella shrieked as Buddy began to bark frantically. "Do you want to get us killed?" She hurried to the window to look out. It was a white Range Rover. "Who is that?" she muttered. The door swung open and the driver stepped out. Ella let out a sigh of relief. "It's Hallie Prince."

"Hallie! What the hell is she doing here?" Stacy demanded.

"I don't know," Ella said. What *was* Hallie doing here? Ella's heart suddenly climbed to her throat. She wouldn't be here unless something had happened. To Luca? Maybe he'd been in a car accident. She threw open the door. "Hallie!"

Her abrupt door opening startled Hallie, and she swayed back, staring at Ella.

"Ah . . . hi," Ella said. She pushed open the screen door, and Buddy bounded out to greet Hallie.

"Don't *hi* me," Hallie said, and paused to pet the dog, then marched up the steps, pushed past Ella, and walked into her house. She twirled around, her hands on her hips, and glared at Ella.

"Is everything okay?" Ella asked. "Is something wrong?"

"*You* are what's wrong," Hallie snapped. But then she drew such a deep breath her shoulders lifted, held up a hand, and slowly released the breath. "Okay, allow me to rephrase that. It has come to my attention that you are not coming to the fund-raiser tonight."

"Umm, no," Ella said.

"May I ask why the hell not?" Hallie snapped.

"Hallie," Ella said. "I've had some stuff come up—"

411

"No," Hallie said firmly, and shook her head. "I'm not interested in your excuse. Just tell me why you can't or won't be there for Luca."

Ella was struck speechless. Where did she begin? She drew a breath to steady herself. "There is a lot you don't know—"

"Hello, Hallie."

Hallie whipped around. Ella groaned. Stacy stepped from behind the bedroom door, folded her arms, and smirked at Hallie.

"What are you doing here, Stacy?"

"You should know that Ella is moving to Nashville with me and my band."

"You're *what?*" Hallie nearly shouted as she twirled back to Ella.

"No, I'm not," Ella said, and glared at Stacy. "Stop saying that. It's not true."

"But you might," Stacy said.

Hallie's anger was suddenly confusion. She looked at Ella with Luca's eyes. "Does Luca know about this?"

"No!" Ella said, waving it off. "I haven't made any decision."

The fury went out of Hallie, and she dropped her arms. "But *why?*"

A better question was why not? "Look, I don't know if I will. But all I've got here is an old house that needs an awful lot of repair I can't afford. My accounting business is not going anywhere. I guess part of me wonders what I have to lose."

"That's not all you've got here," Hallie said. "What about Luca? He really cares for you, Ella. He seems . . ."

Ella's heart began to pound. "He seems what?"

"Heartsick."

That was a solid kick to her gut.

"Come on, Hallie," Stacy said angrily. "You went to school with us. You know who we are. We have *nothing*," she said. "Do you really think it's going to end happily for Ella and Luca? Do you *really* think there would be some big society wedding like yours? Does your family even know that Ella's mother is in prison for trying to kill someone?"

"Okay, all right, Stacy," Ella said. "That's my business."

"I didn't know that," Hallie said softly, and fixed her gaze on Ella. "But I know my brother. Yeah, Stacy, you're right, I can promise you my mother would not like that. And obviously I don't know what's going to happen with the two of you, but I have faith in Luca. And I know that he cares about you Ella, *really* cares, and the last time he cared was so long ago that I can't remember. He has spent his whole life hiding behind a pretty face, but then he found you, and he found purpose for his life, and this is so important to him, and I can *not* believe that you would be so cruel that you'd abandon him now, of all times."

Ella's heart felt like it was spinning. Her limbs felt tingly, the air thick around her. She felt almost ill, because yes, she knew how important this was to Luca. She had never wanted to hurt him. "I know, I know," she said tearfully.

"Then come," Hallie begged her.

Ella shook her head. "It's too late. I don't have anything to wear."

"I figured as much," Hallie said, and quickly pointed a finger at Stacy. "Not a word from you, please."

"I didn't say anything!" Stacy said.

"Wait here, Ella," Hallie said, and hurried out of the house and down the porch steps. She returned a moment later with a long garment bag. She laid it on the couch and opened it and withdrew a dress. Not just any dress, but a pale pink, tea length, spaghetti strap dress. The pale pink silk was covered with a layer of sheer pink nylon that had been festooned with an explosion of red tulip appliques around the waist that faded as they went up the bodice and down the skirt. Under the silk was tulle to flare the skirt.

"Oh my God, it's gorgeous," Ella said.

"I wore this to a charity function in New York," Hallie said. "Which means I can never wear it again, because I was photographed. The trolls are so brutal if you wear something twice."

"*That* is a beautiful dress," Stacy said. She picked up the dress and held it up against Ella.

"Perfect," Hallie agreed. She cocked her head to one side as she eyed it, then dug in the garment bag and pulled out some red stilettos. "I hope these fit," she said.

It was the most beautiful dress Ella had ever seen. "I can't wear this," she said.

"Like hell you can't," Hallie said. "This isn't about you, Ella, or about all your noble reasons for breaking it off with my brother. This is about the one time he's ever really needed anyone, and by God, I'm going to take you if I have to drag you out of here myself."

"I'll fix your hair," Stacy said.

Ella looked at Stacy with surprise. "You *want* me to go?"

Stacy shrugged. "I haven't changed my opinion. He will never marry you. He'll end it when he's had his fun. But we've been dying to see that ranch forever, El. Go. Have a good time. You deserve it."

"You deserve more than a good time, but never mind that now," Hallie said. "I'll send a driver for you at six." She looked at Stacy and said, "Yes, I am rich and privileged, and I can send a car, and my mother is *not* in prison, she's probably stomping around Three Rivers right now and will probably be a bitch to Ella, but then again, she's pretty bitchy to everyone she meets." She looked at Ella again and smiled warmly. "Don't worry. You can handle my mother, Ella. You, of all people, can handle her because you've already handled much worse. Now, I've got to go. I'm in charge of the setup." She started for the door.

"Wait!" Stacy cried, and when Hallie turned around, she said, "Please don't tell anyone you've seen me."

Hallie rolled her eyes. "No chance of that." And with that, she was gone.

Ella looked at Stacy, then at the dress. Her heart was racing along at such a clip she could hardly breathe. *She was going to see Luca again.*

Just an hour ago, she had believed with everything that she might never see him again.

Chapter Thirty-two

There were so many people, so many black ties and glittering dresses beneath the lights strung through the trees. Luca was dressed in a tux and had allowed Hallie to pull his hair into a man bun after she swore on the blood oath they'd taken when they were six that it was the fashionable thing to do when one was wearing a tux. He'd trimmed the scruff of his beard, but he hadn't had the energy to shave.

He spotted Karen in full mother-of-the-bride armor, her hair in very tight gray curls. She was with her husband, Danny, who slapped Luca congenially on the back and made him stumble.

"I know you've got a lot on your mind, but don't forget those golden cheek warblers," Karen said.

Luca smiled—Karen had come around to his choice of reading material after all and had turned into an advocate for the nearly extinct golden cheek warblers.

"Hey, man, great turn out, huh?" Brandon was in the company of a pretty young blonde he briefly introduced. He dated about as seriously as Luca had before he'd met Ella.

Luca saw Blake wandering around behind Brandon, a drink in his hand. Luca hadn't remembered inviting him. They'd spent a lot of time on the guest list, sure to include all the deep pockets in their circle, as well as friendly faces. He had no doubt Blake had badgered Brandon for the invitation.

"Great turnout," Luca agreed.

"Damn sure is. Are you ready?" Brandon asked.

"Yep. You?"

Brandon shrugged his shoulders like a football player getting ready to play a down. "Ready."

Luca moved on, greeting people he knew, being the charming host that his mother had insisted they all learn to be as part of their societal duties. He had to hand it to Hallie and his checkbook—the setting was beautiful. Her magnolia trees had pink flowers and had been strung with white Christmas lights. Peacocks wandered the grounds that had been manicured to perfection. That was especially commendable since Martin had reduced the grounds staff to save costs.

He took a plate from a passing waiter and helped himself to the buffet. Salmon and cucumber twists were served alongside skewers of lamb and tomato, and gulf shrimp with wasabi on rice crackers. Champagne flowed from two fountains at either end of the pool, in addition to the two full-service bars.

Luca spotted his grandmother, dressed in a flowing blue gown, and for some bizarre reason, a tiara. He saw Nick, too, also dressed in a tux, with one arm on the bar as he eyed the crowd with a gimlet eye.

There were many people he knew vaguely or didn't know at all. People he and Brandon had met over the last couple of months, including professors from the local Texas universities they'd approached for funding and the North Texas rancher who had successfully turned much of his land into a conservation preserve. A gentleman from the EPA in the company of a woman from the USDA.

There were people Luca had known all his life—rich people, powerful people. People who had foundations or who guided grant processes for big companies. He'd even extended an invitation to Tanner Sutton, hoping that he'd at least consider doing something similar with the acreage his dad had left him. Tanner was dressed in a tux, but he looked uncomfortable and stood off by himself.

There were so many people gathered tonight who could make their foundation that it made Luca feel a little ill. He'd spent thousands of dollars on this event, had drawn the right crowd. Now all he had to do was read in front of them.

He was not nervous—he was numb.

It was almost time to begin, so Luca decided to have a drink, see if that might loosen him up and let him feel. He walked to the bar where Nick was standing. His brother smiled as Luca ordered a bourbon. "You're looking sharp," Nick said.

"Thanks," Luca said, and downed his bourbon. "So are you," he said. "Another one," he said to the bartender.

"Drink enough to take the edge off, but not enough to slur," Nick advised.

Luca smiled and tapped his glass to Nick's. "Got it."

"Knock 'em dead, cowpoke," Nick said.

Luca started toward the temporary stage the catering company had erected. On the way, his grandmother intercepted him. "There's my handsome grandson," she said.

"You look very pretty tonight, Grandma," he said, and looked to the top of her head. "The tiara is an interesting choice, but it does compliment your pink and blue hair."

"Thank you," she said, patting her hair.

"Have you seen Mom?"

"No, but I'm sure she's here somewhere, getting all liquored up to face this crowd." She grinned. "Now listen, Luca," she said, for once using his true name. "I know your mom can be a bitch sometimes—"

"Grandma," he said, his voice full of warning.

420

"Well, she can," she said with a shrug. "Cordelia Prince has a sharper tongue than Satan. But she's got an awfully big heart. You get that from her, you know. She loves you, Luca, and she is proud of you. She's just not very good about saying it."

That was a gross understatement. But he appreciated his grandmother telling him.

"Your father would be so proud of you tonight," she said, her blue eyes welling. "Oh, how he loved you." She suddenly patted Luca's cheek and shook her empty champagne flute at him. "Time to see if I can find a man to fill my glass," she said, and waggled her brows.

Lord, this family.

Luca carried on to the stage. There were chairs for the other speakers and an outdoor screen the audiovisual service had installed.

It was show time.

Luca stepped up to the stage and looked out at the crowd as someone began to tap a fork against a glass to gain the attention of the crowd.

He stepped up to the microphone. Because of the light on him, he couldn't really see much past the dark shapes of people gathered in front of him. It was strange—he didn't feel as jittery as he had in Karen's living room. He felt nothing. Like his mind had separated from his body. "Thank you all for coming tonight," he said when he'd gained their attention. "Brandon Hurst and I

421

have been looking forward to this for a very long time." He pulled the note cards from his pocket and looked at them. For a moment, the letters danced all over the card, rearranging themselves, and he felt a moment of panic. But he drew a breath and glanced up—and his eyes caught the colors pink and red splattered on a dress. He was stunned to see Ella standing just off to the side. She was wearing a beautiful dress unlike anything he'd ever seen her wear. She looked like a dream.

She had come.

"Dude," Brandon muttered behind him.

Luca dragged his gaze from Ella to the crowd. He cleared his throat and suddenly, without reason, decided he was sick of being ashamed. It had something to do with Ella, and the vague idea that both of them were good at hiding from the truth. Luca smiled. "I'm going to have to ask you to bear with me," he said, and a bit of laughter went up from the crowd. "I've got a few notes written down here, but to be honest, I'm not a good reader. As in, I couldn't read at all until very recently."

People laughed.

"It's true—I'm dyslexic, and I've only just learned how to read."

He heard a murmur of surprise go through the crowd. He could see Karen standing below him, beaming with pride. She gave him two thumbs-up.

"So here goes nothing," he said with a grin, and it felt like something lifted off of him. The ten-year-old boy disappeared, and in his place stood the man. The crowd was silent now, and Luca glanced down at his note cards and, this time, saw words very clearly. He read, *I've spent my whole life on this land.* He looked up. "I've spent my whole life on this land."

He began to give his speech. He was reading his notes—truly reading them. Yes, he stumbled a time or two. Once, he heard Brandon whisper a correction behind him. But he read what he wanted to say, and Ella had come, and she'd seen it all. She'd seen him walk out from the shadow of his fear.

Now it was her turn.

When he was done, he turned the presentation over to Brandon and felt the tension rush from his body.

He watched as they went through the shocking pictures of deterioration and depletion the university had shared with them. He listened as experts talked about what could be gained by conserving land, for ranchers and farmers alike. He admired the pictures from the North Texas ranch, where springs and natural wetlands had been restored, where ten-point bucks and their herds were roaming, where ducks had established new habitats.

When the presentation was over, Luca returned

to the microphone. He didn't need notes for this part. He explained simply that his vision for the land his father had left him was simple—he would return it to the state in which God had given it to the world. "Brandon and I want the world to experience what we were so privileged to know growing up. There's a lot of work to be done, and there is a lot about the earth to be learned. We have formed a foundation with some solid partnerships and hope you will join us."

The crowd applauded. Brandon was shaking hands with people who'd come up to their little stage, making jokes about what they were going to do with all the checks that rolled in tonight. Luca stepped off the stage and very nearly walked into his mother.

She looked as elegant as ever, with her blond hair artfully arranged, her designer dress shimmering in the evening light. And her eyes were filled with tears. "Oh, Luca, I am so sorry," she said, and cupped his face with her hands.

"Why?"

"I'm sorry that I haven't told you enough how proud I am of you. I am *so* proud of you, Luca. What you did tonight—and I'm not just talking about admitting you can't read—but what you've put together has filled me with so much damn pride I can hardly breathe."

"*This* is new," he said. "Thanks, Mom."

"I can't believe you taught yourself to *read,* Luca—"

"No, Mom, I had a lot of help—"

"I am . . . I am so flabbergasted and proud. I was wrong, Luca. I was so wrong and you were right."

Luca was stunned. He knew how much it had taken for his mother to make that apology. He suddenly laughed. "Call the presses—that's quite an admission from Cordelia Prince," he said, and hugged her. "Does this mean you're going to donate to my foundation?"

"Lord, no," she said with a laugh. *"Maybe,"* she amended. "I want to hear more about how you learned to read. For now, you'd better meet your fans," she said. "Who knew there were so many tree-huggers in this state?"

"Thanks, Mom. It means a lot," he said, and turned around to speak to people willing to help them fund the foundation. But he was looking for one person in particular.

He had made it through a throng of well-wishers, had been hugged within an inch of his life by Karen, had slipped through a few people he didn't know, and finally, when he was beginning to think he'd dreamed it, he saw the pink and red from the corner of his eye and turned his head.

He immediately stopped walking. She was a princess in that dress, almost as if she'd stepped out of one of his dreams. Oh yes, he had dreamed about her, had mourned her, and here she was, standing before him, and his emotions were churning.

Ella smiled self-consciously and clasped her hands together. "Are you going to say something?"

He stepped closer, his gaze moving over her dress. "I'm a little speechless right now."

"I'm not. You were amazing, Luca," she said quietly.

"I thought you weren't coming."

She stepped closer. "I know. I'm so sorry. I'm sorry that I ever said I wouldn't come, because I am so thankful that I did. It was incredible. You sounded like a scholar. I am . . ." She pressed her palm to her chest. "I am so in *awe* of you right now. I'm in awe of your courage and your foresight, and . . . and everything about you."

"You look beautiful," he said quietly. "So beautiful." For some reason the admission made his heart feel heavy. He would like nothing better than to take her in his arms and celebrate this night, but after what had happened between them, he didn't trust her. "So why the change of heart?" he asked simply.

"It's complicated."

"It's always complicated with you, Ella. Are you finally going to let me in, or is this appearance something else?"

She looked stung. She glanced around them, at all the people who were milling around. "Now?"

Luca looked at all the people who would help him change the course of his life. But in a way, Ella already had, and he needed to understand what had happened. So he held out his hand to her. Ella hesitated. "Please don't make me beg you again," he murmured.

She slipped her hand into his.

He turned toward the house and began to walk briskly. She had to hurry to keep up but couldn't help gawking at her surroundings, like everyone who came to Three Rivers. When they entered the house, she slowed her step and looked up at a painting. "Is that a Van Gogh?"

"Cezanne." He led her into his father's study and shut the door behind them. He'd not been in here since his dad had died, and by the look of things, no one had. It looked exactly as it had that winter day his father had dropped on the golf course. It still smelled of his father's cigars. He turned around to Ella and folded his arms across his chest. "Well?"

Ella looked pained. "This is your night, Luca. You don't want to hear—"

"Ella. We've danced around this long enough. If you don't want to tell me, then you probably need to go."

Her mouth gaped. Then closed. She nodded. "Okay. All right." She walked to a chair and put her hands on the back of it, almost as if she needed to hold herself up. "You remember my friend Stacy? The one who stole the dress from Mariah?"

He nodded.

"She's in trouble," she said, and began to tell him about her life with Stacy. About her best friend, a shoplifter with a big talent who belonged in Nashville.

"What has this got to do with us?" he asked impatiently.

"I'm getting there," she said. "I urged her to get a job to save money. She got one at the sheriff's office. But he . . ." She winced. She swallowed. "He wouldn't leave her alone."

Luca frowned. "Blake?"

She nodded. "He wouldn't keep his hands off her," she said.

That was no surprise. Blake couldn't keep his hands off any woman, was notorious for it. "Okay," he said uncertainly.

"But one night, he was upset that she kept saying no, so he, ah . . ." She pressed her fingertips to her cheeks. "He forced it."

Luca didn't follow at first. "Forced what?"

"Himself. On her."

He felt the blood drain from him. "Are you saying he raped her?" he asked, his voice rough.

"Tried to. But Stacy fought him off. And she . . . she somehow got his gun away from him and

428

pointed it at him. He told her she better shoot, because he was going to arrest her for theft and assaulting a police officer, and I don't know what all. She escaped with his gun, and she's been hiding at my house ever since."

Luca was stunned. Blake had always been a bastard, but this enraged him. And he was furious with Ella. "For God's sake, Ella, why didn't you tell me? Why didn't you go to the police?"

"Because of who we are, Luca," she said. "Who is going to believe Stacy over him? All it would take is one reporter looking into her past, and no one would believe her. They'd say she's a criminal, trying to get out of trouble. Everyone knows she stole that dress from Mariah's shop."

Luca thought of the many accusations of improper sexual behavior in the press lately. Ella was right—Stacy would be judged. "Couldn't you have come to me? You could have let me help you instead of shutting me out."

"No, I couldn't," she said. "He said I would be arrested for aiding a fugitive."

"What?" he demanded.

Ella told him that Blake had come to her house in search of Stacy and had threatened her, too. She told him that twice, as teens, Stacy had been caught shoplifting when they were together, and she'd been picked up, too, but released. Her name was on the old report, and Blake knew it.

Luca's blood was churning. He thought of that

smug son-of-a-bitch and wanted to kill him with his bare hands.

"I couldn't have let you be associated with that," she said. "I know how these things go, and people would talk about you and judge you, just when you were about to do something as amazing as you did tonight. It would have marred this. And I couldn't let you turn in Stacy, because she is the only family I really have. I'm *so* mad at her, you have no idea. But at the same time, I want to protect her."

"Where is she?" he asked.

"At my house. She's trying to arrange for someone to pick her up so she can go to Nashville." She paused and looked down. "She's asked me to go with her."

Luca's throat suddenly constricted. "Are you?"

"I don't want to," she said. "But I've thought about it. I have a house falling down around me that I can't afford. I can't even keep Priscilla in kibble, and I pretty much blew it with you."

All of that was true, and he wanted to talk about this, but he had a fund-raiser going at full tilt outside. "Ella—don't go," he said. "At least not yet."

"I don't think you understand," she said softly. "I can't see you around Three Rivers and know I lost you, too. I can't bear it. My heart can't take it. This nightmare with Stacy is just one of many unpleasant things that could happen. What if my mother is ever released from prison? What if I can't afford to keep my house? There are so many ifs we haven't even thought about, Luca. Things *you* need to think about. I mean, do you really want to keep doing this?" she asked, gesturing between the two of them.

"If you are asking if I really want to spend my life trying to convince you that I am here for you, the answer is no. Or spend my life wondering if you'll suddenly decide you need another wall between us? Hell, no," he said, his hands finding his waist. "But do I want to see where this thing between us will go without the complication of Stacy? Or Blake? Absolutely."

He stepped forward and reached for her elbow, drawing her in. "We have something great, Ella. And I won't lie; I don't trust you. Nevertheless, all your what-ifs don't scare me. What scares me is wondering if you will ever be able to see past them."

Ella's lashes fluttered as if he'd shouted at her. She glanced down and bit her bottom lip.

He had no desire to hurt her and drew her close. "Don't decide anything tonight," he said. "Promise me you won't go to Nashville. Not yet."

She nodded.

Luca lowered his head and kissed her and immediately felt himself fall into that space where only the two of them existed. He kissed her deeply, to make up for the days they'd lost, to say good-bye, if that's what this was.

He didn't know what it was, honestly. He had to figure out a few things first. But he desperately wanted to figure them out, because he didn't think he could survive if he lost her.

Chapter Thirty-three

The man who had picked up Ella in Hallie's Range Rover—he said his name was Rafe—was waiting for her like a pumpkin right on schedule at eleven o'clock. She caught Luca's eye and waved, rather than draw him away from people who were interested in his foundation.

After their conversation in the study, Luca had introduced her to his brother Nick and his grandmother. She'd dined on fancy canapés and drank good wine instead of the cheap kind she usually bought. She'd talked to people without knowing who they were and discovered at one point in the evening she'd been talking to a senator.

She drifted home on a cloud.

Stacy was waiting up for her. She bolted upright when Ella came in. "Tell me everything," she demanded.

So Ella told Stacy about the house with the hickory wood floors and marble entry. She told her about the massive two-story entrance and the dual staircases that went up into the clouds above. "They even have a *Cezanne*," she said.

"What's a Cezanne?" Stacy asked.

She told Stacy about the pool and how it looked as if it was spilling into the fields beyond, and the magnolia trees that had been brought in and festooned with pink blooms, and the bars and the champagne fountains. "I met a senator. And a local news anchor," she said.

"Yes, but did you meet his family?" she asked.

"His brother and grandmother." She thought about it a moment. "I never did see his mother."

"So? What did Luca say when he saw you?"

Ella remembered how stunned he'd looked. How she'd seen a thousand emotions sail across his eyes. Irritation. Relief. Confusion. Lust. And love. He hadn't said it, but she knew what she'd seen, and she'd seen love in his eyes. "He wanted to know what I was doing there, of course. So we talked a little." Ella did not tell Stacy she'd told him the truth. She didn't want Stacy in a panic.

"So, what does it *mean?*" Stacy asked, bouncing a little in her seat. "Are you back together?"

"No," Ella said uncertainly. "I'm not sure where we are. He asked me to give him a couple of weeks before I decided about Nashville. But he also told me he doesn't trust me."

"Why?" Stacy asked, her brows furrowing.

"Because I can't get out of my own way, Stacy. I am so sure I know what will happen that I go ahead and make sure it does, you know? I should have told him the truth."

"*No.* You were right not to tell him the truth. He doesn't know what it's like on this side of the tracks."

Ella didn't want to debate with her. She understood what Luca meant, and it had made her think. She glanced down at her dress. "I will never have a dress this beautiful again," she said sadly.

"Well, at least you got to wear it once," Stacy said, and smiled.

So did Ella.

"I'm so sorry, El," Stacy suddenly blurted. "For everything."

"You don't have to say it," Ella said.

"I *do.* I always do this to you. I always dump everything in your lap."

"That is so true," Ella said with a sad laugh. "But it's okay. That's what family is for, right?"

Stacy sniffed. "How would we know? I feel awful for the position I've put you in." She glanced down at her hand. "They left for Nashville without me."

"What?" Ella said, sinking onto the couch next to Stacy.

She nodded, and tears began to slip from her eyes. "Wells—he's the guitarist—he said I'm in trouble and they don't want to get caught up in it. He said that if I can get out there by the end of June, everything is cool, but if not . . ." She squeezed her eyes shut.

"If not?" Ella asked.

"They will find another singer," Stacy said tearfully. "I put that fucking band together, and now they're going to *dump* me." Her tears were flowing freely now.

Ella wrapped her arms around Stacy. "We'll figure it out."

"No we *won't*," Stacy said on a strangled sob, and doubled over. "I always do this! I sabotage myself! Why did I have to take his gun? He would have forgotten all about me!"

Ella didn't offer her the usual empty platitudes. They'd both heard them enough times, and Stacy knew the truth. What she needed was a shoulder.

"I don't know why I do it," she said through her sobs. "I don't know what's *wrong* with me."

"Nothing is wrong with you, Stacy. You're just finding your way, that's all."

"Yeah, and what are *you* doing?" Stacy asked. "Building walls?"

"Border walls," Ella reminded her. "Thirty feet high."

In spite of her sorrow, Stacy couldn't help but laugh.

Ella changed out of her dress and found some tequila Mateo had once left behind. She and Stacy and Buddy sat on the floor, Stacy and Ella with glasses of tequila, Buddy snoring. Stacy told her the cold-water handle had come off in the bathroom sink.

Ella groaned and fell on her back.

Stacy lay on her back beside her. "What are you going to do about this place?" she asked curiously.

"Hell if I know," Ella said. "It needs so much *work*. I can't spend all my money on this house just so I can say I have a place to call my own."

"Will you move back to the burbs?"

To her old apartment? That seemed a huge step backward, like she was returning to a transient, belong-nowhere kind of life. "Who knows," Ella said dejectedly.

"You're never coming to Nashville, are you?" Stacy asked.

Ella thought of Luca's hazel eyes and the way he smiled at her. She didn't know what the future held, but the thought of walking away from him was too much. Too difficult. Too heartbreaking. "No."

Stacy groaned and covered her eyes with one arm.

"We're different people, Stace," Ella said as she stared up at her stained ceiling. "You've always wanted the city lights and the travel and to be on a stage. I've always wanted a place to call home and to matter to someone. That's it, that's all I've ever wanted. But you? You have places to go and things to do."

"I know," Stacy said softly. "I know we're different. But that's why I love you, El—you're *not* like me."

437

"Same," Ella said, and groped around until she found Stacy's hand. They lay there like that, holding hands.

"You're lucky," Stacy whispered. "You're lucky that your high school crush turned out to be the one."

He was definitely the one for her. But only time would tell if Ella was the one for him. She had a sinking feeling that the mess she'd made was too big to crawl over.

Ella didn't know when they finally went to bed, but she stumbled into her room and fell facedown, exhausted from the roller coaster of emotions and the mix of tequila with wine and champagne.

The next morning, she woke up to Buddy snorting in her face. She stumbled out of bed and went into the kitchen to make coffee. She didn't see the note on the kitchen table until her second cup. She snatched it up and read it, then ran into the front bedroom. "Stacy!" she shouted, but the room was empty, her things gone.

Love you.

That's all Stacy had written. Ella didn't know how she'd left or when or with whom, but Stacy had taken her troubles and, apparently, the sheriff's gun, and had finally left Ella out of it.

Her abrupt departure made Ella feel incredibly

sad. It felt almost like a death. As if they'd crossed some bridge last night, and Stacy had decided to leave her. But Ella didn't have time to dwell on it, because as always, she had to go to work.

Chapter Thirty-four

Two days after the fund-raiser, Luca sat with Uncle Chet and Nick at the Saddlebush offices. All three of them were silent, thinking. Luca had come for advice, and apparently, it was not easy to give.

Nick broke the silence. "You're asking for trouble, you know that."

Luca nodded.

"And you know Brandon won't accept it."

That was the worst of it. Luca loved Brandon like a brother. "I know."

"He's put in half for your foundation," Nick pointed out unnecessarily.

"I don't care about the money," Luca said. "I care about our friendship. He's been my best friend my whole life."

"As long as you understand the risk, I'm a thousand percent behind you," Nick said. "Blake Hurst should rot in hell."

Luca looked at Uncle Chet, but Uncle Chet shook his head. "I don't know, Luca. If you don't succeed, you're going to have a big ol' target on your back."

Luca smiled wryly. "Where Blake Hurst is concerned, I've always had a target on my back. I can't let him get away with this. Who knows who else he might have done this to? He won't stop on his own."

"That's true," Uncle Chet said. "I never did understand a man who felt the right to take advantage of women."

"You ought to give Brandon a heads-up first," Nick said.

"He'll tip off his brother," Uncle Chet said.

"Maybe," Luca said. "But I owe him that much." He stood up. So did his brother and uncle. "Be careful, Luca," Nick said. "Sure you don't want me to come along?"

Luca shook his head. "Thanks, bro, but not this time. This is something I need to do."

What he had to do was the easy part. All he had to do was get Blake to talk, which Luca knew wouldn't be hard, because Blake liked to brag. Everyone around town knew that most days, Blake had his lunch at Jalisco's. Luca watched for a couple of days to make sure that was his habit.

One the third day, he woke up and decided it was time. At lunch, he parked around the corner from Jalisco's and waited. When he saw Blake go into the restaurant, he called Brandon.

"What's up, buddy?" Brandon said. "I'm about to walk into a courtroom."

"I'll make it quick," Luca said. "First, I love you like a brother, Brandon."

Brandon sputtered a laugh. "Okay. Right back at you."

"But I'm about to do something that's going to put a wedge between us."

"What are you talking about?" Brandon asked impatiently.

"I'm going to confront Blake about his mistreatment of a woman."

"Not Ella," Brandon said instantly, and Luca had the sick feeling that Blake had said something derogatory about Ella to him.

"Not Ella. Someone else."

There was a long pause on Brandon's end. He didn't ask another question. He didn't ask how Luca intended to confront Blake. Or even what had happened. He said, "I've got to go before a judge right now. I'll call you later." And he hung up.

It seemed almost as if Brandon didn't want to know.

About a half hour later, Blake walked out of the Jalisco working a toothpick. Luca got out of his Sombra and walked across the parking lot, intercepting the sheriff just before he reached his patrol car. Blake clapped a hand very dramatically over the badge pinned to his chest. "Damn near scared me to death," he said.

Luca smiled. He was holding his phone, set to record. He slipped it into his pocket.

"So what's up?" Blake asked. "You're not going to hit me up for money to save a salamander, are you?"

Luca chuckled. "No. I saw your patrol car and thought I'd catch you. I wanted to ask you about Stacy Perry."

Blake's expression instantly changed. "So your little sex buddy knows where she is after all, huh? You know I could arrest her for lying to me."

Luca already wanted to punch him. "She doesn't know where she is," he said dismissively. "But she's on me to talk to you. She told me that you tried something with Stacy."

"Yeah, like what?" Blake asked, and folded his arms across his chest.

"She said you got a little fresh," Luca said with a chuckle, as if to suggest women were always complaining about something.

Blake took the bait and smiled. "Well, hell, have you seen her? She's a good-looking woman."

"Yeah, she's hot all right," Luca agreed.

"I'll tell you what, it's a little difficult to concentrate when Stacy's ass goes bouncing by your door." He made a crude motion with his hips and laughed. "Yeah, I might have gotten a little fresh with her, just playing around," he said.

"Sure," Luca said as if they were buddies. "But you didn't try anything, did you? I mean, you didn't do anything she could make a formal complaint about, right?"

443

Blake snorted. "Can't even look at a woman these days without them wanting to turn you in. No. I mean, she came into my office one night, and I'd say things got a *little* out of hand. But that was her fault."

"How so?" Luca asked.

"Just coming on to me," he said with a shrug. "You know how it is."

"Yep, I know how it is." Luca looked across the parking lot. "Actually, what she said is that you tried to rape her." He shifted his gaze back to Blake.

Blake frowned. "Like I said, things got out of hand. But I didn't try and *rape* her, goddammit. She was practically begging for it."

"So she didn't say no, or tell you to stop?" Luca asked.

Blake's eyes narrowed. "Why are you asking this, Luca?"

"I don't know. I just thought it was curious she had your gun."

Blake froze. "What the fuck are you trying to do here?"

"Who, me?" Luca asked with a cold smile. "I'm just trying to figure out if you tried to rape her and she got hold of your gun to stop you, that's all."

Blake stepped up to Luca so they were nose to nose. "So what if I did, you stupid hippie? Are you going to write up a report? Oh, that's right—

you can't read or write because you're a stupid little shit."

Luca stood there, his blood pounding in his veins, but didn't say a word.

"Here's the thing about whores like Stacy Perry. They're a dime a dozen. They come on to you hoping for favors, and then get pissed when you come back at them. Now, you can get in your little tree-hugging Sombra and cry about it if you want, but trust me, when I'm through with her, she's going to be sharing a cell with your girlfriend's mommy. Is that what you want? You want everyone to know about your girlfriend? Cuz I can damn sure make it happen."

It took all of Luca's resolve not to put a fist in the middle of Blake's face. "The guys must have had a good laugh over you losing your gun," he said.

Blake's face mottled with anger. He suddenly reared back and punched Luca in the jaw, sending him to the ground. "You weak, pathetic loser. I always told Brandon he was too good for you. Where is she?" he demanded, and grabbed Luca by the collar. *"Where is she?"*

"I have no idea, Sheriff," he said. He could hear people coming out of the restaurant. "Last I heard, she was in Dallas."

"Sheriff?" someone said.

Blake hauled Luca to his feet. "Get the hell out

of here," he said, his gaze flicking to the people behind Luca. "I'll deal with you later."

Luca casually brushed himself off, rubbed his jaw, and said, "Looking forward to it." And then he turned his back on Blake and walked across the parking lot to his car. He drove away from Jalisco's and pulled into Timmons Tire and Body. He took his phone from his pocket and played it back. He smiled as he listened—he'd gotten every word. He saved the audio, then called Lucinda Hampton, one of the local reporters from a San Antonio station. He and Lucinda had dated a couple of times.

"Hey, Lucinda, Luca Prince," he said when she picked up.

"Well, hello, stranger," Lucinda said.

"How would you like a big scoop about Sheriff Hurst?"

"Who?"

"Thomas J. Hurst's son," Luca clarified.

There was no hesitation from Lucinda. "Where can I meet you?"

By ten o'clock, the story was all over the news.

The next day, Blake called a press conference to say he'd been framed by a Prince, that he had never touched a woman inappropriately.

Two days later, Stacy was found in Nashville and did an interview detailing what had happened. Two days after that, Blake was forced to resign, because as Luca had guessed, women started coming out of the woodwork with their own stories about his predation. And every time a story ran, there was a link to Luca and his foundation. Their brand new website had so much traffic they had to increase the bandwidth.

Luca did not escape unscathed. He received a few death threats, delivered via social media. People threatened to bring legal action, seeing as how he'd recorded Blake without him knowing. But Blake had much bigger problems than Luca Prince.

Luca tried to call Brandon a few times but, predictably, got no response. By the end of the week, he received a letter from Brandon's attorney telling him he intended to withdraw his support and his pledge to the foundation. There was no personal note.

When his mother heard about it, she shrugged. "Well, I'm sorry that you and Brandon are on the outs. But you can do this without him, Luca. It's your passion. Let that lead you."

That might have been the most stunning development of the week.

Chapter Thirty-five

Ella heard the news about Sheriff Hurst from Big Barb when she delivered the mail one morning.

"You haven't heard about it? He's been forced to resign." Big Barb practically shouted, seeming a little put out with Ella for not keeping up.

"I don't have TV out here," Ella said apologetically. Plus, her hot water heater had gone out, and she'd been a little caught up in that drama.

Once the hot water heater was fixed, Ella had to make a trip to Lyle's, because a gauge on her dash kept flashing a red warning sign. "You're going to need a new radiator," Lyle said.

"Are you kidding me?" Ella asked, and leaned over the car and banged the hood with both fists. "That's *it!* I'm putting that stupid house on the market right away, and then I'm going to sell this piece of crap because both of them do nothing but cost me money!"

"I've been telling you to get a new car," Lyle pointed out.

"Well, Lyle, if only I had wads of cash to throw at a new car," she said irritably.

He smiled. "I'll keep an eye out for a bargain. In the meantime, if I have to, I'll fix your radiator and you can owe me."

"Nope. I'll pay you."

"I won't say no to you throwing wads of cash at me. So *hey,* the sheriff is making a splash around town, eh?"

"Yeah, so I've heard."

"Always did think he was a jerk," Lyle said.

Everyone was talking about Sheriff Hurst. But Ella was thinking about Luca. She hadn't heard one word from him. He hadn't come by the Magnolia or her house. He hadn't called her or texted her. It had been more than two weeks since the fund-raiser, and it had been radio silence.

Well, she'd blown it. There was no other explanation.

She consoled herself with Hostess cupcakes and cold showers. Even Buddy had finally moved on, just like she always feared he would. One day, he went out the back door, and he didn't come back. Three days had passed since she'd last seen that damn dog. Three days had passed since she'd seen the horses, too. Like they all had packed a bag and said, "See you! Wouldn't want to be you! Sad sack!"

One Saturday morning, she heard something under her house, and with a flashlight and base-ball bat, she went to have a look. Lo and behold, the damn barn cat had found a friend in the wilderness and had given birth to a litter of kittens. Priscilla was interested in the weeds at Ella's feet as she checked out the kittens, and kept nibbling at her ankles.

Ella shimmied out, fetched some water for the cat, and went back in to place it nearby. She was half under that porch like the Wicked Witch of the West when her phone rang. She bumped her head hard on the porch underneath as she tried to get out. "Ouch!" she shouted, and shimmied out once more, brushing spider webs and leaves from her as she stood up and grabbed her phone.

"Hello?"

"We got the deal!" Stacy shrieked into the phone.

"Oh!" Ella cried. "Oh my God, Stacy, really?"

"Can you believe it?" Stacy said happily. "Even after all the publicity about the sheriff."

Ella paused. "The news about our sheriff came up in Nashville?"

"Of course it did! I'm the star witness. Please tell me you saw me on TV," she said.

"I don't have a TV," Ella reminded her.

"Oh, for fuck's sake. Didn't Luca tell you?"

"Luca? Tell me what?" Ella demanded.

There was silence on the other end. "Ella— haven't you talked to him?"

Ella sank down onto her rump, and Priscilla

450

nudged her with her snout. "Not a word. I blew it, Stacy. I haven't heard a word from him."

"So . . . you don't know he's the one that got the sheriff to confess on tape?"

Ella's mind suddenly went blank. She couldn't make that sentence work in her head. "Luca?" she said weakly. "But how?"

"With his phone. You really need to hear it," Stacy said.

Ella's heart was racing. She tried to think of what this meant. What about Brandon? What about the foundation? "Tell me," she said.

Stacy told her. And by the time they hung up, tears of gratitude and love and disbelief were streaming down her face.

Nick had caught two of the mustang a day or so ago, but the stallion had escaped and was running around with a dog, he said.

"Black and white?" Luca asked. They were watching one of the vaquero's Martin knew work to break one of the horses. Luca's mother stood on one side, Nick on the other.

"How'd you know?" Nick asked.

"That's Buddy."

"Well, if you know Buddy, tell him to quit enticing that stallion to run off," Nick said.

Luca swallowed. He wanted to say that Buddy belonged to Ella, but he wasn't able to talk about her just yet. He was still trying to figure things

451

out. He'd needed a moment after the thing with Blake and Brandon.

"So what is—"

Luca's mother started to say something, but she didn't finish, because the sound of metal screeching startled them all. They turned from the paddock and looked up the long drive. Luca's heart dropped—there was an old beige SUV in the middle of the road, with smoke rising out of the engine.

"What is *that?*" his mother asked.

"That is Ella," Luca said. "I don't believe it."

His mother glanced up at him. "Your girl?"

"Actually, I'm not sure," he said. His heart had climbed to his throat, and he felt a bead of perspiration slide down his temple. They watched Ella get out and kick the door closed. Hard.

"You better go find out if she is or she isn't," his mother said. "But either way, that car needs to go."

"Right," Luca said. "Excuse me."

He strode across the lawn to the drive. Ella spotted him and moved tentatively to the front of her car. How was it possible that she looked even more beautiful than before? Even though she looked like she'd been dragged behind that SUV? Her shirt had what he hoped was mud on it, and she was wearing her rubber boots. She'd stuffed her hair up under a sunhat, and her cotton shirt was open to her breastbone.

He stopped walking, uncertain how to proceed. He had lain awake almost every night, trying to decide if he could trust her. He loved her. But he didn't know if he could trust her.

They stood about three feet apart. Neither of them spoke. She looked like she was trying to, but no words came out.

"What are you doing here?" he asked at last.

"I ah . . ." She rubbed her nape. She looked uncomfortable. "Have you seen Buddy?"

He swallowed. "Did you lose him again?"

"Looks like," she said, and dragged the back of her hand across her forehead. "Any chance you might have found three horses?"

He stepped closer. "I've seen two of them. They're here now. One of them is still running loose with Buddy."

"Oh," she said softly. "That explains it." She took a step closer. Her eyes were searching his face.

"So, you drove over here to ask about your dog?" he asked.

"Not really. But I suck at this, and I'm a coward at heart. I drove over here to tell you I . . ." She swallowed hard, and Luca steeled himself. *I can't do this. I'm moving to Nashville.* "To tell you that I love you, Luca. I love you so much. I always have."

Luca's mind went blank. He tried to take those words in, to feel them in his heart, but so many questions swirled around them. The same questions that had kept him up at night.

She bit her lip. "I hope I didn't say something wrong."

Luca didn't know yet. "Lyle said you told him you were selling your house."

She looked confused. "I did?" She thought about it, then nodded. "Oh, right, I did. In a moment of frustration, I said I was going to sell it right away. I was being dramatic."

"Dramatic." He took off his hat, ran his fingers through his hair.

"But I was never moving. Or going to Nashville. Especially not after what you did for Stacy. And because, you know, what I said. I really love you, Luca."

"I didn't do it for Stacy," he said. "I did it because Blake Hurst is the biggest goddamn bully I have ever known, and I was happy to see him get his due."

"Oh," she said. "What about Brandon?"

Luca shrugged and looked down at his hat. "He won't answer my calls, and he's pulled out of the foundation." It pained him to admit it, that he'd lost his best friend.

"I am so sorry," she said softly, and took another step forward. "After all the work you put into it? I can't even—I am *so* sorry. This is my fault. If you'd never met me, you—"

"If I'd never met you, I wouldn't know how

hard a conversation like this is, Ella. It's not your fault. I didn't have to do what I did. I *wanted* to bring that bastard down—he's abused enough people. But I'll tell you what is your fault, if you want to know."

She took another tiny step closer to him. "I definitely want to know," she said. "But don't feel like you need to spell it out. I mean, it's pretty obvious you're through with me, and I don't blame you. Since your fund-raiser, all I've done is think about what I would say if I were you, and hate myself for what happened. But go ahead," she said, and gestured with her fingers for him to speak. "I've been waiting for it."

"Thank you," he said, inclining his head. "It's your fault that I haven't had a good night's sleep in weeks. That I've been tossing and turning wondering how the hell to scale your walls or if I even want to."

She frowned. "I totally understand," she said quickly. "And I think that—"

He held up his hand. "I'm going to do the talking for a minute, if it's all the same to you, because I've thought about this, Ella. I've thought about it a *lot,* and I've got a few things to say. I don't know how or why you got under my skin, but you did, and I can't dislodge you even if I wanted to. I tried. Couldn't do it."

"Oh. Well, that's the—"

"Still talking," he said. "I don't care that your

455

mother is in prison or that your best friend took off with a sheriff's gun or that you lived in umpteen foster homes before you were eighteen. I don't even care that you've built a fortress around your heart, because I like a challenge, and I'm going to crawl over it. What I *do* care about is having you in my life. But here's the rub—I don't know if I can trust you. I don't believe you aren't going to get some idea in your pretty head that things ought to be a certain way. I mean, that's what you did, and you left me holding the bag."

Ella's lips parted. "I understand, and that's why—"

"Nope," he said. "Still not finished." He was going to get this off his chest once and for all, let the chips fall where they may. He moved closer and pushed the brim of her hat back. "I've thought about this, long and hard. And Ella? I want to be with you. Not just for the time being. Forever. Now, I know that proposing marriage would probably send you into a tailspin of fear, but if you really aren't packing up and moving out, then maybe, just maybe, you could see your way to dating me.

"I will apologize up front for being a lot richer than you, and not being able to read very well, and just losing half the start-up funds for my conservation effort, so I'm kind of back to square one, and I drive a Sombra that I can't unload because no one out here wants an electric car. Still, my idea is we date. We take it slow. And we promise each other we will not assume we know what the other can bear. If you can't commit to that, then we need to say good-bye. Oh, and one last thing. I will always be on your side. Never against you. So if you would please just open up the goddamn door and let me in, I swear I'm not going anywhere. But I need to be able to trust you."

A single tear slid down her cheek. "I get it. Wait—is it okay for me to speak?"

He nodded.

"First, I need you to know I won't be able to survive if you leave me. You will be the one who puts me in the ground, Luca Prince. Just so you know, I've thought long and hard about it, too, and I know I have these irrational fears, and I'm trying to take down my walls, but some of them are pretty damn thick. And yet, I've knocked part of it down. I truly have. Because no matter what, Luca, no matter what else is happening in this crazy world, I have fallen for you. Hard. I can't even pick myself up from missing you."

He eyed her critically. Was it possible he had scaled a wall? "I wanna make sure I heard you right. You're saying that you have fallen for me."

She nodded. "Like an asteroid. I fell the first time I saw you, did you know that? You were my first love, and you're definitely my last love.

I fell hard the moment you sat next to me in algebra class. I swooned then, and I swoon every time I see you, and not only have I fallen, I think this obsession I have isn't as weird as I thought. I think it's just what love is."

He drew her closer.

"I mean it. I love you, Luca. I came to beg your forgiveness and tell you I love you, and then just . . . *love* you. I swear on my miracle dump of a house, on Buddy's head, on Priscilla's snout that you can trust me. I swear to you that I will never leave you holding the bag again. I get it now. I get what it is to be so in love and not fear it."

She was looking at him so earnestly that he believed her. He could see her emotion and affection in her eyes, and he believed that he had, by some miracle, finally scaled that damn wall around her heart. That was two miracles in the year—he'd learned to read. He'd learned to love. He wrapped his arms around her. "Do you mean I've been sweating what I would say to you all this time and you loved me all along?"

"Every moment. Bad enough that I actually drove over here to tell you at your big fancy house, and now my car is broken down, and I'm not even completely ashamed." She laughed. "Only a little."

"Ah, Ella," he said, and sighed with relief and happiness, with a lightness he'd not felt in weeks. "Is everything always going to be this hard?"

"Probably."

"Good," he said. "I've had it too easy." He wrapped his arms tightly around her and kissed her.

"I can't breathe," she said when he lifted his head.

"Better get used to it, because I'm never letting go," he said, and kissed her again.

Epilogue

SUMMER

Cordelia had Martin install a sun umbrella at the family graveyard, and she was sitting beneath it, in her lawn chair, wearing flip-flops. She had never in her life owned a pair of them, had said disparaging things about people who wore them, but there they were, staring up at her from a big bin at Walmart.

They were pretty damn comfortable.

"So I like her," she said to Charlie. She could see Luca and Ella in the pool. They were having a barbecue today, a family affair, to introduce Ella to the family. "Seems pretty serious," she said. "Luca told Hallie he'd be married by the end of the next year."

She flicked off her flip-flops and dug her toes in the dirt that still covered Charlie's grave. "Her mother's in prison. Dolly and I Googled her the other night, and you should count yourself lucky you didn't hook up with *her,* pal."

Somewhere in the cosmos, Charlie snorted.

"Nick seems to be doing better, but his resentment is *pret-ty* obvious. He tries to hide it, but he stomps around here like he's going to put a fist through every wall. Have at it, I say. Sometimes the best way to get rid of frustration is to wail on something. I wish I'd wailed on you a time or two."

Somewhere in the distance, she heard a rumble of thunder.

"It was a just a joke," she said. "And Hallie? I wouldn't say this to anyone else, but something isn't right with Christopher."

She glanced at Charlie's tombstone. "I know you liked him, Charlie. But I'm just saying. I get a vibe off him that I don't like. But whew boy, try and tell that to Hallie. She gets her back up quicker than that old dog we had when we first got married. Remember him? The one that ate all our chickens?" She laughed.

"Looks like rain!"

Cordelia rolled her eyes, then glanced to her right. Here came Dolly, carrying her own lawn chair. She'd made Cordelia take her to Walmart to get one. She set it up right next to Cordelia.

"Do you not see an entire graveyard before you?" Cordelia asked, gesturing to the breadth of the family cemetery. "Why do you have to sit right next to me?"

"What's the matter, do you stink?" Dolly asked,

and plopped down. She had a bag over one shoulder and pulled it around to her lap.

"I like my alone time, Dolly. I like sitting up here *by myself* for a reason."

"Do you hear that, Charlie? No respect," Dolly said, and pulled two wine coolers from her bag. She held one out to Cordelia.

Cordelia eyed it suspiciously. "Where'd you get that?"

Dolly giggled. "*Walmart!* Can you believe it? They come in all kinds of flavors, too."

"You know what Walmart needs is a bar," Cordelia said, and took Dolly's offering. "Think about it—big slushy margaritas while you shop." She unscrewed the cap from the bottle and drank. "I think I'll write them with that suggestion."

The two of them were silent for a time.

"Nothing like a family barbecue," Cordelia said at last.

"Got that right," Dolly said, and tapped her bottle against Cordelia's. "You know, we're pretty damn lucky our kids want to be around us."

Cordelia watched Luca pull Ella out of the water and wrap her in his arms and kiss her. She thought her kids were lucky that they had the chance to know the strong kind of love she and Charlie had had in spite of everything. Of course, she wouldn't say that out loud. As far as Dolly was concerned, everything that had happened to Cordelia and Charlie was Cordelia's fault.

"I hope they don't put barbecue sauce on those burgers," Dolly said. "Did I ever tell you about the food poisoning I got at the governor's mansion? That'll bring a barbecue to a halt, let me tell you."

Cordelia cast a look at Charlie's tombstone. *Thanks a lot,* she mouthed as Dolly launched into her tale.

Books are produced in the United States using U.S.-based materials

Books are printed using a revolutionary new process called THINKtech™ that lowers energy usage by 70% and increases overall quality

Books are durable and flexible because of Smyth-sewing

Paper is sourced using environmentally responsible foresting methods and the paper is acid-free

Center Point Large Print
600 Brooks Road / PO Box 1
Thorndike, ME 04986-0001 USA

(207) 568-3717

US & Canada:
1 800 929-9108
www.centerpointlargeprint.com

8-19